Historical Note

Much of the history alluded to in the novel is correct, including the details of the Kildonan Clearances, and the Brora coal mines, which were indeed closed in 1828, and not reopened until 1872. A visit to the Brora Heritage Centre will tell you all you need.

The Kildonan gold rush existed exactly as stated, lasting for a mere year, ceasing on 31st December, 1869 by order of the Duke of Sutherland, following many complaints about the noise and damage caused by the panners.

The Brora Bowls can be seen in the fantastic musem at Dunrobin Castle, as can that first nugget of gold found by Robbie Gilchrist.

For those who know the area, forgive me for the slight liberties I have taken with distances between Kildonan, Helmsdale and Brora. Sometimes you have to bend the truth a little to make it fit!

Acknowledgements

I would like to thank the Scottish Arts Council (now Creative Scotland) for the Writer's Bursary that made the writing of this book possible, and Laura Longrigg at MBA for her invaluable comments.

I would also like to thank Melissa for all her support, and the absolutely fabulous cover design.

The BRORA MURDERS

By

CLIO GRAY

CONTENTS

PREFACE: *His lord is buried by the darkness of the earth*

Part 1

Storofshvoll, Iceland

8.43 a.m. September 2nd 1855

The air smelled of snow, though Lilija Indridsdottir doubted it could be so, for surely it could not fall so early, not when the ground below her feet was so warm she'd taken off the clogs she'd been wearing and slung them on a string about her neck. She looked for the dog, who was nowhere to be seen, wondered why there were no chickens pecking and chafing about the yard. She went out to the cattle to give them their feed, found them all snorting and snuffling together at the back end of the paddock, apparently unwilling to come forward as they usually did to greet her, remaining there even when she'd lugged out and loosened several bales of summer straw, scattering it enticingly about their feeding trough.

'Hi!' she shouted in encouragement, and 'Hi!' again, but the usual scrum was unforthcoming, and the cattle stayed resolutely where they were, milling about as much as they were able in the confines of the crowd from which they seemed unwilling to break free, hooves pawing restlessly at the mud and spilt faeces, bodies jittery and jumpy, eyes large and white-rimmed when they raised their heads. Something must have spooked them; she understood this, and looked around her, but saw nothing out of the ordinary – no strangers, no foxes, nothing. She shrugged, and left them to it, went off towards the rye field to inspect the stooks. Even at this distance she could see the huge flocks of greylags and pink-footed geese that had settled upon the field, milling and moving restlessly, rustling like the wind through autumn leaves. At their farthest end was a line of whooper swans, white necks erect, yellow bills upturned, their melancholy calls soon drowned out by the increasingly shrill crescendo of the heckle and cackle that was beginning to break out amongst the geese as they stirred and shuffled and yet did not take to wing. Again she looked about her, looked up into the sky, searched for eagles, for harriers, for anything that might have given all these animals such alarm.

Her eyes traced the lines of the hills that surrounded the valley, and then she saw it, saw the great dark burst of ash that was coming out from Hekla's summit, rising like a thundercloud, bright flicks here and there of burning embers and pumice, moving and dancing in the currents made by the heat that was coming up from beneath. She stared at the silent spectacle, a quick short gasp escaping her lungs as her blood began to thud beneath her skin, her mouth as dry as the straw she had just loosened for the cattle, her hands shaking, moving involuntarily towards her throat. The darkness moved as she watched it, grew and spread, went up in a great plume above Hekla's craggy neck, a sound like breaking thunder just then reaching her ears, and that was when she ran, her clogs flying off from her neck on their string as she covered the ground, realising only now why it felt so warm beneath her feet, cutting her soles on the stones and gravel as she ran and ran, the sounds of her livestock now unbearable, the shrieking of the cattle, the grackling of the geese which all of a sudden rose up and shook the air with the concerted effort of their wings, went up as one, went as a throng, before starting to separate into desperate single ribbons as one phalanx met another, and the superheated ash began to darken their outspread feathers, caught their wings alight as they tried to navigate the unfathomable darkness that had descended upon them with no moon, no stars to guide them, and one by one, they began to fall out of the sky.

2

Lilija Indridsdottir did not stop; she heard the plunking of birds hitting the ground all about her but could not see them. The sun had disappeared, and her world reduced to twilight in a moment, the only light coming from the embers that had embedded themselves into her clothes, into her skin, and from the bright halo about her head as her hair began to singe and then to burn. She could no longer see the path that led down to the village, but was pushed on by her own blind momentum headlong into a rock that broke her foot with its contact; she heard the crack of her bones even as the impact knocked her sideways, sent her off into a skid further on down the hillside, sliding into something warm and wet as cattle-shit, though she could smell nothing except the sulphur of Hekla exploding somewhere up above her, and knew now why the old folk called that mountain the gateway into hell.

Birds were falling indiscriminately all about her, all kinds, not just geese, but sparrows too, buntings, larks, thrushes, many still alive as they hit the ground, though not for long. A swan crashed down two yards to her right, neck bent and contorted like a gorse root in the hearth, tail feathers flaming, ash-blackened wings still beating, beating, as it tried in desperation to clear the ground, its white burned into black, its flight turned into immobility. Lilija reached out a futile hand towards it, but stopped mid-stretch; she could hear a kind of arrhythmic thumping and struggled to understand this new thing, the message of the beating drum, and then the sweat broke out upon her forehead, making grey rivulets through the ash there as she realised what it must be. She struggled to stand but could not, and instead flailed out with her hands, caught her wrist on a boulder and began to drag herself towards it, heaved with all her might to gain its protection, curled herself up tight against its solidity, beneath the slight overhang, an acorn trying to squeeze itself back inside its cup. And then they came, several score of steers and milkers broken free from their paddock, stampeding headlong away from the farm, down the hill towards the river. She could feel them coming, feel their movement in the ground, in the soil and in the bones that were shuddering within her skin, and then they were on her, passing over her in a chaos of tangled legs and panicked hooves, several tumbling as they hit the obstacle of the rock scree, crashing into their neighbours, tripping up the ones that came on behind. A hoof caught Lilija on the shoulder with the strength of a sledgehammer swung onto a fencepost, smashing a clavicle, breaking an elbow, and she whimpered as she tried to pull herself further inward, terrified by the burning of the ash, the thickening dust, the mud scooped up by the fleeing cattle, the snorts and bellows of those still running, the anguished screams and cries of those that had been brought down, and she felt the weight of them all around her as they crashed into the earth, felt her world breaking a little more with every fall.

In the river beyond the village, seven fishing vessels had not long been pushed from the pier to take advantage of the outrunning tide. Above the creaking of their oars, of wood on water, of ropes being pulled through badly oiled winches, sails rising up into the wind, the sailors heard other sounds, and looked up to see the vast cloud that was spewing out of Hekla. It came at them with the speed of an avalanche, a great black tongue unfurling down the mountain towards them, wiping out the morning as it blackened every stone, every field, every roof, every blade of grass, doused the day completely, subsumed them into night. Every man on every boat began to shout, to call out incoherent instructions or pleas, some tugging at the rudder ropes, unable to gauge direction, sails coming crashing down as knots were left incomplete, untied, everything unravelling, and soon came the crash and splinter of wood on wood as one boat ploughed into another, forced a third into what they called the Shallows, a sandbank at the river's middle where the tide insisted on depositing tree boles, rocks and boulders, after every winter's storm.

The air about them thickened, darkened, and men began to fling themselves into the water, lashing out for bank or pier, hurled on by thoughts of wives or children, treasured livestock or possessions, the water beginning to crust about them, sizzling and boiling with the fling of molten rocks, scalding their arms, their faces, the ash clogging their clothes and hair and lungs, weighing them down, narrowing their vision, constricting their breath. Into the cauldron went Lilija's brother, tripping up the man they'd called the Bean Counter, who went headfirst in behind him.

And then above all the pandemonium, the crack of wood, the panicked shouts, the clashing of oars, the splashing of men in the water, the crashing of unsupported rigging, above it all there came another sound as of a bell at the starting of its tolling, a bell so vast, and its peal so low, that it came first as a vibration, making the smoother surface of the downstream water begin to shiver as the air compressed and began to move in gusty, unaccustomed ways, pocking at the sails that were still erect, growing in strength, as every tolling bell will do, until the noise of it was vast enough to become the whole world, as if every boulder on every hillside had begun to shift and roll, as if the earth itself was roaring. Hekla yawned and then was woken, breathed out another mighty exhalation, a new turret of burning ash that rose then fell towards its southern slopes, spat out a tarred-black rain that leached the light from the sky, swallowed the sun; released it, grey and greasy, for seven long and weary months into Storofshvoll's future, vomiting out the last plume of ash from its cracked and broken summit, the last eruption of Hekla, at least, in the lifetime of Lilija Indridsdottir and her village.

September 2nd 1855, it had started. Nine o'clock in the morning, almost to the second.

April 5th 1856, when the last plume died.

Seventeen minutes past three.

Storofshvoll grey as granite, an uninhabitable tundra, everything buried beneath half a year of Hekla's winter-compacted ash.

Spring-time, early 1859

Three years now since the eruption, three years with no more ash but plenty of storms, welcomed where they had once been cursed, sweeping away the worst of the loose ash with their wind and their rain and their ice and their snow, lifting it up in great black maelstroms and carrying it out to sea, dropping its dark ruin onto Scotland, England, France and Spain, wherever the winds took their way.

Tiny pinpricks of grass were beginning to struggle up through the new grey soil; previously buried farmsteads began to re-emerge roof tile by roof tile, timber by timber, then wall by wall, an inch of plank here, a foot of plank there, as they were washed free by wind and rain, storm and spate, as ice and snow gave way to successive springs, and the small brief blooms of the intervening summers.

Another spring, this time in 1860, and now several of the original, surviving villagers returned, began to dig out the old homesteads in earnest, abandoning those too badly damaged, concentrating their excavations on the few that appeared intact and airtight, hammering away at the outer crust with picks and shovels until they had broken through the pumice casing, finding a chink, a window, a doorway, inside. And when they finally gained ingress, it was like walking through the interior of a blown egg, a going from day and into twilight, out of noise into utter quiet. A thin layer of ash covered every surface, every boot that stood by every door, every coat that had been slung on every hook, every piece of fish that still lay in the smoke-holes dug into the inglenooks by long-dead fires, every piece of fur and blanket that lay on every bed, every pot and pan that hung from every hook in every ceiling, every cheese and jar that stood on every shelf in every pantry. All was as it had been before, yet had undergone a subtle transformation, a kind of quiet sleeping, a hibernation that felt as if it could have gone on without end, and gave the eerie sense that it belonged to an entirely separate world that was neither waiting for, nor wanting, anything to change.

The men who crashed into these silent worlds felt like stomp-pigs, large and loud, intolerably intrusive, and they did not stay long, at least not the first time. It was the women who came in later who broke the spell of these abandoned burrows, stirred them up with their brooms and cloths and dusters, brought in great pails of water and washing soda and wiped away the secret lives of these abandoned rooms and replaced them with their own normality, brought in with the noise of toil and graft, their clicking knee-joints, and the scrub, scrub, scrubbing of their brushes.

Amongst these women was Lilija Indridsdottir, a lopsided version of the woman she had been before, with one shoulder angled towards the sky, the other dipped towards the ground, right arm stuck in an awkward crook at an elbow that gave her no mobility, her left foot splayed, every bone broken in it and badly mended, flat as a frog's. She'd not been able to help with the harder work, and spent most of her hours down at the pier, sorting through what had been salvaged from the boats that had been wrecked upon the Shallows, bones and possessions and trade-wares entangled as if in a beavers' dam, encased in a shell of ash that only the ever-flowing water of the last few years had been able to breach.

The population of Storofshvoll had been more than decimated, and less than a tenth of its surviving members elected to return; all others chose to stay where they had taken refuge with outlying relatives, or had already migrated into Reykjavik where they had decided to make their new home. The ones who chose to return and stay spent all their time repairing pumps, harrowing fields, digging out old crop cellars, living on whatever sacks of grain, dried peas, beets and roots had been found beneath the old houses they had managed to excavate from the ash, still preserved, just as they had been five years before.

At the end of the summer of 1860 these few survivors, Lilija amongst them, moved back into what they had dug out of the ruins, broken and blackened constructions they unimaginatively christened the New Storofshvoll, and made their own constitution, the basic tenet of which was *Give help where help is needed.*

And there is no better foundation on which to build a new society, no matter how small.

The citizens of New Storofshvoll came across some disturbing sights during the following months of excavation, especially when they began to dig out several of the farms on the outlying slopes of the village, where the ash from Hekla must first have fallen; they found people inside them, friends and relatives, who had been unable to get out in time, who had been suffocated, baked alive, by the smoke and ash that had poured in through their open windows, through open doorways, down chimney flues, through cracks in the roof, gaps in the wall joists.

One such family was discovered huddled in a heap in the middle of the room, bodies and clothes intact and discernible, eyes closed, arms around each other's shoulders. The outside men who had dug into this desolation did not speak, but withdrew by common and tacit consent and retreated, one of them taking up a wooden tablet from the pile they had ready, someone taking his knife from his belt and carving out the names into the wood of those within, before hammering it into the ground outside, and moving on. Maybe one, maybe more, of these men would return later, anyone related to that lost family, or a neighbour who had known them well, to shovel in as much ash as they could through the windows or doors they had opened during their earlier expeditions, trying to make of it more of a burial, more of a grave, than it already was.

It was different with the bits and bobs of bodies they discovered tangled in the wreck-heaps stranded on the Shallows, because they were only scraps of bone and tatters, flesh and clothes having long since been devoured by sea or fish, or by the acid of the ash that had plummeted down upon them. Nothing much of the remains of those who had been on the boats marked out one man's body or belongings from another, so instead the decision was made to collect together every bone, every rag, every button, every scrap of paper, of leather, everything collected at the edge of the site of the new cemetery, the old one having disappeared without a trace.

It fell to Lilija Indridsdottir, with her gammy shoulder and splayed-out foot, to sort through this pile of dead men's detritus, a fortuitous decision, because it had been in her barn that the man had bided, giving her and her brother a bit of extra rent, a bit to gossip about, and also because she was the only person in the whole of the world who knew where he'd been going, and why, on the morning the sky had exploded.

She had puzzled over the old battered travelling case when she unearthed it from her pile of rubbish, scrutinising its rusting edges, its balding leather, wondering why it seemed so familiar. It took her several minutes to realise it had belonged to the man they'd called the Bean Counter, on account of his habit of tramping up and down the coast, visiting villages and towns, ticking off who went to this church, who went to that, how many and how often, scribbling down any other, older beliefs any of them might still hold to, the tales the old women had of ghosts, of the *huldufolk*, who supposedly lived beneath certain stones, guardian spirits who took the forms of birds or bulls.

Counting beans, was what they'd said of him then, that man who went around their island country counting souls, adding everything up for some purpose they didn't know. But he'd been a nice old stick, she remembered, and she pondered about this bag and what to do with it, remembered what the old Bean Counter had said when he'd told her he was finally leaving.

'Where will you go next?' she'd asked him, and he had sighed deep and low, shoulders sagging, looking as tired as if he had just dragged his own cross to Rifstangi from the Holy Land itself.

'Home,' he had said, and she remembered that the deep crease between his eyes had softened as if he was about to smile, though he did not.

'Home,' he'd said again. 'If home will still have me.'

It struck her back then as such a very sad and lonely thing to say, and now, five years on, it seemed all the worse because she knew he had never even got out of the harbour, that he had never gone home, that he had gone down with Anders and all the rest on the boats that had been boiled into the river when Hekla had done her worst. And she felt for him, for this stranger, for this man she had hardly known, and for the family at the home he had never managed to reach. And so she took hold of his case that had been dragged from the Shallows, wedging it awkwardly against her bad shoulder so she

10

could get at the rusty clasp with her one good hand, managed to snap it open from its rust without much fuss.

'Well now, Mr Bean Counter,' she murmured as she opened it up. 'Let's take a look. See if there's anything left of you inside.'

PART 2

THE HELMSDALE PICK

The Bean Counter's name had been Joseph Lundt; he had been born in Sweden, brought up in the traditions of the Lundt and McCleery Mining Company, schooled in its histories and languages, in English, Swedish, Russian and Norwegian, from the age of three.

His first job for the Company came when he was fifteen, a secondment to the opencast iron-works of Dannemora, just outside Uppsala, where a vast cleft had been hewn out of the ground into which disappeared the ends of cranes and hoists, pulleys and cranks, men on platforms suspended only by a couple of ropes anchored to the ground up above. Across the maw of the chasm, across its hundred foot depth, narrow boardwalks had been slung with spectacular casualness, over which workers, Joseph amongst them, had to crawl and sway from one side to the other, though never in high winds.

By 1826, when Joseph was twenty-one and newly married, he had proved his worth enough for the Company to send him solo over to Sutherland, in Scotland, to advise on the coal mines at Brora with a view to the Company taking over a permanent lease from the Sutherland Estate, who owned both the land and the mineral rights.

He'd been happy when he'd first arrived at his new home in Salt Street in Brora, but it is sadly axiomatic of life's disasters that they rarely give warning of their arrival; an avalanche can be triggered by the tiniest slip of ice, and so it had been for Joseph Lundt.

By the start of 1828 he had already conducted a comprehensive geological survey of Brora and its hinterlands, of the mines that were in use, and the places he thought warranted investigation for further workings. He had also submitted a minutely detailed report of the machines and innovations he believed the Company could make use of to maximise the profit and productivity of Brora coal, and on top of that, his wife was about to give birth to their first, and, as it would turn out, only child.

He'd been given no indication at all, either by the Company or the Estate, that communications between the two had been deteriorating rapidly over the past twelve months, both parties arguing that the other had financial responsibility for implementing the modernisations Joseph so eagerly recommended. The relationship had soured irrevocably by the time Joseph first heard anything untoward, when he'd been in Trondheim attending the annual AGM, and it was there that he was informed, without preamble, prior consultation, or explanation, that the alliance of the Sutherlands with Lundt and McCleery's was at an end, and that he would no longer be required to oversee the mine workings at Brora because they had already been declared permanently closed. Joseph couldn't understand such a decision, just absolutely couldn't understand it. He'd been thorough in his work almost to the point of obsessiveness, had engaged the opinion of not only the best geologist the company had to offer but also two independent experts who had local knowledge; he had meticulously detailed all the potential profits that could be expected once the new equipment was in place, had advised on the optimum positions and digging depths needed to improve the quality of the coal being dug up, had detailed forecasts that the projected investment would be returned twice over within five years, and doubled again in the few years following that. But all this was ignored. Any opinion he had on the matter was neither asked for nor wanted, and there had been no discussion. The decision, he was told, had already been made, and was final.

Joseph Lundt had never known such anger, nor truly understood the nature of rage, the kind that makes a man feel as if his blood is about to boil right out of his skin, that makes him rash to the point of irrationality. Not that this rage was reserved for himself, nor for his own change in circumstances the Board's decision implied, nor that it meant his recall to Sweden while his wife was so gravid she could hardly move an inch from her bed back in Salt Street. What made him so incandescent was that neither the Company nor the Sutherland Estate had so much as considered for a second what such a closure would mean for the populace of Brora and the surrounding areas, for the people they had already swept off the land a decade before with as little concern as wind blowing chaff from the corn; the same people who had been promised a future in the new township of Brora, where work was to have been provided for them in the mines. Mines that had already been declared closed, no matter that they depended on them for their survival.

And by God, how Joseph had fought for them, for those men and women so far away, for the disenfranchised, the people who had no representative here but him. He had stood up at that AGM and tried to explain the situation calmly, but was soon called down, after which he had let loose the dogs of war, had shouted and bellowed, tried to make them all grasp the implications of what they were doing, of the terrible consequences their decision would bring, and had they no concept at all of what they were condemning those people to, that they were setting a whole population onto what had become known throughout the Highlands as Destitution Road?

But for all his words, Joseph's pleas were ignored, and in the end he had walked out of the meeting, and was not welcomed back, not even when he had returned the following morning, simmering still, but under control, to

14

offer apologies along with a detailed plan he begged them to listen to, an option for salvage that would cost them so little but be a way of rescue for all the people that the Sutherlands were about to dispossess. He had been only grudgingly admitted to the assembly, and only after Elof John McCleery had reminded them that under the Company's constitution Joseph must be accorded the right to appeal his case if only for the legislated two minutes granted by said constitution. Joseph had got his two minutes, and two minutes only, after which time his proposal was summarily thrown out by the Board after barely a moment's deliberation.

Joseph had left Sweden two days later, was back in Brora within the week, had come into the town in storm and fury to find the mines already boarded up, and a dreadful despondency settled upon the town like a dreich and drawing rain. Men were gathered in dispirited huddles about the docks, below the bridge, by the ice-house, talking in low voices, some angry, others fatalistic, many unwilling to believe that the Sutherlands could be so blackhearted as to do this to them again, not after what they had already done. Why, such men had murmured, would the Estate deliberately clear them from off their lands into these new townships, only to turf them out less than twenty years later? It seemed a decision without sense, and no more had it made sense to Joseph Lundt, who hadn't even taken the time to go home and wash after he had alighted from the ship from Scandinavia, had just run, dishevelled and crumpled, into those small crowds, urging them to bang on every door in Brora, gather every last man they could wrangle onto the east beach of Brora by Salt Street, where he, Joseph Lundt, would deliver the one bright strike of hope these men had been praying for, but had never believed would really come.

15

'For those who've had service in the mines or the quarries,' Joseph had shouted out to the huddled masses before him, 'there is a possibility, maybe not for all, but for many, that berth will be given on a ship going over to Norway, and employment thereafter provided for them at several of the mines in the east.'

A stir had gone through the crowd at these words as if its members had just awoken, all of them trying to move forward, pushing themselves upwards on tiptoe, shifting from one side to another in order to get a better glimpse of the yelling man, to make sure it really was Joseph Lundt shouting out this message of salvation and not some joker; their faces were creased in concentration, wanting to make sure they hadn't misheard. Joseph's voice had been scratchy, a little hoarse, had an edge to it that might have been ground on a whetstone; every face tipped up towards him where he wobbled himself onto a hastily upturned barrel to cast out his words.

'There are not so many places as there are all of you,' Joseph had called out, 'and though the jobs will not be good, and the work will not be easy, they are there, and for some of you, and for your families, there is at least a chance.'

Two mornings later, Joseph saddled up his horse and rode out into the dawn, driving the animal as fast as he could take it up to Helmsdale and its harbour, three-quarters of the population of Brora trailing on behind him, piled high on every wagon, cart and dray they could muster.

As soon as Joseph rounded the brow of the hill that led down into Helmsdale, he could make out the ship at anchor and the flurry of activity on the wharfside, the piles of bricks, the barrels of lime, the pallets of wool already being loaded, and he cursed in every language that he knew, for this was not as he had planned. He charged breakneck down the hill and swept onto the cobbles of the wharf, did not waste time tying up the horse that was sweating and snorting, its froth exuding in wild billows about its nostrils, too tired to do anything but clop aimlessly here and there amongst the stevedores. Joseph Lundt did not tarry, but went straight to the wool merchant's warehouse and hammered at the boards until at last the man came out, and was no sooner out than he was in again, Joseph's fist against his shoulder, and him shouting, shouting, right in his face. The other man quavered against Joseph's anger, trying to explain that it hadn't been his doing, that his wool had been right and ready just as Joseph had required, but that the ship's captain had a signed order for not only the wool, but for the other, heavier stock that needed to be loaded first.

Joseph let him be then, turned and strode across the wide street and charged up the nearest gangplank, shouting all the while and at the top of his voice for the work to stop, though no one took any heed, not until he took out his knife and began to cut the ropes that were hoisting the pallets and barrels onto the deck of the waiting ship and into its hold. At the sounds of the pallets crashing against the sides of the ship and into the water, the captain at last appeared and stood barring Joseph's further passage, several of his crew fighting to keep this Lundt man still.

'We had an agreement, you bastard!' Joseph spat his words out at the captain, who looked on stalwart and unmoved, before cocking his head as he replied.

'Did we now?' he murmured. 'Must have forgotten some of the details.'

'You're three hours early,' Joseph persisted. 'You were supposed to lie out at anchor until I gave the signal for you to come in.' He had shaken himself free of his captors, his fury still raw, his muscles twitching with the effort of keeping himself reined in, knowing he needed to be calm, use reason and not threats, bribes and not butchery, not that he had the option of the latter, much as he might have wanted it. The captain looked askance at Joseph, put up a hand and rubbed his eyes.

'Must've got the time wrong,' he said mildly. 'Thought you were late, thought you might not be coming, and that I'd better rethink the barter and make a start.'

Joseph felt a stiffness to his fingers as he'd flexed them before balling them into fists, knew he was outnumbered, outgunned, out-argued, so kept them closed against his thighs, breathed in deeply, closed his eyes for a moment.

'It's me that's paying the most of this journey.' He tried to keep the abject agitation out of his voice, keep it steady, rescue something of the shambles into which his master-plan had been reduced. 'And it's me that you'll to be listening to from now on. You'll stop the lading now, this minute, and we'll proceed as we had previously discussed.'

The captain did not reply, just gazed steadily at this piece of string called Joseph Lundt, standing like a frayed rope before him, and had to admire his commitment, if nothing else.

'Have some pity, man,' Joseph Lundt tried again. 'There's men here who've nothing, who've already had it taken away from them once before. They've families, they've bairns, for God's sake…'

And at that very moment, the first of the Brora waifs and strays came clattering down the cobbles from out below the bridge and down the track, spilling off their wagons and drays like unwanted seeds, heads bowed, eyes downcast, offloading small children and bundles, clutching each other's hands and shoulders, all standing distrait upon the harbour walls, others piling on behind them, having to shift to make room for still others coming on at their backs. And yet despite the crowds and the inevitable push and shove as people moved and came forward, they were as cowed and subdued as beaten dogs. There was little noise, only the snorting of the dray animals, the clattering of hooves, a few shrieks of younger children and crying babies, an undercurrent of sighs and whispers, a weariness that seemed to emanate from the waiting families like a wave sinking beneath the bow of a ship.

They'd reached a compromise then, had Lundt and the captain, the latter being adamant he would not unload what he'd already got stowed, but agreeable to taking nothing else but wool and whatever of Lundt's human horde there was space and weight for, and with that, Joseph could do no more. They'd shaken hands, and then the captain had retired to his cabin and his bottle, after telling his first mate and bosun to take charge and to keep an eye on Lundt, who was striding the decks like a panther, gazing alternately down into the hold and at the paper he was holding in his hand, busily scribbling, recalculating, reducing, referring to the first mate several times, being forced to rework, recalculate, reduce one more time.

When he was finally finished, and the first mate had agreed to his numbers, Joseph's perfect three hundred had been reduced to eighty-seven. Eighty-seven families, not one more, not one less. Two adults, two children below the age of thirteen, no leeway, no aspect for argument. And so Joseph had organised the placing of two barrels of sand alongside the harbour wall, and straws to be buried in them up to their necks, some long, some short, so that they could not be distinguished. After that had come the long line of Brora family representatives, and others from Port Gower, Clyne and Faskally, all of whom passed the barrels by, one by one, each plucking out their straw as they went, those who tugged up the longer being ushered straightaway towards the waiting ship, whose anchors were already lifting, tow ropes loose, sails already flapping in the slight breeze. The most who drew the short straws went another way, back from the harbour, back from the wharf, went to line the few streets that wound up the brae, knowing they had no choice now but to head away from Helmsdale and from Brora, take the bad

19

hand life had dealt them, take the destitution roads that led to who knew where and who knew what.

Joseph Lundt felt his heart slowly tearing within him as the awful procession passed his barrels by. No one complained. No one protested at his fate. Each had pulled his straw and abided by the rules, the long-shanks heading doggedly towards the ship with only minutes left to gather the family they were taking with them, deciding in a moment which son or daughter to take and which to leave behind, some too agonised to make the decision, standing dithering inside the circle of their kin, others changing their minds, unable to accept the gift they were being given, unable to tally the cost, swapping their prize with short-strawed neighbours, whose effusive, muted thanks rose up like quiet prayers into the morning.

The ship's bell soon began to toll, the signal that the gangplanks were about to be lifted, and for a few moments a lamentation rose, like the sound of a hundred thousand birds rising together into the sky, and Joseph Lundt had to hide his face, had begun to cry, couldn't bear to watch that stepping up, that stepping away, listening to that last screeching of wood on wood that meant the last gangplank had been raised and withdrawn, all decisions made now, and unable to be undone.

He remained with all the rest, standing in mute abandonment upon the wharf of Helmsdale harbour as the captain gave his order, and the ship began to drift away from the harbour's sides; he heard the shuffling of the ship's sails as they were hoisted and manoeuvred to gain a better draw of the wind, the scuffle of people reaching up their hands in a salute of farewell, the softer sounds of sobbing and sighing of those left behind; he felt the pressure of many hands as they touched his sleeves, his shoulders, his face, in thanks for what he had tried to do, for what he had done, and he couldn't bear it, slipped away then up the brae, took his place upon the bridge that overlooked the harbour, jammed in with all the townsfolk who were watching, watching the departing ship and the people who were still lined up on the wharf like broken flags, a motley jumble of humanity below on the quayside, still weeping, still waving, still there almost half an hour later, unwilling to cease their vigil or look away until the ship that had taken away their nearest and dearest was but a scratch upon the horizon, until the last of it was almost, and then absolutely, gone.

1869

Chapter 1:   *The Wanderer begins to tell his tale*

TRONDHEIM   October 9th 1869

Minutes of the meeting of the Junior Board Members of Lundt and McCleery's Pan-European Mining Company

Knut Elofsson: So we're all agreed then, that this Kildonan proposal should go ahead?

Jens Hansun: We are, though I back the motion that the woman's connection to her father be noted in the minutes.

Harald Aasen: For Heaven's sake, man! That was forty years ago. What possible relevance could it have to the present situation?

Knut Elofsson: Nevertheless, it is a family connection that must be borne in mind, and will be noted. To move on, then. Aasen, who do you propose for the initial survey?

Harald Aasen: Brogar Finn has to be my first choice. He's done all that can be done at Tana Leva, and is first rate. Plus he comes from that neck of the woods, or did. His personnel files indicate his family originated from close by before they emigrated to Holland. From a place called....yes, here it is. Brora, I believe.

Jens Hansun: But is Finn not too valuable an asset to be wasted on such a minor event?

22

Harald Aasen: He would be, if we had anywhere more promising to send him at the present moment, but we do not. And besides, the man has worked like a mule for the Company for almost fifteen years. It would be good policy to give him a couple of months at an easy target, in a place he might even remember from his younger days, and he is in easy reach if we need him urgently. Scotland is not so far away from us these days.

Knut Elofsson: Finn it is, then. But Jens is correct. Kildonan is unlikely to become a major asset, if it turns out to be an asset at all, and although we should not ignore it, neither can we afford to locate such a valuable man there for too long. He needs an assistant to speed things up. I gather his last one is indisposed?

Jens Hansun: More than that, sir. The man is dead. Got caught up in some bar brawl in Kiev and got his throat cut.

Knut Elofsson: I see. I was not aware of those facts. Was Brogar Finn himself involved in this incident?

Jens Hansun: Not that we know of, sir, though witness statements are rather thin on the ground. Still, I do believe we need to team him up with someone a little more…well, perhaps a little more academic than he is used to. Someone to keep him on the straight and narrow, so to speak.

Harald Aasen: A man of whom the priests would sing, perhaps?

Knut Elofsson: Harald?

Harald Aasen: Longfellow, a foreign poet, talking of King Elof and Nidarholm. Actually, though, I do have someone in mind. We've another Scots descendant on our books, right here in Trondheim. He's Swedish born, of course, but he's a brilliant linguist, wasted where he is, and we could do far worse than put the two together. It would also mean that in future we could deploy Finn much further abroad than he's been before, make better use of his talents.

23

Knut Elofsson: Any objections, Jens?

Jens Hansun: None at all.

Knut Elofsson: Right, then. We are agreed. Brogar Finn and—

Harald Aasen: Sholto McKay, sir.

Knut Elofsson: Very well then, Brogar Finn and Sholto McKay, both for Kildonan. Can I leave the arrangements up to you, Harald?

Harald Aasen: You can, sir. I've already made enquiries and Finn can leave immediately. He's already in Vardø, awaiting my word, and I've a replacement lined up for McKay, who, pending unforeseen problems, will be able to join him within a couple of weeks.

Knut Elofsson: Good work, Harald. And now for other business…

Chapter 2:   *Sorry-hearted, he moves along the waterways towards the ice-cold sea*

VOSNOI   October 10th 1869

He had begun his life as a spider amongst the rigging, had been small and lithe enough from the age of five to scamper out amongst the shrouds and cross-trees, the halliards and haulers, the stoppers and the stays, and had never feared the awful drop below him, nor what would happen to him if he fell. His father had done the same before him, and his father's father before that: a family of mast-makers settled in Archangel for generations, one of the oldest crafts in the oldest port of the Russian Empire, a town whose houses were built of wood, and whose streets were paved with timber, never mind the risk of fire, which was no great risk in such a place of wet and cold, where five months of winter froze the sea in its docks and the river into its banks. They were survivors, these men, these children, who scampered amongst the riggings of the ships as if they were play-yards, who had chosen such a life by remaining in Archangel, and liked the way they lived.

And he too would have remained, had he not been over at Vosnoi on that particular morning, evaluating an estimate on the decking-out of several whale-ships that had been crushed into the ice earlier that season, vessels that had somehow staggered on through the summer, and then through another autumn's fishing, ships that could not go out again in the spring until they'd got their broken tenons seen to, their steps and stern-posts properly fixed. He'd not even been listening, had heard what he'd heard only because he had ears, and because the men all about him were loud and shouting, going on and on about the gold rush in Tana Leva. Even then, he'd tried to blot them out, preferring to work in silence, trying to concentrate upon the types of

25

wood he would need to do the fixing, on the elms and oaks he'd already earmarked in his head, the trees in the forest he would need to fell, the particular fir he envisaged to best to replace the mast of this one ship. But then he'd heard that name, and had heard it quite clearly, and the years fell away like an ice floe from a glacier, and he forgot all about the bibs and brackets he'd been trying to figure, no longer worried about the mast or its hounds, had no more care for these men nor the ships they were bound for, only for that one name.

'Lundt and McCleery's,' those crewmen had said, plain as day, or as plain as the day ever would be this time of year, it being the middle of October and the sun already getting low, cutting itself off from them, pulling its own winter sail across the sky.

Lundt and McCleery's.

A name enough to jog him from the rut he'd inhabited but never been content with, a name that woke him from his slumber, and brought him back to life.

TRONDHEIM

Sholto McKay near jumped out of his skin when someone knocked at his door.

No one ever came down here.

He worked alone in his little basement office, with its tiny dirty window scraped out of one wall, looking out onto another wall beyond, onto a crooked flight of steps that, although they led up to the street, had no function anymore and were never used. Every morning he entered the main office upstairs, collected the latest file of dispatches, descended to his room, worked his way through them, from seven through till four, and then went up again, depositing his finished work in the secretary's out-tray, a man who seemed more often absent from his desk than he was present.

26

Luckily for Sholto, he had a whole world locked up inside his head that he could freely roam. Every report, every memo, that came in for him from Poland or from Prussia, from Georgia, Germany, from the farthest outreaches of the Russian Empire before it spilled into Chinese soil, all gave him licence to conjure up the places described by the men who had actually been there; he could envisage the layout of the land, the contours of the hills and vegetation, the proximity of the villages, their various ways of life, the languages he had only learned from books, which, along with the ethnography of their usage, was his real passion. He talked to himself sometimes in those varied tongues, practising their differing syllables and intonations, poring over their idiomatic usage, studying the dialects they encompassed that sometimes varied so much from one region to the next they were almost a different language unto themselves.

Sholto stood up abruptly when Harald Aasen entered his sanctum, embarrassed at what he perceived as mess, where others saw only tidy stacks of books lined up upon his floor space, white paper flags marking the gaps in his book shelves where one volume or another had been removed.

'I've a job for you, Sholto,' Harald Aasen said, without preamble. 'Do you think you'd be up for a bit of fieldwork?'

Sholto was so shocked he could not immediately answer. For the past five years he'd hardly set foot outside of Trondheim, had only gone from his lodgings to this office and then back again, occasionally diverting to the city's libraries, or to the booksellers with whom the Company had an account, allowing him to purchase any research volumes he might require. Every now and then, on his days off, he would take a little trip outside the city, to visit various archaeological sites, or to study one of the many standing rune stones scattered up and down the country, or meet up maybe with other like-minded men of the Linnaean Society when they would discuss some paper or other he or they had been writing for their own in-house, or other, professional, journals.

It was a large part of his job, at Lundt and McCleery's, to scan such journals, study other men's papers, look out for signs of where the next big strike of minerals might come, be it halite, talc, or some precious metal or stone, translating and collating all the reports sent back by the scouts and ongoing agents in the field, reports he would later send up to the Board. That he himself might ever be one of those sending in the reports rather than reading them, had never occurred to him.

Harald Aasen looked at his basement-dwelling protégée. He had long admired McKay's broad-ranging talents, his meticulous attention to detail, his ability to interpret the figures he was given and grasp the underlying structure of places and lands he had never set foot in, and had, for quite a while now, been reconsidering the man's situation. He noticed how pale Sholto's skin was, how the man's shoulders sagged from the constant lean he must take over his desk, his books, his translations, noticed that the startling white streak in Sholto's otherwise black hair that had so marked him out at his first interview, alongside his impeccable qualifications, had faded now into an indistinct, and somehow disappointing, grey.

'You've been too long down here,' Harald said, and meant it, regretted he had let such a man be buried in this dull cage, between these foursquare walls; he saw the outline of the street door blocked and bricked, the grimy window that grew cobwebs about every corner, its lower ledge littered with the carcasses of flies and beetles, butterflies and moths, the unpleasant, greasy looking light that managed to filter through the single clean circle at its centre, where Sholto must have brushed his sleeve against it; he had a vision of this man trying to peer out bleakly from that dirty window, and seeing nothing on the other side.

28

'It is time, my friend,' Harald went on, 'that we sent you out into the world.'

'You've a while yet to kick your heels if you think you're up to it.' Sholto's head had begun to nod, his eyes fixed on Harald's as if waiting for the punchline, afraid that this was all some elaborate practical joke.

'It's real, Sholto,' Harald said then. He moved forward into the room, took Sholto's arm and elbow and guided him to his chair, made him sit, felt a tremor to the man's limbs that he hoped was from excitement, and not fear.

'You've a week to make your decision. We've a man coming in from Oslo to take up your duties here if you choose to accept our offer. You'll need to spend a day or two with the man, train him up, and then you'll be off. Next berth to Scotland I can get you on. Are you up for it?'

Sholto was sat in his seat, and then was up again, shaking Harald Aasen by the hand and shaking it hard.

'Am I up for it? By God, yes, I'm up for it! Am I ready, sir? Yes, I promise you, and thank you. Thank you. I won't let you down.'

Sholto's eyes were already scanning the shelves for the books, maps and journals he might need to take with him or take notes from before he left; he was already calculating the space he would have in the trunk that had been ready waiting in his lodgings for years in case this most extraordinary occurrence might ever happen. That it actually had, he was almost unwilling to believe, and as he watched Harald Aasen disappear beyond the frame of the door and down the corridor, he wondered for a terrible second if he had imagined it all, if he had fallen asleep and been dreaming, if Calderon's *La vida es Sueno* was just that, and that life was but a dream and none of it real. And then he saw the piece of paper Harald Aasen had left on Sholto's desk, saw the space that required his own signature, the clause that stated that if he became disabled, maimed, or incapacitated in the course of his duties for the

Pan-European Mining Company of Lundt and McCleery's, he would forego all legal avenues in favour of reasonable claim, and he understood that this was really happening, and that he, Sholto McKay, had actually been chosen from amongst the rest, and that if he got on well enough with the man he was to aid and interpret for on this one mission, that if he did this one job well enough, he might be given the chance to go on to do all he had ever dreamed about, shrug off his inconsequential existence in this hole and get out there into the real world, explore it, live in it, do something worthwhile with his life, and maybe even something good.

There'd been a piece of wood he had worked on two years before that had been dug out of some Icelandic peat bog by one of the Lundt and McCleery team and sent back to base. He'd been fascinated the moment he'd heard of it, had begged leave to see it, touch it, study it. It had been Harald Aasen who had given him the go-ahead, had delivered the ancient piece of wood into his hands. It had looked nothing special, could have been any old shovel blade chucked into a bog because it had outlived its usefulness, cracked right down the middle from blade to shaft, stained almost black with the tannins of the bog water, could have been any old blade, from any old time. Could have been, but wasn't, for this one had a line of runes carved crude but deep along one side of the crack, as if the crack itself had been used as a ruler: one single word of Sami that Sholto knew meant 'Come to me,' followed by a name and another word, though these last were not in Sami but in Old Norse.

He had puzzled over those runes, those words, that name, had examined other artefacts recovered from the same region and found no fit. It had posed a mystery to which there could be no definitive answer. It was likely to be five or six hundred years old, judging by the pots and bones it had been found with, and if it was that old, it was the earliest recorded example of the Sami language so far found. He'd even had a couple of letters about it after he'd had his piece on it published in the Linnaean Society papers, after which it had been picked up and published too by several other journals in Germany, Holland, and even by Blackwoods in Edinburgh. And yet the central rebus of those runes remained. Why was such a man in Iceland at all? What was he doing there, apart from carving plaintive runes into the spade of his broken shovel? And how had such a man managed to cross from Finland to Iceland so long ago, and over such notoriously barbarous and storm-ridden seas? Sholto understood it would be a riddle he could never solve, and yet there it was. Every time he'd thought on that shovel, that man, those runes, he'd felt the mystery of it like a yearning in his stomach, a longing to tread in the footsteps of that man long dead. And now – he could hardly believe it – by the grace of God and Harald Aasen, that time had come.

VOSNOI

He'd gone home briefly, stocked up, delegated duties, gone out to the forest to mark out the trees that would need to be felled, kissed his two sons and his nephew on their cheeks and foreheads, and poured out generous tots of vodka to toast them and baptize them into their new responsibilities. The three of them had been bewildered, had asked questions, demanded reasons for this sudden aberration in his behaviour, but had got no answers. He had just left, gone for Tana Leva, sled-strap braced across his chest and shoulders in the old way. He had not deviated, but made his way directly across the rough terrain of the Kola Peninsula on the quickest route, skiing his way along the tracks scoured out of its ice and snow, through its forests and scattered villages, across its frozen lakes. It had taken him three furious days and nights to reach Tana Leva, only to find out that the Lundt and McCleery man had left a couple of days before.

There was an odd sort of language spoken throughout Kola and all along the edges of the White Sea as far west as Hammerfest; it was called Russenorsk, a sort of *lingua franca* employed by the mix of men who worked on the ships in those regions, an amalgam of many languages, mostly Scandinavian and Russian, but carrying a smattering of words from other languages: English, French, Dutch and Lapp. He was used it to, based as he was in Archangel, and employed it often, liked that it made of every man an equal; he had, therefore, no difficulty in asking the locals at Tana Leva what had happened to the Company man he'd been seeking.

It didn't take him long to establish that the man was named Brogar Finn, and that he'd been at Tana Leva for several weeks before establishing that the gold in the river was only good for panning. Finn, apparently, had hung around several days after he'd sent in his report, drinking, having a good time, but as soon as he got his call-back notice, Brogar Finn had been gone.

'Gone where?' he'd asked.

'Gone to Vardø,' he'd been told, off to join some ship to who knew where.

He'd not hesitated then, but had sold his sled and all extraneous baggage, taken only skis and backpack and headed off upon Finn's trail. Once at Vardø, he had gone straightaway to the several shipping companies that were berthed upon its quays; it took only half an hour to establish that yes, the Lundt and McCleery man had got here a couple of days before, and yes, he was booked onto a ship due to leave the following morning, but no, no one had any idea where the man was staying now, nor what he looked like, or rather that he had looked like all the other men who hung around the ports looking for work, or waiting for their next sailing – he was stocky and strong, badly dressed, big jumper with holes in it, fur hat, fur coat, his only distinguishing feature being that he'd a bit of scar upon his face, and spoke Russenorsk rather badly.

For a while then, he sat on the quay, watching the ships, looking out at the dark roll of the sea, wondering what he should, what he could, do next.

Lundt and McCleery's, he thought. *How long has it been since I even heard that name? Ten years?* He shook his head sadly, knowing it had been nearer fifteen, and that a whole lifetime had passed between the old days and those he inhabited now. He'd a family, a home in Archangel, had once had a wife he'd been fond of for the few years she'd been alive, still had the two sons she'd left to him. He'd a good profession that had done him well, as it had done his father, and would do so for his sons after he was gone. He'd taught them everything he knew about wood and ships and masts, which trees to cut down and how and when and to what purpose their wood should best be used, how to barter and get the best prices with the ships they did business with. And it had been a satisfactory life up till now, but that was all it had been: satisfactory. And just the mention of that name, Lundt and McCleery's, had been enough to bring back all the old dissatisfactions, the never-quite-lost itching of his feet, that hankering after going somewhere new, not knowing where the day would take him, or where he'd be at its end.

Fourteen and a half years had passed since he had travelled with Joseph Lundt, years during which his life had shrunk into the humdrum, sunk back into the everyday. There'd been nights when he'd lain on board the ship he'd been working on, or when he'd been out in the forest, nights when he would look up at the sky, watching the stars wander the heavens; nights when he heard the tick, tick, ticking of his life as it trickled away through its hourglass, one grain following the next without interruption, one day, one week, one month, one year... always that tick, tick, ticking, tick, tick, ticking, until it became unendurable, and he'd had to jump up and stamp his feet, or begin to pace a decking, or rub that harsh mixture of snow and pine needles into his face just to remind himself that he was not so numb that he couldn't feel cold or pain, that he'd once had a life worth living.

Now he was sitting on the quay at Vardø, and that ticking was louder and more insistent than it had ever been, and the hole in his heart was so great, the urge so strong, the craving so deep-rooted in him. And by God, how he wanted one last throw of the dice. He watched the sailors and the stevedores loading up or winching down their cargos, saw the seagulls wheeling, heard them screeching around the ballast holes, saw them diving into the stink-rotten water that spewed from one ship's hold only to be drawn back into the one berthed alongside. And he felt his carefully constructed life unravelling, rushing out of him like line from an unstoppered reel. He saw a goldeneye duck flip below the water's surface, envying its agility, the simplicity of its life, its ability to down-and-dive or up-and-off, waited for it to break surface, which it did, but only twenty-five seconds – to his counting – later, coming back up with its cheek-patch white as bow-spray, feathers black and glossy as new-dug coal.

He watched that bird go down, come up, go down, come up, maybe nine or ten times more before he pushed his feet up from the harbour and headed for the office, decision made.

'I've no money for the trip,' he said, 'or at least, not enough.'

'Mast-maker, you say?' the clerk answered encouragingly, nodding. 'Could get you on the short haul then. Pay for that, but you'd need to hop yourself off at Trondheim. Always work of your sort there. Place is as big as it gets and ships by the barrel load, and you'll soon get another one over the water.'

He thought for a few moments, looked at his boots, considered his options. If he was really going to go through with this, then this was as good a plan as he would get. The alternative was to trek back home again, pocket a bit more cash, face questions he didn't want to answer, waste more time, but now that he'd started this journey, he couldn't bear the thought of being diverted, so Trondheim it would be. If he was a couple of weeks behind the Company man then that would have to do.

'If I take a ticket, can I sleep on board tonight?' he asked. 'I've nowhere else.'

'You can,' the clerk told him, taking his money, issuing a chit, telling him to present it to the bosun once on board. 'There's no berths, mind,' he warned. 'S'a fishing vessel, not much more. Takes a bit of grain and booze over south. Kip on deck if you're wanting. Might wanta take a blanket or two. Nights is pretty nippy.'

The clerk shoved a stub of paper over the desk towards him, the words he'd written on it sprawled and almost indecipherable, as if they'd been caught in the rain. '*Vatanger*,' the clerk said, as if in explanation. 'East harbour. Can't miss it. Look for a bucket made outta rust and you got it.'

He frowned then, waited a beat, wondered if he'd heard right, if a Company man could really be crossing over to Scotland on such a base ship.

'Sudelundt,' he queried. 'This is the one going over to Sudelundt?'

The clerk nodded sharply. 'Man you were asking after? He was in a bit of a hurry, and it's th'only one out this week. Off on mornin' tide about three. Calls in at Hammerfest, like I told you, and Lofoten and Trondheim after that, and then nothin'. Nothin' at all but the sea and a lot more of it, until you reach Sudelundt, the land of the Scots.'

Chapter 3   *Seeking those who knew his kinsmen, and could give him comfort*

He boarded the *Vatanger* that same evening, and found it just like the clerk had said: a short, squarish-looking vessel held together by rusting bolts and rivets that had sunk several inches into the outer planking, sails hanging dirty, like unenthusiastic shrouds. It didn't look promising, but then again, what adventure ever did, right at its start, especially when you were setting off into the darkness? So much Joseph Lundt had taught him, and now that he was on his way, he no longer hesitated.

He was shooed off deck by the working crew, pushed into a corner at the back of the poop where he tried to find a stretch to roll out his sleeping bag that was not slick with fish oil, or wet to the core with barrelling-brine and sea water puddling through dips and warps in the wood. He tried to find a spot where he could see other men boarding, but couldn't get in plain sight of the gangplank, and eventually settled his body into a crick of the decking, half sitting, half standing, hunched in a blanket, his sleeping bag still in his rucksack to keep it dry. He closed his eyes and breathed deeply of the scents he was so used to, tar and wood, fish and salt, net and weed, listening to the creaking of the *Vatanger* as it moved lazily against the harbour walls, the lapping of the water, the flap of unfilled sails, ropes settling down around capstan and winch. He spent his time wondering just exactly what he would do when he reached his goal, and if it would be a time of rejoicing or of retribution; he prepared himself for both.

Fourteen years was a long time to bear a promise, carry a grudge, and he needed to get it straight in his mind just how he should go about it, though he doubted it would be hard to find her, not with a name like hers, not in a place like that. The hard bit would be what to do when he *did* find her. He'd never

36

been one for direct confrontation, not until all the facts were in hand, but if push came to shove, he knew he would act. He had his own priorities, his own loyalties, and they lay foursquare with the father, not the daughter, and if she got in his way, then so be it. If it turned out she really had betrayed them both, then he wouldn't be stopped. He already had his suspicions, had carried them with him long enough, had waited too long for that letter, that acknowledgement to arrive. That it never had meant one of several possibilities, none of them good – that Joseph had never got home being the least of them, that Joseph was dead, being next in line; that Joseph was dead and the manuscript irrevocably lost, being the worst. He hoped the truth would lay tangled somewhere in between, stranded, and waiting for rescue.

He unbuttoned an inner pocket of his jacket and took out a small wooden case, unhinged it and held it open. It was too dark to see the face of the icon painted on the inside, though he could glimpse the small shine of its gold. He kissed it gently, refolded and then hasped it, put it back inside his pocket and buttoned that pocket up.

'Whatever it takes,' he vowed. 'I'll do whatever it takes.'

Brogar Finn had left one of the run-down harbourside inns and boarded the *Vatanger* half an hour before it was due to sail, having paid a boy to listen for the bell being rung halfway through middle watch to alert crew and harbour men of the turning of the tide. You needed a good push to get out of shallow water and clear the headland, and the best time was a half hour into turn when the tide was pulling away from the shore, the water dragging back into the main off-shelf currents, taking any boats out with it, with time enough to get their sails hoisted and turned fair to the wind.

It was a good night for it, Brogar noted, as he made his way down the narrow flight of stairs, bumping into a crowd of men lashing out of the bars, drink still heavy on their breath, pulling themselves up from the tavern floors on which they had allowed themselves a few hours sleep upon dry land before heading back out to sea. Lamps had been lit along the harbour walls, and Brogar bypassed the line of men pissing out their alcohol in the dark pools between them, their hands leaning against the wall to stop them falling while they yawned and fumbled with their trousers. He stretched his arms and shoulders as he went, hoisting his bag upon his shoulders, heels clicking on the cobbles, exhaling a tiny ice-cloud about his head, and he smiled into the darkness, happy to be on his way, happier still at where he was going, wondered if he would remember any of it when he got there, if there was any part of it that still remembered him.

An hour later, the *Vatanger* slipped out of harbour into darkness. The night was calm and cool, wind blowing favourably, taking them round the headland with ease. The following day they reached Hammerfest, and then went on down the side of Norway, skirting fjords and rock-shoals, craggy inlets where the water crashed without cease, throwing up a mist of spume about the cliffs.

The master mast-maker hadn't enjoyed the voyage. He'd spent all his working life on ships and amongst their crews, but only when they were stationary. He hated the crush of men, and longed to be alone, completely alone. It was nothing like when he'd travelled before with Joseph Lundt, for the most of their days had been spent walking, trudging along endless tracks and paths from one far-flung village to the next, sometimes with sleds, sometimes with skis, occasionally with dogs who pulled them fast but needed keeping in order and were always yap yap yapping at the end of each trip, baying for the bundles of dried reindeer meat they carried with them, tied up with the sinews of the same beasts slaughtered to provide the meat. The best times had been when it had just been him and Joseph plodding on from one place to the next, talking about the birds and trees and clouds, or anything else that came to mind, all to keep them putting one foot in front of the other, always wondering what it would be like when they got to wherever it was they were going, often setting their direction by the merest dot of information, a scrap of a name, a hint of a tribe, a slight path already walked by someone else in the snow.

He disembarked at Trondheim, and found the Vardø clerk had been right. The place was bristling with ships and sails and masts, and he knew he'd find work as soon as he could spit. Chances were there were men here he'd worked with before, or others who'd heard of him if they'd ever been to Archangel or Vosnoi. All the same, he wished he hadn't had to leave the *Vatanger* at all, wanted to get on, felt the pull of the wild, of the sea, as strong, maybe stronger, than it had ever been.

'Not long though,' he told himself, promised himself, a week here, two at the most, to earn a bit of money, and then he'd be off.

Just one short week.

He could do it, had to do it, but then he'd be back on her trail.

'She'll be going nowhere,' he reminded himself, 'not with the Company man arriving so soon at her door. And wherever she is, I will find her.'

Once past Trondheim, the *Vatanger* had swung out into the true province of the sea, a bleak and frightening vista to those who were not used to it, where waves darkened into grey and grew in size, became huge, haphazard, and unpredictable, pulled by tide and winds that made the ship rise and fall without warning. Not so for Brogar Finn, who revelled in it, leaning dangerously over the sides as the *Vatanger's* prow dipped and surged through open water, laughing as the spray hit his face, soaked his hair, left lines of salt upon his jacket. God, but it felt good to be back out at sea, as free and unreined as the waves themselves.

There was no fishing to be done on the way over, the holds already laden, but occasionally the boil of fish just below the surface was too enticing to ignore, and the crew threw out their nets and hauled them in, got out their knives and split them belly to head and threaded them on lines strung between the masts and housings, so that the boat looked decked out for some fiesta, the smell enough to twist your guts, and then too strong to even notice, overwhelming every man on board, seeping through their clothes and skin, until the fish were crusted over with salt from the sea-spume and packed back-on-back, belly-to-belly, into a few spare barrels that were topped off with brine, sealed, and loaded back into the hold.

The evening before they landed, out came the caustic soda and the potash, and every man on board, Brogar included, scrubbed himself down from head to foot, along with shirts and trousers, the latter sent out to air in the wind like flags. Some of the crew were left arsing around bollock naked until their only articles of clothing were dry enough to put back on again – having been too lazy, too drunk, or forgetful back at Vardø, to have brought any extra with them – their skin as white as fish-bellies, laughing as they bared themselves to the world. Brogar Finn laughed with the rest of them at this escapade; he had seen the same thing many times before on other ships going other places, and revelled in the freedom it gave these hard-working, hard-cursing, hard-drinking men that had been let loose upon the sea, untrammelled by the society of women and the rules that confined them when they were consigned to solid land.

At 11.34 a.m. on the morning of October 13th 1869, a mist rolled over the *Vatanger*, threatened to becalm them, smothered every noise, clung to the sails and the rigging, dampened the faces of the crew and their newly washed clothes, but it stayed where it was as they moved on, as if latched to the surface of the sea, and they soon passed through it, and by 12.32 were out again, and as they did so, land was sighted, and two hours later, at 2.57 in the afternoon, the *Vatanger* sailed into view of Helmsdale harbour, and was soon docked.

Chapter 4   *For his friends have been slain within their mead-halls*

Brogar Finn was completely unaware that he had picked up a companion back at Vardø, and that, like the tail follows the dog wherever it goes, the man would follow him into Helmsdale, landing one week to the day after Brogar had done himself. Unlike Brogar Finn, though, this man had no exact idea of where he was going once he'd got there, only that he was on the eastern seaboard of Scotland, somewhere to the north. He'd some idea of the name of the place he had landed in, but no notion of where to go next. Coming off the gangplank, the master mast-maker had found his legs still swaying with the movement of the sea and had to sit himself down on a capstan before he fell. By the time the nausea and dizziness left him, the wharf was practically deserted, half the crew having already disappeared into the warehouses that lined the harbour, many others into the taverns, only one or two left standing guard upon the boat – another rust bucket – shuffling disgruntled from one foot to the next, impatient for their shift to be over, so that they could begin their own carousing.

It was the rain that roused him, spitting in a sudden squall from off the sea, a great low roll of cloud moving behind it, across the surface like a silent wave. Minutes later, the haar had slunk across the harbour, reduced visibility to a few yards, and all the screeching of the gulls, the lapping of the water against the stone, against the boat-bows, was diminished. He closed his eyes, felt the clamminess of the mist against his skin, the great hush that had fallen all about him, and took peace in it, felt not afraid, nor disoriented, but at the centre of his universe, as if the rest of his life had been sucked inside itself, reduced to this one point in time, and that, like a needle pulling thread through a sail-seam, wherever he went from here would be the start of something new, something other, some great voyage of whose purpose he was not yet fully aware, and nor did he know where it would take him, only that it had at last begun.

He pulled himself to his feet and managed to locate a single man weaving his way along the wharf through the mist. His English was non-existent, but he hoped the two words he knew would be enough.

'Solveig McCleery?' he asked, though it had not sounded to those Scottish ears how it was meant, had come out more like 'Sulvig Mag-livee'.

The man shook his head, but pointed up the brae that went past the Artillery Hall, and he trudged up its slope, noting its barred windows just as Sholto would do a week later, unaware that half a century previously this was where the Sutherland factors had barracked their men, had them resting up, cleaning and loading their guns, prior to marching like an enemy force up the glens to clear out the uprising population who were refusing to leave.

He walked the couple of streets of Helmsdale up and down several times before spying one shop in particular, large gold letters written across its glass. He didn't understand the words, nor even recognise the letters, but he did know what the large sieves in the window were used for. A small bell rang as he entered the dingy shop, and he saw straightaway the prominent set of scales on the countertop, the small scoops of the pans, the tiny weights, that were used for the measuring of gold that came not in nuggets, but in dust.

'Sulvig Mag-livee?' he asked the small bespectacled man who had appeared at the ringing of the bell, his pince-nez halfway down his nose, staring at the stranger, at his odd appearance. He'd been some-time jeweller, most-part pawn-broker, to Helmsdale and the surrounding area for years, but this last year had been an absolute godsend, and he'd made more money in the last ten months than he had done in the same number of years. Add to that the

43

amount he had made from supplying the aspiring panners their panning sieves, the coats, boots, canvas, cooking equipment they had for the most part landed without, and he was beginning to count himself a rich man who had only to stick it out another few years before he could retire. He was patient, therefore, with this tongue-twisted newcomer, and took his time to understand what he was trying to say. It took a while before he figured it was a name the man was asking after, not just the usual, 'What way to Kildonan?' but after ten or fifteen repetitions he grasped the man's meaning, and was pleased to draw him a map when it seemed he understood nothing else.

'This way,' he told the man as he handed over his sketch, pointing out the line he had drawn that went up by the river to Kildonan farm and the site beyond, that was called the Baile an Or, from where the panners fanned out across the hills. He felt a little sorry for this foreigner, who had obviously come a long way to get here, arriving rather late in the day, and the year, when most of the other panners had already quit, knowing that the weather would only get worse from here on in.

Still, whatever gold this stranger might find would eventually find its way to his shop, in one form or another, and so he held up a panning sieve, hoping for a sale, but the man had waved his hands to say no, only picking up the sketch, bowing with relief and gratitude. The stranger had then taken a coin out of his pocket and held it up, and the shop-owner had taken it from him, studied it with his eyeglass, couldn't make any sense of its markings; he hadn't come across anything like it before, but he took it anyway. Who knew where this man or his money had come from, but money was money after all, and maybe the rarity of this single coin would earn him a little hard cash from the Duke of Sutherland, who popped in every now and then, and was well known for collecting the odd and the curious.

The master mast-maker from Archangel took the small sketch, and the shop-owner stepped out from behind his counter, went out the door with him and pointed him in the right direction. The map wasn't detailed; it just showed the river and the road running beside it, the route he needed to take coming to an end at a place name, Kinbrace, that he couldn't read, and a large X-marks-the-spot.

He'd no idea of the distances involved, but it was good enough for him, and he started walking away from Helmsdale and its harbour, and gone on for several hours, deviating a few times to climb at least partway up the hills to the north of the river, wanting to get an overview of the area, a feel for this place that was unlike anything he was used to: too green for the time of year, too verdant, and too soft. This spying out of the land was something he had been taught to do by Joseph, back in the old days, a safety mechanism, a way of surveying the surrounding area with a view to how best they could proceed.

He made his own additions to the shop-keeper's map as he went, pencilling in rises and ridges as he passed them, the starts of tracks where they led away into the hills, walking a little way up and down one or two of them, sitting sometimes just to pass the day, watch the clouds, study the plants, the few trees, drink from the odd stream. In all his time walking, he saw no one else. He came to a fork in the road and stopped, could see a farm away to his left, and a decrepit-looking church beyond it, its graveyard unkempt, partially hemmed in by broken stone walls. He paused, uncertain whether he should go on or wait out the night somewhere nearby and take the last leg in the morning. There seemed little activity going on in the farm buildings, but he'd got through the pack of rye bread and hard cheese he'd brought with him, had finished the last of it on the ship that morning, and this afternoon's walk had made him hungry. The obvious thing to do was go down to the farm to ask for milk, bread, maybe some eggs, though the lack of language would hamper him, and he realised only now how serious a problem it might be.

While he was standing at the fork undecided, a dilapidated cart trundled up the track behind him and came to a stop at his back, a man calling out to him, greeting him kindly, as far as he could tell, asking him something, or so it seemed to him from the intonation, perhaps if he needed directions.

The master mast-maker smiled, shrugged, held out his map to the man who clambered down from his cart; he got out his pencil and sketched what he hoped looked like a loaf of bread and a mug on the edge of the paper, pointed at his illustrations and then down to the farm. The newcomer looked at the map, took it from him and looked again, scrutinising it closely before handing it back, then surprised him by holding up a finger and going back to his cart, pulling a blanket off the back to reveal several sacks of grain, various stoppered earthenware jugs, a few wooden crates crammed full with foodstuffs, and a barrel leaking brine from the stop-hole high in its side. The man lifted out a trencher of bread from the topmost crate, along with a greasy package held together by a wisp of string, and a couple of slabs of salted bacon that he scooped from the barrel, which he slapped onto the bread that held it like a plate, soaking up all the salty water that was leaking from it.

'Here ye go,' Andrew McTavish said, not that the mast-maker understood, merely shook his head, pulled a pocket inside out to indicate he had no money with which to pay for it, or at least none that would do service in these parts. But again the man surprised him, and Andrew, smiling broadly, thrust the package into the stranger's hand, made him fold up his map and take the bread plate with the other. 'New here, I'll warrant,' Andrew said, patting the stranger's shoulder as if they were old friends, steering him down the track towards the farm, pointing to the dilapidated building that lay

46

beyond it on the side of the river, saying slowly and with exaggerated mouth movements, 'the kirk. You need to get on to the kirk.'

The mast-maker understood where Andrew was pointing him, and began down the track towards it, turning several times to watch the human embodiment of generosity heaving himself back into his cart, waving heartily several times before disappearing around a bend in the road. He couldn't know that Andrew was the man who kept the stores up the road, and that the reasons for his benefaction had been twofold, firstly because he had felt genuine sympathy for this stranger – yet another washed up on the shores of Sutherland in hope of gold – and secondly because he knew that the moment this new prospector settled in, either at the Suisgill or the Kildonan camp, he would be dependent on Andrew for his services, unless he did what skinflints like Willie Blaine did, and took the trouble to go down to Helmsdale for his provisions where they were undoubtedly cheaper. A little good will on Andrew's part now would be sure to reap rewards in the coming weeks and months – if the man stuck it out, that was, and Andrew had the feeling that this man would, for he'd a resolve about the way he held himself, a bearing that said, *I've worked hard all my life, and will carry on working as hard as I can until I drop.* Not a man, certainly, to be put off by the first scrape of frost on the grass, or a little glouf of ice-cold wind from the hills, especially not as he was obviously foreign, and had probably travelled many miles to get here.

Andrew whistled as he went the way back up towards Kildonan, glad he'd made the decision to take a punt on the gold rush, leaving his sister in charge of the bigger store they owned down in Helmsdale, gladder still because since he'd been up here he'd seen so much more of Moffatt Murchison, an old friend from way back when, the kind of old friend when it didn't matter a wisp that they'd not seen hide nor hair of each other for getting on thirty years, because once back together they'd rabbited and smoked, drunk and joked, just as if the clock-hands of his watch hadn't been round their circuit forty thousand times since the last day they'd met. He was a happy man, was Andrew McTavish, as he went back up the road to the stores, a man who knew his life was going good and would only get better, at least as long as this gold rush lasted.

And he wasn't the only one in the best of moods, for his largesse to the stranger, the mast-maker from Archangel, had seemed to the latter a sign of better things to come. It had been a strange day, a strange week altogether, one in which he had crossed peninsulas and seas, moved from one language, one country, one land-mass to another. But he didn't regret any of it, not for a second, and this single act of kindness from this one man on this first afternoon of his landing in this strange land had been all the confirmation he needed to validate his actions, an omen of the sort you did not question, did not try to figure out, but just accepted. And as Andrew made his way back to the stores, so the master mast-maker made his own way down the track to the old Kirk of Kildonan, and whatever future awaited him in the days to come.

Chapter 5   *Carried away by wars and wolves and ravens*

In a curl of the Suisgill burn, a huddle of canvas had been erected over sticks and branches to shelter the men who went out hacking at the banks, loosening the gravel, sieving it for gold. Their pickaxes, better cared for than their tents, were regularly oiled and cleaned, methodically wrapped in waxed sacking to keep them from the rain. Every morning they left the camp at daybreak, returning with the setting down of the sun. It was hard work, unremitting, unrewarding and dull, barely yielding enough to pay the next month's licence, the last month's food, enlivened all too rarely by wild shouts of victory as someone luckier than themselves, somewhere further up the valley maybe, or further back into the bank, uncovered an actual nugget, no matter how small, or a rich seam of grit with plenty of discernible dust. And then their tired hearts leapt with hope, and they all piled on down to camp to celebrate with their new best mate, take a little share in his good fortune, breaking out an illicit keg of beer or spirits, quietly swearing they would carry on until their own little piece of luck found them, for God knew, there was nothing much else in their lives they had to look forward to.

The Kildonan gold rush had never amounted to much, but at least it had been something. Willie Blaine had started early doors, only a few weeks after his old mining mucker Robbie Gilchrist had started the whole thing rolling by finding a nugget the size of a baby's fist, and gone running to the Sutherlands with it. And if Robbie could find something here, in this very river, then it stood to reason there must be more, and Willie had not been alone in thinking that sudden riches had come within his grasp. Over two hundred licences had been issued back in June alone, with men coming from as far abroad as Elgin and Aberdeen, for if Robbie had found such a nugget, then why couldn't they all?

49

That it had all gone to crap was what Willie Blaine was thinking as he set out that morning a little earlier than all the rest. He hadn't wanted company, hadn't wanted to chat, had just wanted to get on with it, get it over. He hated it here, had almost quit the day before when he'd been interrogated by that bastard Tam Japp, who had come up to inspect the Suisgill miners, suspicious that none of them'd been down to the Baile an Or this last week to declare their findings. That he'd singled out Willie in particular had been no coincidence, for it had been noted that Willie had taken several trips down to Helmsdale these past few months, and it was presumed he'd been cashing in his gold dust there directly, bypassing the cut he was due to the Estate for the pleasure of having grafted so hard to find it. Which, of course, was exactly what Willie Blaine had done – and why the hell not?

By Christ, but he was sick of the lot of it.

Sick to the very back of the teeth he no longer had very many of.

Sick that he'd slaved his life away for nothing, and that there was nothing ahead but more of the same, more hard graft, more pandying to people he'd no respect for, more handing over of his hard-earned cash for little return. He'd have upped and quitted already had not the man from Lundt and McCleery's rolled up a while before, a geologist no less. His arrival had given Willie renewed hope, for surely there really must be gold of some amount to be found in the Suisgill and Kildonan, for why else would they have bothered to bring in somebody to investigate it? And just because of this, he had given himself one month more to go the course, one month, no more, no less, and though he knew the chances of striking it big within that time frame were so minimal as to be almost laughably non-existent, he couldn't entirely dismiss the hope of it. He longed for a reprieve from servitude and poverty, for an escape from the family he'd not wanted and didn't care for, from the pretty little thing he'd hooked up with in Helmsdale that first trip, who was so good at winkling from him the little bit of cash he'd managed to earn.

He was a man who had lost in life, and he knew it, felt the shame and waste of it rotting him from the inside out. He listened to the *krekking* of a corncrake somewhere down in the hay fields towards the broader river into which the gold-bearing burns of Kildonan and Suisgill finally flowed. It was late in the season for such a bird, King of Quails, to be abroad, at greater risk from the gamesmen's guns the longer it stayed, and he felt a sudden urgency for it, wanted to force it into flight, wanted it to take him with it wherever it was that it went over the long winter months, though where that was, he had no idea.

But Willie Blaine wasn't going anywhere.

Willie Blaine had got exactly as far as he was ever going to get.

The man on the knoll just above him had already raised his boulder and let it fly.

No last words.

No *Bless me Father, for I have sinned.*

Nothing left from one second to the next.

Willie Blaine falling like the rain all around him, nowhere to go but down.

Willie Blaine wiped out in an instant, like dog shit from a shoe.

Chapter 6   *Regret and sorrow, cruel companions to the friendless*
October 30th 1869

The ground was rumbling, sounded filled with bees or the inrushing of a strong tide. All along the links, small plumes of dust rose up through chinks in the old shaft-heads, stones rolled from their overgrown turf banks, small pebbles plinked up and down on the beaten drumskin of the earth, water shivered in the cupped palms of derelict saltpans. The seals, who had been resting away their sun-filled day on the outlying rocks of Brora's East Beach, blinked in alarm, flopped gracelessly back into the safety of the incoming tide, heads bobbing up a few moments later, whiskers pricked and quivering like new-plucked harp strings, looking with suspicion towards the shore.

Another muffled *booooom* came in quick succession, gave way and sank, brought the mallards uprising from the stream, a whoosh of wing-slapped water hurtling them up in garbled hue and cry, sending them flying low and straight towards the bluff of the shallow cliffs, the seals backing off into the grey slack of the sea, slipping in arcs, sliding in circles, disappearing below the waves. Solveig, daughter of Joseph Lundt, widow of Elof John McCleery, both late of the Lundt and McCleery Pan-European Mining Company, looked at her watch, and was pleased the explosions had gone off on schedule, only one minute apart, just as Brogar Finn had instructed. That Finn wasn't here had been the matter of some argument between the two of them. He'd arrived two weeks before on her invitation, his remit from the Company being to investigate the small gold rush happening in the valleys of Kildonan and Suisgill, just as she had asked, just as she had hoped, when she had gone to the Company, cap in hand.

What she hadn't told them was that she had taken out a private firman from the Sutherland Estate to try to reopen the coal mines here at Brora, hadn't told them precisely because she'd known they would not have agreed to such a proposal, not after all the brouhaha back in 1828, when the Company had been complicit in their closure, a closure that had led to her own father being ignominiously sacked from their ranks because of his objections. But she'd history here, and had history with the Company, and when she'd first heard about the gold rush she had blessed it, had worked night and day to instigate herself into its future, had been successful in persuading the Sutherlands it was worth bringing in Lundt and McCleery's, volunteering to make the approach, do the groundwork, be their go-between. With the Company itself, she had pleaded the Sutherland's case, put herself forward, played her history card, knowing she could play it only once.

When Solveig had got the letter containing their reply to her application, had seen their crest, their seal, she had held it in her hand for a minute, maybe two, and then had taken a deep breath, broken it open and quickly scanned the words before going back to the beginning and starting all over again. Once she had finished reading it a second time, she had stood there with the letter in her hand and closed her eyes, lifted her head. Against all her expectations, they had agreed, had accepted her back into their fold, at least temporarily. And more than that, the man they had chosen to send over was no other than Brogar Finn, and she knew his calibre, and also that she couldn't have chosen better herself. She'd kept up with the Company's activities over the years, and knew he was a man more experienced with copper mines and coal than he was with precious stones and gold. Perhaps they thought they were sending over someone not entirely suited to the task just to make things difficult for her, or perhaps he just happened to be available, but whatever the reason for their choice, she had rejoiced in it, for she alone knew that he was just the man she needed.

Brogar Finn had arrived quicker than she had anticipated, landing at Helmsdale not on the usual trade ship as might have been expected, but dropped off from a fishing vessel that had seen better days and had precious little to unload or barter for. And without her even knowing he had arrived, he'd apparently made his own way up to Kildonan and Kinbrace and to the Suisgill beyond, Solveig only finding out he was there at all because Tam Japp, the Sutherland Representative of the sites, had sent a messenger asking why he'd not been informed beforehand of the man's arrival.

Solveig had gone at once the several miles from her home at Kinbrace up to the Suisgill, and had to go another two miles upriver before she'd finally found him up to his knees in the burn, sifting through the silt like any of the many other panners who, back in the warmer months, had been as thick in the water as flies on an uncovered corpse. She'd marked him out from the few still remaining only by his uncovered head, his oddly coloured clothing, and the entirely unusual animation with which he was going about his task.

He'd been a bit of a surprise in more ways than one, the first being that he'd greeted her as he might have done any other colleague, either so wrapped up in what he was doing that he hadn't noticed she was a woman, or not caring. The second was that he was fluent in the language, so fluent in fact that he'd either picked up an accent in the two days it had taken both her and Tam Japp to realise he was here, or else it was native to him, or to parents who had come from not so far away. She'd known his name was Scottish, Highland even, but she'd expected him to be Scandinavian, possibly Russian, as were most of the Company men. She also knew her history as well as the next man, and that there'd been Scots in Scandinavia, and Scandinavians in Scotland, practically as long as either as had been in existence. There'd been Carnegies, Ramsays and Sinclairs expatriated to Sweden for centuries, men who'd gone as mercenaries and ended up as district governors, men who'd

54

sired whole dynasties abroad that were still in existence now. Likewise there'd been Vass's and Greigs in Sutherland and its surrounding counties for just as long, breeding just as often and as well.

But what surprised her most about him was that when she'd brought up the subject of the mines at Brora with the hope of dropping in the plea that, as a geologist, he might be interested, perhaps able to spare a couple of hours to give her some advice as to that venture, Brogar Finn had been enthusiastic to the point of insistence.

'The coal mines?' he'd asked as soon as she had mentioned them. 'The coal mines at Brora?'

He'd a lopsided face, a nose that had obviously been broken several times, one cheek bone flatter than the other, the both of which gave his face at ease an expression of curiosity that it did not necessarily possess, but that he was curious about the mines, Solveig had not been in doubt.

'They were closed years ago,' she'd answered. 'But I believe there's still life in them yet, and it would do the local population no end of good if we could get them up and running again.'

She had paused then, just as she had rehearsed, for this had always been her plan, whichever man the Company might have sent, but she had the feeling that her previously well-thought-out subterfuge had become irrelevant, and that this man, this Brogar Finn, was already on her side. She'd decided there and then that honesty might be the best policy, and almost before she'd thought them, the words were out of her mouth.

'The gold rush, Mr Finn, was a ruse.' He'd said nothing to that, only tipped his head slightly to one side in expectation, and she had no option but to go on. 'My father was brought over to Sutherland by the Company years ago, to ascertain and advise on the possible productivity of the Brora mines. They, and the Sutherland Estate with them, chose to ignore everything he'd worked

55

for, and closed the mines down in '28. My mission, Mr Finn, is to carry on where he left off, get them reopened and functional. Give back to the population that remains of Brora what they were robbed of forty years ago.'

Several hours later, the two of them were standing in Solveig's father's study, its large south-facing window looking down towards the water meadows and the river beyond that ran them by. Solveig had one hand on her father's desk, but was not behind it, leaving the view open for Brogar Finn of the map she had spread out upon its surface of the comparative geology of Brora and Fascally, the name that was given to the stretch of river one step up from Brora. It was the same map Solveig's father had made, the one that indicated the positions of the older mines and of the stone quarry and how the latter could be expanded to aid the brickworks, his scribbled notes dotting the paper like dead spiders, the mines marked with faded red ink along with notations indicating which of them had been functional back in his time, and several others that he had caused to be started dug, other viable spots marked with Xs on his map.

'Very impressive,' Brogar had murmured as he'd leaned over the desk. 'Very impressive indeed.'

And now here Solveig was down on the foreshore of Brora's East Beach, the ground moving beneath her feet with the explosions Finn had advised, hoping they were blowing the old mine workings into submission, giving her no more worry about the sea washing up on a high tide to endanger the whole project, or flooding the new workings she and Brogar had already agreed should be sunk much farther up the seam, farther upriver, farther up land towards Fascally and Clyne.

56

Her ears were ringing, but her feet were still firm on the ground, and after twenty or thirty seconds she became aware that the noise had ceased. She looked over to where her men were moving about the openings of the old mineshafts, thought how good it was that she was a part of this project, and not just a part, but its instigator. She watched her men closely as they went about examining the collapsed openings of the mine-pits closest to the shoreline, saw them knocking here and there with picks and hammers, trying to gauge how closely packed the rubble was down below, whether it would be sufficient to keep out the incoming depredations of the tides.

She wished Brogar Finn were here to oversee these events, remembered him pointing out that in the past forty years since the mines had been worked, the sea had already pushed the sand so much further up the shore that the Marches – the line of large boulders that marked off the neighbouring farm from the coal-lease – had its tail-end right out upon the foreshore, when once they'd all been sited on grass and green. She sought out those boulders while she waited, found a calmness to their order, a strength to their straight line and their implacability in the face of the tide, even if that tide was now up to their knees.

Then several things happened at once.

She felt the ground shifting beneath her feet, although the explosions had already blown and settled, felt a strong vibration setting her teeth on edge, saw her men flinging down their picks and running, jumping off towards the Marches; saw also that there was a young boy heading in her direction, moving quickly alongside the shore, keeping to the very edge of the grass where it tipped into the sand, saw that he had stopped completely and dropped to his knees, hands held up above his head, and then a huge, bone-jarring, stone-turning, earth-moving quake came roaring and rippling across the foreshore, a crumping sound so loud and strong that it pushed the air out of Solveig's lungs. She knew this must be the aftershock Finn had warned her of, had told her the explosions might trigger off an underground turbulence that might take up to fifteen minutes to reach its conclusion, but the sheer strength of it shocked her, and knocked her off her feet. She was dimly aware that the men who had been running towards the foreshore had been thrown down to the ground, as she had been; she feared that the grass might part beneath her feet, gulp her down like a gannet does a sand eel, though this last dread did not come to pass. The minutes rumbled, rumbled, and then faded as the rocks settled somewhere down below, leaving a thin pall of dust hanging suspended in the air like timid haar, before it too was drawn back into the ground.

There were a few moments then of complete silence, followed by a growing crescendo of shouts and anxious laughter as her men picked themselves up, brushed themselves off, slapped each other's shoulders as if they had not all, a few moments before, been as agitated and unnerved as hornets in a storm. The only one who did not move, at least not immediately, was the small boy out on the foreshore, who was still as squat and compact as he had been before, his arms wrapped about his head as if afraid all his hair might suddenly fly off and leave for pastures new. When he finally uncurled, his face had the odd shine and colour of a cooked egg white, and his trembling was visible even from a distance. Solveig stood up, getting shakily to her feet and waved her arms at him encouragingly, and seeing her, he came on, though it took a while for him to reach her, and when he did his eyes were too wide, and he didn't seem able to get enough breath.

Solveig waited, in no hurry herself.

'Is it safe, miss?' he finally managed to gasp, his heart still thudding like a runaway horse within his chest. He'd got so panicked he almost forgot what he had come to tell her, but eventually handed Solveig a crumpled note with a wavering hand, spoke the words he had rehearsed, but only flatly, and without any of the dramatic flourish he had practised all the way here.

'They've found a body, miss. Up at the Suisgill, and Mr Finn says you've to come at once.'

Solveig had been about to answer, but was halted as she looked up and over the boy's head, saw several of her men waving at her in agitation, one of them holding something up in his hand, brushing at it spasmodically with his dust-besmirched coat, tilting it this way and that so that it caught the light, flashed as only metal can. The man was gesticulating wildly, his mouth moving wide and loud though she could not make out any words, her ears still filled with the ringing of the rocks, and the thundering of the ground as it settled beneath her feet.

Chapter 7   *Where now is the horse, the young rider?*

God, but the smell was appalling.

Finn quickly wrapped his kerchief around his mouth and nose to stop the most of it as he moved towards it. He had spied the sack first through his eyeglass as he glanced it over the hills and down the watercourses, had seen the smooth, clear water stumbling over the obstacle and around it, the dark blush that was bleeding from out one side.

'Hi!' he had shouted to the other searchers, bringing the rest of the men converging down upon him, flushing themselves out of the heather and sidings, from the gullies and streams they had been combing for the source of the sickness that had struck them down at the camp these last few days, keeping several men from work, knotting their stomachs into cramps, turning their skin a sweaty and unpleasant grey. The contamination had slowed everything up, forcing those not so far affected into boiling every drop of water they wanted to drink or cook or even wash with.

Brogar looked at the slump of the sack with dispassion, assumed it to be the carcass of some deer poached from off the hills, guessed it had been at one point stashed on the high, flat ledge immediately above where it now lay, that it must have slipped down with the scree that had formed a miniature dam against its furthest side. Soil-creep, he thought, and now that he was closer, could see the slight escape of writhe and winding of what could only be intestines, dipping and swaying in the water. The sight of it made him blench, and he turned his head away, sought out the breeze that was spooling down from the hills that lay all around.

He was wrong about the deer, but right about the infection, and, several hours later, had done all that he could. The sack and its contents had been

60

lifted with difficulty and distaste into the barrel he had ordered up from camp and brought back down again, and Brogar looked now from the barrel to the cart from which it had not long been unloaded, doubting that anyone would want to use that cart again, except for burning. The smell was strong and rank, and nobody wanted anything more to do with it, for although they'd managed to fit the most part of the corpse into the cask and topped it with an ill-fitting lid, they had already ascertained that it was no kind of deer at all, but a man, and in such a state of decomposition, identification was impossible. They'd tried to treat the remains with the respect they thought it due, but had not been able to stop some of the body's more liquid parts from escaping, trickling in small, abhorrent tracks out of the tiny cracks in the barrel's base, soaking into the planks of the cart as they had ferried it down the strath to Suisgill.

Brogar Finn, though, had not been daunted, had taken over and ordered the men into teams, set them to digging out what he called a sluice pool. He'd come across this same situation before, he told them, and not once but several times. For out in the badlands of Russia, he said, it had not been uncommon to come across some erratic prospector dead within his licensed grounds, killed by either cold, animal attack, starvation, or by some other miscellaneous misadventure, and the procedure then had been to clean up what was left, lighten the load, and carry the remains back to the nearest habitation. Once there, they would try to establish the body's identity, return him to any home he might have had, or to the nearest burial ground if he had none.

To the Suisgill workers, Brogar Finn's actions seemed an extraordinary act of human kindness, but to Brogar Finn himself it was nothing of the sort, only the desire to treat others as he would choose to be treated himself if found in similar circumstances, which, given his occupation, was not so unlikely.

He watched the men go at the ground with their picks and shovels, the first team excavating a channel leading away from the burn, the second digging out a large pit, and the third hacking out the other end of the channel that would soon connect pit to burn. When all was ready, the neck between the Suisgill and the channel would be broken, and the water would flow down into the pit into which they would place the man in his barrel, letting the water do what they could none of them bear to do: wash away the parts of the unknown man that were already beginning to liquefy, sift the clothes and flesh from his bones, leave what remained of him and his belongings on the base of the sluice pit, as if he had been sieved.

Brogar Finn was uneasy, as were the rest of the men at the Suisgill camp, for it wasn't every day you came across a body tied up in a sack, and it didn't take much imagination to realise that it wasn't something a man could do to himself. He felt uncomfortable to be left with the load of it, had already sent word to Tam Japp, the Estate Representative down at the Kildonan site, and got word just as swiftly back that neither Japp nor the Estate would have anything to do with it, that the jurisdiction lay foursquare upon the shoulders of the Lundt and McCleery Mining Company, and on Finn in particular, being their man on the spot. The Suisgill men had warned him this would be the reply before he'd even sent his message, and so, to be on the safe side, he'd also sent a man down to Solveig's house and the crude telegraphy system she'd had installed there, that linked her home into a triangle between Brora and Helmsdale. He just hoped there'd been someone at either end who knew how to work the new-fangled contraption, and that Solveig had received her message hours back, and was already the most part of her way up to the Suisgill.

He'd heard the booming coming out from Brora a long while back, at least an hour before he'd discovered the sack, a sound that shook the sky like thunder and reverberated from rock to rock, and hill to hill, a strange rumbling that lasted for well over ten minutes. And despite the situation, he hoped Solveig's day was going well, and that his advice on when and where to blow the explosives had achieved its goal.

He'd liked Solveig the first moment he'd met her – a short, rather formidable woman, maybe five years younger than himself, with a spark about her, an intelligence that was as obvious as it was understated, like a glow-worm in a dirt-pile, the only woman he'd ever met who knew the difference between greywacke and greensand, though he couldn't for the life of him remember how such a subject had cropped up. She'd welcomed him with enthusiasm into her home, made him instantly at ease, had taken him into her study where together they'd laid out several large-scale maps of the Kildonan valley, including a copy of the famous Roy map made for the military some years before, and the astonishingly detailed geological surveys of the area that her father had undertaken, and to which she had added over the years.

She had talked quite candidly about her real purpose in getting him here, had told him how she had lied to the Company, with whom both she and her husband had apparently fallen out of grace, despite her being a Lundt and him a McCleery, and how she had petitioned them with the legitimate lure of Kildonan gold. The Company had been interested – of course they had, for this sort of mineralogical anomaly was right up their street. They had assigned Finn to the case – of course they had, knowing full well he had links to this land, and would have the advantage over other investigators of already knowing the layout, not to mention the language.

Whether they'd divulged this detail to Solveig he rather doubted, or if they had, she made no mention of it, neither on that first night nor any following, and had never remarked upon his name, though it was as Highland as they came, and common as crowberry in these valleys. Or had been, he reminded himself, fifty or sixty years before.

When he'd first been given this assignment, read the name of the place he was being sent to, his heart had jumped hoops. He'd only been a boy when he'd left, one strand amongst the many who had wound their way out of these Highlands straths over the years, their ex-landlord's boot hard up their peasant arses kicking them on, an enforced and ongoing exodus down the roads, both north and south, that those leaving had later had called Destitution, on account of what lay at either end. Brogar's family had chosen to go in 1825, heading south to the coal mines of Lanarkshire, hoping for a more profitable life, and had struck good and lucky and managed to better themselves, making enough money to emigrate to Holland a few years later, settling into a better kind of life. Brogar had known nothing of the draconian closures of 1828 until Solveig told him of them, nor had he realised just how many people and families had had to up-sticks because of them. What he did know was that of all the many thousands who had left this valley over the past fifty odd years, he was one of the very few to have returned.

Chapter 8   *Where now the seats at the feast, the revels in the halls?*

Sholto McKay too felt his landing in Helmsdale as a kind of homecoming, knowing that his parents had left this very harbour forty-one years before, that he was setting foot on the same stones they might have stepped on, stones more worn than they had been then, a little more concave, holding a little more water when it rained, or when the sea was forced over the walls by a storm.

He arrived on the day of the explosions down at Brora, and the wharfside had been tumultuous with men reaching out their hands, yelling for the ship's ropes and painters to be thrown over, all smaller fishing skiffs having been hurriedly backed up and bunched into the river below the bridge like a crowd of clogs over which you could have walked from one bank to the other without wetting your feet.

Sholto had hardly got himself onto the harbour before he was assailed by offers of food and coffee, men talking terms and tariffs at him, mistaking him for one of the several foreign merchants who routinely arrived on the monthly trade ship from the Scandinavian lands. He was tired, confused, his head aching from lack of sleep; he began to long for the solitude of his basement office, wondering why he had agreed to step foot from it; perhaps expeditions and adventures were not for him after all.

He was rescued by a short, sturdy woman, who appeared like an arrow from the frontline straight towards him and, having ascertained his name and that he worked for Lundt and McCleery's, had taken his elbow, steered him roughly through the jostling crowds towards a pony trap into which he was quickly bundled. No sooner had he got his balance than it started up, forging its way through the pandemonium of the harbour and up a short, steep brae, Sholto looking rather wildly about him, latching onto a large sandstone building with barred windows, the words 'Artillery Hall' carved in large bold letters across its lintel; he had a brief urgent fear that he was about to be clapped in irons. But they had passed it by in a blink, gained the top of the brae a moment later, and a minute after that appeared to have cleared the entire town, and were now trundling along a track that paralleled a wide river.

His companion suddenly turned to him and smiled.

'I'm Solveig,' she said. 'Solveig McCleery.'

'My baggage…' Sholto replied weakly, envisaging hordes of harbour-hungry vagabonds ripping through his precious book trunk, scattering its content to the winds.

'They'll be taken care of,' said the woman Solveig. 'I've left a man there with instructions to bring them on.'

Sholto was relieved, managed to relax a little, tried to get his bearings, take in his surroundings, turned towards his rescuer and thanked her deeply. Only then did he notice she was covered head to foot in fine dust, and couldn't fathom why.

She looks like she's been down a mine, he thought. He saw that beneath the dust she looked worried, or perhaps puzzled, certainly preoccupied, and had not registered his thanks, but was gazing off to her right, which suited him fine. He was happy to remain in this silence, immensely glad to be on land in any capacity rather than on the water, and took pleasure in the landscape through which they were clattering, the trap boy working the brace of ponies hard, Sholto enjoying the sounds of the river to their right, and the clear, complicated call of a robin marking its ground somewhere in the scrub that lined its banks.

He didn't have long to rest up, for after a few minutes Solveig suddenly came to life, began rustling her skirts beside him, fishing through hidden pockets, eventually bringing out a piece of paper that she held out towards him.

'I've had a rather bizarre communication from your Mr Finn,' she said, as if all the usual pleasantries of new acquaintance had already been gone through and business was now the order of the day. She looked at him, but said nothing else, just thrust the piece of paper towards him. Despite the jogging of the trap he managed to take it from her hand and unfold it, ran his eyes down the script, couldn't make head nor tail of it.

Fnd dd mn in sck

Nd advc

Cm qck

BF

He creased his brows, looked at the note again, and then at Solveig, who sighed, took the piece of paper from him and refolded it.

'Found dead man in sack…need advice…come quickly,' she recited, obviously having memorised the words. 'It came by telegraph this morning,' she added, as if this explained everything. Her words came out in hiccups as she was jolted against the trap sides, against his shoulder and the hard backs of the seats, by the potholes in the road. He couldn't think of anything to say, could smell the ponies' sweat and the worn leather of the tack, and the faintest whiff of something else, something unsettling and yet oddly familiar, like explosives residue.

They cleared a sudden curve as the track veered in a hairpin away from the river over a tiny bridge, and at last the track began to level out, the wheels running smoother, the trap settling into a more manageable rhythm, allowing them both to get their breath back, allowing Sholto to finally speak.

'I have no idea what any of this means,' he said apologetically. He was truly floundering; he had expected a sedate surveying trip, and was not prepared at all for what this might actually entail given the contents of the note. Solveig was looking at him curiously, but said nothing, so he went on. 'This is my first time out. My first trip away from Trondheim. My first time on a boat.' He recognised the slight edge of rising panic to his voice and clutched at the trap side, breathed deeply, trying to calm himself.

'You've never been abroad?' Solveig asked him gently.

'Never,' he said, gulping slightly, aware that he had somehow disappointed this woman who was covered head to foot in dust and smelled of explosives, aware that she had probably had more excitement in one week than he had had in a lifetime.

'And you've never, then, met Mr Finn?'

'Never,' he agreed again.

'Well,' Solveig said, placing her hands as best she could upon her lap without losing balance, wondering how much to say, how loyal he would be to the Company rather than to her and Finn, what he would say about Finn helping with the mines. She had assumed they had worked together before, that they were colleagues, if not friends, and that there would be no difficulty with Finn continuing to help her on their covert mission. The communiqué she'd received from Harald Aasen the previous day had confirmed what she had already supposed – that Sholto would arrive on the usual monthly trade ship – and she had already dispatched the trap there to meet him there and convey him back to base. The coincidence of Finn's message arriving that morning about dead bodies in sacks had been the only reason she'd had cause to leave Brora at all, and she'd thought it a small courtesy to divert through Helmsdale to collect him personally, rather than take the shorter route to Kildonan over the Loth. And now that she had him, a captive audience if

68

ever there was one, she might as well take the opportunity to soften him up, give him her views, lay down the groundwork, try to make him understand why she had gone behind the Company's back, and how important it was, both to her and to Brora, and to the area as a whole, that she be able to continue her work. There could be no harm, she thought, at least in trying.

He was a rather strange looking man, now that she actually looked at him, trying to weigh him up, gauging her best strategy. He was thin, a bundle of bones beneath a coat that was too big for him, and his skin had the same grown-beneath-trees look that wood anemones had – very pale, with the veins showing through them, looking as if they would tear if you so much as looked at them wrongly. But his most pronounced feature by far was the shock of grey hair running through black, giving him the look of an anaemic badger, one that has spent too long underground, with the faintly startled expression of having come unexpectedly into the light.

How much to tell him, she was thinking, and how to start, though eventually she did.

'There's a lot of history attached to this valley,' Solveig began, pointing out an old boundary stone as they passed it, directing his gaze to the tumbled-down heaps of cottages that littered the broad lands of the valley on either side of the track. 'Seventy years ago,' she went on, 'almost two thousand people lived in this valley. Can you imagine it?'

Sholto McKay could not, and was shocked. For one thing, he could not see how so many people could have survived in such a place and make even a rudimentary living on the few hundred yards of fertile fields that bordered the river, beyond which the hills went up without relent, the topsoil good for nothing but heather and bad scrub.

'The first were moved off at the beginning of the century by the Countess of Sutherland,' Solveig explained. 'She'd always had big plans for this area, and once she'd married into English money, she had the means to carry them out. Fifteen thousand people she cleared off in the end. Fifteen thousand,' Solveig said again, trying to imagine every last one of them standing single file in front of her, saw them stretching up the valley for mile upon mile. Sholto was thinking that if he'd been living here, he'd have been at the front of the queue.

'The Sutherlands built up the Brora and Helmsdale townships specifically to take them all in,' Solveig said. *Good on them,* Sholto thought, but Solveig wasn't finished. 'Shoved them down the mines, put them to work in the quarries and the lime kilns.'

Sholto shook his head. He knew the stories. His father had spoken about them often enough, though Sholto hadn't really listened or understood. He'd always wondered why, if their life here had been so hard – and patently it had been – they hadn't been more grateful for the chance to leave it, and taken advantage of the opportunity to start again somewhere new. But looking at this wide-bottomed valley as he travelled through it, at the great, broad brush-sweep of river that ran through its base, at the tumbled-down cottages, the overgrown patches that must once have been vegetable plots, he had an inkling of what it might have meant to them to have had to leave here.

Solveig was still talking quietly, though he'd only half an ear open; he knew very well what was coming next, and sure enough she said it, sighed it, dropped it at his feet.

'Eighteen twenty-eight,' she said. 'That was when it all ended.'

Sholto nodded, though he was not agreeing with her, and did not look at her, was thinking only, *1828, not the end for me, but the beginning.*

70

By the time they'd reached the Suisgill, Solveig was cricked in her seat, wishing there was an easier way to travel that did not involve being ground like peppercorns in a mill. Brogar Finn was there to meet them, striding forward, taking a strong hold of her elbow to help her down, before nodding over at Sholto.

'You'd be McKay, then,' he said, by way of introduction.

'Sholto,' said Sholto, bracing himself for the inquisition he supposed would come about where he had worked before, at what, with whom, knowing he would have nothing to offer in return, would eventually have to say the brief word 'office', which would say it all. Brogar Finn though said nothing more, and had already started to lead Solveig off even before Sholto had managed to untangle his satchel strap, which had inexplicably got caught in the spokes of the trap's back wheel as he had tried to dismount.

'He's in the sluice pit,' he heard Finn saying. 'I expect you'll want to see.'

He was taking Solveig off to a plateau than ran beside a good-sized burn, away to one side from a motley collection of canvas-hooded wooden struts that looked as miserable and dirty as the mud that ran between them, clogging up their doorways, churned into clods and pools by the evident passage of many heavy boots whose semi-submerged imprints ran thick and oily with water that was black as peat. The whole place reeked of hard times, hard work, sweat and grime, burned-out fires, charred food, wet leather, dirty clothes. He recognised the faint undertow of urine you always seemed to get wherever a group of men were holed up too closely together – on every dockside he had ever frequented, every tavern he had ever walked by in Trondheim. It had the same feel of the cheapest of boarding house, where men were packed in by the dozen, skin and clothes doused with paraffin wax to ward off fleas and lice, the stink of damp straw that passed in those places for beds, the stale dregs of strong drink such men who stayed there needed in order to get even a few moments sleep.

He shuddered as he realised this was most probably the place he would be quartered, tried not to think about it, followed on instead in Finn and Solveig's wake only to be assailed by a stench that was far worse than anything he had ever smelled in his life. He could feel the blood draining from his face, and had to put his sleeve across his mouth and nose to stop himself from vomiting on the spot. Solveig and Finn joined a knot of other men a few yards beyond him, and he saw a dark ripple of water, a dirty bubble popping with difficulty through the water, as if its surface were coated with fat.

He swallowed, approached Solveig, who too had begun to cough as he had; he noticed the skin of her face had gone even paler than the colour of the ash that still remained on her clothes and hair, even after their trip up from Helmsdale.

'That smells absolutely dreadful, Mr Finn,' she finally got out, saying the words Sholto could not, not without taking away his sleeve.

'Doesn't it?' Finn replied jovially. 'You should've been here when we first chucked him in.'

His enthusiasm didn't seem shared by the tatterdemalion group of men who circled the sluice pit, some sitting on their haunches, others further away, perched on stones, carefully cleaning the shovels they were holding upright between their ankles, not looking up. These were the men who had been here the first time the sluice pit had been filled to the brim, who had had to roll the barrel containing the body across the short grass and kick it into the water, who had been told by Finn then to go at the barrel with their picks to release the body from its staves, and had seen it, once released, unfurl like a foetus, moving in the water like an oversized baby, limbs uncurling, so vulnerable, so unaware.

'Either way,' Finn went on unabashed, apparently unaware of everyone else's discomfort, 'there's no chance of contaminating any of the groundwater or it getting back into the burn. I did a few surveys of the underlying aquifers last week, and there's a separate spring beneath here that should leach away the run-off with no problem.'

'I'm glad of it,' Solveig commented, having apparently already accustomed herself to the circumstances of stink and rot. 'No more sickness amongst the men, then?'

Brogar Finn beamed. 'No more of that, and we can say definitely that this was the source of it. Nothing else in the water remotely like it all the way up the burn.'

He pointed into the pit, him and Solveig standing directly on its edge, looking down at the de-barrelled corpse as if they had worked all their lives in an abattoir or a charnel house, and spent their leisure hours attending the anatomy lessons that were all the rage across Europe, from London to Petersburg. Sholto could not share their enthusiasm and hung back, hoping this was not the normal day of a man spent in the field; he had imagined casual, maybe sunlit afternoons, jotting down notes about geological formations, mineral strata, figuring out the various outputs of ore-bearing rocks according to the layout of the seams they had been found in.

He'd not for a single moment imagined field work could be anything like this, not for all the reports he had read and transcribed, some of which had included deaths, of course they had, and not always pretty ones – if death could be at any time referred to as pretty – but they'd all been just words to him, marks upon paper, no hint of the smells and sights he was encountering now, of the man down there in Brogar's sluice pit, a man who had once been a child, a toddler, who had struggled through all the diseases childhood could throw at him and come out the other side, who had gone on to grow and live through all the other hardships brought on by adulthood, only to end up like this.

Sholto felt sick, and began to retch, a thin dribble of spittle hanging from chin to sleeve. He felt someone tugging at his coat, and turned to find a boy of about sixteen thrusting a pewter tankard of water at him. Sholto took the mug, but looked suspiciously at the water. It looked clear enough, but God knew, as must have done the boy, where it had come from. The boy in question watched him curiously, a smile twitching at his lips, before putting Sholto out of his misery.

'I wouldn't do it, sir, honest. I wouldn't. I've been sick three times today already, and that water's clean as a clam.'

He had a different kind of rhythm to his words than Solveig did, but Sholto understood him well enough. He'd spoken, in fact, just as his own parents might have done.

'Thank you,' Sholto said gratefully, but the boy was already walking away.

'I'd scarper a bit further if I were you,' he said as he went. 'Pool's draining pretty sharpish and'll need refilling, and really, mister, you don't want to be here for that.'

The lad was right.

Sholto could already hear Finn shouting for the neck of the channel to be broken again, saw a couple of the men who had been sitting idly around the pit levering themselves up off their boulders with their pickaxes, heading glumly for the burn. Sholto took the lad's advice and was moving away, when Solveig intercepted him.

'I should like to see exactly where the body was found. Shouldn't you?' she asked. 'I think we could both do with the air. Mr Finn!' She raised her voice a little, and Brogar Finn left the pit-side, and came to join them. 'The site of the body's discovery, Mr Finn,' Solveig said, as if it was the most natural thing in the world. 'Will you lead us on?'

Chapter 9   *Where the companions, forced to leave this middle-earth?*

An hour's walk brought them to the place where the man in the sack had been found. Finn had been garrulous most of the way, updating Solveig on all he had been doing since he'd arrived here, of the boreholes he had sunk, the surveys he had carried out, pointing out to them both how the gold prospectors had mettled the track they were walking as best they could with sand and stones, planks of wood, the places the same men had hacked into the high banks to left and right of the burn, bringing down the coarse grit in barrow-loads before sifting every last grain of it for gold.

'It's all alluvial, of course,' Brogar was saying as they gained the high ground, the track now twenty yards above the level of the burn. 'Just as at Tana Leva.'

Sholto nodded then, recalling the very last report he had filed before he had left Trondheim, had been about to allude to it, ask an intelligent question, but before he could come up with one both Finn and Solveig pulled ahead, while he, not used to spending his days walking muddy tracks and up steep braes, was left lagging, and was happy enough about that. It gave him time to look about, admiring the low roll of heathered hills that ran away in every direction, their uniformity marred only by the occasional outline of lean-tos erected by prospectors, desperate shelters knocked together from branches torn from the odd birch or rowan tree that nestled in the gullies that had been gouged out by spate, thin and weedy branches laid over with heather and bracken, in which men could huddle away their nights, maybe kindle up a small fire, all to save the long walk back down to base and out again the following morning.

It didn't bear thinking about, thought Sholto, and it was clear that this was a way of life that was not for him. He couldn't sleep in such places, he told himself, not even back at the camp itself. It was all too unsanitary, too much being with other men, too much close companionship with people he didn't know, and didn't want to know. Why on earth had he ever thought he could be a field agent in the first place? How could Harald Aasen have contemplated for even a second that he could take this kind of life? He was a linguist, for heaven's sake, a man who might have been a mole for all the time he had ever spent in the world. That his own mother and father had come from a place such as this, he was finding equally hard to contemplate.

He was tired, wanted to sit down, wanted to close his eyes and wake up back in his little basement office in Trondheim, see his desk, his bookshelves, all his files, standing just so, just as he had left them. That someone else was there in his office mucking through his papers and books, reordering his desk, was suddenly too much, and he felt lost and alone, tears prickling at the back of his eyes, made worse by the shame of them being there at all.

Brogar Finn was maybe a hundred yards along the track in front of the sniffling Sholto when he suddenly veered off towards his left, skidding sideways down the brae towards the burn. He let out a loud *whoop whoop!* as he went, and Sholto saw, with some dismay, that Solveig was following after him, sliding down the slope on her boots, skirts hitched into her belt, hands held out to either side to catch at the heather to slow her fall. He'd no option then but to follow them, and by the time he had made what he considered a terrifying descent, they were already fording the burn by means of step-stone boulders, Finn soon halfway up the steep bank on the opposite side, Solveig struggling on behind him.

Sholto landed on his tail-bone, the wind knocked out of him, but he ran to catch them up, slipped on the boulders, filling his boots with water, in time to give Solveig a last unseemly shove as Finn dragged her up by her wrists, and soon they were all standing on a ledge fifteen-odd feet above the burn, that was three, maybe four yards long, a little less in diameter. They were all puffing after their exertions, but Brogar Finn soon found the breath to start talking again, gave a wide sweep of his arm that encompassed the ledge and what little lay on it, which wasn't much: no rabbit or deer droppings, no moss, no pebbles, no grit, nor sand, looking rather as if it had been lately swept clean, apart from nine or so large stones that seemed to have been placed there with some deliberation, for they were all quite evenly spaced about the perimeter of the ledge.

'Found this place,' Finn said, 'after I'd noticed the scree and the soil-creep when we were waiting on the barrel coming up from the Suisgill. Reckon the sack must have been secured up here and only fallen over into the river by mistake.'

'A rood ground...' Sholto murmured. 'It looks like a rood ground.'

Brogar Finn looked at his new assistant, at this Sholto McKay, and waited for more, though it did not come. He scratched at the back of his neck; he had had many assistants over the years, all with the same specifications – they knew languages, had a working knowledge of geology, and could adapt to the harsh circumstances Brogar would often lead them into. Only one had ever come up to scratch as far as Brogar was concerned, and that had been the last one, who'd been idiot enough to die a stupid death in a duel he could never have won following a bar brawl in Kiev. Others had merely fallen by the wayside, or resigned their commission, heading back to nearest town, unable to take the bleakness of the life he was offering them. And this new one, this Sholto McKay, he doubted would last a month. He'd seen him turn green as goose shit at the sluice pit, puking up his guts, and he didn't care why Harald Aasen had chosen to fit him up with this baby, only that if he didn't turn into the real deal and soon, Brogar Finn would make short shrift of him. He needed a man by his side to do the parts of the job he couldn't do:

78

the translating, the tedious writing of reports, all the anthropological stuff the Company required for their papers, but he also needed someone he could get along with, someone who could move with the situation, take risks, not tut him every time he swung himself down a mine shaft or threw himself off a cliff on a winch and a tattered length of rope.

This train of thought was interrupted by Solveig, who was crouching down beside him, touching the stone that lay nearest to her feet.

'But look at this,' she said. 'It's got scratches of some kind on it…'

Brogar Finn looked down at the stone she was indicating, and then at another that lay nearby, kicking it gently with its boot, rolling it over.

'This one too,' he said as he peered at the rock he had turned.

'And this one as well,' Solveig added. 'And another!' she said excitedly, moving to the next stone, getting perilously close to the edge of the ledge.

'Be careful, for God's sake!' Sholto warned, worried the whole section might break off beneath their weight; he could easily see how the sack, assuming it really had been up here in the first place, had ended up where it had. Water must have flooded down over this barren, flat-iron of a rock-ledge, shifting the sack by inches, pushing it out towards the overhanging lip which had finally given way and sent it tumbling down to the burn below, and might still do the same for them.

Solveig hadn't acknowledged Sholto's warning, but she had stopped, and was bending down again, studying the rock that lay closest to her foot.

'Mr Finn,' she said, a slight quaver to her voice as she repeated his name. 'Mr Finn. Will you take a look at this?' Solveig's face had gone rigid as she pointed at the stone.

'Is that what I think it is?' she asked, looking up briefly as Finn craned down over her shoulder, their faces almost touching. Finn grimaced, the shadows thus produced making him look to Sholto like a badly carved gargoyle that

79

had jumped down from the guttering of an ancient country church. A fleeting impression, dispelled when Finn straightened and began to speak.

'Can't quite make it out,' he said, though there was a look of puzzlement to his face that suggested otherwise.

'But can't you see it?' Solveig persisted. 'It's like at the chapel…'

'Maybe you should let our resident linguist take a look,' Finn countered, staring now directly at Sholto, as if daring him, or testing him, or maybe both.

The walk back to the Suisgill had been a quiet affair, and once there, Finn stayed a short time to supervise the final filling in of the sluice pit, while Solveig and Sholto walked on the few miles to Solveig's home. She led him down the lane and over a bridge, through a gate, along a narrow path that led to a slightly menacing-looking building set against a tall backdrop of trees, whose four walls formed a perfect square, its rook-dark roof was tailored with precisely cut slates. This building, Solveig told him, had been built by her father several years after the events of the Helmsdale Pick back in 1828. It was a chapel of the Holy Apostolic Church, of which her father had become enamoured in the years after The Pick, and into which he had later ordained himself a minister.

'He went a bit off the rails after the '28 closures,' she elaborated. 'At least so my mother told me. I don't remember him much. He was always away a lot, though he came back for visits every couple of years, until about twenty years ago. Soon after that, I stopped waiting.'

'It must have been hard for your mother,' Sholto said, trying to sound a sympathy he did not truly feel for this newly met woman, whose past was so tied up with his own.

80

'We had a small stipend from the Company,' Solveig told him bleakly. 'It was enough.'

They walked a few more steps until they came to the door of the chapel, now converted into a guest house where Brogar Finn had been invited to make his home, she said, but he had chosen not to, preferring to stay on site at either the Suisgill or Kildonan, wherever he was working. Sholto shivered, unsure which would be the worse fate – staying in the mud and pits with Brogar Finn in what the Suisgill miners called home, or here, all alone in this dreary building, that had an air about it of pushing away everyone that came to its doors. And by those doors they both were now, and Solveig halted abruptly.

'It's the same,' she said, directing Sholto's gaze up to the lintel, and Sholto looked up at the two-word inscription that had been blocked out in the stone by a mason's chisel.

'Sukkiim,' he murmured, looking at the copy he had made of the Hebrew letters scratched out on the stone Solveig had found up on the ledge. They'd been as uneven there as they were clear now, with their transliteration added helpfully beneath:

קפיים

SUKKIIM

'The Dwellers amongst the Rocks,' Solveig added. 'A tribe in the Bible, and what father always called his congregation.'

Chapter 10   *Each day brings new desertion and decay to the walls of the city*

Up at the Suisgill, several men had gathered about the sluice pit, watching intently as the last of the water from the final, fifth baptism of the dead man ebbed away into the ground beneath. Brogar Finn had left for Solveig's home, but they had been given explicit instructions to be on hand when it finished draining, and also on what they should do next, which was to go down into the dead man's pit and pull him out, place him on a blanket and roll him tight, first removing whatever they could of his clothing, which they were to place in a secondary blanket, along with whatever bits and pieces the water might have sieved from out his pockets and person and left upon the base of the pit.

It was not a duty any of them took lightly or with enthusiasm, though they recognised its necessity. The whole process had given them a deeply unpleasant glimpse into the future; they, and everyone they cared for, would one day end up looking as uncompromisingly dead and decomposing as the remnants of the body in the pit. From high above came the cave-empty crawks of several pairs of ravens outlined darkly against the chill blue of the sky, wing-tips exploring the wind currents that kept them up there, outstretched feathers moving to keep them circling right above this one spot, as if they had nothing else to do, as if they just had to bide their time, could stay there suspended for as long as it took for the down-below keepers of their carrion to get bored, desist, and depart.

One amongst the men on the side of the sluice pit began a mumbled prayer, at which all the rest removed their caps, and a few crossed themselves, glad for the interim it gained them, the slight reprieve before the final *amen*, before they had to do what they had been dreading. When the moment finally

82

came, they all stood waiting, hoping someone else would do what they did not want to do themselves, as someone finally did.

'Oh for Chris'sake,' Dougall Meek exclaimed, as he jumped down into the sluice pit, ordering someone to hand him down his shovel and a couple of bits of wood he could use as tongs. 'Let's aye get this done,' he said without preamble as he landed. 'Soonest done, soonest buried.'

The rest above him nodded, hurried into action now that someone else had taken the lead, a couple of others daring to jump down beside Dougall, slotting their shovels below the dead man as Dougall had already done, inching the loosened package of his flesh and bones onto the flattened surface of their blades, the green slough of his skin and shirt and trousers staining their shovel blades as they brought the corpse up with some difficulty, his body unwieldy, bending in places they had not expected, and with a weight they had not anticipated. There was one alarming moment when they'd got him up to head height and almost onto the blanket, when one of the shovel-holders could no longer take the smell and began to cough and retch, his shovel dipping, and the corpse with it, making it look like a flayed and distrait mannequin, which movement started a high-pitched giggling in the youngest of the dead man's top-side tenders, as one Robbie Weavers cracked and couldn't handle what he was seeing, went on and on as if he would never stop; he had to be slapped across the face and pushed to the ground before he was broken and silenced, was told to go and set a fire, get it lit, put on water, make a brew. Even ten yards distant, the rest of them could hear the odd hiccups and choking sounds young Robbie couldn't stop himself from making as he heaved and spat his way back to the fire-ground. He had a few others turning their heads and doing the same, a survival mechanism they were unable to overcome.

Down below, Dougall Meek twisted his mouth in annoyance, having no time for the young, and certainly no time for their theatrics; he had smoked a pipe since he was ten, and in consequence had absolutely no sense of taste or smell. When they'd finally got the body lifted and out and the clothes raked from off it with their shovel blades, Dougall began to poke about at the mud left behind by the corpse's departure with no more emotion than if he had been looking for winter-hidden toads, at least until he found something that really did give him cause for consternation. Dougall wrinkled his nose up in concentration at his discovery, putting his wooden paddle beneath what he had found, and flipping it out onto the bank. He was looking at it now, at head height with it, making his assessment. And then the great unmoveable Dougall sighed deeply, and spoke.

'It's Willie Blaine,' he said. 'I think it's Willie Blaine.'

And though he couldn't quite comprehend that this unidentifiable sack of rot he'd been shovelling up and poking at had been a living man, let alone someone he'd known since a boy, and had worked with, played cards with, chatted and gossiped with for so many years, but for all that, he was sure.

'It's Willie Blaine,' he said again, with a bluntness he could not disguise. 'From Port Gower.'

Everyone else above had stopped, had wondered how he could know this, given the state of the corpse, yet not doubting that old Dougall, of all people, could be wrong. The men who were local enough looked down at what Dougall had just brought up with his stick and flicked upon the ground beside their boots, saw the small, tattered book lying on the bank, just as Dougall had already done.

'It's the same lettering...' Dougall was saying as he hauled himself up and out of the pit, sliding his shovel blade below the pathetic limp of the leather and lifting it up, thrusting it towards one of the men in the waiting crowd, who backed away, holding up his hands. 'It's the same lettering,' Dougall repeated, shoving it closer to the cowering man. 'Tell me it's not so.'

The other man could not. He was shaking, but could not move from his spot, not with that stinking shovel directed right beneath his nose, and the book that was splayed out upon it.

'It's his,' he stuttered finally. 'Yes, you're right. It's his. I seen it plenty times. Always took it with him wherever he went, ever since the chapel...'

Another man pushed forward, looked carefully at the book held out on the open palm of Dougall's shovel and began to retch, went down on hands and knees and started heaving.

'Oh God.' He sicked up the words with the bile he couldn't stop, the saliva hot in his throat. 'Oh God, oh God.'

And the smell of his vomit was bad enough that all the others had to move away or join him. Only Dougall Meek remained, unaffected by the stench, curious about what must come next.

'The church, then?' he asked innocently.

'Lundt's,' another volunteered.

'Lundt's Apostles,' said another, backing away into the descending gloom of falling night.

'Ha!' exclaimed Dougall as he jumped back down into the pit, went back to turning over the mud at its base, found a few other bits and pieces and brought them up, though it was not much: a couple of buttons, a small rusted penknife, the unmistakeable stumps of several non-too healthy teeth, a stub of pencil, a blunted awl, a whetstone. He also found Willie Blaine's pouch, the tight-tied leather purse they all secreted about their persons to keep their dust in, or any small nuggets, if they'd been lucky enough to find any, each burning his own initials onto its skin to mark his claim. The upside men opened it gingerly with their knives, no one wanting to touch it directly, seeking out the initials WB, which they found. They also found that Willie's dust collection was still intact, at which point an uncomfortable silence followed, each wondering if they could decently do what they were all thinking, which was to divide the spoils and pretend it hadn't been found. They looked towards Dougall for direction as they helped him up from his second time in the pit. He looked back at them, and shook his head.

'Funeral's to be paid for,' was all he said, and they got back to their work, put all of Willie Blaine's last possessions, including buttons, teeth and book, with the clothes they had stripped him of, rolled up the first blanket and then the second, washed their boots and arms in the burn before settling back to the fire Robbie Weavers had got going for them, settled themselves upon bum-easy rocks and began to break out tobacco and the renegade whisky they were not supposed to have.

'Who's to tell his widow?' someone asked into the evening, the smoke of their pipes drifting on between them.

'The two of them, you mean,' another added, several nodding their heads, Robbie sniggering, all knowing that Willie Blaine had a proper wedded wife in Port Gower right enough, along with another, prettier, girl tucked away in Helmsdale whom he saw on occasion when he went down to cash in his gold, times when he avoided Tam Japp like the plague. They all recalled the dressing down Willie'd got a couple weeks back from Japp, which was how come they'd not noticed his disappearance, because Willie'd already said then that enough was enough, and that he was not standing for it, and would soon be gone. Quite how gone, they'd none of them anticipated.

'Well I'm not telling no one,' someone answered the original question.

'Nor me,' said another, and a few more besides.

'That Finn'll have to do it,' said old Dougall, settling the matter. 'Told us to do all this, so he did, and we did it. Let'm all else do the rest.'

And so it was left.

Just ten men sitting smoking and drinking companionably around the fire they soon had burning high and bright, only the youngest not with them, Robbie Weavers told to leg it down the road to Solveig McCleery's, tell her what they'd found, and that the dead man was Willie Blaine, and that he'd been made as comfortable as they could make him in his blankets – one for bones, one for everything else – and they had already lifted him onto the trap he had already spoiled with his bringing down from the Suisgill in his barrel, for they were all God-fearing men in their own way, though not in the same way Willie Blaine had been, they had all agreed about that. They trusted Solveig would know what to do with his body, him being one of her father's folk, and as close to the chapel as any of them had been. There weren't many of the Holy Rollers left, not now the valley had been almost completely emptied, just one or two scattered here and there, up and down, a couple in Brora, a few in Helmsdale, several stalwarts who had clung to Joseph Lundt's beliefs like ants to a small raft of grass while their nest is washed away by the spate-time floods.

They filled their pipes, did those men, filled their cups, passed around a flagon, but as far as the remaining Suisgill miners were concerned, Willie Blaine was neither missed nor mourned, apart perhaps by old Dougall Meek who remembered him well, remembered their shared childhood more clearly than he had done last week, and only old Dougall had the grace to raise a silent salute to his old comrade with his cup, and bid him farewell.

Chapter 11   *The weapons, thirsty for slaughter*

Solveig closed the door to the chapel, and though it was still passably light outside, it was dark as a sloe inside the chapel itself. The only external source came from the line of tiny windows pierced into the topmost section of the altar wall, showing now as dull grey pinpricks above the shadows. Solveig quickly moved her hand to the right of the door, dipped into the niche there and took out candles and tinder. Once the first tallow was lit she made her way to the second niche that lay beside the first and took out lamps, and in a few minutes she and Sholto were down at the front of what had once been her father's chapel, standing by a large table, wide and broad, still functional, though no longer as an altar.

'You must be tired,' Solveig said apologetically. 'I'm sorry it's turned out such a long day for you, and your first one here.'

Sholto was indeed tired, but also oddly invigorated; he felt as if his head had left his body behind. The weakness and tears he'd almost succumbed to earlier on the walk up the Suisgill had been replaced by curiosity once they'd reached the rood ground, and then been completely overtaken by an entirely unexpected euphoria on the way back again, as he realised that his own mother and father might have walked the same tracks, the same paths, more than forty years before. And now that he was in the ex-chapel of Solveig's father, he was overtaken by yet another emotion that he'd not had time to identify: he was looking about the walls, seeing the shelves of books lined up on one side tailing off into gloom, a line of rather badly painted landscapes on the opposite wall that had been hung above several cot beds that had obviously been hammered into being from the remains of old wooden pews, the brass holders for candlesticks still apparent at their ends, at their bedsteads.

He hoped Solveig was not the artist of the badly painted pictures, or that he would be expected to churn out false praise for them, but Solveig had already noticed his line of sight lingering on them, and interposed.

'My mother's,' she said, an apologetic note in her voice. 'She wasn't very good, I'm afraid, but it's so easy to hang onto things, hang them up, and better here than in the house.'

Sholto recognised the note of levity to her voice, appreciated it, smiled, was thinking of a similar legacy his own mother had given him, a kidney-shaped pebble, *from the old country*, that she'd strung on a leather thong and made him promise he would always wear. And he had done, though he'd had to restring it several times over, and always wore it below his shirt where no one else could see it. But he realised now that he really was back in the old country from which that stone had come, and he put his hand up to his chest, fingered its old familiarity through his shirt, understanding why Solveig had kept these ghastly paintings; like his mother's stone, they were a fragment of a life that had passed, too ugly to look at every day, too precious to throw upon the fire.

Solveig set her lamps upon the large table, and pointed out where several more could be found. 'I'll leave you to rest while I go and prepare some food,' she said. 'Mr Finn assured me he would join us here soon.' She started walking back up the chapel, and then turned back, just before she reached the door. 'I hope you'll be comfortable here, Mr McKay, and I'd be grateful if you could get Mr Finn to agree to stay here too for the rest of the duration of your work. It would make me so much happier to know you were both here in relative comfort, rather than staying down with the miners. God knows, I've tried to persuade him before, but he's never so much as set foot in the place.'

Hand on heart, Sholto could agree to that.

'I'll do my very best, Mrs McCleery,' he said, his voice loud in this darkness, and sounding even to his own ears incredibly relieved. Thank God, he thought, that he was not expected to stay down at the makeshift shanty town of the Suisgill, the very idea of which still appalled him, and the thought that for the past two weeks Brogar Finn had preferred that place to this frightened him, made him wonder what he had let himself in for, exactly what Harald Aasen expected of him, and if he would fall at the first hurdle, if his nerves would fail him, if he would have to go crawling back to Trondheim, begging for his underground lair, become a troglodyte again, and spend the rest of his life reading about what other people did, instead of doing them himself.

Solveig was still standing there at the chapel door, and though the most of her had been swallowed up by the shadows and the gloom, she was still holding a candle in her hand, and it lit up her face like a foresters' moon, the kind that looks too big when you see it balanced on a hillside or against the backdrop of long-familiar trees. She was smiling, and the smile in the candlelight made her look almost beatific.

'Well,' was all she said. 'I'm sure that if anyone can persuade him, it will be you.'

Exactly what she'd meant by that, Sholto didn't know and didn't ponder, because, tired as he was, there was something that was puzzling him, and when a man like Sholto got puzzled, as Harald Aasen well knew, it was a hard task stopping him going at it until he had figured that puzzle out.

When Brogar Finn arrived at the chapel a quarter of an hour later, he opened the door to find the place in darkness, excepting the several lit lamps right at the other end that showed his new assistant, Sholto McKay, poring over some pieces of paper he had laid out in a circle upon the large table, behind which he was standing.

90

'Hi aye, there!' Brogar announced, in the manner he had learned was the right form of greeting in these parts. That they were both foreigners to these shores never occurred to him, for both spoke the language as easily as Brogar could manage the Dutch or German he'd been brought up with, and was aware from Harald Aasen that Sholto had at least seven European languages under his belt. He got no response, even when he closed the door loudly behind him, started stamping his boots down the main thoroughfare towards the table Sholto was leaning so assiduously over.

'So what've we got here?' he tried again as he got within spitting distance and took up a stance on the opposite side of the table, looking properly for the first time at the man who had been assigned as his new assistant, noting how dark the rest of his hair was compared to the streak of grey that ran through from widow's peak to ear. He wasn't a great one for physiognomies, knew his own face left much to be desired after having been smashed to a pulp by a falling mine beam here, a knife-stroke there, but he found something faintly ethereal about this Sholto's slight build, the way his cheekbones seemed to flute away from his eyes as if they had somewhere else to go. But then his attention was caught by another spectacle entirely – the great glass case of Solveig's father's geological collection, backlit by the lamps on Sholto's table.

He moved quickly, snatched up one of the lamps, heard Sholto tutting in annoyance and was about to remonstrate at that most irritating of qualities he had found in other men, other assistants, until the light of the lantern let him see properly the contents of the glass case, and instead he let out a low whistle.

'Have you seen this stuff?' Brogar said to no one in particular. 'But this is fantastic! Look at all these fossils! There's Ganoid fish scales here, and

Coccosteus. And just look at this Cupressocrinus crassus…and you can still see the resin streaks in this fossilised wood section…'

Sholto had of course noticed the introduction into the chapel of his new boss, but wasn't listening; he had his own collection of wonders to study in the form of the notes he had made of the marks upon the stones where the body had been found. There'd been nine in all, including the one which Solveig had recognised as the Hebrew form of the word *Sukkiim*. It was puzzling enough that such scratches had been made on the stones at all, and more so because although they'd fathomed that the body must have been dead at least a week, probably more, the scratches on the stones had quite patently been relatively fresh. There'd been dust on them when he'd picked them up – he could clearly recall it gritting the surface of his fingertips – and how could that have been so if they'd been there for more than a couple of days? Surely the rain would have washed such dust away, and he knew it had rained three days before, because he had asked, which meant that whatever had been scratched on the stones up at the place Willie Blaine had been stowed, had only been done in the last few days.

Which seemed ridiculous, but nonetheless true. A message had been left up there, waiting patiently to be found.

He'd taken note of all the scratches on all the stones up at the rood ground, and had recognised something of the language they'd been written in. Apart from the Hebrew of the word *Sukkiim*, everything else was in Gaelic, he was sure of it. His parents hadn't had the luxury of being able to read or write, but they had possessed a tatty old copy of the *Tiomnadh Nuadh* – the New Testament – through which he had flipped from time to time, enjoying the oddness of the words. He'd even spoken the language as a toddler – his parents' language – long before he'd started to attend the local school, at which point he had switched to the Norwegian spoken by everyone else, and had become the teacher to his parents who, despite their many years in Finnmark, had struggled with the rudiments of that foreign language ever since.

Consequently, and from all his previous training, Sholto had written out each separate set of scratches on each stone on separate pieces of paper, and had placed them on the table roughly as they had been found on the ledge, aware of the shortcomings of this procedure, it being likely that several had been moved, or had gone over the edge with the body. Still, it was a start:

קפיים   ABAIR

                        DUINE   BITH

AIDH   GAIR

FAOD   AR

                                                 BEN

He could grasp a small part of their meaning. He knew that *ben* meant mountain, and thought that *duine* was probably a man, assuming it was pronounced *doon-a*. As for the rest, he couldn't even decide if they were whole words or merely parts. His eyes had scanned the bookshelves that lined the chapel wall as he wondered if there was a Gaelic dictionary hidden away in there, if such a thing had been written yet. Neither Solveig nor Finn had recognised any of the words, at least they'd not mentioned it up on the ledge, although it was true it had been hard to see them in *situ*, their scratches crude and uneven. It had taken Sholto quite a while to decipher his own copies of them, get them ordered and sequenced, turned the right way up or down. He glanced up at the small windows as he moved about the table, saw how dark it was outside, how quickly the evening had set in, how the surrounding hills must have closed these valleys off from daylight far sooner than the flatlands that were, paradoxically, further north.

Up at the Suisgill, the miners were used to this swift down-falling of the night, and liked the excuse it gave them to finish working, the comradeship they could look forward to between end of shift and time to sleep, a gap before they had to be up and working again. In the summer months it was a different story, for there were times then when the sun barely sank, when they'd be up as early as four, and out for the gold dust hunt at five, and not back to camp until seven, by which time they were so exhausted it was all they could do to boil up a bit of stew and scoop it into their mouths with crusts of bread, before collapsing onto the bunks built rank-by-rank and plank-by-plank inside their shacks and tents, boots still on their feet, clothes still wet with sweat and rain, no thought in their heads but the hope that the following day would prove more successful than the one that had gone before.

This particular evening though, had been different, for they'd none of them had a full working day by any means, not after what had been discovered up at the burn that morning, and all that had followed after. Their muscles didn't ache, they'd had time and energy to wash, and most had shifted shirts and socks if they had them to change into. And now it was all done, they felt calm and comfortable, warmed by the soft flames licking up from their fire, enjoying the soft, aromatic scents given out by the piles of damp heather and dying bracken they'd collected, throwing handfuls every now and then upon the embers to keep the fire stoked. They liked the heat it was giving to their bodies and the bottoms of the boots they had stretched out towards it, and they enjoyed the amiability it gave them leave to enjoy; they puffed at their pipes, for once awake enough to play a few games, the only noises the irregular clacking of thrown dice, the flip of cards, the occasional sing-song one or other of the men about the fire broke into, the gentler sounds of

94

hedgehogs and voles snuffling in the reeds, the constant tumble of the waters of the Suisgill.

Robbie Weavers had been sent off to Solveig McCleery's with the news that they now had a name for the murdered man, and that it was Willie Blaine – hard-bitten, long serving prospector here, and a former member of Solveig's father's church. For himself, Robbie had been glad to leave the company behind, eager to distance himself from the dead man now rolled up in his blanket, but he kept having to spit as he went, still with the taste of decomposing corpse-flesh in his mouth, the scratch of bile at the back of his throat, and he'd legged it eagerly down the road, keen to be as far away in the shortest possible time.

He'd negotiated the track without difficulty until this past fifteen minutes or so, when the duplicity of twilight had made it hard to see exactly where he was going. He was having to take it slow despite knowing the track well; he had maybe a half mile yet to go before the turn-off to Solveig's house.

He took care as he went, didn't want to snap an ankle in a rut-hole, or veer off into the ditches that had been recently dug either side of the track to heighten it, level it, create a channel for the run-off of autumn heavy rain, and make it stronger for all the extra traffic the gold rush had afforded. He stuck instead to the track's middle, his eyes measuring off the lines on either side to keep him steady, and had kept off lighting his lamp until the very last minute, not wanting to waste his oil. He lit it in the end, hadn't had the choice, and had to slow his pace to shield the lamp from the breeze that had crept down from the mountains with the evening, and as he did so, he heard footfalls coming towards him through the falling darkness, though could not yet see the other traveller for the bend.

It cheered him, this as yet unseen companion – obviously a man coming up to the Suisgill for the night so he could start panning early morning by first

95

light. Probably come, not from Kildonan itself, but from the old abandoned church just down the road by the farm, where a lot of men had been staying these last few months, though it had a bad reputation as being a way station for wastrels, for men who had given up on the panning, but had no place else to go. Robbie was not much of a judge of the gold rush as it stood, but he was of the firm opinion that there was much yet to be found, and that the Suisgill would probably yield the better return in the long run than the Kildonan, and he silently applauded the approaching stranger for his judgement, and his better turn of mind to come this far up the valley.

'Hi aye!' Robbie shouted out, to give the other man warning, didn't want to startle him as he rounded the bend.

'Hi aye!' came the reply, without hesitation or mistrust. 'Am I nearby Kinbrace?'

Robbie smiled, carolled out into the by now almost impenetrable night. 'You're almost past it, sir, though not by much. I'm just at the Glen Loth turning now.'

He was surprised then to hear his own name being called.

'Robbie Weavers? Is that you, lad? Son of Duncan-the-Weaver at Crakaig?'

Robbie was glad to be recognised, for so few of the panners who'd remained here were local, and he happily shouted out his credentials.

'Aye! That's me, Robert, son of Duncan.' He realised he'd been louder than he'd needed, as the other man suddenly materialised from out the dark, and was standing right in front of him.

'Well,' said the other, his voice now quiet. 'Then I'm truly sorry for it.'

And before Robbie had an inkling of who was standing there or what was happening, the lamp had been struck from his hand, the glass smashing into shards upon the track beneath his struggling feet, splashing his boots with its oil that quickly caught alight, all the while the man, who was not much taller than Robbie, though far stronger, was grabbing at his elbows and pinioning them behind his back. Robbie cried out with the pain both in his arms, and then his legs as the flames began to lick at his trousers.

'Down to the river,' the man said, right into his ear, 'and let's put out your burning.'

And Robbie stumbled eagerly alongside this stranger in his shock, bleating all the while as his skin began to singe and sear like a partridge on a hot skillet.

'Robbie,' he kept saying. 'Robbie Weavers of Crakaig,' as if it might somehow change things, as if this man's knowledge of him would put an end to whatever was happening, none of which he understood. And then they were down the bank, and into the water Robbie went, feet first, the relief immense as the cold water swirled about his ankles and his knees, putting out both singe and flame, but as quickly as he was relieved he was terrified again, for his assailant had taken something from his pocket, and Robbie could see the glint of glass in the big brown hands, and those hands coming closer and closer to his face.

'Please, oh, please!' Robbie could hardly speak for his fear, knew that this was not something that would do him well.

'Wheesht lad,' was all his attacker replied, but gently. 'It'll all be over soon, and I'll make it easy.'

Robbie was crying now, his face and neck wet with it, but he had ceased any sort of struggle, had slumped down onto his knees into the cold, dark flow of the water, the man leaning over him like a towering cliff. Robbie began to cough as he smelled something chemical on the man's hand, and his throat began to burn as it came closer, as if he had swallowed fire, and suddenly he began to fight, started flailing in the water, but one of the man's hands was clamped onto the back of Robbie's neck and began to push him downwards, the man humming a small tune as he carefully held Robbie's face beneath the water, stroking at his hair as the boy struggled, struggled hard, but could not free himself, and soon had no more fight. His attacker turned Robbie face-upwards, and placed two small plugs of felt into Robbie's nostrils, gently as he could, didn't want the lad to suffer more than he deserved, before rolling him back again into the water, where Robbie stopped breathing air and took in water in its stead. A few lax flaps of Robbie's arms, with no more strength in them than a drowning bird, and then all movement ceased.

'Go gently into the night, my young friend,' the man murmured, hooking Robbie's foot through a bankside root before standing up, moving easily in the dark, practiced as a fox, night vision honed enough to tell one shadow from the next, the moving ripple of the water from the sway of grasses on its bank, the darker streak of the track just above him that made its way between Kildonan and the Suisgill, the slight white catch of the house on the other side of the bridge where Solveig McCleery lived. And he blessed providence for this path that he had taken, though he was not a religious man, believed instead in the rightness of a world fit for its proper purpose, and kept to the beauty of its hidden ways. He felt a sorrow for young Robbie and that he'd been so shy of years, and might yet have changed his life's purpose. But then again, he knew from long experience that a man, or a boy, would almost always stay upon the same course he had been put to, and that only the wisest ever chose another path. And Robbie Weavers, he knew, was not wise.

The sea of death will always take its own, he thought, and started humming up that tune again, some old hymn that incorporated something of those words. It was far too dark now to start carving messages into stones, but he'd come prepared, and extracted the piece of paper from his pocket. It was strong paper, and good ink, should last out any rain, and then he had another thought and smiled at its relevance, put his hand down to the ground until his fingers touched what they sought, brought it up, made a couple of extra pencil marks on the paper, though it was difficult in the dark, then took out a penknife, and scratched a few symbols on the bark before carefully wrapping the piece of paper around it. He looked about him then, selected a spot where he was pretty certain his little clue would be noticed, tucked it in against the roadside edge of a stone. It might not be found at once, but that didn't matter, only that it should be found at some point, and thereafter find its mark.

Knowledge, he thought, as he had so often done before, *is a truly wonderful thing.*

He had turned then, though only briefly, to watch the dark hump of Robbie Weavers soodling in the current somewhere down below, and then had taken his way.

And while by while, the clouds drew down upon the hills, uplifted the half-moon's pale face as it continued its accustomed arc across the sky. Robbie Weavers, though, did not rise, did not stir, stayed face down in the burn, head bobbing slightly as the shallow water ran about him, ran on and away from him towards the bigger river, mirroring his own journey towards a different, though perhaps no kinder, sea.

Chapter 12   *His spirit is separated from the bounty of the earth*

Solveig returned to the chapel a few minutes after Brogar Finn's arrival, bringing with her a tray of cheese, cold mutton, butter, oatcakes and newly baked soda bread. On her arrival inside, she was soon diverted by Sholto's question about a Gaelic dictionary, and set to finding the small book her father had started to compile soon after he'd arrived in Brora, finished in a fever in the few months following the Helmsdale Pick, in tandem with the small handbook he'd been hell-bent on producing and printing, an aide-memoire of all the parts of the Bible he'd considered might be of most comfort to all those who still remained after the closure of the mines, all painstakingly translated into Gaelic and distributed not only amongst his new congregation, but given away free of charge to any else who would take them in.

She joined Finn and Sholto at the altar table, as fascinated as they both were now by the messages that had been scratched upon the stones. They had begun a rudimentary translation of several of the words, confirming *man* and *mountain*, adding a few more, when Solveig straightened suddenly, hearing a noise coming from outside.

'Listen,' she said, and both Finn and Sholto held themselves still, Sholto's hand still hovering above the page in the dictionary he had been about to turn, and then they heard it too: a distant rhythmic thumping: a *bam, bam, bam,* and then a short silence before it was repeated. *Bam, bam, bam,* it came again, and then there was the sound of boots coming quickly up the path towards the chapel from the house, and they all exchanged glances. Finn was first to move, though Solveig was quick behind him, but it was the outsider who reached the chapel door first, and they all plainly heard the knock knock knocking, and the creak of the wooden door as it began to open, swinging

100

inwards, revealing a man halfway in, halfway out of the low mist that roamed about the lawns skirting the chapel, the air above it cold and sharp with tiny shards of frozen mizzle, giving the intruder an eerie, unworldly effect he was entirely unaware of.

'Mrs McCleery?' His voice was hesitant, rising deferentially, his cap lifted as he spoke, the mist settling on his shoulders in droplets, suspending from his hair, dripping down his collar. He tried again. 'Young Gilligan telt me you'd be here?'

Solveig was trying to place the voice, knew she knew it, though could not quite give it a name, came up behind Finn, a little irritated at the exaggeratedly defensive posture he had taken up, a little glad for it also, for she still did not recognise the man who stood in rain and shadow at the chapel door.

'I'm here,' she called from behind Finn's back.

'Thank goodness,' the man replied with obvious relief. 'Please excuse the lateness of my calling. I'd've gone anywhere else if I'd've been able. If it were nearer, I'd've gone straightaway to the farm, but my lamp…I broke my lamp.'

His voice was Highland, though very soft in accent, drained away by his years of working abroad, only lately come back home to Kildonan on the back of the gold rush.

'Moffatt Murchison!' Solveig exclaimed, recognising the man as she neared him, slotting his voice into place, shoving Finn's barely yielding body out of her way. 'Whatever are you doing out there, and in the rain? Come in, come on in!'

And in he came, and told them slowly that he'd been walking his way up first from Kildonan to the old kirk by the farm where he'd been planning on sleeping the night with the throw of other panners who bided there, men who

101

were sick of kipping out in the open, preferring the stinking hug of unwashed bodies heaved about their paltry fires, its damp and abandoned walls blackened with their smoke, the air thick with the stench of alcohol and tobacco and the mess of common stew the men made out of anything that came handy, fish and meat boiled together with spuds and barley gleaned from the fields, or brought in from the stores at knock-down prices because they were already mouldering.

Solveig was sickened that Moffatt had thought to stay in such a place, for she recognised him now, and said so. Told him he'd only have had to ask and he could have stayed here, insisted that he did so now. Everyone knew that the men within the old kirk's walls were the dregs of the hopefuls the Helmsdale valley had been host to, who had arrived entirely unprepared for the hardness of the life they had bought into for the price of a monthly licence, men who thought nothing of defecating amongst the tombstones of the old kirk's yard, where Solveig's own husband was buried. Moffatt had stopped there only moments before deciding to go on, had got just past the turning to Glen Loth that led down to Solveig's house when he had found what he had found. He was obviously upset, and Solveig took Moffatt's arm, tried to guide the old man back towards the table where the lamps were brightest, but unexpectedly, Moffatt resisted, stayed resolutely where he was.

'I've not come for succour, Solveig,' he had said, blinking slowly and with deliberation. 'Not at all. I don't know why I went down there, just that I could hear the burn wasn't running right. Heard the water sort of stumbling. And when I got there, well – that's when I found him. Dropped my lamp, I was so surprised. Tried to get the poor laddie oot, but I couldnae manage it ….'

They left the chapel on a run, went back to the house only to gather storm-lanterns and oilskins before heading off into the rain that had by now scuffed itself into sleet, felt it shivering and melting against their faces, pushed on by a gusty scour of wind. They found the boy, just as Moffatt had described to them, a few yards above the turning of the track, saw the muddy churns where Moffatt had tried to haul the dead boy up the bank, leaving him a sorrier sight for it, only the top half of him out of the water, his face upturned towards the sky like a tarnished penny, the rest of him swinging like a metronome as the current caught and pulled at his legs, bedraggling the skinny remnant of his body, entangling him with fallen leaves and small branches, making him appear like a badly made, and now broken bridge, anchored at only one end to the bank.

'But he's so young,' Solveig murmured, as Sholto racked his knees into a crouch beside the body, Finn holding both their lanterns above him, the unsteady light giving a strange ripple to the dead boy's skin as it jumped and flickered in the wind and rain. An odd sort of rigor had taken hold of his upper limbs where Murchison had grabbed at him and tried to heave him out of the water before finding the task too much and going instead for help. It had left the boy's arms slightly crabbed across his body, had pushed his shoulders out of joint and out of socket, had sunk his chest like a gully between them, giving him the look of having had his centre all scooped out, hollowed like a neep at Halloween, lips drawn back by the cold into an unnerving, unswerving smile. But there was something more disturbing about him still, Sholto thought, as he bent down closer and caught sight of what had been lodged inside the boy's nostrils, and took a sharpened pencil from his inner pocket and hoicked out first one, and then the other, laid the small plugs of matted felt upon his palm like new-pulled teeth, sniffed at them, and then briefly closed his eyes.

103

'And how was he when you found him?' Sholto asked, looking back up at Moffatt Murchison, who seemed unwilling to come closer, was standing several yards beyond the brief circle of light cast by Finn's illuminating lanterns, his hat lowered and clutched between his fingers in a mute gesture of despair. 'I mean exactly,' Sholto added. 'Was he completely in the river, or laying alongside it?'

Murchison's face had turned a tired grey, like an overblown cep, the water in the air now running freely down his skin, dew-dropping the sparse and unkempt prickles of his beard.

'He was sort of lying alongside, in the water. Like a log,' he finally managed, and Solveig looked at Moffatt, wondered if he was remembering what she was, remembering the day they had first met, when he had taken a little time out of his life to make hers better, when she'd been seven, or maybe eight, and her two-month-old kitten had been run over by the milk cart and he had found her staring at it and its weak mewling, not knowing what to do, and he had knelt down beside her and picked the animal up, snapped its neck and put it out of its misery. How afterwards he had taken her down to the river bank and told her to put the thing into the current, and let it go.

Sholto creased his brows, cricked up to standing and looked about him.

'So how did you even come to see him at all?' he asked, the slight tone of accusation completely passing Moffatt by.

'I didn't see him exactly,' Murchison answered slowly. 'Heard him, like I said. Heard the water moving badly. Then saw summat white and sort o' shiny right by the track-side, down by them reeds. Thought it might've been an otter's leavings. Got a whole half salmon nearby here just such a way.' Moffatt had the grace to cough and glance at Solveig at this last, unintended disclosure. 'Years back, that were,' he added, though such a minor enpoachment was quite beyond Solveig's care at this moment, or ever.

'And it was what?' Sholto persisted. 'This shiny thing. What was it?'

Murchison looked surprised. 'Why it weren't nothing. Just a lump o' rolled up paper. It's still there, look, where I kicked it.'

And then he pointed a little way to his left, a further few feet beyond where he was standing, the small white patch a dull gleam in their lamps. Finn got there first, and lifted it from its lying-place, was just about to start uncrumpling it, when Sholto stopped him.

'No, Finn. Leave it till we get back to the house. It's already been in the rain for a while. No point in soaking what little there might still be legible inside.'

'Inside?' asked Murchison. 'What do you mean? It's just paper.'

Sholto didn't say anything; he was already busy totting up the accumulated evidence in his head: another body, a boy this time, a boy whose nostrils had been plugged with felt soaked in ether – or something very similar – a smell persistent enough to still be detectable some time later, at least by Sholto, despite the boy's immersion in the burn, though how long he had lain there Sholto did not know. Long enough, he thought, for the body to have cooled to the ambient frigidity of the water. Long enough for the dragged-out upper torso to have descended into some sort of rigor by the cold and sleet of the night after Murchison had dragged him up there barely half an hour before. Not long enough, though, for the rest of his body to have gone the same way, maybe too busied by the movement of the water to have followed suit.

Sholto wondered if the intention had been for the boy's body to have been found early the next morning, for he had been close enough to note what the others had not, that the boy's left ankle had been entangled in a root spool protruding from the bank in such a way that was highly improbable to have occurred naturally. He thought of the other body, the ledge, the stones, the rood ground.

Two bodies within two weeks, both put out on display.

105

One set of cryptic messages scratched out on stones nearby the first, and now this balled-up fist of paper by the second. He carefully put this last into his pocket, his fingertips touching the two small plugs of ethered felt as he did so, and at the touch something jumped into his head, snagged a memory. He creased his brows, narrowed his eyes, touched finger and thumb to the corners of his lips, but the memory would not resurface. It would come, he knew. You had to let these things go before they came back to the surface, like bubbles from mud, or a body in a sluice pit, of their own accord.

Chapter 13   *So he is bound by sorrow*

They brought the boy's body back from the river on a plank of wood. The night was dark and wet and uncomfortable, but to leave the lad there bobbing halfway in, halfway out of the river had been, at least to Solveig's mind, unthinkable. Finn had argued they should just haul him out of the water and collect him at first light, but even Murchison, ex-crofter, hardened miner, had quailed at that suggestion, knowing all about the nip and gnaw of night-hungry mice and rats and voles, and of the swift-swooping down of owls that could strip a head of its hair, divest a socket of its eye, not to mention the wild cats that were twice the size of their domestic relatives, grey-brindled from tip to tail, who could rip a sheep carcass apart without compunction, and would do the same to this poor dead boy. Moffatt had stated quietly, but with a certainty nobody argued with, that he would carry the lad back upon his own shoulders if that was the only option, and had he not spoken up first, Solveig would have said the same. Instead, she had delegated Finn to go the half mile back to her house, shake up the two boys who looked after her sheep and cattle, and get them to fetch up a serviceable plank of wood from the workshed.

While they waited, Moffatt and Solveig talked softly up on the track, drifting slowly, if unintentionally, back in the general direction towards the house where Finn had already gone. Sholto was left alone with his lantern and the dead boy and the ever falling mantle of rain that seemed to breathe itself out of a near empty sky, the drift of mist so faint as to be almost not there at all. He'd once read about Herschel's visit to South Africa in the 1830s, and the comet he had seen and sketched there, and how he had discovered that its tail was not composed of fire and brimstone as had been previously supposed, but was more like a bridal veil, vast and diaphanous, hundreds of millions of

107

miles long and so infinitesimally diffuse that you could still see the stars on the other side, even as it passed you by.

There seemed a similar kind of awe to this night as Sholto sat, marooned in darkness, unable to see the roll and fold of the valleys and hills he knew were all about him, gazing up to where the stars shone so startlingly bright, despite the hesitant rain. Every now and then a half-wink of moon would emerge, hooded by the clouds that shone weakly with its light, and once, as it did so, he saw a splash of rain hit the dead boy's still opened eyes, made him appear to blink, giving Sholto such a shock that his heart beat so loudly he could hear it. In the same moment recognised this face, this child: it was the boy who had given him water up at the Suisgill that very afternoon, and the thought of it tightened his throat to such an extent he could hardly breathe, and a small sob escaped him. He was not used to dead people. Was not too used to people of any kind, and wished he had the courage to put out his hand and pull the lad's eyelids closed, but he did not.

He couldn't say how glad he was to make out the bobbing of lanterns as Finn and his two-boy crew came back along the night-dark, rain-drenched track, nor how heartened he was by the latter's excited chatter and the clatter of their boots as they ran and stumbled through mud and rut towards him, so loud, so life-affirming, that they motivated him into standing, and he was only just in time to set his lantern against the grass by the dead boy's head, and far too late to let out the warning that had only just struck him as being apt, that these boys coming from Solveig's house might actually recognise this dead one, just as he had done. That this was the case was soon obvious as the two boys, still chirruping, plummeted down the bank towards him, the others staying as dark shadows up above.

'Oh my,' said the first, skidding to a stop beside Sholto, clutching at Sholto's arm to stay his course, seeing finally what he had been sent to fetch back upon his board. 'Oh my,' he said again, just as his friend landed down beside him, finding no such lucky catch against Sholto's arm, colliding straight into the sodden corpse. This second boy grabbed at a young-grown stump of alder, its dying leaves purple-black against the faint gleam of light that came from the lamps, spun up from the river and the reflection of the moon, and having finally stopped his skid, was almost comical in his turning, in his double-take of what he had just seen, and then went the colour of a fresh cow-pat, bent away from Sholto and his friend and the dead boy and was spectacularly sick, throwing up his evening meal of lamb and potato stew enlivened with a few chews of the carrots that had been meant for the horses, and the dark sludge of sugar-beet meant for the same, all liberally lubricated by the two cups of beer that was every servant's due after a hard day's work.

It wasn't pretty, and the smell was bad, but at least it led the first boy to look at the dead body for distraction, and after a few moments staring, he gave up his name.

'Jeezo,' he said, still clutching hard at Sholto's arm. 'Yon's young Rab Weavers.'

The second boy had stopped throwing up, and had wiped his face down upon his sleeve as curiosity overtook him. He got himself up on shaky legs to take his own proper look, delivered his own thin-voiced affirmation.

'Aye, that's him right enough. Fast-handed little shite.'

His bravado, and his uncharitable view, was echoed by Gilligan, the first boy, the non-thrower upper.

'He'd nick anything as wasn't screwed down,' he added helpfully. 'Stole my dad's baccy right out of my pocket once,' he said, not noticing the hypocrisy implied by such a statement. 'Never did get it back.'

But for all their condemnation of Robbie Weavers, the two boys both removed their caps and remained silent whilst Murchison and Finn got him strapped onto the plank of wood, and up the short brae onto the track, and began their slow and steady walk back to the house. Their progress was so wet and funereal that it prompted Sholto into speech, asking the two boys what else they knew of Robbie, or young Rab, as he was known to them.

'He used to work at the stores till he got pinched for thieving oatmeal,' Gilligan supplied.

'And his old man got flogged for poaching a while back,' the other boy, Hugh, was quick to add.

'You didn't like him much, then?' Sholto enquired, at which the two boys exchanged glances.

'No,' Gilligan said slowly. 'It wasn't like that. He were fun to be with. Allus a wee bit kicky, if you ken what I mean.'

Sholto didn't know exactly, though grasped enough of it as Hugh went on.

'Aye, that's right enough, that is. Mind that time when he ground up them buckie-faulies and put them down his ol' man's breeks?'

The two boys began to giggle, a strange sound in that dark night, with the wind whooshing low through the short brakes of trees that grew at them on either side, strange rustlings coming up from the leaves as the water voles ran their hidden paths below.

'His bum went reid as a rowan berry with all that scratchin',' Gilligan chortled. 'Showed it to half the port he did, thinkin' he was after catchin' some scabbit disease!'

Behind them, Solveig smiled. She might not have known Gaelic, but she knew well enough the language she'd been brought up with, and she translated briefly to Sholto.

'Rosehips,' she elucidated shortly.

'Itchy-coos!' Gilligan snorted. 'And mind that other prank he paid on the Jappster earlier back this year?'

110

Patently Hugh did, as he too laughed, telling the tale of how Robbie had nicked a huge lump of iron pyrites from one Reverend Joass, who had come up from Golspie, on hearing of the gold rush, to conduct his own geological survey, and had young Robbie Weavers accompanying him as bagman. Young Rab had apparently pinched the sample of Fool's Gold, which looks as near the real thing as the name implies, and had placed it nearby the track where Tam Japp was tramping down behind them and he had, surreptitiously, and predictably, scooped it up and taken it back with him to his desk, before impatiently logging the panners' finds of the day, weighing out their dust, extracting his employer's due.

'That was never him!' Solveig exclaimed, for she too recalled the event of how the sullen Tam Japp, quite out of the blue, and for the first and only time, had condescended to go out panning one afternoon soon after, and had come back yelling how he had found the biggest nugget of gold ever found in the burn. A nugget that turned out, on closer inspection, to be nothing of the sort. It had afforded a great deal of sarcastic merriment amongst the panners, who had never liked Japp, or, more specifically, the long arm of the Sutherlands that he represented, and Japp had smouldered like a dying fire at his humiliation from that day to this.

Even Moffatt Murchison smiled sadly at the reminiscence, before telling the boys to wheesht, which they did, as did they all, the realisation dropping down on them like a stone that the glad-hearted boy who had done such things was nothing now but a flaccid-skinned corpse on a rain-wettened board, and that whatever he had been, and whatever he might have become, had been abruptly ended far before his time.

Chapter 14   *The counsels of his lord have been lost to him*

They arrived back at Solveig's house in silence, Solveig dismissing the two boys after thanking them for their help, telling them that though they could take a few extra cups of beer back to the stables where they slept, she expected them up not more than one hour later than was usual to look to the animals that were in their care. The rest went on to the big barn where they laid out Robbie Weavers' body on a bier of straw bales, before retiring back to the chapel. Moffatt went with them; he had no stomach left to take the journey on up to the Suisgill, even if Solveig would have allowed him to. 'You'll stay here,' she said, 'and for as long as you need. For as long as you're working up at the Suisgill, any road.'

She brooked no argument, and Moffatt was too weary with the night's proceedings to protest, and remained in the chapel with Finn and Sholto whilst Solveig went back to the house to heat up some soup, replenish the food tray she had previously supplied with jugged hare and more mutton. In the meantime, Finn uncorked a couple of the bottles of wine she had left with them, and when Solveig returned, she found the food on the tray partially demolished, and the three of them clustered about the altar table, supping at the wine, poring over Sholto's notes.

'So, Mr Murchison,' Sholto was saying.

'Moffatt,' Murchison interrupted politely.

'Moffatt,' Sholto went on. 'Can you read it? The Gaelic, I mean?'

There was a brief silence, a few dead moments passing slow as leaves dropping from an autumn tree, during which Solveig poured her own glass of wine and approached them.

'There was a time,' Moffatt cleared his throat, looked down at his glass but did not bring it to his lips. 'There was a time,' he went on, 'when anyone a

112

stone's throw from this house could do the same, when everyone from th'east coast through to the west was happy at it. But not the new ones, not the young loons, not once they'd given us the schools.'

Solveig nodded, knew the rules, knew that Gaelic was not the language the schools had been told to teach in, that it had become more or less forbidden within their walls. Sholto too creased his brow, rubbed his nose; he knew a lot about dead languages and how easy it was to bury them, knew that power was the source of their persecution, the vanquishers denying the vanquished what had once marked them out, fearing their differences, the mutterings of rebellion in a speech they could not understand, felt the same drumbeats of emotion that had begun earlier, when Solveig had been pointing out the tumbled-down homesteads, the abandoned villages, the rough-racked stretches of green behind and before them that indicated this had once been a land ploughed and planted, where people had spoken whatever language they liked.

Solveig saw this brief passage of what she thought might be anguish passing across Sholto's face, as if something inside had just stopped, frozen like a leaf on an ice-bound pond.

'Mr Murchison,' she said quietly, easing her way up to the table. 'Can you help us?'

Moffatt shuffled his feet, uneasy to be so near a woman in so informal a way, no matter that he'd known Solveig since a bairn; he still recalled the kitten-killing incident, and the other afternoons that had followed, when she'd trailed him after his visits to her father's chapel, latched on to him, cajoled him into teaching her the Gaelic names for the animals and plants she'd found around her, names she had always repeated, but never seemed truly to have learned.

'I can,' he finally said, 'though I'll maybe need a little space for it.'

113

Solveig obliged, moved away, went to get more wine, and Moffatt breathed easier, began walking slowly around the altar table, looking at all of Sholto's notes. It didn't take him long. Finn was only on his third piece of mutton, his fourth scoop of hare, when Murchison announced his findings.

'It's a proverb,' he said. 'A Gaelic proverb, though one that's been jiggered about with a little. Och, it's quite simple,' Moffatt Murchison went on to tell them. 'Of common use hereabouts, or used to be. Just means that any man can be happy in the hills. *Faodaidh duine 's am bith gair a dheanamh air cnoc,*' he said easily, the words sounding right in his mouth. He turned then to Solveig, a small crease deepening down the middle of his brow as if someone had struck his head through with a chisel. 'Matter o'fact, lassie, now as I think on it, it was something your da used to say a lot, once he'd learnt it, and once he'd learnt what it meant. One o' his favourites, so it were.'

Sholto had come back from the tray of food, though empty handed, and now asked Moffatt for the actual, literal translation of the words upon the stones, and the order they had been placed in. Moffatt obliged, and what he said was this:

Any man, Sukkiim, will find himself laughing on a hillside.

It had been early evening when Moffatt Murchison had first arrived at the chapel, and much later by the time they'd returned with Robbie Weavers' body; later still when Moffatt had made his small revelation about the Gaelic proverb that had been scratched upon the rood ground stones. None of them, apart from Brogar Finn, were used to anything of a particularly dramatic nature happening in their lives, and all were feeling the strain. Solveig was beginning to doze on her feet, and Moffatt was on the point of collapse, bewildered by all the questions Sholto was firing at him about the Gaelic

114

words he had used and how they were spelled, and why were there so many silent vowels, let alone silent consonants, questions to which he had no answers.

Unusually, it was Finn who broke up the party, though it went against the grain, but even he had been a little drained by the discovery of two dead bodies in the span of a single day, and he was tired, and he saw the same look on both Moffatt's and Solveig's faces, though Sholto didn't seem able to let up.

'Sholto,' he finally said, 'as my new assistant, I admire your level of commitment, but as your boss, I am ordering you to quit your questions and go to bed.'

Solveig and Moffatt looked at Finn gratefully, and Solveig left, refusing all offers of accompaniment back to her house. Finn had already flopped onto his chosen bed, and Murchison gladly went to the adjacent one, lay down upon it without even taking off his boots, so that it was with mild surprise that Sholto found himself a moment later standing all alone, the lamps having gone out, only two candles still alight but futtering, one of which went out the moment he moved, leaving him in almost perfect darkness. Making as little noise as he could, he quickly scratched out a last note, hoping it would be legible in the morning, then plinked closed the top of the inkwell, made his way to his own cot, and curled himself fully clothed upon it, pulling the eiderdown up to his chin.

He couldn't sleep for a while, kept seeing Robbie Weavers handing him that pewter jug of water, kept listening to the small wind riffling loosely through the browning leaves of the trees behind the chapel and the barn, the reed stalks creaking in the water meadow, the bracken as it bent down beneath the weight of water freezing on its fronds. There was a murderer out there, he was sure of it, who maybe hadn't done for Willie Blaine but had certainly put

115

him in a sack and dragged him onto that ledge, and who had later waylaid
Robbie Weavers on the track not far from where he was lying, and done him
to death.

Those two plugs of felt, he kept thinking, those two small plugs of felt...

Inside the big barn behind the chapel, Robbie Weavers lay on the squared
bier of his straw bales, and opposite, on her own bales lay Solveig McCleery,
her lamp still glowing dimly where it hung from a hook on the wall just
above her head; her eyes were closed, her sleep shallow and sporadic though
unrepentant for having made it here. She could not have left that small boy,
dead as he was, all alone in the dark.

And further on down the valley, the men inside the old kirk had finally drunk
and smoked and sung themselves to their own sleep, grumbling when they'd
had to move the odd limb here and there to accommodate the late-arriving
stranger who was even now picking his soft footfalls through the debris and
detritus and the scatter of broken clay pipes and those that had been
fashioned out of neeps and carrots; moving carefully about the flagons of
upended beer, the grease-smeared bowls and discarded bones picked clean of
flesh. He cocked his head a little, listened to the coughs and grunts, the snorts
and farts, the shuffling of night-weary bodies, and realised that the rain had
finally ceased. He retraced his steps then, and reached the door, took a step
outside and breathed deeply of the clean, sharp air that carried the scents of
the clear running water of the river that ran twenty yards to the south, and the
soft, sweet smell of deer musk that came at him from the hills, the occasional
barks of the bucks sounding strange and unfamiliar, not having the same
pitch or timbre as the ones he was used to back home. He made his way
round to the lee-side of the building so he was shielded from the low but

constant wind, and took out his blanket, unrolled his elkskin sleeping bag that had been double-lined with fur, and tied himself in. He supposed he could have dug a pit, made a fire, but it didn't seem all that cold to him, not compared to the onset of the Russian winter from which he had so recently departed, and soon he lay warm and cosy, wrapped in his furs outside the old Kirk of Kildonan parish, a little disoriented by the different positions of the stars up above his head, a little unnerved that there was no glimmer of aurora on the horizon, no shine of blue ice nor snow, no groaning of bears or bellows of elks out in the forests, only the shuffles and scuffles of the men huddled together on the other side – the inside – of the wall of the old kirk, the sounds of them coughing and creaking within their makeshift beds, kicking off their boots, one of them humming something every now and then as he turned in his sleep.

But he was happy, felt at peace, knew he had been right to come here, and thought of Solveig McCleery, who'd been a Lundt when he'd first come across her name, not that he was in any doubt it was the same Solveig, the same daughter, the same person who was somehow at the heart of this place, just as she had always been at the heart of everything he and Joseph had ever done.

'My daughter, my life,' Joseph had once said when he'd been asked how he could spend so long away from his family on his travels, his holy mission, his mast-maker – only an apprentice at that time – at his side. 'My daughter, my life,' he had said. 'I pray that she never has to bear the cross that I do.'

She was always at the heart of everything Joseph ever did, and he thought how odd it was that this girl, or this woman as she must be now, this person he had never met could nevertheless have been so stern a pilot of his life.

And he wondered how it would all end up, and whether the ending would be good or bad, and he felt for the small icon latched within his pocket, kissed

117

his fingertips and touched them to its wood, then slowed his breathing, closed his eyes, and slept.

Chapter 15   *Time passes under cover of the night*

Sholto was first to wake; he broke the thin skin of ice on the water in its basin, dashed a little of it on his face before disappearing outside to relieve himself amongst the tree break, a respectable distance from the chapel. He'd no idea what time it was, only that it was early, the edge of the half-moon still shining brightly like a new-struck coin in the sky, a cushion of pink clouds rising over the eastern hills. When he came back into chapel no one else had stirred, and he needed to take a couple of candles from the niche and get them lit to navigate the gloom. He returned to the altar table and looked for the notes he had scratched out in the darkness the night before, not that he needed reminding – he knew well enough those last two thoughts he'd had when everyone else had switched off, forced him too to bed.

Chck wth BF about the Geologist

Ask S abt Helmsdale Pick?

After a couple of moments, he underlined the first words, put parentheses about the next. That was something that could wait, he decided, for the primary duty here must certainly be the murdered boy. He could take a good guess at how the boy had died, but had no inkling of the reason, only that it must have taken place sometime late the previous afternoon, probably early evening, judging by the partial state of rigor the boy had been found in. Still, the fact remained that he had been killed, and Sholto wanted to know why. If he could solve that problem, it might go a long way to impressing Brogar Finn that he was fit to be his new assistant, and stop the rest of them being pushed off the short pier of life into oblivion.

And there was something else too – there was the scrumpled piece of paper Murchison had seen near Robbie Weavers' body and kicked away, retrieved by Brogar, but too soggy with rain and drizzle last night to do anything with.

119

Sholto had left it by a lamp to dry out gently of its own accord, and as he studied it now, he realised the paper must be of good quality, well made, expensive, for it hadn't just collapsed in on itself or disintegrated, but was dry enough for him to get out tweezers and a pencil, begin to tease it open, ease its edges back. And when he did so, he realised there was something inside. He wheedled at the corners and folds, and finally freed the hidden kernel: a small piece of bark, rough outer edge slightly curved, smooth inner surface marked by larvae that had left small lines across its surface, like snail trails on stone. It seemed nothing special, didn't even look fresh, looked just like any other piece of alder bark you might find lying on a river bank. Quite why it had been wrapped in the piece of paper he had no idea, so he put it to one side, turned his attention instead to the paper itself. Using the tweezers again, he picked it up by one edge and wafted it in front of the candle. Behind the steam he could see there were words written there, and he repositioned the paper, placed another candle to one side to make it easier to see.

Three lines: first two Gaelic, and neatly written.

He knew enough of that language from the last message, and from his explorations of Solveig's father's dictionary, to recognise it, and he tried to read the words, mouthed out each cursive syllable as he thought it might be pronounced. After a minute or two, he moved to the last sentence, saw that this time it was in English, though it was hard to make out at all, was a mere twitch of pencil against paper, and again, he mouthed the words as his eyes wandered across the letters.

And then he stopped, gave out an involuntary gasp.

'This can't be.' He spoke out loud, his voice was hoarse, a harsh whisper, and he looked again at the paper, then picked up the little piece of bark again, studied it carefully this time in the candlelight, saw that what he had taken for larvae tracks weren't that at all.

'This just can't be,' he said again, the bark dropping the several inches to the desk as his hand went involuntarily to his heart which had begun to beat far too fast, so hard he could hear it thudding within the confines of his chest. He was breathing quickly, sweat popping out along the line of his scalp. He closed his eyes, made a conscious effort to slow his breathing, and after a few moments he was calm enough to begin his investigation over again. He knew the rules of philosophical enquiry, of logic and debate, had had them drummed into him over all his years of schooling, and later at the university, and later on still at the Linnaean Society. He understood the importance of comparing appearance with actuality, and knew that whatever this appeared to be, however outlandish, there must be an explanation for it, and that he needed to come at it from every side, divide and conquer, make sense of each individual part.

He reached over to where Solveig's father's dictionary was lying and leafed it through, searching the annotations to get an approximation of the first two lines, the Gaelic lines, hoping they would cast some light upon the third, for he knew those final words, and how they related to the bark, and knew that there was a line being drawn here, with him at one end and Solveig at the other, and possibly Brogar somewhere in between, but what he needed to find out was what this line was made of, and, most importantly, how it had come to be drawn at all.

Moffatt Murchison coughed, coughed again, and was awake. He opened bleary, red-rimmed eyes to unusual surroundings, took a couple of minutes to remember where he was. He saw Brogar Finn still sleeping soundly on the cot bed to his left, turned creakily to his other side, felt the arthritis in his hip and cursed it, saw the other cot empty and began to raise himself upon his elbow. His feet felt heavy, and he realised he still had his boots on, wondered how bad his socks would smell if he took his boots off now, and decided against it. They'd been on far too long; everything had been on far too long – his clothes, his socks, his boots, the stubble on his chin. He could hear a voice, someone speaking quietly, but he recognised something of the words that were being spoken behind the falter and hesitation of the way they were being said, and he pushed himself to sitting, saw Sholto McKay through the gloom, dimly lit by two candles where he was leaning over the altar table, running a finger along a piece of paper, along a line of words he was obviously trying to read. Moffatt watched in silence as Sholto went back to the beginning of the sentence he had been trying to unravel, and started all over again. This second time, Moffatt listened intently, and though Sholto was stumbling over the words, mispronouncing them in places, Moffatt knew them well enough, had heard them often in this same room, back when it had been a chapel and he a member of Solveig's father's church, back when everything, for a few years at least, had seemed to make some kind of sense, when he'd been a young man and The Pick a few years behind him, The Pick that had stolen his family from him, leaving himself and his older brother to fend for themselves, standing with all the rest on the harbour at Helmsdale while the ship disappeared to lord knew where.

Solveig came out of the barn and went at once to the water pump, washed her face and hands, shook her feet loose from her boots and washed them too. She saw a man sitting on the wooden bench outside her front door, smoking casually, his pipe bowl cupped in rugged hands, a sack nestled between his feet. If he thought it odd that Solveig had emerged in a such a tatter from the barn, he gave no outward sign of it, merely tapped out his pipe when he saw her coming, straightened his back, stretched out his legs, and stood to greet her.

'Eri tonn ar ushgy balv...' Moffatt listened to Sholto's mumblings, surprised they sounded even faintly recognisable, most people struggled for several years before they could even begin to read Gaelic correctly from the written page. He dipped his finger into the little pouch of salt and charcoal that hung from his belt and rubbed it against his teeth, rinsed and spat several times to clear his mouth of shilp and sharrow, the bitter tastes he always awoke with, then heaved himself off his cot and began to approach Sholto, who looked up at the noise from his grim concentration, the creases about his mouth hinting at his frustration, and, Moffatt thought, maybe even fear.

Solveig greeted Lachlan McLachlan, her mine overseer, with a sigh of weariness, wondering what else could have gone wrong. She had so much to do today already – two burials to organise, approaches to be made to Tam Japp with an update he could pass on to his masters, a visit down to Brora to decide how next to proceed with the filling in of the old mines and the excavation of the new. She hoped Brogar Finn would agree to accompany her, give her some guidance, ascertain whether or not the shore mines had been collapsed enough in on themselves as thoroughly as she had yesterday hoped. She didn't think she could bear to take on any more.

'Good morning, Lachlan.' Solveig spoke without enthusiasm, and was surprised by the wide grin that cracked across Lachlan's weather-beaten face, revealing two uneven lines of tobacco-stained teeth that had seen better days a long time since. 'Morning, Missus,' Lachlan replied amiably, then stooped down and pulled up the sack he had brought with him as if it was a rabbit just plucked from a snare. He held it out to her, but Solveig did not take it, not straightaway, not until Lachlan gave it a slight shuggle to show her there was nothing nasty in it, saying as he did so:

'You're gonna wantae take a right lang look at these.'

As if summoned by a breakfast bell, Finn was up and rubbing his hands the second Solveig came into the chapel bearing a tray stacked up with hot, freshly made oatcakes, buttered brose, honey, and a large pot of coffee. 'Ah,' he exclaimed. 'Food!' and leapt up behind her as she made for Sholto and the table. 'Get that stuff shifted, Sholto,' Finn added. 'We've more important things to do at the moment than huff and puff over your little scraps of paper. Ah!' he said again, scooping up an oatcake from Solveig's tray, scraping it across the top of the pat of butter, leaving a trail of crumbs like yellow spraint across a field of snow. 'Now this,' he commented, chewing vigorously, 'this is what mornings are all about.'

'There's more,' Solveig said, and smiled up at her visitors, her weariness gone. She left them briefly and returned to the door, picked something up and came back with it from the threshold. She was carrying the box that Lachlan had brought in his sack, and she laid it carefully on the table and lifted the lid. It was filled with straw, and she brushed the topmost layer aside with her fingers, revealed the convex bases of three bowls that looked to have been forged out of gold.

Down the river, less than half a mile away from Solveig's door, a man was walking. The river tumbled alongside, and he could see a small group of deer striped amongst the reeds on the opposite bank, several lithe and skittish does, their white scuts bobbing, turning nervously this way and that as they caught his scent, corralled between two stags who stood their ground like statues, noses lifted, antlers bared, flanks red on top, the colour of dying

124

grass beneath, their breath clouding about their muzzles, eyes fixed upon him, daring him, challenging him, unwilling to give up any ground.

'The men found them when the topsoil was blown away after the explosions,' Solveig was explaining. 'They're very old, and these are only three of them, the most extant. There were seven in all, apparently, nested the one inside the other.'

'Quite a find,' Finn murmured.

'They're beautiful,' Sholto added, stretching out a tentative finger towards the upturned bowls. Beautiful they certainly were, and obviously delicate, maybe made of copper or bronze, or some kind of alloy of the two.

'Lachlan says Tobar Strabane's the man to ask about them,' Solveig informed them, pleased at her somewhat dramatic entrance, that she had managed to surprise people who were so much more travelled than herself.

'Tobar Strabane,' muttered Moffatt Murchison, who had hung back a little, wasn't sure his heart could take any more surprises, the bowl-bottoms looking uncannily like the heads of new-born babies to eyes that were not so sharp as they once had been. 'Now that's a name I've not heard in a while.'

Solveig looked over at him. 'Nor myself,' she said easily. 'Though I do recall him coming here sometimes, back in the day.'

'Aye,' Moffatt agreed, his eyebrows lifting slightly. 'That he did. Thought well of your father, as did we all.'

Solveig acknowledged the compliment with a slight smile, before asking, 'Does he still live in the same place, do you suppose?'

Moffatt put his hand up to his mouth, rubbed his lower lip between forefinger and thumb, felt several days' worth of stubble rasping at their lower edges and regretted he'd not taken the strop and razor from his pack, the time to go out to the pump and scrape himself smooth; he felt dirty and shabby, and

125

embarrassed that Solveig should see him so. He cleared his throat, glanced over at the box again, at the straw and the treasures that it held, blinked and raised his eyebrows once again, all in one movement.

'Has done for as long as any of us can recall,' he finally replied. 'And since I've been back, I've have heard nothing different, and Andrew would surely have known it, and told it, had it been the same.'

And so it must be, Moffatt thought, for no one moved in or out of these valleys without Andrew McTavish hearing all the details, least all of a man like Tobar Strabane, who'd always been tight with the bigwigs at Dunrobin, rented his steading from them for a peppercorn, as everyone knew.

Money sticking to money like shite on a stick, he thought, knowing as he did that Tobar's father had been friendly with the first Duke, and that their two sons had continued that acquaintance after the old Duke had died in 1833. Knew also that Tobar had plenty of wealth behind him despite the way he lived, which was about as close to the earth as you could get without being buried in it, living from the land in the old way: catching fish, keeping a kine or too, snaring hares, hoeing potatoes, weeding barley, burning peat. Yet true enough, Moffatt thought, if anyone knew anything about these old bowls then it would be Tobar, for it was common knowledge he'd been better educated in his youth than the rest of the valley put together, and that he knew a deal about anything and everything that had ever been dug up in these parts, was rumoured to have a stockpile of books up at his shack at Scalabsdale that would make another man's mouth water, if he cared about such things, which Moffatt did not.

But he envied the man's solitude at that moment. For some reason he had dreamed the previous night of those days, those many months of his life spent in with the huddle of men he didn't know, didn't like, in the holds of ships taking them all to the gold fields of Australia or back again, everyone

126

living so close together, cramped back-to-back, their mingled piss creeping up their trouser legs day by day, week by week, time measured by their tide-marks, the boils that grew in groin and armpit and nowhere to wash, nowhere to separate themselves from the herd. He didn't know where all this had come from, except perhaps from the words he had translated the night before, about how a man can be happy on a hillside, because the moment he had read them he'd known the truth of them, and that though he was back to the grindstone and the panning, he was happy to be back home.

'I'll take them to him,' he found himself saying, moving closer to the straw-box, looking for the first time closely at the baby-headed bowls. 'Might be glad of a bit of company from the old days,' he added, though exactly whom he'd meant by that last comment, himself or Tobar, was moot. Two men, he thought, and two whole lifetimes to catch up on; two men, he thought, how different could they really be?

The deer scattered as he took a small move towards them, leaping easily up the slope of the brae that leant away from the river, up and over the heathered tussocks, the dying bracken, the spines of blackthorn that grew in the ditches by the flood plain. Up and away towards Glen Loth they went, taking its winding, stone-littered tracks back into the hills. He smiled as he watched them go, no sound to them, only the familiar grace of their going, the languid movement of their backs, their stopping further up and looking down on him, seeing him for what he was: a stranger in a strange land.

Chapter 16:   *And in sleep he lays his head upon the knees of his lord*

In the old days, kirk-yards had been places of meeting and merriment, of boys frog-hopping over tombstones, men laying down their load on the lickerstanes provided for the bier whilst they partook of food and drink, the richer families laying on funeral feasts for all comers; a time of rejoicing, a feasting for the poorest members of the parish that sometimes lasted several days, attended by all, ignored by none.

All that was in the past, thought Solveig sadly; the church had tightened its straps and laces after The Great Disruption, become too po-faced and serious-minded to allow a bit of joy over dourness, preferred recrimination and regret over rejoicing. Walking funerals were still commonplace, when the deceased was carried from house to grave, family, friends and neighbours trailing on behind, but there weren't that many houses left, nor inhabitants, and the old burial grounds were mostly forbidden them, placed on the wrong side of the fence, reserved for a better class of corpse.

Modern-day funerals, Solveig thought, weren't a patch on the old, but she would do her best for Robbie Weavers, and for the man they had found up at the Suisgill, whose name was Willie Blaine. She'd learned this earlier that morning when she'd gone up to the workings with news of Robbie's death. The men's reaction to the boy's murder had been strong, and not good. He'd been their junior by many years, and it seemed he'd become a kind of mascot to them all – a rascal, no doubting that, but one they'd all liked and who had lightened their days, had maybe reminded them that they too had once been young. They considered themselves his family, it was as simple as that. His mother, they told Solveig, had died years before, his brothers and one extant sister long since scattered, dispersed by work and marriage, his father scarpered to who knew where to escape the noose, if the rumours could be believed. Robbie had been only sixteen, maybe less, no one knew exactly, no more had the boy himself, and when she'd suggested she arrange his burial in the small plot outside her father's chapel, somewhere in the sheep-clipped grass that led down towards the water meadows, they had all agreed. It was a pleasant place, she'd told them, somewhere she could keep an eye on him, see his grave properly tended, and as near to any home as he'd ever had, far better – no argument about that either – than in the yard of the abandoned, besmirched, church down the road.

Willie Blaine was a different matter. It was made plain to Solveig that he'd not been a man well liked, that he'd kept himself to himself, had a morose demeanour that was depressing, and his loss was unmourned. The prevailing feeling was that he had more or less had it coming, and there was little more sympathy for the widow he'd left behind in Port Gower, who was unanimously branded a harridan and a harpie, a woman who had occasionally appeared at the camp during the last year demanding her due, shouting the house down, forcing Willie, if he was there, to fork out his own rations into her sack before she finally shut up and went away.

Not a happy marriage then, and such a terribly sad summation, Solveig thought, of two lives badly spent, both husband and wife. Maybe better, she thought, to have been a Robbie Weavers, to have been young and fun and missed now he was gone, to never have had to go the extra miles, the extra years, that might have turned Robbie Weavers into Willie Blaine.

However it stood, Solveig knew they both needed burying, that they couldn't be kept above ground much longer, no matter the nip of frost in the air this last week, or how cold her barn was. There was the added fact that they'd both suffered unnatural deaths of one kind or another, and there was talk of every last miner walking off site, either to go back down to the Baile an Or, or quitting altogether. Mutiny seemed in the making, which would have serious consequences for her own plans for the mines, Brogar Finn only being here because of the gold. Only old Dougall Meek seemed to be keeping a level head, though even he'd had a hard time persuading the rest of them to stay.

'Any bloody excuse,' Dougall had muttered angrily as he'd watched his fellow miners shilly-shallying, shuffling feet. Even before Solveig's arrival they had refused to set out for work as usual, kept glancing at Willie in his blankets, and once they'd heard about Robbie, there was even more unrest.

'Bunch of lazy-born incomers,' Dougall had commented to Solveig. 'Never mind as we've all paid licences for the month, and it's anyway almost up. Might as well throw away money as chuck in a few days early.'

He was right about that, Solveig thought. It was only a week shy of November, and at the start of every month a new licence had to be applied and paid for, Tam Japp handing out the chits of paper that told the miners they could carry on working and where that should be. There'd be time soon enough to stand and stare, for back of November was usually first snowfall, and that could only make their work harder, colder, less easy to bear. There would be a let up in the weather mid-December, if all went as it usually did, but January was always a kicker for blizzards and the cold, and only got worse in February.

Standing in the mud of the Suisgill, Solveig couldn't envisage working even a week here, let alone a month or a year, and although the gold rush wasn't her primary concern, she truly hoped Brogar Finn and his new helper would come across something useful in their surveys, maybe even locate the actual source of the gold that trickled its way so grudgingly down these rivers, give these men a better target, a more robust likelihood of striking it rich, shortening the time they had to stay here.

In the meantime, she'd asked that they put Willie Blaine on a cart and bring him down to Kinbrace, and had left the men at it, still grumbling, still finishing their piece, their cups of tarry tea.

When she was nearer home, she halted on the bridge that stood a hundred yards or so from her house; she could taste the saltiness on the wind coming up the valley from the sea. She turned her face northwards to where Sholto and Moffatt Murchison had disappeared a while before, her line of sight obfuscated by the stubby birches and half-axed alders that lined the ditches of the road. She'd felt troubled even before she'd woken, as if the business end of a sledgehammer had been dropped onto her chest while she slept. The weight of duty seemed just as acute when she'd awoken moments later, and though she'd negotiated the day so far without trouble, she needed a few moments grace before carrying on with it, and she gazed down into the water below the stone parapets of the bridge, envying the unconcern of its flow, enjoying the cool spools of mist that rose up from the spume about its ramparts.

She looked down the length of the valley towards the old kirk, where it was hidden by the curve of the river, the push of field that came out from the farm, the huge boulders that had been fissured through by years and years of waters coursing about their shins. It should have calmed her, but instead she had the same uneasy feeling she'd had earlier that morning on the way up to the Suisgill when she had several times turned around quickly, thinking she'd heard a footfall not so far behind. She had stopped once, twice, a third time, studying the frost-raked track, the low branches of the leaf-scant trees. She'd seen nothing then, and she saw nothing now, but could not shake the conviction that she was being watched, felt the hairs on her neck and

131

forearms bristling, was jittery as a hare that smells the hunter but cannot see him, and had the urgent need to run and hide.

And then she did see something.

Only for a second, but she was sure of it.

A man, ducking down behind one of the old sheep byres in the field that separated her from the farm, and the farm from the old kirk. So certain was she that she didn't wait to confirm it, but turned swiftly, ran all the way back up the track to her house and steading and went straight into the yard, saw Brogar Finn standing by Gilligan and Hugh, who were tacking up the trap and pony, and threw herself in.

'It's getting late,' she said, a little breathlessly. 'If we don't go now, we'll not get back again before it's dark.'

Brogar Finn didn't register any surprise at Solveig's sudden appearance and apparent haste, just got in beside her side, handed over the reins, and with a quick switch of her lash, they were off.

'How big is the world!' Sholto thought as he looked about him, gratified to see absolutely nothing of human habitation, and elated because of it. There was a hush to this landscape, now that they had cleared Kinbrace and Kildonan, following Murchison's lead up the tiny tracks that led into the hills. There was a pleasing modesty to this landscape, a comfortable lack of drama, a kind of yawn that rolled on and on, as if the need for words such as hurry and worry had never existed. There were no trees to disturb the rolling hills, the shallow valleys, no shrubs, no sheep byres, no drove roads, no houses, and despite the lack of them, or maybe precisely because of that lack, he felt completely at ease, found it homely in some way he could not quite define.

They had left Solveig's steading an hour or so earlier, himself and Moffatt Murchison, cast adrift on a couple of short-necked, broad-backed horses, carrying the Brora bowls up to Scalabsdale and possible elucidation by the mysterious Tobar Strabane. Nothing here of murder or bad deaths, of scrumpled-up notes and little pieces of bark. Not that he'd entirely forgotten all that had happened in the past twenty-four hours, only that out here, everything seemed so much less significant, as if the earth had better things to do, and was working to a different beat, a slower rhythm, one that would always go on regardless of anything he, or anyone else, might ever do.

Out in his sheep byre, the master mast-maker waited. He was patient, could bide his time, had left the old kirk almost before first light and followed the river to the place the shop-keeper had marked with a cross upon his map, and which had a reasonable view of the single white house that lay beyond the bridge, where Solveig McCleery lived. Before he'd left the old kirk he'd spent a few minutes prowling about the graveyard, stepping through frozen lumps of human faeces and overgrown weeds, looking for Joseph's name on the unkempt stones, though he had not found it. The only one amongst the rest that was well tended belonged to Elof John McCleery, the man that Solveig must have married and who had predeceased her by several years.

He hadn't lingered, had made his way upriver, and less than half an hour later was in sight of the bridge and the house. A man came into the courtyard, hadn't bothered knocking on the door but made himself comfortable on the small bench just outside it, taking a couple of nips from his flask, a couple of pinches of tobacco to stoke up his pipe. Several minutes later, a woman emerged from the barn that lay on the other side of the courtyard. She had gone to the pump and washed her hands, extracted herself from boots and stockings, washing first her feet and then her face. His heart had almost

133

missed a beat then, for even from this distance there was no doubting at all who this must be. She had her father's same broad forehead, the same darkness to her hair that was so unusual in the place they had both come from, the same measured way of moving, the same way of straightening her back, lifting her chin.

He'd wished he'd had the borrow of that man's flask, but calmed himself nonetheless, needed now to watch, to see where she went, what she did, become familiar with the patterns of her life, and, most importantly, when he could catch her on her own. He'd been right behind her, though sticking to the undergrowth, when she'd started up the track towards the Suisgill, was used to moving quietly through forests so as not to alarm bears or boar, knew how to keep himself hidden, had tailed her up and down again unseen, had just got back to his sheep byre when Solveig had unexpectedly stopped at the bridge and turned towards him just before he'd time to drop down beneath the line of stones. And she'd seen him, stared at him for the sliver of a second it took him to duck down, but by then it was too late, and she was already turning, running back up the track towards her homestead, her pigeon-grey skirts hampering her speed, though all too soon, he'd figured, would come the hue and cry, and so he'd upped and abandoned his hidey-hole, running fast as he could towards the copse of beech that was at his back, quickly winding his way through the trees until he reached the track beyond, jogging its length a hundred yards, two hundred, almost three, before sifting himself back into the tangle of alder and birch that grew alongside the banks of the river, following it up a way until he found a place he could ford without too much difficulty, had forged his way across the current that ripped the river's middle, its waters swollen by spate, deepened by earlier autumn storms, emerging ten minutes later on the other side, his bag held high above his head, his body soaked from splash and spume, sodden from boots to belt.

Once on the other side he doubled back, went up the short hill through the heather, bending low. It hadn't taken him long to spy a place that would give him the vantage he needed, a small hillock below which the land bowed out about the bend of the river inside of which lay everything of Solveig's steading: the house, the barn, the water meadows. He went belly down then, crawled the last few yards to the brow of the hill, gained it, settled himself in, laid himself flat and immobile amongst the heather and the crowberry, caught the scent on the wind, the hint of salt, the faint tang of something burning. And looking down from his knoll he could make out another edifice he'd not been able to see from the sheep byre, saw the squat and square of it, the black tiles above, the solid walls below, the single line of small windows pinpricked along its gable end, and knew it for what it was, and his skin began to tighten across his chest, his breath coming quick, his blood running fast with recognition, for this was it, he was sure of it, the place Joseph had told him of: his sanctuary, the sanctuary of the Sukkiim, the home for all those who had been cast out, the one place that the Dwellers amongst the Rocks could call their own.

Chapter 17   *Who was his gift-seat and his throne*

Sholto had been more than happy to accompany Moffatt up to Scalabsdale that morning, and Solveig had made it an easy invitation for him to accept, by explaining that she and Finn must return back down to Brora and the mines, and packing up a saddlebag of provisions for Sholto's and Murchison's upcoming expedition.

'I've put in a few extras,' she'd told them. 'A few gifts for Mr Strabane – a jar of honey, a block of beeswax, some tobacco…well, I needn't tell you all. Your own provisions are in the right-hand pouch, his in the left.'

'Thank you, Miss,' Moffatt had replied, touching his cap with his fingers. 'That all sounds grand. Any particular message for Mr Strabane?'

Solveig had smiled then. 'I've written a short note of explanation,' she'd said, 'also in the saddlebag. But you could ask him, if you would, that he would be most welcome to accompany you both back this evening. I've already prepared a meal and it needs only cooking. We can talk about the bowls properly then, if he knows anything. Talk about the old days…'

Talk about my father, she might have added, everything of late seeming to be conspiring to drag him out of the past where she had confined him for so long, what with the mines, the message of the Sukkiim, the harking back to the chapel with Murchison and Strabane. Murchison understood, and touched his cap once more before hauling himself onto his steed.

'We'll be off then,' he announced. 'Should be an easy enough trip there and back, and we'll be returned before sundown.'

Solveig had smiled at them as she'd watched them go, held up her hand in farewell.

They were a while outside of Brora when they heard the ringing of pick on stone.

'The quarry,' Solveig elucidated. 'Good blocks to be had for building, and on the riverside there's plenty of clay. We've already got the brickworks up and going, though only on a small scale. Two hundred a day once the clay's been washed and pressed. We've got our first clamp pit already laid out like you said it should be, and it's been going for almost the full week. Should be ready to break open today.' She turned to Brogar Finn and smiled. 'I thought it might be something you'd want to see,' she said, and was gratified by the look of surprise upon his face.

'Of course!' Finn agreed enthusiastically. 'The brick clamp,' he added, noting the dark plume of smoke that crept above the small rises of the nearby braes, spreading out and down the ginnels and watercourses, being somewhat heavier than the surrounding air. It was a method he'd heard about, a cheap way of curing bricks without a kiln, one that he'd spoken to Solveig about the first night he'd been here when she had told him about the quarry and the mines. But he had never for one moment imagined Solveig would put his theory into practice, and now she had gone ahead and done it without telling him. He looked at her with renewed admiration. She was an unusual woman, no doubt about that.

'We excavated a pit three yards by fifteen,' she went on. 'I hope that was big enough?' She looked at him questioningly, and Finn nodded sagely. He was a traveller, constantly updating his own experiences with others that he came across, adding to them, embellishing them with his own experiences and knowledge; he had hit upon the idea of a brick pit somewhere or other, though he could not remember where. Apparently Solveig had taken him at his word, had dug the pit, lined it with wet clay, laid on the coal, placed the bricks on top and set it going, sealing up the whole thing with more wet clay

137

so that it stood on the flat of the river valley like an ancient, burning cairn. Finn coughed as an acrid drift of brick-smoke cast across the way as they came closer, making his eyes water, filling his nose, his mouth, with dust and grit, getting thicker with every few yards they took towards it.

Christ, I hope it works, he thought, though not, in this instance, for himself, not for the kick it would give him to have his methodology proved sound and right, but because this woman he'd only known a short while had trusted him, acted upon his ideas, and he wanted more than anything, for her sake, that it would go right.

They followed the Kildonan Burn a few miles before bearing away to the right and skirting the Craig nan Gearr, the Chair of the Child, going up and up, before dropping down into Scalabsdale and the kidney-shaped loch that was settled between the surrounding peaks. They were so much higher here than they had been down in the valley that Sholto and Murchison could see clear through to the northern and western mountains, and the streaks of snow that struck down through their gullies where the sun could not go. A little way further and they saw several well-maintained habitations that adjoined and overlapped like a staggered Z, saw smoke rising from the chimney of the first one, and an odd shimmer of steam breathing out from the seams of the last. As they approached, they could make out someone hitching into the small jetty built out into the loch, the boat rocking slightly as a man bent down over the rowlocks, securing the oars, lashing the mooring ropes into the rings of the pier. He clambered out shortly and looked towards them, towards the noise they were making as they trotted closer, and did not seem disturbed or surprised, and nor did he desist from his task, but carried on tightening his ropes, unloading a creel from the bows, decanting the silver

138

slip and flip of live fish into a meshed wire cage, lowering the lot back down into the water, securing the cage's ropes as he had secured the boat's.

Sholto and Moffatt came to a stop and dismounted, began to walk their horses on. The man stood up as they drew level with the jetty, his left hand cricked into the small of his back; he pushed out his chest, rolling his shoulders, ironing out the creaks.

'Mr Strabane?' Moffatt called out, and then again. 'Tobar Strabane?'

The man didn't answer, but came towards them, off the end of the jetty, motioning them to follow, and went towards the cottage. Once there he turned, caught their horses' reins, hitching them easily to a post, then disappeared briefly into the cottage, returning with two snaffle bags of oats and hay. Only then did he look closely at his two visitors, shading his eyes with one hand as he studied them, his brow deeply creased, his face the colour of the water that gathers in a bog after all the peat has been cut away.

'Is that you, Moffatt?' he asked finally. 'Moffatt Murchison?' And then he clapped Moffatt hard on the shoulder as if he'd been some long-lost son. 'By God, but it is! It's Moffatt Murchison!'

'Aye, it is, sir,' Moffatt answered, blushing slightly, astonished to have been recognised, but glad for it. 'And this is Mr McKay,' Moffatt added. 'Sholto McKay, of the Lundt and McCleery Mining Company.'

'Well, you're both very welcome!' Tobar exclaimed. 'Very welcome indeed. Come along, come along and sit you down.'

He didn't take them into the cottage, led them instead to a seat that had been neatly cut into an overhanging peat bank by the pier, the seat's surface carefully laid over with flat popplestones.

'One moment,' Tobar advised them, held up a finger, leant down and snatched out a sack from a niche secreted somewhere beneath the seat, began to scatter handfuls of dried heather onto the stones. 'But don't just stand

139

there,' Tobar urged. 'This is a welcome day, for it's not often I get visitors. Come on lads, sit you down, and I'll get us something to warm our skins.'

Moffatt and Sholto exchanged glances, but did as they were bade, Tobar Strabane swiftly disappearing back into his house.

'He's maybe a little eccentric,' Moffatt said apologetically as he and Sholto sat themselves down, the dried heather scrunching beneath their weight, releasing a faint smell of mowed hay and honey. Sholto nodded, made himself comfortable; he had read about men like Tobar many times in his reports – men who chose to isolate themselves, men like Brogar Finn, who, though he stayed within the system, patently didn't want to be a part of it any more than was needed. They waited in silence, listening to the distant pocking of a grouse as it was upped by some alarm, watching the concentric circles radiating out on the loch just below them where some ferox trout or pike had briefly surfaced, saw the scuffle of the caught fish in the cage that Tobar Strabane had secured to the pier, gazed upwards to where the broad spread of an eagle slewed its arc high into the sky above their heads, maybe looking down on them with its sharp eyes of gold.

Odd, odd, it seemed to the master mast-maker, that Joseph Lundt had once referred to this confined place as his home, meaning not by that the outlying house or the steading, nor the fields that surrounded it, but this single enclave, this one space, this dimness that stole its habitation between the darkness and the light.

He was in the chapel.

It was dark, hard to make out any shapes. The pews had been stripped back, leaving a central space like a living room, or a library. He stood still, feeling the uneven surface of the earthen floor beneath his boots, watching the light that came in through the tiny windows up above the eastern wall like cart

140

spokes stabbing into the gloom. He saw the outlines of several paintings on the left-hand wall, three small cot beds further up, a great glass case at their end inside of which he could make out shadows and blocks of stone, one of them glittering dimly. The opposite wall was lined with shelves crammed from one end to the other with books and box files. The draught from the door was cold at his back, and he rubbed his fingers against his thumbs, thought of the ice that gathered about mast tops in winter, great lumps that could only be shifted by someone climbing up there and going at them with mallet and chisel.

He moved forward towards the big table, lifted a piece of paper then let it drift and drop, studied the several books that had been opened and flattened face down, spines to the roof like the backbones of birds that had fallen, wings outstretched, unable to rise. The lectern loomed off to his left, and he climbed the two steps that led up to it, placed himself behind it, gazed into the darkness of the room, imagined it still peopled with pews and men, looked up into the eaves, at the wood that hung suspended there like the ribs of an upturned boat. He wasn't sure what he had expected, but it hadn't been this. This was a sanctified place, but one that had now been violated, and that could mean only one thing: that Joseph Lundt – his hero, his mentor, his life before life – was truly dead.

The words rattled like cold, hard pebbles in his head, and though he had long suspected the truth of them, the pain of their actualisation was so acute, so raw, that he found himself on his knees before the old lectern, his hand crossing himself in the old way, the Orthodox way, fingers moving from one shoulder to the next, from forehead to stomach, resting there for a moment before alighting on his lips. A blessing should have followed, but all he found there was a name and a curse. The name was Solveig Lundt, and the

141

curse was upon her for the violation she had wrought upon her father's greatest work.

Chapter 18   *The path of exile has twisted him like gold*

They had reached the quarry a half hour before, and Solveig, obviously nervous, had been talking almost non-stop ever since. She'd pointed out to Finn the openings of the new mines she'd had dug into the river cliffs at Faskally, according to his advice, that they could just make out over the smoke of the brick clamp, Solveig quoting to him all the while the way they'd been shored, the coal samples that had been excavated from them in the last two weeks, the different gradings they'd achieved, how much had gone into the brickworks, how much better was the quality of the coal now that they had taken the direction he had told them to go, which was back along the fault-line towards Brora.

Brogar Finn was a little overwhelmed by the immediate way Solveig had acted on his prognostications after that first night's consultation in her father's old study, when he had studied the maps, made suggestions as to the way he thought the coal must be running, pointing out the lines and seams he couldn't see on the map, but could guess at from the way the rest of the geological understructure stood. Since then, he'd spent most of his time at his first duty, which was the gold survey up at Kildonan and latterly the Suisgill, and he simply hadn't been prepared for anyone going ahead as impulsively as he might have done himself. He was used to being constantly kept in check, used to fighting his way out of the Company's orders and his assistants' protests, so that he could take the initiative he craved – crawling down holes that had been dug into cliffs or caves, lowing himself down unstable shafts, setting dangerous boreholes – instead of spending his time making maps, submitting reports, having them sent in and approved of or more probably dismissed, by which time he had usually lost interest in the eventual outcome, having already moved on to the next assignment, rarely seeing the net results of his findings.

That Solveig was a different kettle of fish altogether was apparent, and he liked it, found her enthusiasm gratifying, endearing, and latterly rather frightening, realising, as he now did, just how much she was relying on his opinion, and that she was pinning the survival of an entire town upon his back. And not just any town, but the one he'd been born and raised in. And he was truly fearful when they finally reached the brick clamp – the one that he had so blithely pronounced on, but had no idea she had actually gone ahead and built and put into use. He feared she might ask him for a speech as its progenitor, but once close by, the smoke and heat were so intense that there was not a hope of anyone standing still long enough for such a thing.

The clamp itself seemed vast. He knew the coal-burning course must be a yard down into the earth, assuming Solveig had gone by his specifications, and there was no reason, given everything else she had done, that this would not be the case, and yet the bricks had been piled so high above it that they reached almost to his shoulder, everything slapped over with a last layer of clay so that it appeared like some misshapen bee-skep that was in the middle of its winter smoking-out. A group of men were gathered about it, most having tied pieces of sacking around their faces and hands, big lengths of wood at the ready, all blinking with the smoke, tear tracks running down their black-smudged cheeks, the tightness of their skin making them seem to grin like maniacs beneath their masks.

'Shall us go in as yet, Missus McCleery?' one was coughing, even as they closed upon the scene.

'Gotta think its fired as far as it can go,' another shouted, his makeshift kerchief muffling his words, his neck like whey about his collar where the dust had not yet settled, in staggering contrast to the rest of him.

144

'We cannae jus drouk it oot,' another commented. 'Best way's to broach it all at once, and do it lickity.'

'Time's a-nigh, missus,' the first man said, sounding so like a boy at a fireworks display that Finn almost laughed. Still, he thought, they had good reason to be excited, for only two weeks back these same men had pressed the first bricks to be made on Brora soil in four decades, pressed them and left them to dry – maybe only the standard straights, and not the more complicated splits, pups or arches any competent brickie would have been able to make without breaking sweat – but only one week after drying, here they were, every last one placed for curing in this crude kiln, fired by the first coal to be excavated in Brora for forty years.

Solveig's face was shining with perspiration and anxiety. What if it didn't work? What if all the bricks had cracked and broken? What if the coal hadn't burned evenly and the most part of them were spoiled? Her mouth had gone dry, her heart beating quickly, the tips of her fingers twitching with the pulsing of her blood.

'Shall I?' Finn asked her, placing one hand upon her shoulder, at which she nodded gratefully, and so he raised his other arm, holding his hat high in the air. 'I take full responsibility!' he shouted loudly. 'And I say the time is now. Let's have at it, lads!' And then he dropped his arm suddenly, let the cap fall, and all the men took up their sticks and whooped, started through the smoke and the heat, began battering away at the steaming stack, breaking the cooked clay that encased it.

'But these are astonishing!' Tobar Strabane was saying. 'Truly astonishing. And you found them where? On the East Beach, did you say?'

'By one of the old shore pits,' Moffatt answered, though he knew no more than that.

'Have you ever heard of the Coygan Cave find?' Tobar asked, though did not wait for an answer. 'There was a colander there too, rather like this one, found around 1810, and that's the only other one I know of anything like this. It's astonishing...' he repeated, continuing to examine the outlines of the bowls where they lay in the straw, unwilling to lift them out yet for they were so delicate; he was amazed they'd not been broken into several pieces by their exhumation, let alone the journey they had suffered from there to here. 'I'd hazard a guess that they're from Roman-times,' he began again, gently teasing one up so that by leaning down and over he could see the rim and parts of its inner surface. 'It's not generally known they came this far north, but Tacitus talks of it, as does Ptolemy. He mentions an *Ila fluvii ostia* somewhere on the northeast coast, and some scholars believe that name can be linked to certain pre-Norse appellations in this part of the world, most notably Strath Ilidh, or Ullie – the old name for the valley, and Dun Ilidh, by which the tiny hamlet that became Helmsdale used to be known.'

Sholto was astonished too, not so much at the bowls, though they were interesting enough, but by the depth of knowledge spilling out of a man who lived all alone in the middle of mountains and moors, and he studied Tobar with interest, noting that though his hair was long and unkempt it was also clean, as was the back of his neck below his collar, the latter having ridden back as the man leaned forward to study the bowls.

Tobar looked up, caught the expression on Sholto's face, his own cracking open in a smile that revealed strong, if crooked, teeth.

'You look a little sceptical, my friend,' he said warmly. 'Why don't you finish off that drink and come inside?'

So saying, he lifted his own cup from the ground and slugged it back in one, Moffatt following suit, coughing as the rough spirit caught his throat.

146

'Made from rye,' Tobar commented. 'Got a still out back. Not strictly legal, you understand, but there's plenty more.' He winked at Moffatt, who smiled nervously, feared a session coming on and didn't like to think of the ride back to Kildonan if such was the case; he wasn't too good on his pins after too much strong drink, though thank God at least they had horses who knew the way home.

'We've a few gifts,' he remembered with sudden hope, thinking food might stave such a happening off, and began to unpack the saddlebag. 'Come from Solveig, right enough,' he added, and Tobar nodded.

'Always was a good one, that Solveig, always was,' he said, going on to admire the clarity of the honey, the soft colour of the beeswax, the carefully wrapped packages of meat and oatcakes; he seized at the tobacco with delight, but plainly was still eager to get indoors, more eager to lift up these bowls from their straw, lay them out, to see them in all their glory.

The clay pit had been broken open, and the smoke that had initially billowed out in great, throat-searing guffs and goffs had subsided, not that Solveig's men seemed unduly affected by it. Their air of good humour was apparent in how hard they were working, their forearms shining with sweat where they had rolled up their sleeves, their faces black with the dust that inhabited the air, settling on every inch of them. Still they laboured on, using shovels grafted onto sturdy poles to lift out the bricks course by course, laying them down on the surrounding earth, the grass having been gradually singed off it by the previous week's burning.

Solveig hung anxiously at one side, darting forward every now and then as one of the men cried out as he lost the grip on his shovel, or a hot brick toppled off and fell onto his boot, burning a stripe across the leather. Finn kept his distance, mostly so that he could carry on breathing, but also because

147

he didn't want to get in the way of so assiduous a work force. It reminded him just how much was riding on this experiment; the success of this one endeavour would give them all the surety these men so desperately needed to hear – that the mines, new and old, could still be productive, if only to provide clinker for pits like these, which would mean that both brickworks and shafts could be started up again on a scale that might not be properly industrial, but would be enough to give work to the men of the township of Brora and the outlying areas, enough to wean them away from the precarious employment offered by the fishing and the Sutherland Estate. If it could be kept going, Solveig had told him, and if Brora could in such a way be guaranteed a future, then it might be enough to stop the rest of the post-clearance families melting away, might even provide the means for bringing back some of those who had left years before.

By God, Finn thought, as he watched the men going at the brick clamp, *but how proud my father would have been to see this, to see me standing here at this moment.*

His eyes had begun to water and he wiped his hand brusquely across his face, told himself it was the heat and the smoke, and that a man like him did not do crying of any sort, and that there was nothing to greet about in the first place. He'd been so young when he had left here, had always been rootless, had enjoyed the feeling of not belonging, of otherness, that it had always given him, enabling him to shift and shally from one assignment to the next with no regrets for leaving any of them, nor the people, the men, the various women, he'd called friends while he was there. He was remembering something his mother had once spoken of, however briefly, a kind of melancholic nostalgia you could have for the place that you had left, no matter how hard your life had been whilst you were there.

Cianalas, she had called it, the only Gaelic word he'd ever heard her utter, at least to him.

Sholto and Moffatt followed Tobar into his cottage, finding the first room claustrophobic, walls and roof-space blackened with smoke, a stall at one end, inside it a pair of heavily pregnant ewes leaning their bulk against the wooden rails, knees down on the floor, chomping at the hay and slurry in their troughs. Even Sholto, who was by no means tall, had to duck down through the opened door, tripping over the flood guard, narrowly missing stumbling into the large table that was set only a yard or so from the threshold; no windows here, only the fire burning slowly in the grate, the walls alive with moving shadows as the flames jittered with their coming, a single bed built coffin-like into the right-hand wall beside the inglenook. Tobar did not dally here, but led them on through the low room, past the ewe-stalls beneath a clumsy arch that had been fashioned out of wattle and daub, leading them on into the next. But once beneath the arch, Sholto gasped, for this room was so different from the first that he found it hard to get his breath. There was another fire burning in another grate, but that was not the only light, for here were windows, large windows, each set deeply into the east- and west-facing walls, the other two being made up entirely of bookshelves that consisted of a rough framework of planks built from floor to ceiling, and one corner to the next. In the middle of the room was yet another set of bookshelves, this time freestanding, piled high from top to toe not with books, but with broadsheets, journals, string-wrapped bundles of papers of every size.

'My God!' he said, as did Moffatt, who had just emerged behind him, and was bumping at his back in the confined space they had gained. Tobar, a yard in front of them, gave out a brief laugh at their surprise, a sound so exuberant and rich in this so unexpected of places, that neither Sholto nor Moffatt could help but smile.

'It's something, isn't it?' Tobar said, evidently proud, in the way he said his words, to have shown them something they had not expected to see, gifting them entrance into his holy of holies, his sacred ground. 'There's a whole lifetime of learning locked up in this room,' he added. 'My whole lifetime, at least.'

He left them both agape upon the threshold whilst he made a swift but careful way along the tiny maze between his bookshelves, seeking out the several amongst the many that he was trying to find. It took him less than sixty seconds, and as soon as he had his several tomes bundled between armpit and elbow, he gestured his visitors to back up, tutting slightly, though with amusement not annoyance, as both Sholto and Moffatt tried to obey, turning themselves awkwardly between the books and shelves, beneath the confines of the arch, finally got themselves back past the pregnant ewes, at which point Tobar pushed past them and spilled his findings out upon the large, self-made table, the axe-marks still evident on the wood, in the pegs that held the trestles to the top-boards. He took a spill from the shelf above the fire and got it lit, and with it several lamps that he placed at intervals about the table, then began flicking through the pages of the books he had tumbled out before him.

'Moffatt,' Tobar said, though he only slightly raised his head from his pages and papers. 'Will you nip outside? Go down to the jetty? You'll find a cut-out bit of bank just to the left of it. It's got a door of sorts, a few bricks of peat. Take a few away and put in your hand, bring us back another bottle.'

Moffatt Murchison didn't move, not at once, was still entranced by the fact that Tobar's library was not as mythical as he had always supposed, and only took his leave when Tobar spoke again.

150

'Come on, man, you're not in chapel now. A bottle, man! We need a bottle. And while you're at it,' he added, 'why not bring up the pen and pull out a couple of those trout? We'll have them grilling on the fire in a moment.'

'Anything I can do, sir?' Sholto asked anxiously as Moffatt bolted for the door.

'Aye, lad,' Tobar answered. 'There's a skillet on the hearth. Get in some dripping from the pot in the larder and get it good and hot.' And then he stopped, straightened up, looked more closely at Sholto, looked Sholto bang in the eye. 'You're not from around here, are you, my boy?' he asked, and though Sholto would have liked to have rebuffed the appellation of 'my boy', given that he wasn't so young as it implied, and Tobar himself maybe only mid-fifties, he said nothing of that.

'No,' he answered noncommittally, 'not exactly. Why do you ask?'

Tobar looked a moment longer at Sholto, at the streak of badger in his hair, and then looked away, smiled that warm smile again, as he waved his hand.

'Ach, it's nothing. Just the way spoke your words is all. Reminded me of someone, from way back when.'

Sholto did not reply. He went instead in search of the larder, found it consisted of several rough planks hoisted on bricks at the back of the room, away from the heat of the fire. He found the skillet, scooped out a ladle of dripping into it then steadied it on the embers. After that, while waiting for Moffatt to return, he sat himself down on one of the several stools set about the table, and watched Tobar's large, workmanlike hands as they lifted the first of the bowls from the straw, saw how strong and scarred those hands were, hands that must have hewn this table, probably this whole habitation, and marvelled that they could be so deft with something so delicate, that they possessed a gentleness towards these bowls that he had rarely seen before; maybe only once, maybe only that time at the meeting of the Linnaean

151

Society back in Trondheim a couple of years before when Peder Steffenson had returned from some plant-collecting mission in Madagascar, when he'd chosen to show to them the spiders he had caught there, gassed and pinned to a velvet stretch of diorama representing all the plants those spiders had been found on, when he had lifted up one carefully preserved leaf to show another that had been cut and curved and sewn into itself like a canoe.

'And this,' Peder Steffenson had said, as he had put just one tip of one finger beneath the first leaf to show the second, 'is the first example ever seen of the nesting behaviour of the spider I have chosen to be named after myself...'

But Tobar Strabane had nothing at all about him of Steffenson, not of his pomp nor of proprietary exclamations. There was something quite opposite going on here in the way that Tobar was investigating these bowls, in the way he lifted them up, making sure that the straw came with them, that they were never given a sudden jolt; he had an attitude of humility towards them as if they were something of far greater value than they had seemed to be to anyone who had so far seen them, Sholto included. And he admired this care, and the way the man went about his work, his careful sketchings, his application to his books, so that it seemed almost an affront when Moffatt returned ten minutes later with both bottle and fish.

They'd cleared the clamp of bricks as much as they were able. The lower courses just above the coals were black, impossible to shift, at least with any ease, their bases having melted in the heat and welded to the clinker beneath, and hot as hell.

'We should maybe leave this layer to cool for a bit before we rake it over,' Finn started to say, but was stopped by the look of incredulity on Solveig's face and the smile that was seeping through the grime that encased her from head to toe.

'Leave it?' she said, laughing. 'These men'll not leave it! There's three days heat here for their families and fires, maybe more. They'll shovel it off and take it away anyhow they're able.'

And he saw that she was right, saw the line of women and children that had mysteriously materialised at the backs of their men, saw the coal scuttles, cauldrons, pans, earthenware bowls, they had brought with them; they were already battling the ferocious heat, using ladles, paddles, pieces of sticks, anything they could get their hands on, anything to shovel up the still burning embers into any vessel that they could. A couple of women already had their pinafores go up in flame and were being rolled on the ground by their children, but no sooner were the flames out than they were back up again, shovelling as if the devil were on their tail, grabbing for their homesteads all they could secure.

'It's coal,' Solveig said simply. 'It's been here all along underneath their feet, and they've all known it. But getting it out, that's a different matter. There's men here've tried to go back into the mines on their own over the years and been killed by falls or fumes. But if we can properly get at it, and get it out, then its only right their families should get some of it, even if it's only like it is today.'

She was right, Finn knew it. Coal would always burn longer and hotter, better and brighter, than did any kind of peat, no matter how deep these people dug into their bogs to retrieve it. Solveig's plan to improve their lot was audacious, and no matter, Finn thought, that she was going up against the Company by doing it, he would back her all the way.

The fish were sizzling in their skillet. Both Sholto and Moffatt had glasses filled to the brim with a spirit they were neither of them too keen to take too much of, had the overwhelming stench of warm sheep shite in their nostrils, and their eyes smarting as the smoke of the fire crept its way about the room, keeping company with the draughts that shifted every time the sheep chose to buffet and bleat. Tobar Strabane, by contrast, was entirely at ease. His books and papers were spread the length and breadth of the table, consigning Sholto and his notebook to one corner, and only a few square inches at that. Tobar himself was far too busy taking his own notes to notice his guests' discomfiture, and wasn't put off in the slightest by their presence. What interested Tobar was the bowls themselves, especially after he had lifted out the first of them, the colander, as he called it.

And it was beautiful, no doubting that. It was also almost broken in two, creased like a piece of paper down its middle. Tobar had held it with its bundle of straw still intact for only a moment before replacing it, left the table briefly to fetch out some thick woollen socks from a drawer which he balled into a woollen circle and placed beneath the colander, removing the straw stalk by stalk until the metal was cupped about the sock-ball, and only then did he lift the whole and place it, oh so gently, down onto the table so that he could study it whole. He copied out meticulously the patterns made by the tracery of holes pierced over its sides and base, making note of the riveting, of the patterns on the rim, did all this and more before moving on to the next artefact, the first of the two bowls, giving it a similarly thorough and reverential treatment, as he did also to the third.

Sholto had occupied himself during this lengthy occupation by making his own notes, marking down his own take on the patterns, leafing through each book as Tobar discarded it. Every now and then he glanced at Tobar, studied the creases at the sides of his eyes, his mouth, the way his lips moved slightly

154

as he was reading. At one point he'd asked if he might slip off and take a quick look at the library for himself, and Tobar had nodded his agreement.

'Just don't touch anything on the middle stack,' he'd warned. 'It's stuff I've not had time to catalogue properly, and I don't want it moved.'

Sholto had passed the sheep, patting one of them vaguely on the head as he passed it by, wondering about Tobar Strabane, and how he had he managed to accumulate so many books in so faraway place, and who delivered all these piles of periodicals that were buckling down the centre shelves with their weight, and how it was that such a man as Tobar knew about Ptolemy, and Roman artefacts. This last question was answered easily enough as soon as Sholto began reading the titles of Tobar's accumulated library, many of which were concerned with archaeology of one kind or another, and most of which were in Latin or German. This, Sholto soon realised, was not the library of an amateur, this was the library of a scholar, of a man who regarded such things as the bowls dug up in Brora as serious stuff. He'd been rummaging through the books for maybe half an hour, when Murchison's voice summoned him back to reality.

'We'll need to leave soon, Tobar,' he said, his voice loud, presumably so that Sholto could hear it too. 'Mrs McCleery, as I mentioned before, has asked us to ask you back down for dinner.'

Tobar didn't react at all, Sholto saw, as he came back past the animal pen into the room. His head was down, and he was scribbling furiously onto his notepad.

'It's well past two,' Moffatt tried again, though still with no response.

Sholto decided to lay the bait, for he too was keen to get back down to base.

'She'll maybe have brought the other four bowls back with her from Brora,' he said with as much insouciance as he could manage, though it had the

155

desired effect, Tobar looking up sharply, his body stuttering slightly in its seat.

'You mean there's more? Not just these three?'

Sholto cleared his throat in satisfaction. 'Not all in such a great state, sir, but yes, there are more. Seven in all, though not so well preserved.'

'And you never thought to mention it before?' Tobar said, and for a moment looked like there was a thunderstorm brewing deep inside him, his lips tightening into a thin white line. But then he relaxed, nodded his head, stood up and slapped Sholto's shoulder.

'Quite right, young man,' he said. 'Quite right.'

And again, Sholto had the irrational urge to explain to this man that he was not so young, nor should be spoken of as such, but the moment came and went, for straightaway Tobar agreed to pack up, got his fire banked with clinker and cinders so it wouldn't go out during the night he would be away, got his horse tacked and was up on its back within the space of ten minutes, though not before securing the three Brora bowls to his own exact specifications back into Sholto's saddlebag, socks and all.

'Mustn't keep the delightful Solveig waiting,' Tobar called back as he rode on ahead, keeping up a fast pace hard for both Sholto and Moffatt's rides to keep up with, and it escaped neither that Tobar kept looking behind him all the way he went, maybe checking the safety of the bowls, or maybe, Sholto thought, because he was already missing his small wild place in the hills.

Chapter 19   *And bereft him of his homeland*

Brogar and Solveig were also returning, coming back with a brief detour through the Baile an Or, entering the small shack Tam Japp liked to call his office. Tam was sat now behind his desk, looking as scruffy and dirty as any of the panners who passed daily by his desk, but none the less officious for all that. On seeing Solveig enter he stood up automatically, nodded, rubbing his hands nervously together. They were big hands, used to rolling over sheep that had got stuck on their backs overnight and needed shifting, or holding those same sheep still against his brawny thighs to get them sheared.

His rise from sheepsman to overseer to panning secretary had been a good one as far as money went, though it had only come about because his predecessor had succumbed to pneumonia back in February, and the Sutherlands therefore needed someone on the spot and quick. Tam had been the Estate's go-between by then down at the docks in Helmsdale, logging the sales of wool, the receipts of grain and wine, and had been scrupulous in his dealings with both the Estate and the merchants they were doing business with; he knew that he had earned this post, no matter how many grumbled behind his back, and was proud of it.

For other men it might have been a drawback that the job meant living out in the sticks with a load of world-weary panners, but not for Tam Japp who had, at least at first, rather liked it. He'd found he missed the hubbub of men all around him that he'd had when he'd been at the sheep. He'd no wife, no family, and no friends, not here anywise, most of the men at the Baile an Or despising him for his job, accusing him of cheating them, of skimming from the top. He knew it wasn't so – or not always. Sure, he'd done it once or twice, but only when the find had been big, the loss to the panners or the Estate negligible, and every job had it perks, and this was the only one he'd found. And as men went, he thought he'd lived his life well, performed his jobs honestly, though this last had left his strong hands itching for action, as he felt the physical prowess he'd always been proud of waning, but had enjoyed it anyway, had even been under the delusion for a while that he was getting accepted, pally even, with some of the miners.

That had changed, of course it had, after the incident back in the summer when the Reverend Joass had visited to do his survey, the time Tam Japp had, quite literally, thought he'd struck gold. When it turned out a trick, he'd been livid, embarrassed and humiliated, and now everyone treated him with even more contempt, sniggering behind his back if not to his face. That the boy he was certain had been the perpetrator was now dead, he regretted almost as much as the next man, but he wasn't going to go out of his way to find out why the lad had died. Life in these valleys had always been hard, brutal and short. That Robbie Weavers' had been harder and shorter than most was not something he took pleasure in, but certainly wasn't going to lose him any sleep. Any number of boys died young and early, blown from a fishing ketch into the sea, falling drunk into rivers and drowning, or slipping in snow, banging their heads on the way down, dying all alone in the cold. That was just how life went, and Tam Japp knew it. And knew that the Sutherlands, bigwigs as they were, knew the same, and that the jurisdiction for any investigation into such meaningless deaths was on Solveig's shoulders, or at least on the Company she represented. But he was not a cruel man, nor overly vindictive, and he had done his duty, indeed had done far more, and had double-checked, sending a man up to Dunrobin – the Sutherlands' seat outside of Golspie – for written confirmation, even suggesting that the provost should be sent for out from Dornoch, the nearest Royal Burgh. But, as predicted, the deaths of a couple of gold panners were not of particular interest, and anyway the Sutherlands had already gone south, taking the Duke's own personal railway to Inverness and on from there to their country seat in England to ride out the winter in more beneficent climes.

But now Solveig McCleery was here in his office in person, her companion waiting outside, setting the horses to the water in the burn. Tam Japp felt obscurely embarrassed for his employers that they had let her down in such a way, and at such a time. She was a small woman, fierce, and with a formidable reputation. Everyone knew what she was doing about reopening the mines and the brickworks, and everyone was thankful for it, including Tam Japp. It had taken Brora a long time to recover after the closures of 1828, which had stripped the township right back to its bones. The families who had stayed had struggled hard to remain, some living off the fishing, some on trade with the boats, the rest on the sheep farms. Four decades on and it was still hard going, but here was someone, and a woman at that, trying to do something about it, trying to breathe a little life back into the place, put a bit of flesh on those old bones, and you couldn't help but admire her for that.

'Ma'am,' he said, holding out his hand then withdrawing it, seeing the dirt that had accumulated beneath his nails, in the creases of his palms. He might be a man of some authority here, but he still bunked the same way the rest of them did, on a piece of planking at the back of his shack, covered in wool blankets and sacking, still had to wash in the river if he wanted washing, clean his clothes the same way, still had to dig his peat from the riverbanks to set his fire, wrestle with dead bracken and dying heather if he wanted to keep even halfway warm, the whole inside of the shack covered now with a film of ash and dirt.

Solveig looked at him, and then smiled, a sight so unexpected it made Tam Japp blush.

159

'Mr Japp,' she said, surveying the small room, the man's discomfiture, the lack of anything that could make this place a space fit for living in. Tam squirmed, moved around his desk, offered her his chair. She thanked him, and took up his offer, sat down, and he could not have been more surprised by what she said next.

The ride back down to Kildonan and Kinbrace from Scalabsdale seemed half the length it had taken them to get up there.

'Short cuts,' Tobar told Sholto. 'Know them all. Been trekking up and down these hills my whole life. You get to know every stone, every deer trail, every ditch, after you've been doing it as long as I have.'

He had insisted on spending most of the journey riding side by side with Sholto when he was able, primarily, Sholto thought, to keep an eye on the bowls, judging by the way he kept glancing anxiously at the saddlebag they had been so carefully packed into. They hadn't spoken much, but Tobar had at one point asked him where he came from.

'I was born not too far from Dannemora, in Norway,' Sholto had answered truthfully. 'The family moved up north to Finnmark some time after.'

Tobar had not looked surprised, had merely taken one hand from his reins, rubbed his chin with it, and said, 'Were you now,' though it was not a question, and Sholto wondered just how much the man knew of the Helmsdale Pick, for he was of an age when he must have known of it if he had been living here then, which Moffatt had said he had. And he thought back to that comment Tobar had made back up at Scalabsdale, about the way Sholto had 'spoken his words'.

It had never occurred to him before that he might meet people in this valley who had known his parents, or maybe his grandparents, that there were people here he would have known himself if his parents had never left, although given that scenario, Sholto was of the firm opinion that he would never have been born at all.

'I need your help, Mr Japp,' Solveig was saying. 'I need to ask you to look over your ledgers, or let me do it for you. I need to find out just who was up at the Suisgill when Willie Blaine and Robbie Weavers died, and who was down here in the Baile an Or. I need to know if anyone has made any complaints about either of them, if there were any accidents, injuries or fights I should know about.'

Tam Japp was stood on the wrong side of his desk. He looked over at Solveig. He fidgeted, felt exposed, wanted to be sitting back down in the seat she now occupied, didn't like the way her fingers were tapping the cover of his Book of Licences, wasn't sure if he should argue or just hand everything over. Solveig stayed silent, waiting for a reply that did not come. She closed her eyes briefly and then opened them, looked straight into Tam Japp's own.

'You do know men have died?' she began. 'I say men, but one of them was only a boy. Robbie Weavers. I believe you knew him?' Tam flinched, wondering how much she knew about the incident back in the summer, though her face gave nothing away. 'Understand, Mr Japp,' she went on, 'that I am not accusing anyone. But it was you who told me, was it not, that if any investigation was to be undertaken into these deaths, then it was up to me to do it?'

Another question to which he didn't have an answer.

Tam Japp began to sweat.

Outside, the temperature was falling fast, clouds the colour of granite beginning to swell upon the horizon, smaller yellow offshoots scudding fast across the sky. Tam could see his exhaled breath forming its own small cloud as he opened his mouth and then closed it again. He had no idea what he was supposed to say; he needed some kind of prompt, and did not feel any of the authority he was supposed to have. Solveig coughed once into her closed fist and then looked up at him. She was a small thing in her chair, in Tam Japp's chair, but right at that moment the world fell away from him, and there was nothing outside of him but her. 'Willie Blaine died, or more probably was killed,' she said quietly, 'tied up in a sack and put on display on a rood ground.' Her words were brutal, meant to shock, and she had not finished. 'Robbie Weavers was subdued, pushed into a river and left to drown. Is there anything about this that strikes you as unusual, Mr Japp? Anything about this situation that leaves you in any doubt about what the right thing is to do?'

Solveig had been harsher than she'd intended, mostly because the man's inability to make a decision, or say anything at all, had infuriated her. She'd been a little lurid in her descriptions of the deaths, but knew she was not wrong, as Tam Japp began to shuffle his feet, and finally spoke.

'Just take them, missus,' Tam Japp said. 'Take anything you want if it'll help at all.'

And as he spoke, all Solveig wanted to do was laugh. She couldn't help it. Kept thinking of the story Gilligan and Hugh had told her of how Robbie Weavers had done in this Jappster with his jape about the gold. She started to laugh, knew how inappropriate it was and put her hand up to her face to stop it, then she realised she wasn't laughing at all, but instead had begun to cry, suddenly finding that everything was far too much for her to bear.

Tam Japp stood before her like a monolith, didn't know what to do. Had never known what to do, had only ever done what he'd been told to, and none of it had prepared him for this. And his legs began to move of their own accord, and in seconds he was back around the desk and he was patting his stocky hand clumsily on Solveig's shoulder.

'It'll be all right, missus, you'll see it will.'

162

It was pathetic, but it was all he had, and amazingly it seemed to do the trick, for Solveig's outburst ceased, and though she still held one hand over her mouth and another to her throat, her sobs were soon stifled, and in another minute she managed to speak.

'It's nothing,' she said brusquely. 'Just the dust from the brick clamp. And all that smoke.'

Aye, right, Tam Japp thought, though he kept his peace. He'd found the episode, short as it was, acutely uncomfortable, and yet was rather glad to know that Solveig really was a woman just like any other, and could take to tears as soon as the next.

'Someone's been here,' Sholto said. 'No doubt about it.'

'Couldn't it have been the wind or something?' Moffatt asked nervously. He was exhausted by the day's trip, wasn't used to all that riding, and certainly not the drink. All he wanted to do was lie down and forget the last twenty-four hours had ever happened, forget he had ever found that poor wee laddie down and drowned in the water. He wanted to go to bed and dream of the warm days and nights he had spent in Australia, forgetting that all the time he'd been there he'd hated the place with its heat and flies, and that the only dreams he'd ever had when he'd been there had been, paradoxically, of here.

'It's got to be the bowls,' Tobar Strabane stated with such certainty that for just a moment Sholto had been ready to believe him. But only almost, for a second after Tobar had said it, Sholto knew it could not be so, for there was no one knew the bowls might've been here to find. Lachlan McLachlan had brought them out from Brora only that morning, the only man, as far as they knew, who'd been bothered enough to think them worthy of Solveig's further attention after they'd first been found. Not even Solveig had remembered their existence; she had been far too focussed on dead bodies to think on anything else. And even then, Lachlan had only brought three of them to Kinbrace, had left the rest back in Brora – completely unguarded and out in the open – for her to collect the next time she went down there.

'It can't be,' Sholto said then. 'No one knew about them. It's got to be something else, and the only other thing that has happened around here is that two people are dead.'

A silence fell in the chapel, or would have done, if Tobar hadn't at that moment been removing said bowls from the saddlebag he had insisted on bringing in himself, telling them that the bowls were too delicate to be handled by anyone who had no prior experience of such precious artefacts, distracting both Sholto and Moffatt by the scratching of straw and socks and the scrunched-up paper he had them wrapped in on their journey down to Kinbrace.

'Maybe one of those stable boys has been in,' Moffatt offered. 'Or some housemaid tidying up.'

Moffatt didn't know much about housemaids, but he knew that tidying up was what they did, and he'd already noticed there was some food missing from the tray that had been left them in the morning, and that the spare inch of wine he'd left in his cup had been drained. Every job has its perks, he'd thought, echoing Tam Japp's observations earlier that afternoon, then looked up to see that very man suddenly appearing in their doorway.

'Halloo!' came the cheery cry of Brogar Finn as he pushed past Tam Japp's nervous form, pulling that resistant participant on. 'Ho, Sholto!' Brogar exclaimed as he came down the ex-nave of the ex-chapel, apparently of the opinion that Sholto would be just like all his other ex-assistants, at least in one respect. 'You'll like this,' he added, in a sarcastically hushed reverential tone that made Sholto want to hit him. 'For look,' Brogar went on unabashed, 'I bring you books.'

164

Chapter 20   *Alas for the bright cup, and the splendour of his prince*

Sholto was alone in the chapel, and apart from the sounds of the gathered starlings squabbling on the outside roof tiles as they vied for space next to the warmth of the chimney stacks, all was quiet.

No wind.

No rain.

No people.

It was the first time since he'd left Trondheim that he'd been truly solitary, and he should have been glad for it, should have been content, but he was not. When everyone else – Tobar, Moffatt , Brogar and Japp – had drained away to Solveig's house on her invitation, he had chosen to remain a while, looking carefully about him, without the clutter of other men, and now he was absolutely certain that someone else had been in the chapel, and the fact of it chilled him, and that memory he had been seeking the night before suddenly jumped its way into his consciousness, and all at once he knew why he had found the discovery of the plugs of felt in Robbie's nostrils so disturbing.

It had been years ago, not long after he'd started working for Lundt and McCleery's, when he'd been curious about exactly what they did and the kind of people they employed. He'd been reading through the works of the various geologists who had even the vaguest connection with the Company, and had stumbled upon the fact that there seemed a remarkably high number of suicides in that profession, at least recently. There'd been George Richardson, who had slit his own throat open in 1848, and Gideon Mantell, who had deliberately overdosed on opiates in 1852. Then there was the Scotsman Hugh Miller, inspiration for a whole generation of following geologists, who had shot himself in the chest in 1856 on Christmas Eve in a

166

fit of mania and unwarranted paranoid delusion. This chance discovery had led him on a small trail of curiosity, and found a few others of their ilk who had previously shifted from eccentric to stark staring mad, Buckland and Hawkins being the most famous, but then there was the one who had stuffed his nose up with plugs of ethered felt and stood on the edge of a riverbank, waiting there until the ether did its business and he fell unconscious into the water and drowned. Sholto couldn't remember that last man's name, but knew he had worked at some point or other with Brogar Finn.

And having slotted that piece of information into place, another, more disturbing one came to mind, to do with the note and the little piece of bark he'd found by Robbie Weavers' body. He shook his head. The foundations of logical enquiry had always taught him that coincidence was an assumption to be mistrusted, and by God, he knew to distrust it now.

Solveig too was alone for the first time that day.

With the arrival of both Tam Japp and Tobar Strabane, she had invited them all into her house instead of the guest chapel, to sit around a proper dining table to eat, and had left the men talking and drinking while she excused herself to her kitchen to finish preparing their meal. Like Sholto, she too would normally have been gladdened by this brief interlude into solitude, that being the usual way she spent her life, and she should have taken joy in pootling about her kitchen, left to her own devices. But her mind wandered also, and though at the start it had gone in a completely different direction than Sholto's had done, it had ended up in the same place. At first she had worried about the bricks that had come out of the brick clamp, and whether they were good enough for building, if the brickworks could support the mines and vice versa.

And then she'd thought about the murders, and had visited the barn on her return, looking on the two bodies lying there, lighting a couple of candles well away from the straw for vigil, had noticed that Robbie Weavers' body had stiffened, the rigor drawing his limbs back into his body, pulling his lips away even further from his teeth, the lids from his eyes where she had closed them so gently the night before. She had brought in a sheet and covered the most of him, though not his face – could not bear to cover that – and despite him looking the more grotesque for it, had left it at that.

Willie Blaine had begun to smell again, and so she had sprinkled more quicklime over his blankets, set some camphor and sage burning in a small portable grate she had brought into the barn, but his decomposition still clung to her clothes, her hair, and she could smell it even now as she went about her tasks: grilling pheasants, skilleting grouse and woodcock, preparing a mash of neeps.

Just one more night, she thought, just one more night, and then tomorrow they would both be buried below the earth. Tam Japp had surprised her by volunteering to stay over and dig the graves in the morning, and the minister, by means of the telegraphy system, had agreed to come up from Helmsdale. She tried to remember if her father had ever buried anybody when he'd been his own self-appointed minister here, but if there had been such an occurrence she could not recall it. She would mention it, though, to Moffatt and Tobar, for it seemed fitting to her that she should abide by any burial rites the chapel might once have adhered to. It was not a great legacy her father had left her, but duty and respect towards others had not been the least of its parts.

Tam Japp felt queasy and ill at ease.

He was not used to company, not this kind of company at least. He was used to the shuffling lines of dirty, working men quibbling and complaining as he issued their licences, weighed their finds, scribbling it all down in the ledgers he had been at first unwilling to let go of that afternoon, electing to bring them himself here to Solveig's, bringing too an old suit left behind by one of the miners who had suddenly upped and departed, thinking it might be of use for dressing the dead Willie Blaine, because he knew enough of the man to know that the only suit he owned was the skin that was no longer wrapped about his bones.

He looked at the bright white of the tablecloth, and could not help but think of the sheet that had been placed over Robbie Weavers' body, Solveig having opened the barn door and practically pushed him inside when they had got here. Seeing them there had sickened him, particularly Robbie, who, just as Solveig had reminded him down at the Baile an Or, had really been so very young, and the sight of it had scratched at his heart. Willie Blaine, on the other hand, evoked no such pity, only memories of the many run-ins he'd had with the man, the most recent being only a couple of weeks back. He wondered now how nobody had noticed the man had been missing from the Suisgill for at least week, then realised he'd not even noticed it himself, despite it being his job to know just such things – who exactly was where in the valleys and doing what, and for how long. But there'd been so many men to keep tabs on, all toiling away from dawn until dusk, with hands as raw and red as new-mown clover from the chap of grit and gravel, and their constant immersion in the freezing waters of the burns. And for what? For the slimmest of hopes of striking it just over even, if not actually rich, men who came at the start of each month full of enthusiasm and special ways of working the dirt or the water, only to drift away at the end of it, dispirited, with not enough earned to pay another licence, men who'd trudged off down the road to wherever they had come from, not a trace of them left here apart from the scribble of their names inside his book. But not Willie, Tam reminded himself, he'd not been one of those quitters. He'd been here from the very first, longer than Tam Japp himself, ever since the man Gilchrist had started up all this gold rush business in the first place.

Tam Japp had shaken his head at the two rolls of grey blankets, unable to equate them to the Willie Blaine he had known – an unlikeable man who went out of his way to make all his life a quarrel, and yet who had worked so much harder, so much longer, than so many of the others, and to no great reward. And standing there looking at those blankets, Tam Japp had unexpectedly found a regret for Willie Blaine, and for that commitment, that endurance, and that it had brought him to end in such a way.

There but for the grace of God, he had murmured, realising that the line dividing his own life from Willie Blaine's had not been so wide they could not at some point have crossed over, swapped places, their individual lives swerved apart only by a bit of good luck or a run of bad, and he thought on that revelation now, sitting at this table, fingers clasped about the glass of wine he had yet to drink from. He looked towards the door through which Solveig had just disappeared, and wondered why it was that this woman should have taken such a care about two people she had never known, never even met, caring enough to shelter their two bodies inside her barn. He felt ashamed, and for one fleeting moment imagined himself lying in that barn in place of Willie Blaine, and only Solveig's care of his body, his blanket, standing between himself and oblivion.

Pahaa ennustava, a Finnish phrase meaning neither dread exactly, nor foreboding, more like a prefiguration of something that hasn't yet happened, an echo of a future event that has somehow escaped into the past to forewarn

170

of its approach. It was a phrase Sholto was familiar with, and he felt it now, shivered with it, turned his collar up against it, decided it was time for food and drink, and company. He walked the length of the chapel and out of the door, came into the yard and as he did so he looked up towards the trees that marked out the edge of the flat land, the beginning of the brae that led up to the moor, and for a second he thought he saw something glinting there through their emptying crowns, and then a shadow moving quickly on the brow of the hill beyond. He stood quite still and watched intently, but he saw nothing else. Whatever it was had gone, but he had that strange feeling again, that echo, that unshakable conviction that something was heading towards him, and that it was something bad.

Chapter 21   *Alas for the mailed warriors who have been put to the sword*

Andrew McTavish was pleased with his day, pleased with his entire week. He'd had a visit that very afternoon from the McCleery woman, who had settled up all she'd owed him this last month, which had been a considerable amount, having ordered up far more than usual on account of the visitors she had coming, a couple of men from the Lundt and McCleery Mining Company, she'd said, who'd need food and drink for the month or two they'd be staying with her up at the steading. He knew she was being kind, supporting his business, that she was often enough down in Brora to bring back everything from there that she needed. He appreciated her kindness, and that she always paid promptly, including that afternoon, when, on top of everything else, she had placed a stonking new order that had cleared several shelves of stock he'd not been able to shift for months, buying huge amounts of flour and sugar, oats both flaked and pin-milled, three tubs of molasses he'd had with him since March, and as much dried fruit and cured meat as he could muster. He knew why, of course he did, even before she'd explained that she was personally putting on the wakes of Willie Blaine and Robbie Weavers, and was pleased she was doing things the traditional way, inviting everyone who knew the two deceased both from Helmsdale and Brora, as well as everyone in the valley, at least those who still remained.

She was, he told himself, doing exactly what he had done the week before when he had given that stranger a helping hand, though Solveig was obviously doing it on a far larger scale than he had done, making possible an event that would never have happened without her intervention, and which had the added advantage of shoving all that new business his way.

Kindness, he thought, *always comes back to those who dole it out,* and in some obscure way he believed that he was reaping the biblically promised

172

rewards of his own small act of giving, and though it had been a good day business-wise, he wasn't so uncaring as to ignore the fact that people had had to die to make it happen. He'd not known Willie Blaine over well, but he'd known Robbie Weavers right enough, had even employed him briefly at the start of the so-called gold rush. He'd been a rascal back then, had young Rab, and Andrew had caught him pinching from the store not once but several times, only bits and pieces, but each time he'd been confronted Robbie had straightway confessed, held up his hands, offering to work the next few days for free, or sweep the floor or clean out the grain tubs or the privy, or do anything else he could to pay the price. And Andrew had known it then, that young Rab had not been a bad lad at all, only one who, like himself, had been brought up with nothing, and when faced with golden opportunities could not turn away, just grabbed at them with both hands and ran with them.

He'd been more upset by the lad's death than he cared to admit to anyone, even to his old mate Moffatt Murchison, who had called on him early doors to give him the news, asked if he was going to the funeral, made him promise he would close the stores at three o'clock and come up to Solveig's steading to pay his respects. Robbie had been trouble, but he'd been trouble in a good kind of way, the kind that tells you life is there for living, makes you smile, reminds you that you were young once too, and did the same kind of things that Robbie had done. And at the end of it all he'd been but a boy, and one who had been far too young to die.

Andrew glanced at his little Johnson's safe at the back of his store and thought of the small bag of cash that was in there, the one Solveig had given him earlier that day. Tomorrow, he thought, he would take a few coins from the stash, maybe more than a few, take them to the minister, get him to say a few prayers for Robbie's soul. It might be an act a wee bittie Catholic for the minister, but he'd persuade him, because, God knew, it had always been a hard road they'd trodden here in Kildonan, and the minister knew that as well as Andrew did, and could surely not refuse. Andrew sighed, turned his attention to the bottle Solveig's companion had placed upon his counter when he'd come in to pick up the last part of the packages Solveig hadn't been able to manage. He blessed her for it, picked it up, squinted at the label, though was none the wiser for it. It looked expensive, not that he was any judge, but he thought it as good a time as any to pop the cork, make a toast, say a prayer for young Robbie Weavers, and so he took it over to his seat by the peat-burning stove and unhooked his mug from the tiny dresser, pulled the top out with his few remaining teeth, and poured out a hefty slug.

'To you, lad,' he said, raising the filled mug first to the air and then his lips. 'And to all you might have been.'

The dining room was full for the first time since her husband had died. Back then it had seemed claustrophobic, stuffy and artificial, like a museum whose finest exhibit has been stolen away, its curator calling up twenty or thirty inferior pieces from the vaults to try to fill its place. Tonight was different. She'd five men happy to sit in company around her dining table, and though she'd no maid to help her, she was glad of it, pleased to trundle her tray from kitchen to table and back again, pleased to listen to Tobar Strabane, the supposed Scalabsdale Hermit, who didn't seem able to stop talking, although admittedly all he was talking of was the Brora bowls. Quite why he found them so fascinating she didn't know, but both the Company men, Brogar Finn and Sholto McKay, appeared rapt by his monologue, and it was only now, standing as she was in the doorway at a slight distance, the first distance she had really had from them both, that she noticed how different each was to the other. Brogar Finn was dark and sturdy, strong necked, wide shouldered, looking a little dangerous with that oddly unsymmetrical face,

174

the scar that ran from hairline to cheek and chin, and from chin to chest, and the blunt-ended fingers, clutched about a wine glass, that were missing several tips and nails. A man's man, she judged, if ever there was one, and the kind of man that was not for Solveig McCleery.

Sholto, on the other hand, piqued her interest. He seemed taller than he was, but in fact was not too many inches above her own height, which had never been anything to boast about, and he had that rather alarming streak of pale hair that ran through the rest, making him look from certain angles like an angry badger. Yet below that strange hair was another face altogether, one that was bookish and thin, and looked in sore need of a bit of sun. A face, she realised, not unlike that of her Elof John. Sholto, the focus of her gaze at that moment, had been speaking to Moffatt Murchison who was sitting to his left, and she caught his face in profile, saw him rest his chin upon his thumb, elbow on the table, index finger straight up and on his cheek, middle finger stroking the top of his lip, and it was a gesture that was so familiar, so Elof John, that for a moment she couldn't bear to see it in anyone else, and had to turn away, went quickly from the door back to her kitchen, afraid that she would cry again, just as she had done earlier in Tam Japp's office, and been so ashamed, then as now. As it happened, Tam Japp had looked up at Solveig at that very moment, and was witness to the brief burst of grief she had unwittingly displayed, saw an anguish on her face that turned his insides into worms.

Andrew McTavish had drunk his first slug of wine, and his second, and his third. The wine was rich and red, sumptuous and deep, and he decided it was too good to quaff too quickly, needed special care, special drinking orders, so he'd stood up to open the door to the wood-burning stove with his tongs, had lobbed in several cakes of dried peat and the few logs he'd been saving for a special occasion.

He chuckled to see the logs catch to flame so readily, felt a little dizzy, thought he must be a little tipsy then realised that no, he wasn't feeling tipsy at all, but felt rip-roaring drunk in the worst possible way. His head was spinning, and there was a tingling in his gut, in the tips of his fingers and his toes, that he did not like at all. He tried to brace himself, put his hand out first to his chair and then the counter, but found himself unable to gauge the distance needed, and fell crashing to the floor. His head hit the packed earth with a thud that briefly stunned him, but when he came to, he felt even worse than he had before, felt truly awful in fact, spit gurgling at the back of his throat as if he had swallowed a wasp, and a really sharp, hard pain in his lungs. His eyes were open, and from where he lay he could see the bottom edge of the counter, the circles left by the feet of the stool on which he spent his days, the small tracks in the dust made by the mice he had been waging a war against ever since he had come here. If only he could get over to the counter, he thought, haul himself upright using the stool as leverage, get the counter bell ringing, then maybe someone would come to his aid, maybe some passing panner heading up or down the way, maybe Moffatt come back to convince him he should close up sooner, maybe close for the whole of tomorrow for the funerals, give them more time to have a drink and a blether. But there was no one, and though Andrew tried to move his mouth, tried to shout, he couldn't get any words out, only dribble, and though he tried to move, his body disobeyed him, fingers and toes burning like he was being baked alive, and a hot heaviness in his chest like his heart was burning like a cake of peat. And then he understood that something really, really bad was happening to him, and that it no longer mattered if there was anyone out there beyond his storefront or no, nor whether he had the means to raise

176

them, because there could be no help, and that any help that did come would be far too late. And he wished more than anything that he could see one of those mice he had so determinedly tried to exterminate from his store, or a fly, a flour mite, anything at all that was still alive.

Oh God, he thought, *oh God oh God oh God,* and he might have gone on like that forever had not a great uprushing come from somewhere deep inside him, so loud that it drowned out everything else, as if a hundred thousand hornets had chosen that moment for their flight, shrinking his life's horizon to one single line of vision, from which came a great black boil of clouds that was rising, rising, hovering for just one moment as if to gauge its own weight and momentum, before it finally broke free, came swarming across the empty space dividing him from it, pushing the air from his lungs as it rampaged on, enveloping him with a heat so intense that his skin contracted, just as if the door to his stove had expanded and swallowed him whole. There was a smell too, so strong, so bad he would have died just to escape it. And die Andrew did, thirty-one seconds later, the longest and most agonising half minute of Andrew McTavish's sixty-two years, three months, ten weeks, and two days of life.

Chapter 22   *He ponders deeply on the darkness of his life*

'Will you be staying for the funerals, Mr Strabane?' Solveig was asking, the food having been cleared away, several bottles of wine and another of whisky taking its place, Solveig now sitting at the table with the men.

'Funerals?' Tobar asked somewhat sharply. 'What funerals?'

Solveig's brows creased involuntarily.

'Didn't Moffatt mention it to you?' she said, surprised, astonished in fact, that the first thing Moffatt and Sholto had gossiped about up at Scalabsdale hadn't been the two recent deaths, hadn't bargained for the intensity of Tobar's interest in the Brora bowls that had swept all other topics of conversation right off the slate.

Both Moffatt and Sholto were looking uncomfortable, exchanging glances, hardly daring to look at Solveig. Their afternoon away in the hills had been a relief for them both, a time to breathe deep and easy, forget all about bodies and the corpses of young boys. Tobar himself looked only puzzled.

'Someone's died?' he asked. 'Who's died?'

'Not just died,' Brogar Finn put in, a little too merrily. 'But murdered. A man and a boy, and not so far from here.'

Tobar's head swivelled towards Brogar, who raised his glass and took a swig. Of all of them Brogar had been the least troubled by the passing away of Willie Blaine and Robbie Weavers. He lived a life where death came and went like a frequent house guest, for mining of any kind was hazardous, the people going at such ventures taking risks no sane person of adequate employment would contemplate. And Brogar shared that mentality, and though he valued his life, and those of others, he was of the philosophical bent that life and death came and went in seasons, and where one ended,

178

another began. No one was irreplaceable, and it didn't bother him a whit that his life, like everyone else's – whether they knew it or not – was spent dancing on a precipice, for that element of unpredictability and danger was, he believed, the very essence of being alive at all.

Tobar, by contrast, reacted to the news as anyone but Brogar Finn might have done, and looked perplexed, worried, shifting his gaze to Solveig.

'But how? How were these people killed? And why?'

Solveig did not reply, for she had no answers, at least none that were complete.

It was instead Sholto who spoke. 'The first of them was Willie Blaine,' he said, 'killed by a severe blow to the head at least a week ago.'

Solveig looked shocked, for how could Sholto know this?

'I know this,' Sholto went on, as if she'd spoken out loud, 'because a little earlier this evening I took the chance to examine the bodies.'

He'd attended many autopsies and dissections, such events being a staple outing for the Linnaean Society of Trondheim whenever they got the chance, a kind of theatre that Sholto, along with the rest of them, had always found fascinating, examining the executed bodies of criminals, or intestates – those who had no embargo on what happened to their bodies after they'd died.

And so after he'd left the chapel that afternoon, after he'd seen that twitch upon the hill, he'd changed his mind about joining the rest immediately, and had instead taken the opportunity to go into the barn, take a proper look at the two dead bodies, give them a good once over. It had not been an easy task. Willie Blaine's body had been the most unpleasant thing Sholto had ever come across, and nothing like the cleaned-up cadavers of the anatomy theatres, which seemed children's toys in comparison. But Sholto had steeled himself, removed as much of the blanket as he could from the dead man's body, trying not to burn his fingers on the quicklime Solveig had sprinkled over it so liberally to halt the smell. But his investigations had been instructive, and Willie's most obvious, and obviously fatal, injury, had been a section of crushed skull almost three and a half inches in diameter, its radiating fractures still having faint traces of blood and membrane adhering to them, which meant that Willie had been alive when the injury had been done to him.

'An injury,' Sholto now told his attentive audience, 'caused either by a large, heavy stick or, more probably, a stone. 'And unlike Robbie,' Sholto went on, 'Willie Blaine wasn't meant to be in the water at all. He was supposed to have been found in his sack upon what we could call a rood ground, a place where the bodies of executed criminals used to be – and still are, in some regions of Europe – put out on public display after execution, left to rot openly, as a salutary lesson to the rest of the population.'

The sparse light in the room jumped as Tam Japp knocked his elbow against a lamp, his face as grey as the inside of an oyster shell. Solveig, who was sat beside him, placed one hand upon his arm to keep him still, and nodded to Sholto to go on. She'd no notion at all of what that hand meant to Tam Japp, nor that it had been the closest he'd ever come to a meaningful relationship with a woman in all his life, and that Tam Japp's heart was turning somersaults because of it.

'And Robbie,' Sholto said, 'well, he was subdued, placed into the river, fixed to the bank by means of having his foot tangled into an outgrowing root, and held down until he drowned. There is bruising on the back of his neck, and, well, other signs I won't go into at present.' He glanced about him, as if expecting questions, but as nobody spoke, he proceeded to a conclusion that sounded rather more melodramatic than he'd meant it to be. 'And these deaths,' he said, 'these two bodies, two people most likely murdered at

180

random, were deliberately put on display, to give us, or, more precisely, to give Solveig, a message.'

He stopped talking. His mouth had gone dry. He took a sip from his glass.

'What message?' Solveig asked, her voice thin, like a reed stripped right down to its pith. 'And how can you think it's meant for me?'

Sholto breathed deeply, felt the echo of the *pahaa ennustava* rippling out to everyone who sat about the table, including Solveig, and he thought of the Sukkiim, the Gaelic proverbs, the little piece of bark...

'It's you, Solveig,' Sholto said. 'I'm sorry, but I'm certain it all has to do with you.'

He'd been seen again, or might have been, couldn't be sure one way or the other, but couldn't take the chance. The thin string of a man with the stripy hair he'd seen earlier that day coming out of the barn had looked directly at him, and though he was well hidden, and couldn't possibly have been seen directly, he thought maybe the eyeglass he'd bought in Trondheim had given him away, the lens maybe caught by the light of the dying sun, betraying him with its brief beacon. Whatever the reason, he needed to be gone, and it didn't take him more than a minute to collapse his shelter, stamp it down, roll up his pack, and move on.

This time he went right down beyond the brow of the brae, creeping along the edge of the water meadow. The stands of rosebay, bracken and water mint were still tall and tangled, camouflaging him well, tufts of rosebay seeds catching at his sleeves and shoulders, the heads of bulrushes breaking away into lamb-tails, dappling him with their pollen as he passed them by. He went out onto the spit of shingle that licked into the water where the river had been forced into a tortuous bend by the sandstone escarpment on the opposite bank, and he stood there a moment, then waded in, heading for a small cave-like opening overhung with ivy and dying brambles. And inside he crawled, on hands and knees, pulling the ivy tendrils back across the opening behind him. He got himself settled on stomach and elbows, then made a little window through the leaves, for from here he had a clear view across the river, across the water meadows, to Solveig's house.

'But how on earth have you come to such a wild conclusion?' Tobar was saying, speaking for the rest. 'And what possible proof do you have that Solveig is at the centre of anything?

Sholto had been expecting this, and was surprised when Brogar Finn took up the cudgels on his behalf, even gave Sholto's shoulder a hard pat.

'I think Sholto has explained himself admirably. Dead bodies don't usually pile up in a specific place without prior motive of intent.' Everyone looked at Brogar, bemused by the precision of his language, unaware that he'd had cause many times to sit in courts for one reason or another. And Brogar smiled broadly. 'What?' he said, spreading out his scarred and calloused hands upon the white expanse of the tablecloth. 'Am I not allowed an opinion?'

Solveig found her eyes drawn to Brogar's blunted fingertips, the ones without any nails, the leathery wrinkles gathered about the knuckles of his hands, and found herself wondering what those hands had done, and to whom, and shuddered slightly. Brogar was oblivious of Solveig's scrutiny, and was shaking his head.

'Mining is a desperate game,' he went on. 'Anything goes when the stakes are high enough, and I know those games well. I've played them practically since I could walk and talk, and though I've been to a hundred places since, I know this valley as well as the rest of you.' He looked around him, at Tam Japp's raised eyebrows, the questions forming on Solveig's lips, the downright look of disbelief on both Tobar and Moffatt's faces. 'Check the parish registry,' Brogar ended with a flourish worthy of an actor twenty-five years on the stage, 'and you'll find my name there, because this, my friends, is where I was born and raised.'

Five seconds passed, almost ten, before anyone spoke.

'But by Christ, I knew your name was familiar,' Tobar began, looking squarely at Brogar, the glimmer of latent knowledge in his eyes. The table between the witnesses to Brogar's revelation seemed to have shrunk, drawing them closer together as they felt the pull of distant lives, departed families, the scraping of old memories trying to break for air.

'And I remember, too,' said Moffatt slowly. 'It was Clach Mhic Mhios, wasn't it? Alongside Glen Loth?'

Tobar nodded, took off where Moffatt had led on. 'The Stone of the Bad Month,' he said slowly, drawing out his words as the old histories began to surface, the old stories, the old names. 'We used to call you the Winter Family on account of it...the standing stone that wasn't set for summer solstice but the winter one, and your father...' Tobar's face screwed up in concentration, trying to winkle out all those childhood stories. 'Your father...' he faltered. 'The Finnish Winter...that was the name they called him by ...'

Brogar was quiet, almost rapt. He'd thought he'd had the element of surprise, but this information was new to him, and he was as startled as all the rest when Tobar thumped his hand down on the table, kicked back his chair, and suddenly stood up.

'The 1813 stand-off against the Sutherlands!' Tobar shouted. 'Your father was right there! They called him Finn MacCool afterwards... By God, Brogar...' Tobar sat down as suddenly as he'd stood, almost missed his chair, had to grab at the table to stop himself from falling. 'By God, Brogar,'

183

he said again, before subsiding. 'He was a hero to the folk in this valley, the first to stand up against the clearing of the land.'

Brogar said nothing. He couldn't understand why his father had never mentioned such an exciting episode in his past, but it did explain a lot – both why his father had clung on for as long as he could, right up until the last months of 1826, and why he had eventually left. He must have been a marked man, and he wondered how truthful his father had been when he'd told the young Brogar they'd been cleared not by the sword, but by the sheep.

Chapter 23   *On men buried, dreich-faced, into the earth*

The next morning dawned blue and clear, with a frost that made Solveig's heart soar a little, covering as it did every blade of grass, every fallen leaf, every clump of reed, making every stone and tile of her father's bleak chapel seem to shine and sing. She'd woken far later than she'd intended, to find the minister from Helmsdale almost at her door, his dray clattering noisily down the lane and over the bridge, complete with the two wooden coffins she had ordered, and the two girls she would need to help her with all the cooking for the day, and no time at all to think on what she had learned of Brogar and the Bad Stone the night before, or how much it seemed their two fathers had in common.

She dressed quickly, and was just in time to greet the minister, who helped her bring the bodies out of the barn and into their wood, Robbie arranged as peaceful as she could make him, washed and dressed in the ill-fitting, too-large suit Tam Japp had mysteriously conjured up from nowhere the night before, intended, he'd said, for Willie Blaine, until he'd learned there was nothing of Willie Blaine left to hang a suit on, and so it had gone to Robbie instead. She'd asked that the lid of his box be sawn into two hinged parts, so that the top flap could be kept open to show Robbie's face, and though there was no way you could mistake that face for being asleep, let alone alive, he did at least look reasonably peaceful and clean. None of this, though, for Willie Blaine, who was nailed up tight in his corpse-box, shut into his own stink, leaving his life much as he had led it – alone and private, and not for other people's eyes – which was perhaps, Solveig thought, just the way he would have wanted it.

185

Half an hour short of eleven, and there were crowds gathering in her fields. A day of amnesty from work was not to be shirked, and all the miners had come in from both the Suisgill and the Baile an Or, the Suisgill men bringing with them some reminders of Robbie that they placed carefully beside him in his open coffin – a couple of sheets of paper onto which they had arduously written out the words of some of the songs he'd used to sing: The Border Widow's Lament, Jock o' Hazel Green, Young Waters – the untimely death of whom seemed particularly apt – a few pinches of snuff, his cooking pot, his panning sieve, a few sprinkles of precious gold dust Dougall Meek had sacrificed from his own stash, a small whistle whittled out of a piece of willow that had been the one possession they all knew Robbie had been most proud of because he had made himself, no matter that it had never really been in tune.

And so the whole show started, and it had been grim enough at first, everyone crowded around the coffins in the courtyard whilst the minister did his piece, Solveig adding her own recitation, thanking everyone for coming, saying a few words about the tragedy of death brought on too soon, adding that they had died whilst taking part in something far greater than them all – the rejuvenation of Kildonan and Brora, and of Helmsdale by proxy – and that such good work must still go on. Even Tam Japp, as the representative of the Sutherlands, had managed to stutter out the few words that were required of him, and oddly enough it was his words that the men and women gathered at Solveig's steading that morning remembered most.

'William Blaine,' he had said, 'and Robert Weavers. They're names that have been in my ledgers almost since day one, and though they neither of them ever struck it rich, they neither of them gave up either, just stuck it through and through, and I know they would have gone on sticking it, if they'd not been stopped.'

186

Afterwards, both coffins were laid side by side into the ground behind the barn, the filled-in mounds marked by wooden crosses Solveig had promised would later be replaced by proper stones.

Once these formalities were over, the day began to devolve just as it was supposed to do on such occasions, because it was a holiday after all, no matter the circumstances. The farm had provided a couple of sheep for the spit, and Solveig kept up her end too, food flying out of her kitchen as soon as it was baked: oat cakes, griddled scones, soda bread, cheese-and-potato pies, potted brawns and venison, various possets and cranachs flavoured by every dried and bottled fruit Solveig could find in her pantry or had bought at Andrew's stores the day before. There were other offerings too, brought in by the mourners themselves, although these were pitifully poor beside Solveig's bounty, and the sheep roasting on the spits were the biggest draw, very few of those present having tasted it for years; all lined up with knifes and trenchers at the ready, carving off thick chunks as soon as the flesh was sufficiently baked, crackled and cooked.

Halfway through the afternoon, Solveig was overworked, hot and tired, didn't want to be a part of any it, of any crowd. It was too much a reminder of when Elof John had died, and all she'd wanted then, as now, was to be left alone. She recalled the first letter she had penned to him, the one written in such anger after her discovery of the file her father had kept on the Helmsdale Pick. And she remembered clearly the first letter Elof John had written back to her, knew every word by heart, could hear him speaking those words now as clearly as if he had been standing at her shoulder:

'You are a battleship amongst coracles,' he had written, a comparison she had not thought particularly flattering at the time, until he had gone on. 'A rudder amongst oars, a polestar amongst unfriendly constellations.'

187

He'd been a bit inclined to the florid, had Elof John, but by God, how she had loved him for it, especially in those early days when all they'd had between them was words, several weeks between each letter, and every one a new revelation during which she'd discovered that far from being her father's enemy, Elof John had in fact been his only ally, her father's inside man, and it had been him who had been the battleship in the end and not her, electing marriage over disinheritance, Solveig and Scotland over Sweden and family.

In the courtyard and fields about Solveig's steading, the crowds were loosening, beer flowing freely from the farm-donated kegs, and fiddles were soon broken out and playing, the mining men going at the songs Robbie had used to sing. It was all too much for Solveig. She needed to get away. She took herself to the chapel, stood a moment or two beneath its stone lintel, below the name of the Sukkiim. But she could hear voices, and anger, inside, and she pushed the chapel door open to see Sholto and Tobar facing each other at the altar table like fighters, Sholto's pale face anguished in the meagre light, Tobar squaring up to him as if they were about to come to blows.

She was about to enter, to ask what on earth was going on, when she felt a sudden weight at her back, the smell of damp earth, of rain on leaves, and Brogar Finn materialised, pushed right past her, went down the nave like a log down a stream in spate.

'Explain yourselves.'

His voice was like a rock, and not the kind you could kick casually to one side with your boot, but one which went right back into the centre of the earth. All movement ceased, and Solveig, who was rooted to the spot, saw the action unfolding before her. Sholto was at the altar table's left, looking flushed, like an anxious priest, with Tobar immediately to his right, halted in the action of stabbing his finger at Sholto, only inches from his chest.

188

'Tell me,' Brogar said, and he had no need to place himself between the two antagonists; his very presence forced Tobar to drop back. This power of absolute command was a side to Brogar they'd none of them seen before, and not one any of them felt inclined to challenge, Tobar included.

It was only a few minutes in the telling. Sholto had been trying to explain to Tobar his theories, and Tobar, angered to the point of abuse by the perceived laxity of Sholto's arguments, had fought back, the gist of those arguments being this: that the messages on stones, paper and bark had been directed primarily at Solveig, a notion Sholto had inferred from the mention of the Sukkiim on the rocks, and the fact that the Gaelic proverbs had both been ones favoured by her father, and secondly that Solveig's name had been substituted for that of Ingvald on the bark inscription. He didn't explain himself, for it seemed perfectly clear in his head, and instead just went on, his words tripping over themselves as they tried to get out.

'And then there's the way Robbie died,' Sholto said, 'with those plugs of felt up his nose. That part was aimed at you, Brogar, because it's exactly like the suicide of that geologist…'

Tobar sighed but did not move, stopped from what he might have done by Brogar turning his head slightly towards him, though his eyes remained fixed on Sholto.

'Anything else?' Brogar asked, and Solveig looked at Sholto's face, thought it looked like it belonged to someone who should not be in the real world at all, but perhaps in some monastery, some sheltered place, a quiet arbour from which anger was entirely banished. Not so Brogar, who appeared at that moment to be the entire world, or at least the rule of it.

For a few moments the chapel was completely silent, but for the slight flim and flicker of the candles, and the soft, plaintive sounds of singing coming

189

from outside, and then Brogar Finn sounded out his voice, as both Tobar and Sholto retreated.

'What the hell is going on between you?'

But before he got an answer, and before Sholto could go on and explain himself more clearly, the door to the chapel scraped open again, and Moffatt stood there within its frame, his face the colour of new-shorn wool.

'There's been another one,' he whispered, and had they not been all as quiet as they were at that moment, they would never have heard him. 'Oh God,' Moffatt had whispered. 'There's been another one.'

Chapter 24   *And how cruel are the wounds of his heart*

'Who else knows?' Brogar asked Moffatt as he took charge, leading them all away from Solveig's house, even Tobar shocked into submission. But Moffatt was too agitated to answer straightaway, was having a hard time keeping his emotions boxed up inside his head. He'd seen men dying, sometimes right beside him, men gasping like landed fish in the holds of disease-ridden, water-sparse boats, or crushed beneath beams, impaled by pickaxes, but what he had never done before was leave a wake to go down the road to find out why his friend hadn't turned up as planned, only to find that friend flat on the floor of his shop, a dirty brown foam about his mouth, limbs at odd angles, like only the dead can do.

'It just wasn't like him,' Moffatt finally said, one hand scratching his fingers across his brow so hard they left red marks there. 'He always kept his word – you know that, Solveig. And he'd promised he'd close up shop by three, meet me at the wake.' His voice was edging towards the hysterical, and Tobar moved up beside him, put a hand on his arm, but Moffatt shook himself free.

'The front was locked, but I used the key, the one he always left round back in that empty jar…'

And then he stopped, sat down on a wayside boulder as they came into view of Andrew's stores, and wouldn't budge.

'I can't go in there,' he said softly. 'I just can't. Not again…'

Moffatt had begun to cry, a horrid sound, like a rasp over bad wood, making of him that boy again, standing on the wharf at Helmsdale harbour, watching the rest of his family sail away to a place he would never know, and could never find. The others were embarrassed, moved away, focussed instead on the stores twenty yards down the track and set off in that direction. Only

Solveig remained; she went down on her knees beside Moffatt in the mud, put a hand upon the crook of his right arm where it was lifted against his face, felt it shaking like a leaf that has just detached itself from its stalk and is about to let fly.

'Oh please don't, Moffatt,' Solveig said, pushing her knees against the sharp stones to lever herself up, put an arm about his shoulders. 'Please don't,' she said again, but whatever cork he'd been using, to keep all those years stopped up inside himself for the most years of his life, had been worn too thin by these last few disasters, and every disappointment, every bad thing he had ever seen, could no longer be contained, and the sounds that came out of him were so awful, that Solveig sat down beside him in the dirt, and laid first her hand, and then her head, upon his knees, and felt the wave of desperation that had overtaken him overtake her too. She could see Brogar Finn turning back to look towards her, and after his display in the chapel had the wild hope that if anyone knew what to do in such situations it would be him.

Brogar's look back had been brief, and seeing Solveig beside the broken Moffatt he had felt a fleeting disappointment that he should have buckled with such ease. But he turned back to the task in hand, and though it would be too crude a judgement to say he was pleased by this latest instalment of the drama, there was an undeniable jaunt to his step as he set himself towards it, overtaking Sholto and Moffatt and going in. He found Andrew McTavish just as Moffatt had said, lying behind his counter beside his chair and stove. He'd been dead a while, so much was evident from the colour of his skin, which was an unappealing shade of grey, like badly cured soap. Then in came Sholto, found Brogar sniffing at an overturned bottle.

'No Tobar?' Brogar asked mildly, and Sholto shook his head.

'Said he'd had enough of dead bodies for one day, and has gone off home.'

Brogar nodded. 'Small mercies,' he commented, before taking hold of the pewter mug that sat on top of the stove and sniffed that too, before holding it out to Sholto. 'There's something in there,' he said, as Sholto took it from him but did not look at it, his eyes fixed instead on Andrew McTavish's body, which was vastly more unpleasant at close quarters than it had seemed at the door, the foamy spittle a horrid brown that spoke of blood, and tinged with the green of interior decay. There was too a strong smell of faeces and dried urea, and Sholto had to put his hand across his mouth and nose.

'The mug?' Brogar prompted, a note of challenge there, or perhaps amusement, both of which made Sholto want to spit, but it had the required effect and bucked him into action. He switched his gaze to the mug, lifted it up slightly, could see there was a fine residue about its base, probably precipitated from the liquid it had held as it evaporated from the heat of the stove. He forced himself to look again at Andrew, at the pool of congealed sick in which part of his face was lying, the twisted threads in it that must be blood.

'The wine?' he asked, catching sight of the bottle lying tipped over by McTavish's side, its puddled contents looking thin and innocuous beside the thickened, blood-coagulated stew that had been ejected from Andrew's stomach. For a few moments Sholto couldn't take his eyes off it. He saw chunks of food, hurriedly chewed, judging by their size – potato pasty maybe, some neeps – noted that they seemed to form a separate expurgation, a semi-circular dam into which the thinner, bloodier liquid had been spilled and held, and he began to form a kind of timeline in his head of this man sitting down to eat his dinner, rushing through it so he could get started on the wine that must have been his real pleasure of the night.

The night, he thought suddenly, and knew it must be so, knew it from the going out of the stove, the rigor of the man's body, the spilled contents of his

193

stomach. All night long this man had been here, all last night and all today, locked up, alone and dead within his shop.

Why hadn't anyone noticed? But as soon as he'd thought it, he knew the answer: the funerals. It had been the day of the funerals, and who would have thought it odd in the slightest that the stores had been closed up because of them? He was aware of a slight choking sound at his back, and realised it must be Solveig.

'Don't come in,' Brogar said sharply, though Solveig, being Solveig, did not obey.

'Well,' said Brogar, once she was in. 'Another one indeed.'

'Murdered?' Solveig asked, though was in no doubt of it.

'Murdered,' Brogar agreed. 'And what's more,' he added, picking up the discarded wine bottle from the floor and holding it out at arm's length, studying the label. 'It seems that I, Brogar Finn, am the murderer.'

Chapter 25   *And how he longs for the good times passed*

Another night, another death.

Same barn, same bales, different body.

Rain was falling.

He could hear its gentle chatter on the leaves and banks about him, could smell it on the dying leaves of the bracken, could see it pittering patterns on the river's surface where the water swirled so slow and stately just a few feet below. The black slates of the chapel roof were dark in the distance, iridescent as the massed and chittering swoop of starlings that had swung through the valley earlier that evening before moving on to some other place, some other tree top, to wait out the night.

Again he had the weirdest feeling that he had stepped from one world into another. The funerals that afternoon had been strange to him, like he was an Audience of One at Easter Week, watching some modern mystery play unfold that hadn't stuck to the normal rules.

But it had made up his mind.

This would be the night.

No more shillying, no more shallying, no more lying belly down in the dirt.

There was going to be a time when Solveig's men, whatever their peripheral roles in her life, would either be gone, sleeping, or drunk, and that would be his moment. He'd already rolled up his blanket and sleeping gear in anticipation, had repacked his bag, retrieved *The Succour of the Sukkiim* Joseph had left to him, and had read it through again for the hundredth time, the thousandth time, though knew practically every word by heart, and could have recited any part of it without ever moving a finger or an eye down its

195

page. He stowed it in his pocket in its little leather pouch, could feel it sitting there alongside Joseph's icon. He'd taken the time to sharpen his knife, replacing it with care within the sheath at his belt, for it had an edge to it that could have cut right through the leather. And then he was ready to leave his camp, and it wouldn't be long now before he would make his final move. The last card of Joseph Lundt's life was about to be played, and he was the one who was holding it.

And then everything changed, and by God Jesus, how he swore and mouthed his curses, because this was not at all what he had planned, nor what he had expected. For instead of solitude with Solveig, it was just another night, and another death.

Same barn, same bales, different body.

They'd made no fuss, had made no grand entrance, had slipped like an eel along the lane to the barn with their covered burden, had got there without being spotted by any of the mourners, still occupied as they were with drink and song and talking in the fields about the barn, until the rain began to fall.

Only a few sporadic splotches at first, the odd drop here and there, then another falling on men's jackets and uncovered heads, making them gaze upwards into the sky, as if by looking they could halt its fall. But they could not, and the deluge came on them several minutes later with the nonchalance of a bit-player who has been twiddling his fingers in the wings for far too long, and now that his moment has come is not about to let anything or anyone mar his grand entrance. It came down in torrents, quick and heavy, splashing up from every surface, and within minutes the grounds about the chapel and Solveig's house were sodden with its falling, puddles replacing the men who swiftly deserted, leaving behind them scant reminders of their presence: Solveig's empty platters, the scatter of glasses and mugs, the remnants of the roasted sheep that had been sliced right down to the bone.

He watched it all, warm and dry, from his hidey-hole, knew well enough the weather and its vagaries no matter where he was, and knew that such a heavy downpouring could not last. Back home there would have been thunder and lightning too, but not here, in this pale land, where all the rain did was make everything wet – wet hills, wet grass, wet buildings. Wet people too, and he recognised that once again he had been stymied, and that yet again the Lundt woman would not be alone, because after they'd put the new body into the barn the men carrying it had not gone on to the chapel, late as it was, but instead had dripped and shivered instead into the woman's house.

'For God's sake!' Brogar exclaimed, as he shook himself into the welcome respite of Solveig's porch. The rain had started only a few minutes before, but already he was soaked to the skin, and it was seeping down his neck and back, dripping from his coat-ends and down the legs of his trousers. 'God's sake!' he said again, stripping off the sodden coat, rubbing his face and hands with the towel Solveig thrust at him from a handy pile she kept in a dresser by the door. That these were old dog-towels, she didn't deem it necessary to mention, for they did the purpose just as well for men as for dogs, and she doled them out first to Brogar and then to Sholto. She had a brief thought of Tobar Strabane, who had left them at the stores, deciding he'd had enough of human life, or perhaps of human death, preferring to leg it back into the evening and the hills that were his own personal retreat, and she couldn't blame him for that. She thought too of Moffatt Murchison, regretting she hadn't been able to convince him to return with them to the chapel; she still had the memory of him trudging off up the track, dragging his discomfort and his grief like a disembowelled carcass upon his back.

197

The situation had overtaken her after Moffatt had left, when she had caught up Brogar and Sholto at the stores, Tobar brushing by her as she'd arrived and he had left, declaring it was time for him to go if he was to make it back home in a modicum of light, and could she please look after his horse. Brogar had barked at her to stop, and Sholto had tried to bar her way, but she'd seen enough over his outstretched arm to know that just as Moffatt had announced earlier, Andrew McTavish was as dead as could be, and was not a pretty sight. Brogar had gone to the small outhouse behind the stores and broken the door off its hinges – a feat that took less than a minute due to its flimsy construction – and brought it back, along with a rough and very damp horse blanket that was perceptibly growing mould in all four corners, and he and Sholto had gone in and fetched out the corpse, already shabbily covered with the blanket to hide it from her eyes.

She hadn't complained, and they had carried the door, blanket, body and all, the whole way back to her house without a murmur, though she could see that the old shed door was splintering about its edges and couldn't have been easy to hold for any length of time, its planks bending with the weight of the body, and though she'd thanked them both for what they were doing, neither had replied, excepting that Sholto had shaken his head to flick back that strange shock of greying hair from his forehead, and managed to raise a small smile.

They'd got back down the lane without incident, without meeting anybody, and she had reconnoitred briefly before leading them into the courtyard and then to the barn, for the last thing she'd wanted was that anybody should see them with yet another dead body, fearing the panic that might break out amongst the crowds if they did. But thankfully everyone was clustered about the spits in the field beyond, and they'd only just stowed Andrew McTavish in the barn when the rain came down out of the sky with strength enough to move small stones off the ground, and heavy enough to send all the mourners streaming past them, scurrying back off to the Suisgill, Kildonan, the old kirk, or wherever else they had come from. And for a few moments Solveig, Sholto and Brogar had been left standing in the courtyard, the rain cascading all around them, bouncing from the cobbles, six inches up and then down again, before they'd made their dash past the water pump and into the safe harbour of her house.

The one person she had wanted to see, but hadn't, was Tam Japp, for there was no way around the fact that he needed to be informed of this latest death and quickly, for surely this would be enough for him to finally inform the Provost at Dornoch, no matter what his superiors had already said about the Company – and her – being responsible for any investigation into accidental deaths up at the gold mines. Not that she thought of any of the events of the past two days as accidents, nor had she really performed an investigation of any kind, not having much of an idea how to proceed.

And all the way back from the stores to the barn, she had felt an anger at her impotence that alternately made her want to weep one minute, then bawl out the next that none of this was her fault, and what was she supposed to do about it anyway? She closed her eyes at the thought, stood in her doorway, and after both Sholto and Brogar had taken her old dog-drying towels and moved on into the study, she looked out towards the yard, and began to cry, though her tears were granted anonymity by the still-falling rain, and she listened to it hammering down upon the roof of her house, upon the cobbles, the yard, the barn, the river, knowing it would be muddying up the freshly turned turf of the two new graves, and wondered if she would have dig another, and another, and another after that.

'Mrs McCleery?' Sholto was so close to her that his voice made her start. He reached out a hand, touched her arm briefly, holding up the towel he had been using. When she didn't respond, he put the wet towel back upon the dresser and began to move away. He had reached the open door of Solveig's study where Brogar had already taken up his damp residence and was kneeling down by the inglenook to turn a hastily stacked pile of tinder into fire, when Sholto turned back, and saw Solveig's profiled face still staring resolutely out into the rain and that she was wet with it, and that her face was running over with it, tracking down her cheeks, her chin, her arms. He saw her lift the towel he had just placed down on the dresser, saw her bring it up to her face, saw the brusque way she used it to rub at her cheeks, scouring the rough material across her face, and recognised the gesture, that she was trying to wipe away some weakness she did not want to succumb to, at least not in front of other people, which meant himself and Brogar.

'Solveig,' he said quietly, taking a step towards her, though she did not move. 'Solveig,' he said again. 'You must realise none of this is your fault. You can't hold yourself to blame for the actions of another.'

She wheeled around so suddenly on her heel that Sholto took an involuntary step backwards, as she began to advance upon him.

'You can't know that.' Her voice was low, almost a whisper, but there was a shout in that whisper fighting to get out, and her face was flushed from the self-flagellation of the towel. 'How can you know that?' she said again, her voice now rising far above its normal pitch. 'You said it yourself – I'm at the centre of it. You said it yourself!'

The desperation in her voice was so evident that Sholto could not help but pity her, wanted at all costs to give her the reasons she was seeking, provide the answers that would abnegate her guilt. He'd not known her for long, but he knew the full scope of all she was trying to do here in her little corner of Sutherland, how she was trying to lift the lot of the common man, raise the standard of life for all who fell within the parishes of Kildonan and of Brora, and he felt absurdly thankful for all her efforts, for the sleight of subterfuge she had employed with both the Company and the Estate to get the mines reopened, and the brickworks with them; he knew that if his own parents had not been amongst the lucky few at the time of The Pick, then his own family would most probably have been one the ones that she was trying so desperately to help. And though he didn't have those answers yet, he was beginning to have an inkling of whereabouts they might be found, and he surely wanted to lift the yoke of onus at least a little from her shoulders.

'Solveig,' he said, and would have put out a hand except that her demeanour denied such a possibility, for she was as rigid before him as were the door posts she was framed by. 'Solveig,' he said again, looking beyond her out into the rain, couldn't meet those blazing eyes as he continued. 'There is more I've yet to tell you about these deaths, and I think the time to do so is right now.'

They drew up their chairs about the desk that had once been Solveig's father's pride and place of joy, where he had, many years before, collated all the details and references for his dictionary of Gaelic words and phrases and their English and Swedish counterparts, and composed his little primer *The Succour of the Sukkiim*, and later worked on the tenets of his church.

'I never finished explaining myself earlier, in the chapel.' Sholto stood up as he began to speak, moving towards the big bay window, his figure silhouetted by the water-washed sky, the last light of the evening before it sinking into night. He rested his long fingers on the brass girdle of the globe of the world on which Solveig's father had once marked out his travels, so faded now they could hardly be seen. 'I'd been telling Tobar about what was written on the piece of paper we found beside Robbie, and I never got to tell you, but there was a piece of bark wrapped up in that piece of paper, and

201

something on it that I recognised straightaway. It happened a long time ago, but there was something one of the Company's geologists had brought back from Iceland, and it intrigued me, and when I asked Harald Aasen if I could study it, he agreed.'

Sholto hesitated, stopped speaking, hearing the small scrape of Solveig's chair as she turned the better to see him. Brogar too was watching Sholto closely. Harald had been Brogar's immediate boss when he'd first joined the Company over twenty years before, and he knew him to be an able judge of character and situation, one of the few high-up big-wigs who understood that there were certain episodes in the lives of field men like Brogar Finn that needed, of necessity, to be left out of their final reports to the Company Board.

'It was a shovel,' Sholto went on, 'dug out of a bog in Iceland, and it had on it certain inscriptions, partly in Sami, partly in Old Norse runes. Very important, very ancient, the oldest recorded use of the Sami language ever found. *Come to me, Ingvald, please.*'

He brought out the piece of paper from between two leaves of his notebook, along with the little piece of bark. Brogar lifted a single finger from the surface of the desk and left it suspended in the air, giving Sholto the impression that he was expecting something more, and did not want to disappoint.

'And that same phrase was replicated in the note we found, excepting the substitution of Solveig's name for Ingvald's, which means something very specific, for very few people could have known about something so obscure.'

Brogar dropped his raised finger to the paper, and pulled it towards him, Sholto leaning over and pointing to it while he explained the rest.

'And along with that, there's another Gaelic proverb on the paper that amounts to this: *Eiridh tonn air uisge balbh.*' He pronounced the foreign

202

words slowly, then added their translation, as given to him both Joseph's dictionary and Moffatt Murchison earlier that day. '*The waves will rise on silent waters,*' he said, 'and then the bark has pencil marks on it, rune, and though they're not exact, they are exact enough.'

Solveig leaned forward.

'Can I see?' she asked, and Brogar pushed paper and bark towards her. She read the words, quiet and slow, and as if they were all of one sentence.

'*The waves will rise on silent waters. Come to me, Solveig, please.*'

Sholto dared not move a muscle, not an inch, fearing the effect these words might have on Solveig now that she had seen them written down with her own eyes, and not just as a point in that ridiculous argument he had had with Tobar in the chapel. But Solveig was made of sterner stuff, and only blinked, placed the paper back down onto the table, Brogar stretching out a lazy hand and picking up the bark, which was about half the size of an average playing card.

'It does rather lower the suspect pool,' he commented, apparently without irony. 'For how many men in the world, Sholto, do you think would care about a thing such as this?'

'Not many,' Sholto said. 'But someone obviously does, and must know I know about it too – and those plugs of felt? I know Tobar didn't agree, but it seems to me that was aimed at you, Brogar. So, like I was saying, Solveig, whatever this person is trying to say, it's to all of us, we're all in this equally, and up to our necks.'

It was calm, with no hint of wind now that the rain had fallen, though the air was still saturated with droplets of moisture so slight, so benign, that they scarcely seemed there at all. He had the odd sensation that all his movements had slowed of their own accord to chime in with this stillness, as if this new landscape was beginning to absorb him, instil into him its rhythm, blend him into its hills, its water, its night. It struck him, not for the first time since he had been here, just how quick a process that shift into darkness was, when one moment the sun rested on the tips of the mountains, and the next had disappeared behind them, the light draining away like water down a sink-hole.

He chose his moment well, emerging into the brief gloaming and flitting his way across the boulders that strode the river; he gained the opposite bank, turned to his left and burrowed back through the tunnel his previous passage through the reeds had left. He came out onto the edge of the water meadow, Solveig's house a few hundred yards up to his right. He stopped, straightened himself briefly, put a hand against the small of his back to relieve the crick that had grown there by his bending and crawling like a worried vole, and for a moment was intoxicated by the smell of mint that was coming from the stems and leaves he had bruised by his passing, released into the air by the falling of that small, so slender, type of rain.

He allowed himself to stand tall for a few seconds, savouring the feeling of being upright. He could see the house quite clearly, the big bay window, the silhouettes of the three people ensconced within, two of them sitting, one standing, leaning near the window like a skinny, badly made mast, one that had a bend and tilt to it that gave him the familiar urge to rush forward, get it splinted and fixed. He watched for one second, two, entranced by the sight of those people, before self-preservation kicked in once more and made him duck back down into the shadows of reed and stem, one man battling his way back up the river of his life, trying to find its starting point, its source, the place where it had all begun to have a meaning, the place where he had first found Joseph, the place where it would soon all end, one way or another.

Chapter 26   *The friendless man awakes and sees before him the fallow waves*

'So he knows us,' Brogar continued after an unhurried hiatus.

'Or knows about us,' Sholto corrected, unable to stop the pedant that had taken up residence early doors inside his head. 'Either knows us, or knows about us, maybe someone who knew we were coming here, and has the resources at hand to have done some research on us both.'

Solveig said nothing, content to let Brogar and Sholto winkle out whatever they could from this latest message, though she still had those sparse five words ringing around her head as if they had been regulated by a metronome with a long time to still wind down. *Come to me, Solveig, please.* She understood that the use of her name represented some kind of threat, some unknown menace, but it also struck her as indescribably sad that the originator of those words had been in such a state of want for his Ingvald, that he had carved out those words onto the blade of a broken shovel. Like a prayer, she thought, or an invocation, the forlorn hope that by scratching out those words, they would come true.

She was tired, and, despite all the cooking she had done that day, she'd eaten nothing, and exhaustion came on her so quickly there was nothing at all she could do to stop it. Sholto happened to turn towards Solveig at that moment, saw her face going quite blank, as if a lever had been pulled deep inside her that made everything collapse, her head falling down towards the table, her body following, her elbows slipping from the table's surface as if gravity had suddenly increased its downward force.

'But stop! Stop!' Sholto shouted in alarm, though it was Brogar who was up and over the two yards between himself and Solveig, caught his hands roughly about her shoulders and pulled her back the moment before her head thumped down against the hard wood. The sudden movement jolted Solveig from her stupor, and she opened her eyes, tried to focus but could not, shook her head, or thought she did, though felt she was entirely numb, her mind as empty as a slate after rain.

'Has she fainted?' she heard Sholto's anxious voice way up above her, like a lark madly twittering out its song in the first throes of spring. Brogar didn't answer, just released one hand from Solveig's shoulder, and with it swung her chair around, the scraping of its feet upon the stone of the floor making Sholto involuntarily grind his teeth. Brogar put a finger beneath Solveig's chin and lifted it, crouched down so that his face was level to hers.

'Solveig,' he said quietly. 'You need to wake up now.'

And so she did, quite suddenly. She blinked. Could not account for the situation she found herself in, with Brogar's face only a cubit's reach from her own, and she looked at him, really looked at him, saw the dark eyes, the nose that was flattened at its bridge and kinked to the right, the two thin lines that ran through his left eyebrow, the other scars that marked his face from hairline down to chin.

'You poor boy,' she found herself saying, and the words were so incongruous that Brogar grinned, though a grin from Brogar would have been a grimace in anyone else.

'Welcome back!' Brogar said, as if Solveig had just returned from a shopping trip and not the narcoleptic stupor she had slipped momentarily into.

Welcome back indeed, thought Sholto, wiping away the perspiration that had sprung from his forehead like morning dew. He'd never seen anything like it, though Brogar Finn obviously had, and he wondered what other new surprises working for this man would bring, and despite the rapid increase in his heart rate that he knew could not be good for him, he smiled too, because

206

he realised at last that this was what his life would be like if he carried on working with Brogar Finn: a life of twists and turns and unexpected happenings. And by God, even the thought of such a life felt good to him. He'd never felt anything like it, and despite the circumstances prevailing in Kildonan, he truly didn't want any of it to end.

Soon afterwards, the men went back to the chapel, Brogar insistent that Solveig take herself off to her bed. She had agreed without argument; she felt as if her body had already slipped halfway into sleep.

They'd reached the door of the chapel when Brogar had turned and placed one hand lightly upon Sholto's shoulder.

'I'm very particular about my assistants,' he said, 'and I don't suffer fools gladly, as I'm sure you've already observed.'

Sholto felt his heart sinking.

So this was it.

This was the moment.

This was the now or never, and whatever came out of Brogar's mouth next would decide his fate.

'Luckily, Sholto,' Brogar said, 'it is apparent that you are no fool, and,' he went on, 'I think we'll work well together, you and I. Your probationary period is now officially over. I have only one thing left to say to you, and that is this: welcome aboard.'

Sholto could not hide his pleasure, was beaming, grabbed at Brogar's hand and shook it, and shook it hard.

'Thank you,' he said, and then again. 'Thank you. Thank you. You've no idea what this means to me.'

Brogar laughed quietly as he disentangled his hand, opened the chapel door.

'Come on,' he said. 'We really need to get some sleep. We've a lot to get done in the morning, not least getting this murder business knocked on the head. It's beginning to seriously hamper my work plans, not to mention tearing the delightful Solveig's nerves to shreds.'

Sholto could not agree more and said so, though was at a loss as to how to proceed. Brogar though, had some suggestions as they made their way towards the altar table, and he waved a hand around him to indicate the shelves of books and files that lay catching dust upon the chapel's right-hand wall.

'Just look at all this stuff!' he said airily. 'Your brief tomorrow, Sholto, my new assistant, will be to trawl through as much of it as you can.' He held up a hand as if Sholto was about to protest, which he was not, and carried on swiftly. 'I know we said earlier that it seems as if we two have become objects of interest to our murderous stranger, but I cannot for a moment believe we're at the heart of it.'

Sholto looked at Brogar with some awe. In a single sentence he'd summed up the entire rat's nest of thoughts that had been twisting about inside his head all day, all the strands he'd been trying to reconcile, but could not.

'It's something to do with this valley,' Brogar went on. 'I'm absolutely certain of it.' Sholto nodded enthusiastically as Brogar carried on with his theory. 'Nobody here could have foreseen our coming, and certainly not together, not unless they have some secret spy high up in the Company, which seems more than a little doubtful.'

By God, thought Sholto, by God, he's right – we're just spare cogs that happened to be lying around that someone has decided to make use of. The answer might as well lie here, in this very room, as anywhere else, and straightaway Sholto wanted to start pulling down volumes, combing them through for some clue as to what that could be. Brogar, though, yawned loudly.

'I need sleep,' he said, and made for his bed, kicked off his boots, lay down, and reluctantly Sholto followed suit, blew out the lamp, listened to the night, shivered in the cold, too excited to sleep, wondering what he might discover in the morning, what he might discover in the rest of his new life. He thought he could hear some animal moving on the other side of the wall beyond the altar table and the lectern and the pinpricks of the windows set in the wall above, and was glad for it, that it could move with such ease so close to where he was, imagined some lone deer or fox coming down from the hills to snaffle at the scraps left by the wake that afternoon, pleased that something good would come out of such desolation. And despite himself, he slipped into sleep as easy as a barque pushed out into the dark waters of the night, one that would stay there at peace, until recalled by the tether of the dawn.

Chapter 27   *The rocky cliffs, where sea birds bathe and preen*

Up at Scalabsdale, Tobar was awake, despite the lateness of the hour. He'd got back
just as the sun was going down over the brim of the hills, the sky a luminous gold, the lochan below him so calm that the sky lay there too, every detail of the clouds etched into the water. The beauty of it overwhelmed him, and he sat for a while on his bench sipping a little from the bottle he had retrieved from its hidey-hole. As he sat and thought and drank, he was reminded of another lake that lay to the west of Stockholm. Lake Mälaren, third largest lake in Sweden, seventy miles long, thirty miles across at its widest point.

For Tobar this was no idle comparison, for in that lake lay Lillon Island, site of the ancient township of Helgö, a place extraordinary amongst its peers for being the centre of trade and export in Sweden for almost five hundred years, from the third century through to the eighth. The iron weapons that were made there, the files and hammers, borers and chisels, locks and keys, had been distributed all over Europe, as was its jewellery, its scribers and tongs, its files and gravers, its beads of glass of differing colours. All these things coming from that one artisan township, that one small island, set adrift in the middle of a Swedish lake.

He knew nothing of the existence of a master mast-maker prowling about the valley of Kildonan, but he did know that the first references to the use of masts and sails on European ships came from another Swedish island, from Gotland, seen in the pictograms carved into standing stones dating back to the seventh century, a time when Helgö was at its zenith.

He was thinking about such things because he was trying to place the origins of Solveig's bowls. It was a rare enough turn for him, getting visitors, and he had enjoyed it well enough, but there was no one in the world could have visited him who would have given him more pleasure than he'd got from seeing those bowls. They'd been absolutely extraordinary, similar in many ways to the so-called Coptic bowls, whose remains had been found scattered all across Europe. And similar, in much more significant ways, to those dug up not long ago, in 1837, in a tiny place in Romania called Pietroasa. Five gold vessels had been found there: a jug, two beakers, one large plate, and a golden bowl so similar in cast and size to one of the Brora ones that they might have made at the exact same time by the exact same hand, if not from the same materials. Both had been crafted from a single sheet of metal, gold in one case, bronze alloy in the other, the only surviving tool-mark being a single point at the very centre of their interiors, their rims strengthened by means of two metal strips, one attached to the inside, the other to the out, each secured with solder and a single rivet at the quadrant point of each rim. The Pietroasa beakers had been studded with garnets of a type and colour that were identical to the Scandinavian-mined examples of such gems. And, more tellingly, the colander that had fitted so perfectly inside one of the Brora bowls had punch-holes exquisitely preserved, forming a complex pattern of leaf-like tendrils about a single six-petalled flower, exactly like the scraps that had been dug up at Helgö two or three years before.

He could hardly believe he had been privileged enough to see such rare and wonderful objects, and from his studies of them, there was no doubt at all in Tobar's mind that the Brora bowls were Helgö-made and Helgö-traded, and if he could amass his evidence well enough, if he could make a case for the links between Helgö, Pietroasa and Brora, he knew that by this time next year his name would be attached to the paper that would carve out a whole new direction in the world of archaeology, give a whole new aspect to the already accepted fact that trade between Scandinavia and Scotland had been established since the earliest times. And this was a cause he had spent a large portion of his life pursuing. He lived in Scalabsdale, for heaven's sake, named after a Scandinavian incomer hundreds of years ago, just like Helmsdale was named for Hjalmundal, and Torroboll in Lairg from Thori, and a hundred other examples scattered all across this northernmost part of Scotland, paradoxically called Sutherland, from the Norse, meaning Land of the South.

He knew all about the early years of trade, with timber coming in from Norway, iron from Sweden, grain and wool shipped back from Scotland to both, along with a plentiful supply of foot-soldiers who were deployed by various Scandinavian armies on various fronts. Just look at John Cunningham, or Hans Cunningham as he was known over there, who had left Scotland for Scandinavia in the late 1500s and worked his way up to being an admiral in the Danish army, serving under Christian IV, for whom he had gone on to reclaim Greenland for the Danish throne back in 1605. For this great service Cunningham had been gifted the enormous fortress of Vardø on the edge of the Kola Peninsula, a home-from-home for Scottish traders for hundreds and hundreds of years, maybe even as far back as the heyday of Helgö.

As a younger man, Tobar had once thought of taking a journey in Cunningham's footsteps, going to see the fortress at Vardø for himself, maybe even heading off to Greenland, but to his great misfortune he got sick at the mere sight of a ship swaying gently in harbour, and sicker still if he set foot on one, a sickness he never grew out of, keeping him hammer-bolted into his home.

It hadn't taken him long to get over this disappointment, and he came to the decision that travel was overrated; he could do all he wanted of it in the pages of his books, or by tramping the hills outside of Helmsdale. He'd never been one for close friends or the companionship of others, and through all his adult years there'd been only one person he'd ever talked to on a regular basis, who had been blown, quite literally, into his path on a dour, wind-whipped morning back in 1835 just outside Kinbrace. This stranger had stopped him, and though talking was difficult because of the extremity of the wind, he had handed over to Tobar a book free of charge, which Tobar could not refuse. It had been a self-published primer in Gaelic and English entitled *The Succour of the Sukkiim,* the two intertwined S's on its cover giving it the local nickname, he was later to discover, of the *SS Kildonan.* Tobar had taken the book home, and read it through and through, occasionally laughing here and there, at other times taking notes, and he had eventually taken the extraordinary step of tracking down its author, whose name had been Joseph Lundt.

It was strange, Tobar thought, as he sat there on his bench, sipping from his home-brew, watching the lake below him ripple away its colour and its clouds, the wind beginning to growl now through the heather as night came down on him, stars flicking on one by one as the sun sank ever further below the curvature of the earth, how life was just like that, like a circle, a sphere maybe, with every point on its surface somehow joined up to all the rest. He could not possibly have foreseen that the simple act of accepting a book from a stranger on a windy morning thirty years before would have had such an impact on the rest of his life.

And yet it had done so, and Joseph Lundt had been at the heart of it, just as Joseph's daughter, Solveig, was at the heart of it now. He didn't quite understand how Solveig's life had become so interlinked with his own, except perhaps for the fact that it had been he who had encouraged her father in his involvement with the Holy Apostolic Church. Not that Tobar was a believer – far from it – but he'd understood back then that Joseph was in need of some kind of salvation, a deliverance from what he perceived as a

213

dreadful wrong. And the church Joseph had latched onto was perfect in every way for both of them, for Joseph got to be a missionary, got to spread his word, got to uphold the simple virtues of the early Christian church, and Tobar, well, Tobar thought that in the end he had got the best of it, because Joseph had gone to all those places Tobar had always dreamed of going but never would, and it had been Tobar who had directed Joseph's journeys every step of the way, and Tobar who had done the initial research for Joseph, pointing him to the wilds of Russia, the very edges of Scandinavia and Finnmark, and had stated the case for him going there, laying out his lines like bait on a hook. And Joseph had swallowed it willingly, and the letters he had written back to Tobar had been Tobar's lifeline, his only connection to the outside world he was choosing to withdraw from even then, like a snail from salt, until the only place he felt at peace was here, in Scalabsdale, miles away from anyone, the architect of his own silence.

He could not begin to say how much he regretted urging Joseph not to quit when Joseph wrote that he believed he had done enough at last, that he had just heard from his daughter that she had married, and to whom, and needed to get back, needed to go home.

Just one last trip, Joseph, Tobar had written to advise him. *We've only the Faroes and Iceland left from our initial list, if we discount Greenland as being too far. Why not include the first two as part of your return, for they are surely on your way, at least if you leave from Vosnoi or Archangel on one of the whaling ships?*

And Joseph had complied, had taken Tobar's advice as he had always done, had left Archangel on March the 22nd 1855, sending a letter off to Tobar that very morning, telling him how touched he'd been that every member of the branch of the church he'd established in Archangel had turned out to see him off, and how relieved he'd been to turn his feet back towards Kildonan, no matter the roundabout route.

But what had happened to Joseph after that had been a mystery, for Tobar never heard from him again, no more did Solveig, nor the master mast-maker who had been his constant companion until Joseph had decided to give it all up and return home.

Chapter 28   *And knows that frost and hail and snow are coming from the north*

He reached the trees to the west of the barn and bent beneath them, the rain gathered on their leaves falling sporadically onto his back as he went. It was so dark the only path he could follow came from the map inside his head, but he was breathing slowly, at ease within the framework of the night, and soon reached the other end of the plantation and moved onto the unkempt grass of the field, towards the bulwark of the barn. The clouds gave hurried glimpses of their captive moon only briefly, in slivers, as if through bars, sporadic shards of light in the night, but enough to keep correct his internal compass.

He stopped at the barn's far left corner, leaning against the wood, feeling its strength and solidity beneath his shoulder. The night was perfect, and he knew he would get no better chance; the unexpected crowds of the afternoon had long since deserted and would not be back, the stable boys were flat out upon their pallets, and Solveig's other companions gone a half hour since to the chapel. Another brief hint of light from the moon revealed the courtyard, the pump a skinny crooked man with a dripping nose. The house had only one door, and having assumed it would probably be locked, he had already selected the window through which he would gain entry into the scullery, always left a finger's breadth open to let in the air, keep it cool. He ran swiftly down the side of the barn, cut across the corner of the courtyard, swerved onto the grass that led up to the wall of the house, when something entirely unexpected happened.

The door opened.

She stepped over the lintel onto the cobbles.

She was so close to him that he could hear her breathing, hear her slippers softly scuffing across the stone. She was carrying a single candle, and made her way across the courtyard, past the old-man fountain. He stayed stock still, did not move an inch, fearing that if she turned she would be able to make out his form spread-eagled across the whitewash that still held a glimmer of light upon its surface. But she did not turn, did not hesitate, and was at the barn door less than half a minute later, and, as she pushed it open, he took his chance, slipped around the corner of the house, cold sweat at the back of his neck as he folded himself into darkness.

The barn door closed behind her, and he began to assess his options. Should he carry on down behind the house, retrace his steps, wait out the night, try again the next? Or maybe he should access her house as he had planned? Wait for her there, for he knew there was no one else left inside. The other option was to confront her now, in the barn, assuming it wasn't bolted from the inside, hope he could cover her mouth before her screams alerted the men in the chapel fifty yards distant. Or maybe one of those men was already in there, and the reason for Solveig's nocturnal perambulation in the first place. And then he remembered that there *was* at least one man in the barn, though maybe not a live one, and he understood what she was doing there, and not even he could disturb her in her service to the dead. It had been a central tenet of Joseph's religion, his eighth sacrament, and whatever else he might have done, and whatever else he might still be capable of doing, breaking one of Joseph's sacraments was not one of them.

216

In the barn across the courtyard, Solveig was sitting dry-eyed beside yet another corpse. Despite her earlier exhaustion, and her retirement to her bed, she had slept barely half an hour after Brogar and Sholto had left. She didn't know what had woken her, but the second she'd opened her eyes she'd been fully awake, and had lain for several minutes staring into darkness, her absolute aloneness more acute than ever it had been since Elof John had died, and she found herself suddenly wishing she had got herself a dog again, or maybe two, and promised herself that once this business was over and done with, that was exactly what she would do.

This business, she thought. *And what exactly is this business?*

She'd no idea at all, just couldn't fathom it, couldn't connect the dots, couldn't find any link between the three people who had died, or any link between their deaths and herself, though she knew there must be one. Brogar had been right enough when he'd stated that bodies didn't just pile up in one place for no reason. And she was angry with herself that she couldn't find that reason, thought that probably it was right in front of her though she couldn't see it, and couldn't shake the conviction that she *did* know, yet couldn't put her finger on it.

She'd shaken her head in the darkness, sat up from her bed, pushed her feet into her slippers and lit a candle. She might not be able to do anything about why Andrew had died, but there was one last service she could do for him, just as she had done for Robbie Weavers and Willie Blaine. And it was not so much to ask, as her father had always told her, to keep company with the dead, make sure their last few hours spent above the earth were not spent alone.

'Good night, Andrew,' Solveig said once she was in the barn, blowing out her candle, lying down upon her by now accustomed bale. She was asleep in moments, so deeply that she didn't dream, didn't wake, until the following dawn.

Inside her house, the master mast-maker was moving softly, carefully, had lit with his tinder-flint one of the lamps he'd found hanging just inside the hall. He moved by turns through the living room, the kitchen, the study, saw the large globe there by the big bay window and went up to it, moved it gently with his fingertips until he could see the place that he had come from, the other places he had been with Joseph, thought he could detect a few marks upon its surface flickering in the light of the lamp, thin lines marking those vast stretches of northern wilderness through which they had trod together. He looked closely at the northern tip of Finland, at Vardø and at Vosnoi, and a little further south towards Archangel, from where Joseph had set off on his last trip, heading here to this very house, this very room.

Where did it all go wrong, Joseph? he asked the silent night, but there was no answer, only the soft sputtering of the lamp.

Why didn't you take me with you? And where is the proof you promised me of all that we did? How much more do I have to do?

He was tired. Lord, how tired he was at having no answers to his questions, no end to all the years of pointlessness and wondering what had become of Joseph and their work. And despite his tiredness, or maybe because of it, he couldn't stop the old anger bursting like an unstoppable, all-entwining vine through his veins, and he heard the old words he had used to shout out into the universe, the *keinolla millä hyväsä,* that meant that by hook or crook he meant to have those answers, and have them soon.

One way or the other, he swore that tomorrow would be the day that brought him his truth, and that he would throttle the life out of anyone who got in its way.

218

Chapter 29   *That the hall walls will soon be swept by storm and frost*

The barn door rattled, was opened a moment later by Brogar Finn.

'I suppose you've been in here all night again,' Brogar said as Solveig rubbed her eyes awake, looking blearily up at him. She was embarrassed, covered only by her nightdress, her several blankets having shuggled their way down to her waist during the night, her sleep so deep she hadn't noticed their migration despite the cold.

'I tried the house,' Brogar said easily, apparently as unconcerned by her state of undress as he was by the dead body a couple of yards to his right. 'Look lively,' he added. 'We've a lot to do today. I've got mines to see to, and Sholto's got murders to solve, and you've got the pleasure of assisting at either or both.'

After that he left her, depositing a tray of tea and toasted soda bread upon the next-door hay-bale, an act of kindness that took her completely by surprise. And as she ate and drank she wondered how much more there was to Brogar Finn than met the eye.

Ten minutes later she was back over to her house, galvanised by Brogar's gift of breakfast and the attitude he had exuded of get-up-and-go, which had convinced her that today might really bring a solution to all they sought. She noticed in passing that a lamp appeared to be missing from the hall, and that some of the papers on the desk in the study had not been as she'd left them, but had assumed this was Brogar's doing, or possibly Sholto's, because one or both of them must have been inside her house that morning to stoke the range, heat the water for the tea, slice yesterday's bread and get it grilled before it had been brought to her.

She went by habit into the kitchen to check the range was stoked enough to last the day, and her eyes fell on the rug in front of it that had been chewed practically into non-extinction by all the generations of dogs who had lived and slept there, the last of whom, Jaspar, died only a week after she had buried Elof John, after which she had not replaced him, hadn't thought then that she could bear to have her heart broken all over again.

Not so now, for after her thoughts of the previous night she was positively alight with the idea of gaining a new four-legged, tail-wagging companion, thought she might even throw out a few lines of enquiry as she went about her errands today, and that she had errands was not in doubt, for unquestionably Tam Japp and his overlords needed to be informed of Andrew McTavish's death, and steps taken to prick the ears of the Provost down at Dornoch, for Andrew had not been a mere panner or seeker of gold, and therefore nominally under her jurisdiction, but a longstanding, well-known, and well-respected member of the mercantile community. And that had to be a kick up the arse worth pursuing

She could hear Brogar in the courtyard calling to the stable lads to get a move on, get the horses ready, separate ones for himself and Solveig, and she saw the basket of laundered linen to her left, decided to speed herself by throwing on one of the dresses that had been cleaned and pressed by Mrs MacDonald down at the farm, delivered the day before when she had attended the wake. She'd her nightdress already on which would act as underdoings, and the dress she picked from the heap was strong enough, stiff enough, to survive the rigours of the day. Which was just as well for Solveig, for upstairs, the master mast-maker was still lying, rather unimaginatively, beneath her bed, though well hidden by the drooping sheets and eiderdowns she had flung aside the night before, and whose falling he had aided by his lying down upon its vacated warmth, waiting the night through, waiting for his chance, disturbed only by Brogar Finn's noisy entry just after dawn, and his clattering his way into the kitchen down below.

Solveig parted from Brogar Finn in the courtyard, he going on down to Brora, she to the Baile an Or, which had been eerily empty when she'd reached it, the panners, most with sore heads from yesterday's carousing which had continued after they'd arrived back at camp, having already left for the upper reaches of the valley to sift its burns and hack at its banks. They'd been soaked to the skin by the downpour that had doused the wake, but once back at what they temporarily called home, they had built up their fires, stripped off the jackets and trousers that were for most part the only ones they'd got, and carried on where they had left off while their clothes dried and the air about their fires filled with sweat-tinged steam as the men took a bit more drink, had a bit more talk about what was happening in the glen.

The fires had burned down to embers by the time Solveig arrived twenty minutes before nine, ash hanging in the air like dirty mist, the ground ankle-deep in mud. She could hear the striking of the men's pickaxes echoing from the couple of miles up the valley where they were working; strange, disembodied sounds that only added to the dismal and deserted aspect of the so hopefully named Town of Gold.

Tam Japp had been no breezy spirit either, his face an unhealthy grey, framed from cheek to chin by unshaven bristles, skin slack from lack of sleep, eyes tired and unfocussed. That he'd never had the look of a man at peace Solveig knew from previous encounters, but she had never seen him so haggard as he did this morning, and was shocked at his appearance, felt pity for him; he so obviously couldn't cope with the care and worry that had been heaped upon his shoulders in recent days, a burden, she thought sadly, that she was about to add to.

He'd greeted her with a smile that was lacklustre, and had nothing about it of joy, and for himself Tam Japp could see no reason for her coming here, but immediately began to fret about the Book of Licences he'd left at her house, tried to rationalise his anxiety by telling himself, and her, that it had never been out of his ken before, and what if the factor came by, on this morning of all mornings, to inspect it?

'It's in good hands,' Solveig mollified him, assuring him that Sholto would be looking through his book this very morning, and that he could go up to Kinbrace later in the day to retrieve it for himself.

'But what if someone has a really big find?' Tam Japp persisted, and though they both knew such an occurrence was unlikely in the extreme, Solveig realised it was not completely outwith the realms of possibility.

'If that happens,' she told him, 'you must weigh the find and record it on a slip of paper. Here, look,' she added. 'I'll sign one such for you now, so you won't have the responsibility of it if anything goes wrong.' Tam had looked at her then with such pathetic gratitude she'd felt an urgent need to slap him across the face, wallop the self-pity right out of him. 'There is another reason I am here, Mr Japp,' Solveig said, savouring the moment, knowing it would be the blow she had previously envisaged, if not in any physical sense, 'and I am not going to lie to you, nor beat about the bush.'

Tam Japp had raised his eyes to hers, looked at the short, defiant woman who was standing on the other side of the scrappy length of splintered wood that divided their two worlds, his throat tightening.

'The situation is not good,' Solveig continued, 'for there is another man dead. Andrew McTavish, keeper of the stores.'

222

Tam Japp flinched, moved back a pace, looked as if he was about to faint, gripped at the wood of his counter as if his life depended on it. He didn't think he could take any more, felt an unpleasant tingling in the ends of his fingers as the blood rushed away from them towards his heart with this latest shock, yet another he was so ill-equipped to deal with.

Solveig either didn't notice this reaction or else chose to ignore it, and instead pushed two sealed letters across the counter towards him.

'I need you to get these sent on.'

Tam looked at the creamy-white folds of paper she had pushed his way, and although he did not touch them, he felt a jab of hope as he read the names of those to whom they were addressed, Solveig helpfully elucidating as his eyes tripped their way across her handwriting.

'One is to Provost William Fraser in Dornoch,' she said, 'and the other is for the factor at the Estate.'

Tam Japp twitched, wished he had half the resilience of this woman, his voice catching in his throat so badly that she had already turned to leave by the time he managed to stutter out his reply.

'Thank you, Ma'am. Thank you. And if there's anything I can do…'

Solveig turned back to him at these words, stood so still that she might have been one of those stiff, upright stones you found abandoned in fields, put there as grave-signs or boundary markers thousands of years before. She closed her eyes for a second, maybe two, and when she opened them again he saw that the area beneath her lower lashes was wet, felt his own eyes tearing up involuntarily.

'Anything,' he said again, hardly realising he was saying it, his habitual timidity worn away by circumstance.

'There is something,' she said, as she took one step back towards him. 'You could oversee the manning of Andrew's stores. Use anyone you want,

223

anyone you trust. Recall a few men from the valley if you have to. I will see to it they are well recompensed.'

Tam readily agreed, and understood why she had asked him even before she explained.

'It would be a defeat, Mr Japp,' she said, 'if the stores were to close. A conspicuous defeat, and one that I will not brook. The stores must stay open in defiance of whoever is trying to disrupt everything we are working for. And I know it is what Andrew would have wanted.'

Whether Andrew would really have wanted such a thing or not was no concern of Tam Japp's. Before Solveig's arrival that morning he had felt only inability and confusion, completely at a loss as to how to deal with the extreme situation in which he found himself. He was not a man anyone would have wanted at his back in wartime, incapable as he was of snap decisions, a man who needed to be primed and aimed by someone stronger than himself. But now that he had been goaded into action, all doubt was gone. He swept up Solveig's letters, was already working out a roster of men he could use to man the stores; he had been given sail and rudder, and even though it was a woman providing them, he found that he did not begrudge it. It was to be a day of discoveries, and this small revelation was Tam Japp's.

Brogar Finn's, by contrast, was far more practical and of much more use.

He had made his way down to Brora, just as he had agreed with Solveig that he would do while she was away. He was to check on the mine workings, see what needed to be done in terms of new bore holes, the sealing and filling of the mines on the foreshore, the resetting of the brick clamp, take charge of the men who would otherwise be at a loss for what to do, so he took advantage of Solveig's absence to inveigle a couple of the old hands into taking him to the site of the oldest, most seriously unstable mine on the other side of Brora going up to Faskally.

As far as mines went, it was of no great shakes compared to the very many Brogar had been down in his life, was in fact perhaps the most diminutive, and yet for that very reason he was keen to investigate it and find out exactly why earlier projects had pushed it so far and no further, even though production here, as in the rest of the mines, had peaked the year before the closures in 1828.

The shaft of this particular working had an interesting history, and was named The Lady Jane Gordon, after the widow of the 12th Earl of Sutherland who had sunk it as far back as 1529. Prior to marrying into the Sutherlands, this Lady Jane had been divorced from Lord Bothwell, so that he in turn could go on to be the third husband of Mary, the lady they called the Queen of the Scots. Not that Brogar Finn cared a fig for such historical details as were being told him, and said so, loudly; what he wanted instead to know about was the pit itself, the shaft, and he thought it all a pretty poor exploration of what he believed was really down here, his work over the past two weeks indicating that although the Brora coal seam was not massive, there was more than enough of it to turn the town around and give the Company a good profit into the bargain, if only it was handled well.

So he threw himself with gusto down the rope ladder that had been flung down the side of the shaft, emerging an hour later from his explorations black-faced, smudge-kneed, bruised at shoulder and elbow, grinning like a maniac, alive and unburied, unlike some of the men who had previously tried their luck down there, the old pillars collapsing behind them as they went. It was a classic case of long-walling, as far as Brogar could see, where men had hacked through the seam, leaving freestanding pillars of rock and coal for support as the miners dug around them, a procedure that was as unsafe as it

225

was superseded. What it needed, thought Brogar, was proper shoring, so that new passages could be excavated out from the farthest end, and it needed pumps to rid it of sixty years of stagnating, eroding flood water, and a set of tramlines laid to bring out the coal. And when all that was done, this could be the real deal, the true rebirth of Brora coal. He had never been as sure of it as he was now.

And that had been Brogar Finn's discovery.

Sholto McKay's explorations had been of the sedentary kind. Even before Brogar had woken, he'd begun to go through Tam Japp's Book of Licences. It had been conscientiously maintained, if not particularly neatly, with every month's licence noted alongside each applicant's name, his place of origin, which pitch – if any – he had worked before and which he was now being granted licence to dig. Next to these entries came tallies of what each man had found each month, the weight of dust in grams, how much it was worth, how much went to the miner and to the estate. The occasional highlight of a substantial nugget was just that – occasional – and it made for rather depressing reading.

Even so, there'd been a steady increase of panners as the year went on, almost five hundred registered by April 1869, six hundred by June, and well over two hundred applicants per month by July, not to mention the tourists and journalists who had apparently turned up in droves, and whose names Tam Japp had also jotted down, many of them signing his register as they would have done a visitors' book in a hotel.

Come September there'd been a huge drop-off in panners, and by October the numbers were negligible in comparison to those of earlier months, though by then, according to Sholto's reckoning, over twelve thousand pounds worth of gold had been amassed by these various individual panners, mostly in dust, the smallest part in nuggets, a consistent ten per cent of every find going as Royalties to the Sutherlands, on top of the payment of the monthly licences.

Of all these men, only three others, besides Willie Blaine, had been there from the very start of the gold rush back in December 1868 up to the present, Dougall Meek being one of them, and the other two Patrick Skinner and Donald Patience, both from Avoch.

Brogar had awoken then, and there'd been a brief interruption to Sholto's studies while they went across to the house to scour up something to eat and drink, but he was soon back at it again, rummaging through Joseph's books and files. He found notes on Joseph's conversion to the Catholic Apostolic Church, which had begun a year or so after The Pick, Joseph having attended the Edinburgh lectures of one Edward Irving, a Scottish minister with many influential followers, including ex-MP Henry Drummond, whose substantial financing of Irving's proto-church had led to Drummond being ordained by that church as the 'Angel for Scotland' in 1834.

So much, so little, Sholto thought, moving quickly through the next wad of notes – dry documents relating the whereabouts of the missionaries of that Church in later years, Joseph included. He looked up at this point, hearing Solveig's pony trap going down the lane towards the bridge, presumably off to Helmsdale with her grim news of Andrew McTavish's death. He shook his head, not envying her the task, and opened the next box file.

This contained a whole volley of letters from Joseph Lundt to one Elof John McCleery, all of which concerned The Pick, and as Sholto read on he slowly subsided from his standing stance to sitting, had to read the letters over twice before he could take it all in, before he realised he was reading about his own past, his own luck, and that Joseph Lundt had not just been a part of The Pick, as he had previously supposed, but had been the whole of it from

227

beginning to end, and that without Joseph's intervention in Sholto's family's life, in the life of this valley, then he, Sholto McKay, would have had a very different life to the one he was living now, indeed might never have had a life at all.

Chapter 30   *And how terrible it will be when all has gone to waste*

The master mast-maker had spent the night on Solveig's bed, sleeping in that vague way a man can do when he knows that any second he will have to be up and at it, his semi-slumber punctuated by brief visions from his past life too real to be proper dreams.

Consequently he was already awake and sliding himself beneath Solveig's bed when he heard someone knocking at the door of Solveig's house, just past dawn. The visitors knocked several times but got no answer, and instead two men ingressed Solveig's house, talking quietly as they did so. He knew there were two by their voices, and matched up those voices with the men he had watched the previous day: the deeper timbre belonging to the man who looked like he could heft an ox onto a cart and not be out of breath, and the lighter, softer voice to the one who looked like a scholar.

These two had moved through the downstairs rooms back and forth several times, though had made no attempt to broach the upstairs, and no particular effort to remain quiet; they must have known by then, just as he had known the night before, that Solveig was not in the house at all, but out in the barn. He'd heard them in the kitchen, riddling out the stove, piling wood into it, opening cupboards and then closing them; he heard the filling and later whistling of a kettle, the rattle of crockery, and then they had departed, closing the front door behind them, and so far had not come back, no more had Solveig.

He had stayed where he was for almost a quarter hour before deciding to emerge, rolling himself out like a rug from beneath Solveig's bed, standing himself strategically behind her bedroom door, wondering if he had played his game too far, if it would not be Solveig at all who climbed the stairs, if he

229

would have to incapacitate some housemaid he'd not yet figured into his plans.

The front door opened, and he knew it really was Solveig by the quiet way she'd closed the door, moved down the hallway, had the same soft scuffling to her slippers he'd heard the night before. He braced himself, feared and hoped – all in the same breath – that this would be the time. He heard her place one foot upon the staircase, upon the warped and creaking step that had so alarmed him the night before, but she did not come any further, had apparently changed her mind, and went instead towards the kitchen, where she'd rattled a few more bits of tin and crockery, and was silent for a while more, before making her way back down towards the door, apparently no longer in slippers, judging by the heaviness of her tread, and had gone back out into courtyard. He could hear the ox-shoudered man hying up Solveig's stock boys, the unmistakeable sounds of horses being readied, traps being attached to harnesses, the sleepy, hungover stock boys going at their duties without enthusiasm. And then they were away, trap and horses and Solveig with them, and with their departure went his best chance of having a face-to-face with the only daughter of Joseph Lundt, the keeper of his secrets. Nothing left now but to pull back, regroup, and try another day. He'd come so close to Solveig that he was burning with frustration to have come so far and no further. He felt his thwarted anticipation shifting into anger with an ease he'd not anticipated, but felt the stronger for it, and the clearer, and realised there yet was one person here who might yield to him, if only he brooked no resistance, gave him no time, and no choice.

It took Sholto a few minutes to get over his discoveries about The Pick, but it wasn't long before he was up again, grabbing at another file from the other end of the table that he'd leafed through earlier, and, having noted its contents, had put aside as having little relevance to the case in hand. His excitement was such that he found it difficult to get his fingers moving properly, flipping clumsily through the old and brittle pages, but at last he had what he was looking for: a document that had been sparse in its telling, laid out like a legal document with a dense mass of footnotes at the base of each page, along with several bulky appendices, written in what he now recognised as Joseph Lundt's neat handwriting. His eyes moved back and forth over the pages, latching on to a word here, a name there.

And what he read was this:

A Brief Account of the Clearing of Kildonan Valley

1807: Whitsuntide: the first large-scale sheep farm established at Lairg; rent tripled; native population (c300) moved (unhappily) to the northern shores of Loch Naver.

1807-8: Failed harvests in Northern Scotland; famine widespread; many of the moved population of Lairg take opportunity to emigrate to America, but said ship is lost with all hands off the Newfoundland coast.

1809: Old Sutherland factor sacked; William Young and Patrick Sellar brought in from Moray to enforce the new plan of economic advance, establish sheep farms in the interior, increase population on coast, thereby to increase rent and industry for the Estate.

1812: Whitsunday: local tacksmen of Assynt take over new sheep farms; excess population moved out (unhappily) to the coast.

1812: End of year: plans move on to the clearing of Kildonan and Clyne, to general unrest.

1813: First week of the year: Riots in Kildonan – local populace ('savages' and 'banditi', 'poachers' and 'whisky smugglers') eject visiting surveyors, prospective shepherds and factors; sending petition to effect that many of their menfolk in 93rd Regiment abroad fighting, and should hold fast to their land until their return.
Backed by foremost Gentlemen of the County, all agreed on the Expulsion of Strangers from their land.

1813: March: negotiations break down again; Mr Finn from Bad Stone (called Finnish Winter) leads rebellion; troops ordered into Kildonan; six months' notice given to populace until enforced removal.

1813: December: Golspie Inn: Young's auction of Strathnaver to competing tenants; all outbid by Patrick Sellar (as agreed by previous arrangement with William Young and the Countess); Patrick Sellar takes over tenancy from east to west.

1814 & 1815: Four hundred and fifty families of Strathnaver 'arranged in different allotments, rents doubled, and put to a more industrious way of life' (William Young).

1816: Tuesday 23rd April 10am: Patrick Sellar brought to trial at Inverness for culpable homicide, real injury, and oppression, 'whereby the people and lawful occupiers...were turned out, without cover or shelter' and to detriment of life (Naver, Kildonan & Clyne);
Judge: Lord Commissioner of Justiciary, Lord Pitmilly.

1816: 24rd April, just past midnight: Patrick Sellar acquitted

1816: (Summer time?) James Loch takes command of the Highland Estates from Young and Sellar.

1818: James Loch issues Notices of Removal to all remaining tenants of the interior Estates (see attached page).

1819: August: The Flitting, when the last leave (unhappily) their land.

Conclusion:
Population of Kildonan valley
In the year 1811 :   1,574
In the year 1831 :   257

Sholto moved slowly, leafing through the attached notes on Patrick Sellar's trial to what he must have glanced through before but failed to register: a list of complainants, a list of witnesses, a list of men and women who had argued on both sides. Two names he had seen on either side of this divide, two names he knew and recognised. An unpleasant sensation passed through him like a shockwave, there one moment, gone the next, leaving him exactly as it had found him: a thin figure hunkered down over his pile of papers in the dim light of the chapel, the line of pinprick windows above him passing just as quickly from light to dark to light again as a small cloud chose that moment to scud across the face of the morning sun.

He closed his eyes, stretched his head back upon his neck, clenched and unclenched his fingers to ease the tension in them, calm the unsteady tic that was pulling at the corner of his left eye. And then he stood up, decision made, sudden death in this valley seeming now so much more commonplace, and those of the past few days, though undoubtedly violent and tragic, just the last of a long, long line, a line he was beginning to pull at, unsure what he would find at its end, but ready to find out.

He had just reached the door of the chapel when it was opened with such speed and force that it caught him sideways on, sent him stumbling backwards, his head hitting the ground so hard that for a moment he couldn't see anything, feel anything, until of a sudden he was being jerked up by his collar, the edge of his shirt so taut against his windpipe that he couldn't get any breath. He was aware of movement, knew he was being dragged back down the length of the chapel, his heels kicking spasmodically against the earthen floor. A few moments later the back of his knees connected with something hard and straight, and he realised he was being shoved back into the seat he had just vacated, so hard that the chair was tipping away from him even as he folded onto its wood. Whoever had brought him here flashed a hand by his head, caught at the chair arm, brought it back down to the vertical with a momentum that tipped Sholto forward, brought his head downwards to his knees, a burn of bile spraying from his mouth out onto his boots. He registered its dispersal with an obscure feeling of dismay, his eyes blinking rapidly with involuntary tears, but there was no let up yet from whatever bad thing was happening to him, as a hand – maybe the same one that had stayed the chair – cupped itself roughly about his chin and brought it

234

upwards with no gentle movement, stretching the skin across his throat in such a way that made him feel more vulnerable than he had ever thought it was possible to feel.

'Tell me where she is.' He heard the words growl across his horizon, felt the panic of that sound, felt his head begin to sag, the words reverberating like loose gravel in his head, thought he might pass out, thought he might even be dying, though was disabused of that notion by the shock and pain of the quick, hard slap levelled at first cheek and then the other.

'Where is Solveig?' the voice demanded, and the roaring was so much in his head that he would have said anything to keep it still.

'Scalabsdale,' he had croaked, 'she's up at Scalabsdale.'

Later, when everything was over, when all that was about to happen had happened and all was done, he would wonder about that single moment, about those few words he had spoken, about whether they had been born from fear or perspicuity, or both, about whether he had even registered the language the question had been delivered in, the same language in which he had given his answer, wondered how differently things might have gone if he had not answered at all.

Chapter 31   *But the wise man keeps secure the mind-chest of his thoughts*

Solveig felt weary, drained right back to the marrow of her bones, the strength she'd felt earlier that morning all gone. After she had visited Tam Japp, she'd made her way down into Helmsdale, delivered her dreary news to Andrew's family, for Andrew, unlike Willie Blaine or Robbie Weavers, had a family that actually cared about him, and the grief and loss she had caused them by it had been so acute that Solveig couldn't extricate herself from its binding fast enough. Even so, arrangements had been made, and two brothers and a nephew would be up to Kinbrace to fetch Andrew's body home the following morning, so at least she didn't have to worry about digging another hole and arranging another wake she didn't feel equipped to handle, especially now that the stores were empty not only of stock, but of Andrew too.

It was with some trepidation, therefore, that she made out the form of Lachlan McLachlan shambling towards her on his downbeat horse a mile or so before she got back up to the Baile an Or. She'd stopped her trap when she'd made him out, allowing the two ponies that had been drawing it to forage at the grasses on the wayside, waiting for Lachlan to get closer. She had no idea what he was doing so far away from Brora where he bided, though assumed that, given everything else that had happened recently, it must be bad tidings of one kind or another. Maybe Brogar had sent him to intercept her, tell her all had gone wrong with the mines or the brick clamps, or maybe that Brogar himself had been buried alive in one of the old mines she had strictly forbidden him to enter, knowing that he was not the kind of man to be forbidden anything he'd a mind to do, whatever anyone said. Black, then, was her heart and her mood as she waited for him, though the closer he drew, the less likely such dire forebodings seemed to be, for

Lachlan McLachlan appeared relaxed on his shamble of a steed, jaunty even, which was never a word she would have previously used of him.

'A'ternoon, missus,' he said, as he finally got within a couple of yards of where she was so bleakly waiting for him by the wayside.

'Lachlan,' she said, trying to keep the wobble of worry from her voice. 'What on earth are you doing here?'

Lachlan smiled his yellow smile, his teeth clenched hard about his pipe, but did not reply, and began instead to fiddle at his saddlebags, had to dismount to finish the job, finally brought out yet another of his sacks which he held out towards her with some triumph.

'Brought you this, missus,' he said. 'Mr Finn telt me to bring 'em to you direct. Seemed to think you might be wanting them.'

Solveig's skin contracted as she heard the slight metallic clinking coming from within the sacking, withdrew from the shiver of bad news she had been expecting, felt her heartbeat slow and then speed up again as she realised what it was in there.

'The other bowls?' she asked.

'More like bits, really,' Lachlan replied, and Solveig winced, remembering the beauty of the ones already recovered, hated to think of all the rest being tossed into a single sack and served up to her as they were being done, but so relieved at the innocuousness of the gift that she was effusive in her thanks as she put out her hand and took the sack from him.

'Thank you, Lachlan, thank you. You really didn't need to come all this way just to give me these. Can I ask you back to the steading? It's only a few miles up the road. Maybe get you some beer? A bite to eat?'

Lachlan could no more control the expressions that passed across his face at this offer than he could control the path his pipe-smoke took in the slight breeze that drifted in chaotic eddies about them both, and Solveig smiled to see those expressions go – alarm, swiftly followed by dismay, replaced a moment later by grim resignation at having to spend time with his boss – and a woman boss at that – and make polite chitchat all for the sake of a cup of ale. Oh God, how she understood such feelings at that moment, and decided on her own course, her own small rebellion from what was expected of her, what she ought to do, and spoke his mind for him, and for her.

'It's all right, Lachlan,' she said, putting out a hand, patting his arm, a smile rising free and happy across her face such as she'd not felt since they'd found Willie Blaine's body up at the Suisgill. 'There's no need for it,' she continued. 'No need for such civilities. Why don't you take the rest of the day off? Go the long way back to Brora? Take a little holiday. God knows, we both need it.'

It was reckless, Solveig knew it, but she felt as if her day had taken a sudden lift, and why shouldn't Lachlan benefit from it too? He was still puffing at his pipe, looking a little baffled, but so absolutely relieved she wanted to laugh.

'Here,' she said, starting for the ponies, bringing them back from their grass, tightening them to the trap. 'One last job for you. I'm going to take the rest of the day off too. I'm going to take these bowls up to Tobar Strabane, and I want you to take the trap on to Tam Japp at the Baile an Or so he can take it back to Kinbrace. Tell him I told you so. Tell him to give you another mount that will get you back to Brora.'

Then she moved past where Lachlan McLachlan was still shuffling his feet in consternation, and detached his saddlebags, threw them without ceremony onto the open seat of the pony trap, before launching herself into the stirrups of Lachlan's horse, which looked far less startled than did its owner, who was left standing agape in the track, watching as Solveig spurred on up and away from the track onto the moor, her skirts hitched somewhat indecently, the sack of broken Brora bowls nestled securely between mane and pommel.

'Aye, right,' Lachlan McLachlan finally managed to pronounce as he withdrew his pipe, watching Solveig disappearing up the hillside, trying to ease his bulk into the trap before deciding otherwise, ended up leading it, contentedly, slowly, back up the way he had just come, towards the Baile an Or.

'Funny things, women,' he was thinking as he rounded the bend towards the farm and the track that led down to it and past it to the old kirk. 'Never could figure 'em out.'

Brogar had tarried as long as he felt able, had visited the foreshore of Brora's East Beach and checked out the collapsed workings, which had no problems as far as he was able to determine, and had also been back to the site of the brick clamp, that, just as Solveig had predicted, had been stripped right back to the charred earth – not a single piece of half-burnt coal or charcoal left. All the usable bricks had been stacked according to their quality of curing, and stood in piles awaiting his inspection, but all the broken ones – again, as Solveig had intimated – all the ones burned through to the waist by being too close to the hot coals, had vanished as mysteriously as the spoiled coal. A clean-up job, carried out by the impoverished inhabitants of Brora, and one that had been more efficient than anything he could possibly have organised, and that left him in some awe.

He'd remained long enough to pass out some new orders to Solveig's workforce, to carry up more coal from the one mine he'd seen fit to be officially re-braced, re-shored and re-worked for the purpose, laying out the plans for a second bed for the bricks, after which he'd known there was nothing for it now but to head back to Kinbrace, see what Sholto had discovered, knock heads with his new assistant to try to figure out why three people had been murdered so maliciously on what he saw as his watch, and to the detriment of his work.

It was just the back of three when he arrived back at Solveig's steading, to find the place deserted. No Solveig back from Helmsdale, which was not that surprising; he thought probably she'd been held up with Andrew's family and the arrangements for keeping the stores open, which she'd been absolutely adamant must be done as long as his family had agreed that it should be so – and why wouldn't they, seeing as it was obviously a profitable enterprise? What was more worrying was that there was no sign of Sholto either, and when Brogar went into the chapel to look for him, he stepped right into a small, but suspicious-looking, pool of what looked like – and, upon later investigation, tasted like – blood, situated about six feet from the door, which continued in sporadic droplets down the nave.

What was also apparent was that all the papers on the altar table were uncharacteristically without order, and though Brogar hadn't known Sholto long, he'd known men like him, and knew that this was absolutely not the way that men like Sholto operated. More tellingly, the chair Sholto had adopted as his own, on the opposite side of the altar table, had been overturned, and, when Brogar examined it a little closer, he'd been able to make out several dark smudges upon its arms and top rail. More blood. He'd seen plenty of it in his lifetime, spilled from himself and other people in one way or another, and he knew that what he was looking at was not good.

He left the chapel at a run, leaving the door ajar behind him, and entered the courtyard, already shouting for the stable boys, though neither Hugh nor Gilligan had appeared. Brogar looked around him, saw the door to Solveig's house was closed, though not completely, was several millimetres short of its mark. He took a quick shufty inside, found it empty of people, no sign of

240

intrusion, then ran for the stables, also empty, the last two ponies missing. Sholto might have taken one if he had chosen to go somewhere, though where that might be, Brogar was at a loss to know. But why take two? He was turning on his heel in the courtyard, wondering what to do next, when he spotted movement in the pasture over the bridge across the lane, could make out Solveig's cattle-boys leading the herd back home, Gilligan at the fore, Hugh at the rump, both with switches in hand to guide the cattle on.

Brogar waved his arms, exaggerated movements that must have looked like windmill tracks, though he gained from them no increase in speed, no more response than a brief acknowledgement, a slight lift of each boy's arm to let him know they were on their way and would get there just as soon as they got there, which was not going to be any time soon.

He was about to remonstrate, when a pony trap came out of the curve of the trees and began its trundle down the track towards the bridge, looking a little bizarre in that the men who were in the trap were almost as large as the ponies drawing it. He ran towards them, grasped the reins of the pony closest to him, though both had stopped anyway, knowing how close they were to home.

'Where is she?' Brogar asked, in unconscious imitation of Sholto's earlier assailant.

Both men were bewildered, exchanged glances, until Brogar gripped the side of the trap and shook it with such violence that the two of them were tipped forward from their seats, Lachlan's teeth temporarily unclenching with the shock of it, causing his pipe to slip from its accustomed place, dislodging the warm tobacco and dottle, as stem and barrel took an uneven hit upon the trap-floor between his feet. He looked down towards it with what might have been outrage in a more uneven man, and then back up at Brogar. It had been in his mind to protest, to lodge complaint, but he saw in that face a wall that was as blank and unforgiving as the pieces of slate they used up in Caithness to make field-fences out of, and though he had never been a man quick with words or elaborate in explanations, he made an exception now.

'She took my horse,' Lachlan said. 'Telt me to bring the trap to Kildonan, swap for another horse but there was none, so the two of us brought it back together up to Kinbrace.'

He looked at the other passenger, who was Tam Japp, for confirmation and Tam nodded, had nothing new to add, might have said that the few working mounts at the Baile an Or, the only rides that might have been available for Lachlan, had been taken up the valley by the workers, but he did not. He was bewildered, removed his bonnet, scratched his head, fixed his eyes on Brogar; he had only really come to retrieve the Book of Licences and take it back to his shack.

The man looked grim, his features contracted, eyes narrowed, brows drawn together into a single arc that cast the rest of his face into shadow, made Tam Japp shiver just to see it, gave him the same feeling of menace he'd once experienced when a bull had begun to roar upon the hill in the field just above where he was working, a sound so low that his body had absorbed it and reacted to it before his mind had fully comprehended what he was hearing, was already priming itself for escape, muscles tensing, hairs standing to attention upon his arms, the back of his neck, on his scalp, heartbeat quickening, breath coming quick and erratic.

Brogar Finn was just like that bull, Tam thought now, isolated from the herd, silhouetted against the hill with the sky behind it, neck raised in anger, the sound coming from its throat like you've never heard before, that sent panic through your bones, made you suddenly aware of the mass of it, the bulk and strength harboured between its shoulders, the realisation that if you moved, if you caught its eye, if it saw you in its path, in its anger, then the few yards

242

between you and the boundary stones, the fence, the ragged thicket of whin and broom, would be as nothing, because by the time it had begun its charge, it would already be too late for escape.

Tam Japp's voice was arrested within his throat like a fly stuck to arsenic paper; he could only stare as Brogar the Bull stood before him, demanding answers to his questions.

'Where's Solveig? And where is Sholto? Right now, damn it! I need to know where they are right now!'

Tam was saved by one of Solveig's cow-lads bounding over the wall that was adjacent to the bridge, swiftly followed by the other one, both having recognised at last that something unusual was going on, something worth abandoning their charges for, leaving the cattle disconsolate in the field.

'You looking for your mate?' asked Hugh, breathless from his leap, his eyes a little brighter than they should have been.

'Do you know where he is?' Brogar was trying to be restrained, but felt the urgent need to beat anyone to a pulp if they stood in his way.

'Cannae say exactly,' said Gilligan answering for his pal as if they were some kind of double act, 'but we see'd him earlier, going on up the road...'

'Had someone else wi'im,' Hugh chipped in. 'Big man. Thought it were you. Heading up the valley toward Kinbrace, then turned off at the farm, went on up into the hills.'

Brogar took a long, deep breath, knew that the pieces were falling into place like rainwater into rivulets than ran into streams, joined into rivers, though exactly where they were leading he did not know.

Lachlan had retrieved his pipe, and despite the slight crack that ran the length of its stem from its fall, he had replaced it in the corner of his mouth, the familiar action and reassuring feel of it jogging his memory.

243

'She was taking the rest of them bowls up to Scalabsdale,' he said slowly, and just as slowly Brogar fixed him with a gaze that would have sent Tam Japp weeping into a corner. As it was, Lachlan felt supremely at ease; everything was right with his world, pipe back in place, afternoon clear, skies blue. 'The missus said it was by way of a bit of a jaunt, that us needed a break, that I've to take the rest of the day as my own due.'

'And you said Sholto was heading off where?' he asked the two boys, though didn't turn around, his eyes slipping from the calm lacunae of Lachlan's face and moving beyond him, up the track, tracing its path behind the trees that ran by the farm and on up into the hills.

'Didn't say where,' Hugh piped up.

'Don't know,' added Gilligan, the sidekick.

'But it could have been Scalabsdale,' Brogar argued, and again his strong hands closed on the side of the trap and set it rocking within his grasp, got the attention of the two men within. 'Could it go anywhere else, that track up beyond the farm?'

Tam Japp was about to say that it could go anywhere, that you could ride up into those hills and not reach anywhere for days, that you could head off to east or west or north and not see another soul, nor trip over any farmstead, until you reached the mountains that bordered the sea to the west, or the jagged drop of the cliffs to the east, or the wetlands, the wild peatbogs, through which you would need to pass to reach the long, white beaches of the north. And he began to understand that there really was only one place that anyone taking that track might be heading for, at least someone like Sholto McKay who didn't know one stone of this place from another except those he had already passed by, already travelled, and that Sholto McKay had travelled only one way from that path before, when, with Moffatt Murchison, he had gone up to visit Tobar Strabane in Scalabsdale.

244

Chapter 32   *And those who are eager for glory do not boast*

The waters of Scalabsdale loch were blue and smooth as silk, pocked by fish-lips sucking at the flies that landed so lightly upon its surface. Up high, the sky was calm, the few high strata of clouds perfectly white, no wind. All was even and without turmoil, and Tobar Strabane utterly content. The oars were up in his boat, the bit and brace he had used to fix the new rowlock pin laid carefully at the stern, not moving a jot as he to let the boat go where it would, which was not far, with no wind to push it on. It was the kind of afternoon that was rare, even for Tobar, who had spent almost two-thirds of his life in this place, and yet still it could almost stop his heart with a day like this. He cast out a line, watched it lace the surface where he knew the trout would be feeding in the warmer outreaches of the loch.

His hand jerked as he heard a noise that should not have been there, and he cursed as the line swung with the movement towards the rushes, towards the dying heads of bogbean that had keeled over with the early frosts, his carefully crafted fly catching and breaking off as he tugged the line harder than he should have done. With ill grace he turned to look behind him, had to ease the oars back onto the rowlocks, new one included, which could have done with another hour to set, and moved the boat around on its axis, so he could look back towards the shore.

At any other time he would most probably have ignored whoever was now standing on the shoreline by the pier, waving a hand towards him. He'd had more than enough visitors for one year, and didn't care if it was the Duke of Sutherland himself standing there. What he never expected to see was the small, stumpy figure of a woman waving at him, holding something up in her other hand, pointing at it to draw his attention, and his pulse quickened suddenly as he realised who it was, and caught the flash of metal in her hand.

Solveig then, and the rest of the Brora bowls. His breath caught within his throat as he saw her picking up a sack and swinging it at him, wanted to shout at her to keep the damn thing still, minimise whatever damage must already have been done, but he wouldn't shout, not here in Scalabsdale, a place where human silence had always had the grace to let the land be.

Solveig saw Tobar out on the loch, his boat almost static, like a black swan with its head curved down into the water, in no hurry to move on, fly or swim, in no hurry at all. She admired this quality in Tobar, his stillness, his ability to make a home here, doing only the minimum to make himself comfortable, his lodgings built of peat and turf, the roofs grassed over with the years so they were almost invisible, like a grouse upon her nest. But she didn't have much time, had taken far longer than was necessary to amble her way up here on Lachlan's laid-back steed, taking pleasure in the calm it gave her, slipping stoat-like from her skin, sloughing off the duties that awaited her down below, of dead men and dead boys, newly emergent mines and brick clamps, the hope of townships resting on her shoulders. She thought she could detect the slight acrid hint of the brick clamp in the afternoon air, and was sorry for it, that it should have reached a place such as this.

She jumped down from Lachlan's horse with a loud scrape of boot on stone, hitched the reins to the hook outside Tobar's cott, and went back to the jetty. She knew she was disturbing him, could see the black shrug of his back, the twitch of his fishing line as he drew it in, and thought for a few moments he was going to ignore her, so she waved out an arm, one of the scraps of the bowls in her other hand, and heard the grudging creak of oars as Tobar turned the boat towards her.

He would have ignored her, she was sure of it, but never the Brora bowls.

247

Sholto's head was hurting, as were his arms where his unnamed companion had pinioned him to his chair back in the chapel, barking out questions, hitting Sholto hard across the face several times when Sholto failed to give up the answers the man required. He knew two teeth had been dislodged from his lower jaw, could feel them wobbling now as he joggled along on this unfamiliar pony, but in truth he'd been so dazed by the whack he'd got from the chapel door when the stranger had entered first, that he'd been unable to answer anything with any clarity, and only now was he beginning to have some idea of what he had been asked, and what, and why, and how he had replied.

The man stayed resolutely behind him, only a yard or two, far enough so as not to impede either animal's passage, close enough to apprehend his captive if Sholto tried to make a break for it. Not that Sholto would have, knowing only the one line between Scalabsdale and Kinbrace, and veering from that line would have meant choosing to be lost in the vast uninhabited wilderness that comprised this part of Sutherland. Two hours in, he knew, and he'd be utterly lost if he went any other direction than the one he was already on, and a single night of exposure to frost and cold would be enough to finish him off.

Like two parallel tracks, the master mast-maker was also ranging his mind over hill and dale. Unlike Sholto, he saw no threat or hostility here, could detect the small threads of paths and terracettes made by sheep and deer, the running of water through heather and stone. He was galvanised by its emptiness, its anonymity, the ease with which a man could be lost in the folds of its terrain, the promise it gave him that escape was his at any time that he chose. Like Tobar, he too heard the timbres of its apparent silence, saw the depths of its underlying nature, the nuances that made of it a living,

248

breathing organism, allowing both him and Tobar to appreciate it in a whole new dimension, as if they saw a sphere, where others saw only a circle.

And as he closed upon the goal of the second great adventure of his lifetime, as he moved within reach of the object on which he had focussed all the pent-up rage, all the impotence, he had felt for so many years at a task left undone, the wilderness pulled at him like the moon tugs the tides, and strong as the urge was to get out there, to escape, explore and survive, stronger still was the need to complete the mission he had set himself, discover the answers he so desperately sought, even if, by their finding, he was destroyed.

'Solveig,' Tobar said as he brought his boat alongside the jetty.

'I've brought you the rest of the bowls,' she said without preamble. 'I'm afraid these last are rather in bits, though I did instruct Lachlan to have them all wrapped separately so they would be the easier for you to reconstruct.'

'Very thoughtful. Thank you, Solveig.' Tobar's reply was a little terse as he looked at the sack she had placed at his feet, thinking that anyone with half a brain would have found a different way to transport such delicate and important objects, would have separated them at site, wrapped up all the bits in sacking and straw, noting which was found where and with what and in what state; they should certainly not have been brought to him all jumbled together in a sack.

'I've hitched up the horse by the croft. I hope you don't mind.' Solveig was apologetic, knew how much the old hermit must value his privacy, and that two visits in as many days might be one too many. 'I thought I could smell something of the brick clamp we broke open recently,' she added. 'We're doing such good work down there. I should maybe take you down to the mines at Brora when you next visit.'

Tobar understood she was trying to be sociable and polite, and that the quickest way to get her out of here was to let her horse rest the half hour it needed before it would be fit to take her back down again to Kinbrace; the sun was getting low and she'd be keen as he was to get her on her way. He was still angry at the interruption, of the tie-fly he had lost because of her noisy approach, wanted, for an awful moment, just to put his hands around her neck and strangle all that noise out of her. And then the feeling passed, for she'd brought the bowls, and so he swept his arm across the threshold of his cott, and waved her in.

Tam Japp finally emerged from the farm with two fast, fit-looking horses. He'd had to swing a few favours to get them, and was still unsure why Brogar was in such urgent need to get up to Scalabsdale, but in urgent need he certainly was, and had flung himself onto his provisioned horse as soon as Tam Japp had procured it, heading off up the brae before he even knew the direction they must go, which was Tam Japp's part in the drama: to lead Brogar there.

Tam didn't understand what was going on, had serious difficulties connecting their disparate parts as Brogar had spelled them out, hitting the index finger of one hand against the fingers of the other to enumerate them, to emphasise their importance:

One: Solveig had gone up to Scalabsdale with the bowls.

Two: Someone had been in the chapel the night before.

Three: Sholto had been in assaulted in the chapel – there was blood there, and some disarray.

Four: Sholto had later taken the last two ponies from the stable before leaving, also in the vague direction of Scalabsdale.

Five: Sholto had left in the company of an unknown man.

What there was in all this that so disturbed Brogar Finn, Tam couldn't quite fathom, nor why just the mention of Solveig's name was making his own skin sweat and flush. It had been happening ever since she'd put her hand on his arm – an involuntary reaction he could no more stop than he could halt the moon from rising, as it was doing now, a ghostly outline in the late afternoon against the cornflower blue of the sky. For why, he was thinking, shouldn't Solveig go to Scalabsdale whenever she liked? And why did Brogar think anyone had been in the chapel? And even if someone had been there it could have been anyone, most likely Gilligan or Hugh or both, larking about, curious about their visitors, about what they were working on, which, God knew, Tam Japp was a little curious about too. And how could Brogar know for sure that Sholto had been assaulted? A little bit of blood didn't mean anything. Sholto could have cut himself, had a nosebleed, brought in a badly gutted fish, and whoever he'd left the steading with didn't seem of such importance either – probably only Moffatt Murchison taking a day off the panning. He'd been pretty shaken up by Andrew's dying, and what better way to settle himself than take a ride up to see his other old friend, Tobar Strabane? Either that, or it was just some random, late-arriving panner wanting to know the quickest way to the Baile an Or. Although even Tam had to admit there was no way Sholto could know the shortcut from Kinbrace to Baile an Or via the track he had left on; the only place he knew it led to must be Scalabsdale.

All in all, it seemed to Tam a bit of brouhaha about nothing, yet he took his duties seriously as he'd always done, and at the moment this was to guide Brogar Finn up to Scalabsdale, and just the thought of seeing Solveig again made his heart tingle within his chest, so he brought his horse up to speed with Brogar's, and together they clattered up the track, scattering pebbles in all directions with their haste, spattering mud over flanks, underbellies, boots

251

and breeches, and Tam Japp was exhilarated by the flight, by the physical exertion, felt a strength and freedom rippling through his muscles that made him think that life could be so much worse than this.

It was three hours, fifty-one minutes after noon when he had that thought, and by the time the sun had begun its descent behind the mountains two hours later, Tam Japp would come to understand just how much worse life really could be.

Chapter 33   *Are patient, and never weak and reckless*

Tobar bade Solveig sit down at his table, began to heat a few bannocks on his griddle, put out some freshly churned butter, two plates, the honey that had been her gift to him, gratified to see how pleased she was that he had already dipped into its sweetness, and gave her a small nod of thanks. He was itching to get his hands on the bowls, unwrap them, get them laid out and sketched and pieced together, absolutely certain they would add weight to his thesis about Helgö trade with this part of Scotland and how far back it really must go. He was already beginning to formulate the words of the paper he would write in his head, the references he would make to the gallowglasses who'd come from Ireland, and the others who'd gone over far earlier, men like John Cunningham, all engaged by the Scandinavian army for their Protestant wars. And then there was the founding of Helmsdale by Viking incomers, and he could maybe quote a little at this point from the old Norse sagas, from some of the medieval texts he had come across in previous research that strengthened the ties between the two countries, the rune stones that were scattered across Scotland and Sweden like twins parted at birth, that the very word *rune* meant *secret*, that there were similar ones on the Brora bowls as those that had been on the Pietrossa ones, namely the ones spelling out the *gutaniniowihailag,* meaning *'those that are sacred to the People of the Goths.'*

He hadn't realised he'd been talking out loud, though it was something he often did, that the words were spilling from him like milk from an overheated pan, his ideas bubbling up and expanding too rapidly to be kept solely in his head. Not until he saw Solveig nodding her head, eyes bright with comprehension, curiosity, and admiration, making her look suddenly so like her father that he almost forgot he'd not clapped eyes on Joseph Lundt for twenty-odd years, and soon he was giving her a brief history lesson about Vardø, Lake Mälaren and Lillon Island; about the wool trade, the iron and the salt and the fish that had been the bridge across which the Scandinavians and the Scottish had passed so freely from one land to the other and back again. And the bowls. He talked about them too, about how they were his absolute proof – even without looking at all the new fragments Solveig had just brought him – of his underlying thesis, that the Scots and the men of Norseland had been mingling blood for almost as long as either of them had been in existence.

'It's going to be such a fascinating piece when you've written it up,' Solveig said with enthusiasm after Tobar had finally run out of breath and historical expiations. 'And you must give me a copy when it's published. Which it will be.' She had flashed him a smile of such confidence that it made her look eleven years old again, which Tobar guessed was the age she had been the last time he had properly talked to her, apart from the night before, when there had been so many others present. 'You've got to go for Blackwoods,' Solveig continued, alluding to the main Edinburgh publishers of academic ideas, the disseminators in Scotland of all the important London and International journals, 'or maybe the Geographical Society. They've got a chapter in Cornwall now,' she said, which snippet of information made Tobar look at her closely. He'd no idea she kept up with such things, though her father had certainly done so; that had been the reason for Tobar's visits to Joseph in the first place, and for all his later contacts with the man, who'd had a mind like a never-ending valley, always seeking out new places to go.

'I want to open a museum,' Solveig then announced. 'I've told no one else, you're the first. But I want there to be a record of this place, a kind of Cabinet of Curiosities of the past of both Brora and Helmsdale and the surrounding valleys. I want to make sure that everything that has happened here doesn't just disappear without a trace.'

The honeyed bannock Tobar had been about to put to his mouth stayed in his hand, kept at half-mast, for some ideas were just too huge, too important, they did not brook interruption, and this was one of them. He'd thought of doing something along similar lines himself, but never with any of the practicality it was obvious Solveig had employed as she laid out the bones of it before him.

'I was thinking we could house it in the old Artillery Hall in Helmsdale, add in my father's mineralogical collection, and all the fossils they've found in the quarry, not to mention everything Reverend Joass found when he came up from Golspie. We could even bring in Hugh Miller's work. Cromarty isn't so far from here, not these days, not with the railway. And then there's the maps, the early ones of this area, and the ones that Roy made for the English military. And there's the bowls,' she added, taking a much needed breath. 'They'd be the centrepiece, and if we don't do something with them they'll just disappear into the Duke's own personal collection, or to some museum in Edinburgh or Glasgow, and we, the people who found them, and to whom they belong, will never see them again.'

Tobar was stunned.

'We'd need backing of course,' Solveig began again, 'but think of all those well-heeled visitors back in the summer...'

Tobar cut her off. 'But this is a marvellous idea!' he said, and by God, he actually meant it. He'd always known he would not be able to hang onto the bowls himself, had always assumed they would disappear, just as Solveig had predicted, into someone else's collection, but this way they could remain forever within his reach. Tobar smiled, really smiled, not the faint simulacrum of the same he'd manufactured earlier at Solveig's intrusion.

This was a smile he truly meant. He stood up, put one hand upon her shoulder.

'I really think this idea has legs,' he said with enthusiasm. 'I really feel it could work, and I think we need to celebrate in style!'

Tobar was so sincere in his approval that he volunteered to get some of his best home-brew to celebrate, and the next words slipped out without thought. 'Only a quick one, mind. I know you need to get back before the sun goes, and we wouldn't want you to go the way of Andrew in his drink, not after such a grand idea.'

As soon as he'd said it, he'd known it was a mistake, and he glanced quickly back at Solveig as he moved away from the table, made his way towards the sheep in their back-room byre. He saw no dimming of the beam upon her face at his words of encouragement, but his hand shook slightly as he put it to the arch, went through into the room beyond that housed all his books and journals, went into his still-room where he kept his most vintage of bottles stashed into caches in the walls, plastered over with mud so the excise men wouldn't find them if they ever happened to call. He chipped away at one of the mud patches with a chisel, extracted a bottle of '63 and returned with it, wondering if he was imagining a slight change to her demeanour, a stiffening of her back, some misgiving in her reaction as he passed her by on his way to the dresser he had cobbled together out of spare planks of rough wood, saw only that the smile she had had before had slipped into something vaguer, exaggerating the lines about her mouth, and the corners of her eyes.

She knows, he thought. *And if she doesn't know it now, she'll figure it out soon enough.*

He took down two thick glass tumblers from a shelf, poured out two drinks, one for himself, one for Solveig, fetched a small jug too, filled it up from a large ewer by the stoneware sink, pushing both glass and jug towards her.

'It's rather strong, I'm afraid,' he said, his voice even, without intonation. 'You'll most likely need a little water with it.'

She looked up at him, took the glass that he offered her, put her other hand about the jug and topped her drink up by a couple of fingers, the strong smell of the home-brewed spirit making her eyes water.

'Best way's to slug it down in one,' Tobar smiled. 'Let it do its work from the inside out. *Air do Shlàinte*,' he said, 'to your good health,' and then he raised his glass to his lips and drained it, watching over the rim as Solveig followed suit and did the same.

Tam Japp was hot, sweating almost as profusely as was his horse, which champed determinedly at its bit as they went, flecks of foam flying from its mouth back onto his jacket as he and Brogar went at breakneck speed up the track; he was thinking this must be what it was like to be a hound going after a hare, or a rabbit trying to outrun a fox. Brogar had slowed only once, when Japp had directed they go up a steep slope to their right to chop a half mile off their journey.

Brogar had been trying to get it all straight in his head, his breath fast but controlled, his heart beating steadily like a war drum, every sense telling him that whatever was happening was coming to a head, had broken through, surging forward with the momentum of a reservoir forcing its way through a chink in its dam. He'd no idea what Sholto might have discovered in the chapel that morning, but he'd begun to add a few things up himself, like Solveig mentioning, on their way down to Brora and the brick clamp, that she'd a feeling she was being watched, and that Sholto had been so sure that someone had been in the chapel the day before, and then there was the blood, the knocked-over chair, the ridiculous proverbs, the allusions to episodes in all their pasts. And he understood that Sholto had been right all along, and

257

everything really did come back to Solveig and that blasted chapel. He heard Tam Japp drawing alongside, his breathing laborious, his face shining with sweat, red as a bullfinch breast in early spring.

'Will y'nae tell me the hurry?' Tam managed to gasp as he came within Brogar's ken, his words coming out in staccato, like floats on a fishing line, Brogar shaking his head, face dark as the sea when it breaks into deep water, mouth set in a hard line, the exertion of the ride stretching his scars on his face into an unnerving pallidity, exaggerated by the water leaking from the sides of his eyes that seemed to seek them out like well-worn, well-travelled chasms, leading down to the blue-black stubble that encased the lower half of his jaw.

'Will y'nae jist tell me?' Tam Japp gasped again, this time putting out his hand, clutching briefly at Brogar's sleeve where it hung loose and unbuttoned from his elbow, and Brogar turned, saw the concern, the bafflement, the panic, in Tam Japp's face.

'It's Solveig,' he said evenly, 'and it's Scalabsdale. She's going there, and so is the man who's already killed three people and has nothing left to lose.'

Tam's horse chose that moment to skid and slip on the sharp incline at the head of the brae, a spray of pebbles kicking out from beneath his hooves, but Tam Japp had heard all he needed and he cursed at the animal, and then chivvied it, and to Brogar's astonishment soon had it coaxed up the edge of the brae and over the lip and was galloping away like a Mongolian herdsman the last few miles up to Scalabsdale, coat tails flapping, arms out at the elbows to give him balance, knees hammering at his horse's flanks like well-oiled pistons, leaving Brogar for once at the tail, hurrying to catch him up.

Sholto's mind had begun to clear at last, like a river beginning to settle after a herd of stampeding cattle had crossed its ford, his thoughts falling into place like shifted, sinking stones. That the man with him was the murderer he understood, though the reasons behind his actions still eluded Sholto. Clearly it all had to do with Solveig, and a notion was trying to surface but getting stuck in all the extraneous information he had read about the Kildonan clearances, and that little snippet of information that had led him to run so precipitately towards the chapel door in the first place. It struck him for the first time that maybe this man had not even known he, Sholto, was in the chapel; he had a blurry memory of him sifting through all the papers on the desk while Sholto was in the chair, though apparently without finding what he was looking for, and that it was only afterwards that he had swept a good many of them to the floor, and turned on Sholto properly. And all his questions, as far as Sholto could recall, had been about one thing and one thing only, and that was Solveig, and about where she was. Several hard slaps in, and Sholto knew he needed to give an answer, his blurry mind finally coming up with Scalabsdale, because he knew it was the one place she couldn't possibly be. And he knew too, that there'd been something odd about the question itself, about how it had been phrased and spoken. And then he had it, like two cogs coming close enough together to find purchase and begin to turn the mechanism they'd been designed for: the man had asked his questions in that odd dialect that was common only to Finnmark, and Sholto, being as fluent in it as apparently was his interlocutor, had answered in the same.

He pivoted a little in his saddle, risked a peek at his captor.

The man was still there two yards behind him, his face turned away from Sholto and from the earth, eyes closed, skin hard and creased as only a man who has spent the whole of his life outdoors can have, neck craned upwards, as if he were communing with the sky. And Sholto looked around him, saw the hills rimming the horizon, the great blue canopy of the sky coming right

259

down to the ground as if to keep all within it safe, saw the strange white lines of clouds edging into pink as they began to coalesce, change colour, starting to glow as they absorbed the light of the falling sun.

'Why did you kill them?' he asked suddenly, the words out of his mouth before he had properly thought them through. The man's eyes opened, latched straightaway onto Sholto's, gave him an odd look that was midway between curiosity and consternation, as if an ant he had been about to step on had suddenly opened its mandibles and asked him unexpectedly for directions. He dipped his chin, chivvied at the reins although his pony had neither slowed its pace nor begun to wander from its path. He took a long while to answer, maybe, Sholto thought, weighing up how much he should say, or perhaps trying to devise a reason that anyone else but himself could understand. When finally he spoke, his voice was like gravel catching in a dredge.

'People are just people,' he said. 'Who knows why anyone does anything?'

It was hardly the definitive confession of guilt Sholto had been hoping for, and he felt obscurely as if he had been ticked off, as if he had somehow missed the obvious.

'But why the boy?' he persisted, and thought he saw a twitch at the corner of the man's mouth, which could have signified anything from humour through to disgust, though for some reason Sholto chose to interpret it as the latter. Half a minute passed before the man answered.

'What is any boy,' said the master mast-maker, 'but the disappointment of the man he is yet to become?'

And then the man seemed suddenly to come awake, and with no warning his hand went down to the knife that lay scabbarded upon his thigh, and Sholto saw the sharp, cruel blade flashing with its upward thrust, heard the whistle it made as it cut the air beside his ear, had no time to register fear, felt only the

260

warm trickle of urine begin to track its way down the inside of his trouser leg, and had the unpleasant sensation that his blood was curdling within his veins, and then the man and his knife were surging past him, his mount urged into an uneven gallop, his knees whacking again and again at its sides and whipping the spare length of his reins upon its neck so hard that they broke the skin, drew beads of blood along its hide.

Sholto looked, but did not see, looked again, saw only the loch of Scalabsdale emerging from its surroundings, a perfect calm upon its surface, broken only by the boat that was being pushed out from its pier.

Solveig couldn't believe how strong the drink was that Tobar had given her, but was aware that her eyelids had begun to droop, that she was no longer capable of opening her mouth, that her limbs no longer felt joined to her body; she could see her own hand lifting from the table as she tried to make it work, saw it idly move from east to west and back again as if she was trying to make a point that had not been properly understood. The only other time she'd felt like this was back when she'd had the mumps when she was maybe thirteen, and had been confined to bed and sedated, had found herself in a world of white that was something like clouds, but much more solid, and something like soft strings wrapping themselves around her, making her believe she'd been confined to an interminable limbo she was powerless to find a way out of, no matter how far she roamed its immeasurable and unmarked landscape. Her head lolled back upon her neck, and she felt arms going beneath her shoulders and thanked God someone was here to take care of her; she thought it might be her father, though she knew at the same time this could not be so, and yet was thankful for the contact, the support, all the same.

Tobar lifted Solveig as gently as he could, trying not to jog her from the false slumber he had imparted to her in the water she had added to her drink. He wished he didn't have to do this, not to her, not to Joseph's daughter, but she'd not given him any choice. Or rather, *he'd* not given himself any choice, not once he'd mentioned the wine Andrew had drunk the night he died, which was something he couldn't possibly have known unless it had been him who had placed it just outside Andrew's door, waiting for someone to bring it in to him, as someone patently had. And whether or not Solveig had realised the import of his words when he'd spoken them, he knew she would realise it soon enough, and all would be over, though not in the way he desired.

He carried her out to the jetty, laid her down with as much care as he could into the base of the boat, and used the bit and brace that was fortuitously to hand to bore out several holes, plugging them with mud scooped from the foreshore and thickened by the gum he had used to stabilise the new rowlock. He took no pleasure in this task, this final murder, but wondered why he'd not thought to do it at the start. He'd assumed that several random, non-accidental deaths in the vicinity of the coal mines and gold fields would be enough for the Sutherlands to take a closer look, realise what Solveig was doing, and shut the whole operation down. He supposed he'd been a little sentimental in not doing away with Solveig in the first place, for she was the prime mover, the only mover, the sole motivation behind this regeneration of Brora and the surrounding valleys. But there'd been all that history between him and her father that had stopped him from that path, for Joseph had been a truly great man. Misguided, no doubting that, but a great man nonetheless, and one who'd had the courage to go to all the places Tobar had once wanted to go to himself. And The Pick, that had been all Joseph's idea, and had been a great one, whether you agreed with it or not.

262

And so it was with regret that he gave the boat a hefty shove out into the currents of the loch, watched it drifting slowly, spinning slightly, heading towards the deepest water, knowing that the plugs of mud would soon dissolve and the water would come in, and the boat would sink, taking Solveig with it. But *Beiridh caora geal ua dhub* – another Gaelic proverb, he couldn't stop himself – a white ewe may have a lamb that is black, and the highest of plans could have the harshest of results, and what was this but such an exigency now? This land, that had been silence and pulchritude for as long as it had existed, did not want, nor need, the disfigurement of mines or clay-pits or brickworks or salt-panners, did not need the gold diggers, did not need people of any kind. His father had been right to put his own Big Plan to the Duke, and the Duke had been right to take him up on it: clearing off the human herd from the valleys and shifting them out to the coast had been the best thing that could have been done; the Estate had provided them with houses, profitable labour, schools for their children, a chance at a far better life than they would ever have had up the glens. Tobar was only carrying on what his father had not been able to finish; he saw himself as the Overseer of Justice for a wilderness that could not act for itself. He'd nothing in common with likes of Patrick Sellar and his ilk, with their impatient methods, and was not acting out of cruelty or for personal gain. All he wanted was to correct the balance that the wilderness had lost due to the importunate intervention of men – and now women – who should never have been there in the first place. An accounting right and simple, a measuring up of what was valuable and what was not, a separation of the wheat from the chaff.

That was all he was doing, because someone had to do it, and he knew there was no one left to do it but him.

Chapter 34   *Because soon comes storm and darkness*

As the stranger passed him by, knife held high, strong legs straddled about his pony, knees going like a bellows at its flanks, Sholto knew this should be his chance for flight, to turn his own pony round and hightail it back to Kinbrace for reinforcements, though his proximity to Scalabsdale rendered such an escape without practical purpose, and would provide him none of the answers to all the questions that he had shifting about inside him like grains of sand in a glass. And the look on that man's face, as he had passed Sholto by, had not been one of murder, but rather of intense anxiety, as if his wife, or a best beloved Gelert dog, was about to be slaughtered right before his eyes. And it came to Sholto just how many unwarranted assumptions he had made regarding what had been going on at Kildonan and the Suisgill, that all had shaky legs at best, and no legs at all at worst, and that the man who had so ill-treated him in the chapel might have had a far more complex motive than simple murder on his mind. The man had spoken Russenorsk, and was hardly likely to have a strong grasp of Gaelic proverbs, and it was an even further stretch to believe he would know anything of either suicidal geologists or the archaeology of Icelandic shovels, any more than would the panners who hacked at the banks of the Suisgill and chapped their hands day after day, month after month, in freezing water, for a few specks of golden dust.

And now that he thought of it properly, now that his mind had actually cleared, there was really only one man in this entire fiasco who was even remotely likely to be acquainted with the holy trinity of Gaelic, geologists, and obscure runes, and that man was certainly not the same one who had beaten him up in the chapel. Moreover, said beater-upper, his captor, his erstwhile suspected assassin, had looked at the loch as they had rounded the

264

corner, and seen what? What was it that he had seen that had made him take off in such fury and fandango? Sholto looked again, shielded his eyes, could make out the shape of a boat drifting out onto the water, a boat that was yawing heavily to one side, obviously beginning to take on water. And then the hairs rose up on the back of his neck as he detected a flash of white nestled within the boat, and then he too kicked and kicked at the flanks of his own pony with such a cruelty he never thought he could possess, as reason and understanding swept over him, and swept away all the false towers of probability he had constructed, as easily as the sea sweeps away a badly constructed castle of sand.

The master mast-maker did not let up until he reached the lakeside, and even then he did not stop, but slewed his pony round to the left towards the nearest landfall to the boat, his feet kicking free from their stirrups, his body slipping off the saddle when he judged it most propitious, the pony galloping on with its own momentum, with the sudden freedom from its troublesome burden from whom he'd received such ill-treatment in the last ten minutes than he had done in the rest of his life. The man who had been on his back skidded down the brae towards the water, wrenching off his coat as he did so before flinging himself in. The cold of the loch was so intense it made his ears hum with the sudden change in temperature, his muscles contracting into agonising cramps, but he closed his mind to this physical distress and ploughed on at the water like a harrow through a field. He'd been in colder waters than these, he told himself, had swum, once or twice, amongst ice floes after a sauna, dunked himself halfway into an ice-hole to pull up a sturgeon, knew the pain and panic his body was registering was only temporary, that if he could just concentrate, focus his mind, he could reach his goal.

The boat was taking on water fast, was half submerged now, tipping over as Solveig's inert body rolled with the momentum, one edge bobbing now below the surface and then out again, lipping at the water as if testing it, tasting it, deciding whether to stay or go full in. The master mast-maker knew he didn't have much time, that he was still too far away, but he forced himself onwards anyway, tried to think himself into being a beaver cutting through the water with as much ease as he knew his knife could cut through flesh. He forced off his right boot with the toe of his left, but could not dislodge the remaining one, and felt heavy, lopsided, heard his body gasping, his arms as they flailed and fought, saw the right side of the boat as it ducked beneath the water, the cold touching Solveig's chin, her cheek, hoped it would check her slumber, force her body to react, her skin to tingle, her eyes to open; but then the boat keeled right over and she was in the water, sinking one foot, two foot, her body reorienting involuntarily towards its centre of gravity, trapping her beneath the upturned carapace of the sinking boat.

Solveig's eyes opened. Her throat was filled with water, her lungs squeezing shut, her first sensation being an intolerable constriction about her chest, a kind of internal claustrophobia that forced her limbs into action, though without conscious purpose or direction; her skirts were heavy and intractable, wrapping around her legs like weighted ropes, the outer layer of her apron floating up into her face, though only slowly, slowly, as everything seemed to her to be. Everything slow. And everything fore-concluded, as if the fight – if there had ever been one – was already done.

The master mast-maker surged forward, his urgency making him stronger than he had ever been before as he fought against the unwieldiness of his body, the struggle he was having being half in water, half in air, a struggle he broke by ducking down below the surface, eyes open, straining for any sign of Solveig, could make out a vague paleness somewhere up ahead, like a sheet undulating in the wind, saw it sink, saw it go three feet down, then four, then five, until he could no longer hold himself under, had to come up for air, went at the water like a paddle steamer, flapping his arms up and down, up and down, before going back below again, a heavy bodied duck, one that usually feeds at the surface and doesn't understand the mechanisms of diving, doesn't have the gannets' way of swimming beneath the water, saw a fast disappearing maelstrom of bubbles as the boat came down after Solveig, sinking quickly, its bulk a dark shadow that divided him from her.

Sholto arrived at the lochside. He was panting hard, drenched with sweat, as was his pony, his saddle swivelling off to one side as the girth straps loosened, sending him plummeting to the ground as soon as the pony came to a halt and reared its head, switched its back, nickering in protest, or maybe for its mate, which had finally come to rest at the top curve of the loch by the far burn, and was hunkered down now onto its knees, dipping its head into the water to free itself from the green-flecked foam that was so abundant about its nostrils it might have dipped its head into a vat of fermenting beer.

Out in the loch, Solveig was still sinking, heading for the silt and the mud and the toads that had buried themselves there for the winter, where the flatfish lay waiting for their food to waft down to them, anything dead, anything dying, but nothing as large as Solveig, nor the catastrophe that was bringing her their way. The master mast-maker, whose name was Yevgeny Constanenko, had had to surface again, had managed to loosen the laces of his last boot with unwieldy fingers, kick it off with a furious shaking of his leg, before going back down again beneath the water, but was now disoriented, had lost all sight of the vague form of Solveig, pushing himself on anyway, but could not find her. Up again he had to go, take a breath, took the time to study the water's surface, spying out the circle of bubbles where the boat had gone down – where she had gone down – and pushed himself towards it, submerged himself, could at last make out the shell of the boat moving below him through the water, oh so slowly, saw its keel, saw one oar coming free, one rowlock detaching from its wooden body as the new glue gave, saw the bit and brace that had been in the boat's hold floating away with balletic grace as they passed from one state of life into another, from usefulness into rust.

What he could not see was Solveig herself behind the swirls and eddies of the silt churned up by the sinking of the boat and his own frantic movements to reach her, nor did he witness the boat's farthest edge coming down hard on the side of Solveig's head, nor the simultaneous look of comprehension and dread that passed over her face as her mind was finally, unkindly, kicked into gear by that blow, and the stress and the panic caused by that comprehension making every part of her body yell out to her, scream at her, that she should not, could not, be here, and that she wouldn't last much longer if she stayed. Nor did he know that, in her final moments, she could taste her own blood as it flowed past her like a cloud, a medusa, flowing freely from the gash in her head where the boat had hit her, nor what she saw, as she passed from blue to green and then to brown, as she sank to the bottom of the loch, all the incoherent flits of memory that flashed across her mind like the bats she had so often seen flying beneath the dark eaves of her father's chapel, nor the blueness of the afternoon she knew she had just left, but could not account for leaving, nor of the faces she saw, like they were just there, right in front of her, of her mother, and her father, and Moffatt Murchison, his mouth moving, understanding the words she could not hear, and that life – think on that kitten – was always threaded through with death, and she was not the only one to go before her time. And then another face, one she did not recognise, and a hard tug at her collar, and she understood that she was going upwards, felt herself being dragged, thought she could see for just one moment the bluest of blue skies, orange clouds stacking in that weird way they sometimes did here, like puffy plates as they drifted off the mountains, making of themselves something extraordinary, new and perfect, and so beautiful she would have given anything, anything at all, to see them again.

Sholto landed badly, couldn't get his breath, felt all the ribs on his left side cracking with the fall, tried to roll himself to sitting but couldn't manage it, had only glimpses of heather, of cotton grass, of the reeds, of the jetty, of the boiling to its left where Tobar kept his cage of fish. He heard footsteps coming slowly towards him, heard them stop just a few inches from his head. It was Tobar, he recognised his boots, his quietly stertorous manner of breathing, and he understood that Tobar was not here to help him, nor to help the two people stranded out there in the loch, that Tobar would let them sink and drown, and that if they weren't able to manage this simplest of acts all by themselves, he was damn well going to make sure it was done, one way or another. And Sholto knew too that he was not going to get out of this easy either, that this would be his last moment, his last sight of the world, and he tried to draw it all within himself, like a man dying of thirst in the desert tries to drink in the sand, because that's all he's got left.

Yevgeny surfaced.

His lips were blue, his face contorted from lack of air, but he was sure he had her, sure he'd caught her clothing in his hand, had wound the material about his fist, about his wrist, dragging and dragging her upwards; she'd been so far down, and so heavy with all the water in her clothes, but by God, he knew he had her within his grasp, and all he needed do now was to get her head above the water, get her back to shore, pump her lungs, get some air in there, jumpstart her back into life. He'd seen it done a hundred times, but was exhausted from being in the cold of the loch, and was too long without oxygen, could only tread the water with desperation, just to keep them both from sinking. He needed help, and he needed it now, or they'd both be back on the bottom of the lake for good.

'Help!' he shouted, the water flooding into his mouth as he went under. 'Help!' he shouted again, surfacing briefly, his arm wavering beneath Solveig's neck as he struggled to keep them both afloat.

'Help!' he tried one last time, knew he didn't have much left in him, that the cold was seizing his limbs up inch by inch, tried to turn himself towards the jetty, looking for the man who had brought him here, who must surely have realised by now that he was not the enemy, that he was trying to help. He saw a shape by the cottage door, a man standing immobile, staying that way even when another surged up on his pony to the jetty, slumping to one side, crashing off onto the ground and staying there.

The water began to seep and gargle at the back of his throat as he recognised the idiot who had fallen off his mount. It was Sholto – not that he knew his name, only that he was the companion of the man he had been tracking ever since he had left Archangel, the Company Man who had led him to Solveig – and he saw the man from the cottage finally approaching Sholto, one of the ones who had been at Solveig's steading a couple of nights before, and would have breathed a sigh of relief if he'd been able, could only lift his hand above his head to give the signal, hope he'd been seen. And then his arm fell back to the water's surface as he saw that second man raise his boot, give Sholto several vicious kicks to head and chest, before turning calmly back towards Yevgeny, towards Solveig and the loch, and he knew then that all hope of rescue and explanation was lost, and there was nothing to do now but give himself up to Joseph's God, and hope that Joseph himself would be there on the other side to greet him – assuming there was another side, which he was not at all sure of. But if there was, and if he got there, and if Joseph really was there too, he prayed that Joseph would look kindly on Yevgeny for this final act of loyalty, in the sure and certain knowledge that he had tried his hardest, had tried as hard as any man can do, to bring his daughter home.

Brogar hit the corner of the track that brought him into sight of the loch with the masterful panache of a Himalayan horseman who has been doing this all his life. He coursed it with ease, leaning into the curve and then out again, took in the scene with the speed of a peregrine bearing down upon a field mouse tucked within two running lines of corn, saw in a flash there was someone struggling out in the loch, maybe ten or fifteen yards from shore, saw two heads bobbing there, an arm being raised only to fall again a moment later, saw them both disappear briefly below the surface, coming up again a few seconds later, slightly further in. He also saw a crumpled form curled up by the jetty, and knew it to be Sholto by that shock of white that ran so neatly through the other darkness of his hair, and saw Tobar there beside him, saw Tobar raise his boot and give Sholto a serious kick to first his head and then his chest, saw Tobar stumble briefly, but recover, walking fast towards the jetty, picking up a boat hook, jogging off around the loch towards where the other unknown man was now sinking out in its depths, struggling to keep some burden afloat, assumed that burden must be Solveig, and knew that if Tobar got to them before he did, then the outcome would

271

not be good. Exactly what was going on, he had no idea, no idea who was struggling in the loch, nor why Solveig was out there too, nor how she had got into such difficulty, nor why Tobar had turned on Sholto. But the fact that he had was enough for Brogar. He'd never been much good at sums, but knew right enough that two and two added up to four, and that whatever it was Tobar had in mind to do with his boat hook needed to be stopped.

Tam Japp had only been ahead of Brogar for maybe fifty yard before the man overtook him, saw him take the corner with a grace he could not muster, had even less notion than had Brogar about what was happening, but understood from Brogar's previous conversation that Solveig might be in trouble, might be out there in the middle of nowhere with the same man who had murdered Willie Blaine and the boy Robbie Weavers, and Andrew the storesman. He'd not been friends with any of them, indeed had his own reasons for actively disliking the first two, but all three had been in some way within his bailiwick, and more and more he had become ashamed that neither he, nor the Estate he supposedly represented, had done anything to apprehend the man who had caused them to die. Worse than that, they had shoved the onus of such a task upon the shoulders of someone as estimable as Solveig McCleery, who alone was trying to drag this entire area up by its bootstraps, make of it a living place as it had been before all that clearance shite, when everyone had been driven down one Destitution Road or another, a time when his own father had only managed to hang on by the skin of his teeth, and only because he'd been one of the best shearers of sheep in the area, and shearers of sheep were a commodity the Estate, especially after the clearances, had been in dire need of.

Please God, let her be all right. Please God, let her be all right.

272

There was nothing else in the world that seemed to matter to Tam now but the plea of that refrain, and although he'd never been much of a praying man, he swore that if this one prayer was answered, he would carry on being a praying man until the day he died.

Sholto's breastbone had been almost snapped in two with the force of Tobar's kick, and together with the ribs he'd cracked on his plummet from the pony, every breath he took gave him a pain so intense he wished he didn't have to do it at all, but bodies are built for life and rarely give up without a fight, even in the worst of circumstances, and so it was for Sholto now, every moment an agony that expanded and sharpened, becoming more excruciating with every breath he took, but still trying to get up there, still trying to fight, though all he had managed was to make Tobar tumble briefly, cost him barely thirty seconds, before he had begun running on around the loch.

Yevgeny Constanenko inhabited that same universe of pain Sholto did. His hand still gripped Solveig's clothing as if tightened by a vice, would not let her go, not even when her weight began to drag him down and the water began to fill his throat again, and he began to sink below the surface as if the loch was swallowing him as he was swallowing the loch. His world became green and slow, a pressure building in his eardrums and chest until he thought he must implode with it, the silent stream of silver bubbles from his mouth decreasing, and then ceasing altogether, giving him a view of the water and the delicate tracery of Solveig's hair as it freed itself from its pins, unveiling her face that was so close to his own, and he could see how white it was, how filled it was with dread, which sight spurred him into one final kick, one final push, and he broke the surface one last time, felt the moment

273

stretching on as if the loch itself was trying to spit him out, give him one last chance, managed to manoeuvre the crook of his arm about Solveig's neck and heave her one more yard towards the shore, two more yards, was almost within reach, could feel the soft spray of shingle moving just beyond the tips of his toes and let himself sink so that finally he was touching ground, could get some air into his lungs if he craned his neck back as far as it would go, saw the curvature of the loch at the periphery of his vision, the circle of the moors that held the loch, the wider crenellations of the mountains that held the moors, the broad dome of the sky above that held them all. And then, from that sky, a dark shape came down at him, knocked him senseless, and he lost his grip on Solveig, and on both their lives.

Brogar got to the pier, got to Sholto, shouted something Sholto could not understand as he went hell for leather around the side of the loch, just as Yevgeny had done before him. Brogar had seen that Sholto was still alive, could tell it by the lines that contorted his face, the tears of pain that pricked his eyes, the slick of sweat upon his cheeks, but Brogar had already seen Tobar lifting up his boathook, bringing it back down hard upon the drowning man who had miraculously managed to get within three yards of the shore, and rode his horse directly at Tobar, though Tobar did not flinch, did not move, was totally consumed by his task. As Brogar's horse drew level with Tobar he did not try to halt it, but threw out his strong hand, his closed fist catching Tobar on the side of his neck, knocked him flying, him and his boathook, which dropped down halfway onto shingle, halfway into reed. It took Brogar thirteen long seconds to rein in his horse and get it turned, by which time Tobar was already back on his heels, had grasped again at the boathook, was hefting it up in his hands, flinging it out like a fishing spear at the man who was only one part out of the surface of the loch, only the top of his head to be seen, like a log that has soaked in too much water and sunk to the perpendicular, just the diameter of its cut edge remaining visible. This time Brogar was not kind, held out his bunched fist and rammed it straight into the side of Tobar's head like a jouster as he passed him by, had the satisfaction of seeing Tobar slump down onto his knees at the blow, and then fall forward, face down, in the mud. Brogar pulled hard at the reins, whoaed the horse to a standstill, dismounted, ran the short distance back, grabbed the boathook that was still lying in Tobar's flaccid hand, and took it up, flung it out into the water to where the man had gone down, could only hope it would meet its mark, and that the man at the other end had enough wit left, enough strength to grasp it, keep a hold of it, and allow Brogar to pull himself, and Solveig with him, to land.

Chapter 35   *When all that is fleeting is turned to waste*

Darkness fell over Scalabsdale, the kidney-shaped loch calm and serene, impervious to the earlier human shenanigans of drowning men and sinking boats that had churned up the mud and pebbles of its banks. A few ripples emanated from the fish that still swished without haste beneath its surface, displacing the reflection of the deep night sky and the dim light of its stars.

Yevgeny and Solveig were up in Tobar's croft house, the only other point of light within the compass of moor and mountain, Brogar and Sholto with them, huddled in various manners about the table, and on the small cot bed by Tobar's fire. Tobar was there too, trussed like a chicken, arms and ankles securely tied to a chair, his nose feeling as if it had been hit by a mallet, the bone and cartilage of its bridge crushed beneath Brogar's fist. There'd been a few moments, lying face down in the mud, his blood flowing freely, bubbling up with every breath he'd fought to take, when Tobar had thought his life was bound to end. The only reason that hadn't happened became apparent after Tobar had gagged out the mud he had swallowed, and had been able to turn his head towards the loch, and seen Brogar struggling with the boathook, a single hand emerging with it at the other end, which had sent Brogar hurtling, splashing, stamping into the water, right up to his waist, and then to his chest as he hauled at his catch, struggling with it like a hardened whaler, and finally bringing it to shore.

Tobar couldn't move in his chair, and his vision was reduced to a pulpy, red-tinged and foreshortened landscape, shot through with stars that shouldn't be there. The bruises about his eyes and nose had begun the moment Brogar had hit him at the lochside, and had carried on their oedemic swelling unabated, throbbing in time with the beat of his heart. He could hear them talking, the

276

occasional clink of a glass as one or other of his unwanted companions helped themselves to his drink; he was hoping they might all avail themselves of the same small jug of water Solveig had already made use of, into which he had added the tasteless, odourless ether solution whose specifics he had gleaned from a publication, in 1858, a copy of John Snow's treatise, *On Chloroform and other Anaesthetics.* Unfortunately, the still conscious Sholto McKay had raised the alarm, pointing out with a perspicuity he had not credited the man with on earlier meetings, that Tobar had a still, and that a still could be used to manufacture many more things than mere moonshine and bootlegged whisky, and so the jug had been found, the final proof, if any were needed, of his guilt.

'Tobar.'

Tobar twitched at the mention of his name, realised he must have been, if not exactly sleeping, then not awake either, his mind roaming freely, maybe trying to extricate him from the pain his body was going through, from all the bruises Brogar had inflicted on him until he had spilled out every last bean, every last secret, all the stuff he had tried so hard to keep hidden.

'Tobar.' The voice was more insistent this time, and he felt a flight of air pass by his cheek, thought he was about to be hit again, but it was only a moth, passing him by, and through his tiny slice of vision he saw a glass being pushed towards his lips, his head being tipped backwards, could see the administering hand on the horizon of his vision, the one without nails that had caused him such pain, wondered when he'd even had time to notice such a thing, reminding him that the human brain was a splendour beyond compare.

'It's no use,' he heard the blunt-fingered man saying. 'He's still not come round.'

Could be so, thought Tobar, though realised it was not so simple, that he was on some kind of brink, could push himself one way or the other, whichever he chose, and that however badly things had gone for him, he was still in control.

'No,' said another voice, with a finality that brooked no contradiction, had a creak to that single word that sounded like tree branches bending over in high wind, and sent a shiver right down Tobar's spine. 'He's drinking,' the creaky voice continued. 'Can only do that when you've a mind to do it.'

'That's right, is it, Sholto?' said the blunt-fingered man, whose name suddenly popped into Tobar's head, astonished he had forgotten it. Brogar Finn. The man who had brought this whole set of actions into play by his arrival, for no matter how hard Solveig might have tried at her schemes of industry and revival, of noise and smoke and mess and people, she could never have done it on her own, but when the Company became involved, even peripherally, that, Tobar knew, would have been the beginning of the end.

Tobar coughed, couldn't help himself, wanted to spit himself out of this world, away from this unwanted company, had such a craving for solitude he almost wept, realised that what he should have done was not go around murdering people, but withdraw further into the wilderness, taking his books, his animals, with him, and made a whole new home away back in the hills. Too late now. Far too late. He had lost everything, had achieved nothing. And then he did weep, and the sound was terrible in that small space, and everyone turned towards it, even Sholto, for whom every breath was an enemy, every movement an agony, couldn't help himself, feeling as if that keening was coming from them all, seeping from the walls of the cott, as if it were the entirety of the world.

'God's sake, Brogar,' Sholto managed to whisper. 'Make him stop.'

278

And Brogar did, picked up Tobar, chair and all, and kicked the cottage door open with his boot, depositing Tobar outside in the coldness of the night where he could howl at the moon for as long as he wanted without disturbing the rest of them, and had Brogar been in taiga or tundra or any one of a hundred other places where he would not have been held accountable, he would have hurled Tobar, trussed as he was, straight into the loch.

Tam Japp had been sitting on Tobar's peat seat by the jetty, looking up into the stars, eyes wet, throat tight, unable to get out all the emotions that were battering around within his chest. He saw the uneven square of light as Brogar came through the door with his burden in his arms, a burden he hefted without compassion, walking with it twenty yards or so out back of the main building towards the outhouses, thumping it down in the heather, allowing it to tilt, and fall, leaving Tobar like a shot ptarmigan waiting for retrieval, an image strengthened by the sounds coming from Tobar's throat, a low, harsh croaking that grated, repeated, grackled in the stillness of the night.

Tam Japp didn't know how long he'd been sitting here, only that his face was numb with cold, and with the inability to deal with the emotions that had been flooding through him ever since Solveig had been dragged out of the loch. He thought back on those spare moments when he'd finally arrive at the lochside, Sholto McKay groaning in a shrivelled heap, Brogar riding off to rescue a man whose name he later learned was Yevgeny Constanenko, a man who had known Solveig's father, a man who had been prepared to give up his life to save Solveig's, and who, before Brogar got there out of nowhere, had already chosen to go down with her rather than let her go alone.

No one could have accused Tam Japp of being a philosopher. He was literate, but only to the extent that he could carry out his job with some efficiency. He'd never read a book, knew nothing of the great tales of heroism offered

279

up by the legends and myths of every continent, but he recognised the trope just the same in this Yevgeny Constanenko, and had understood that he, plain Tam Japp, was less than a shadow in comparison, a hedge sparrow to his harrier, a pull of sheep's wool caught upon the heather while this man soared above him in every way. Tam Japp's abjection was not diminished by the fact that Solveig would never know of it, that he could never speak of it, that the chastisement, the guilt, he felt because he had not been a part of her rescue, which was absolute.

He had arrived at the jetty just as Brogar's boathook had brought Yevgeny Constanenko back into the air, his hand still gripping at Solveig's collar, trying to push her head above the water; and he had been running towards them even as Brogar had stampeded in to aid them both, thrusting his strong hands towards them, catching at their clothes, dragging them back towards the shallows, hauling them out onto the shingle on the edge of the loch. Tam had been ten yards distant when Yevgeny had started spluttering, coughing, retching, and Brogar had gone down on his knees at Solveig's side, slamming his fist into her chest again and again and again,, and he had reached them just as Brogar ceased his attempts, Tam starting to shout, to protest, though had no idea what he had said, remembered only that Brogar had turned to look up at him, and could still see the slow shaking of his head, which meant that all was lost.

And then had come the miracle Tam Japp had been praying for, and Solveig's body suddenly spasmed, and came back to life, wracking and croaking and vomiting out water from every part of her, from every pore, every orifice, but alive all the same.

Yevgeny had believed her long past help that last time he had tried to heave her up, but still he had not let her go. He knew he should have abandoned her dead weight, tried to save himself, but he could not, had been unable to

280

relinquish his last hold on Joseph's life, on Joseph's daughter's life, no matter that it would mean relinquishing his own. No matter that twenty-four hours earlier he had been prepared to beat the same woman black and blue in order to get out of her all she must know about Joseph, and of the legacy that was Yevgeny's due. For at the moment he'd entered the water, after all his days and nights of watching and waiting, everything about this woman had suddenly crystallised, and he'd known that no daughter of Joseph Lundt – and certainly not Solveig – would have abandoned him, and that there must have been good reason why the Holy Apostolic Church had never acknowledged either of them, never published proof of all their journeys, and all the hardships they had suffered together. And so he had held on to her, and onto this new belief that somehow everything still had a chance to matter, to be explained.

He shivered violently beneath the blankets Brogar had thrown about his shoulders, and despite the fire Brogar soon had roaring in the grate, it seemed to Yevgeny that he could not get any warmer, that he had a chill deep inside his guts that he could never be rid of. He had heard of men who had fallen into the sea that moved languid and cold against the snow-clinched cliffs of the Kola Peninsula, men who had been brought out alive but who expired the next day, or the one following; men who were unable to absorb the heat that their fellows had tried to smother them with, as if the piles of furs thrown upon them were not there to vanquish the cold, but to keep it in. And his jaw ached with the chattering of his teeth, but he could no more stop them than he could have jumped up and danced a jig, and the strong drink Brogar had tried to administer to him had spilled not down his throat, but down his chin. He looked over to where Solveig was lying like a statue on the makeshift bier Brogar had created for her by bringing in three bales of hay from Tobar's barn, and he thought of the times she had spent in vigil beside other corpses, on other hay bales in other barns, and was glad that in some small measure, he was at least able to return to her the favour – not that Solveig was dead, not yet, but she was still unconscious after her dramatic coughing and retching on the shore, and he knew what damage could be done to a person so long under the water, and sent up his prayers, hoping that the morning would bring better news.

So much had been explained to him in the few hours he had been here after having been dragged out of the loch with Solveig, her pinafore still wrapped about his wrist; how Brogar Finn and Sholto McKay had been sent by the Company, following Solveig's plea for help with the gold rush at Kildonan; how she had inveigled Brogar, once arrived, to give her advice on the coal mines and quarries nearby that had been closed for decades. And how much like her father she had been, and how little both he and she must have known it, and how much he hoped he could tell her of her father. And he thought how stupid and bull-headed he had been to have come in stealth and guile; he should just have arrived as a mere stranger from the past, knocking on her door, asking for her help, for surely she would have offered it freely. That much he knew now, and the fact that he had misjudged Solveig so grievously was a deeper pain to him than the cold in his belly.

It had been terrible to witness Brogar interrogating the murderer Tobar, for had an expertise that had been frightening in its efficiency, even for a man as hardened as Yevgeny Constanenko, but from it they had all learned a great deal. Brogar had elicited the whys and wherefores of all the murders, and of how Tobar had done his research as soon as he'd heard that Company men were coming to help out Solveig, spending three days going through all the back-issues of every journal he owned – which were many – looking for references to both Finn and McKay, whose names he'd learned from the Sutherland factor with whom he'd been on good terms for many years. He'd also gone through all the reports he still got from Lundt and McCleery's Pan-European Mining Company, and eventually found what he was looking for, and used their presence to his advantage and his own ends.

So much information, Yevgeny had thought, and yet the most important had come from the chest-cracked Sholto, whose facial bruises Yevgeny himself had inflicted earlier that afternoon.

'Yevgeny,' he'd said later on that night, after Yevgeny had spoken of Joseph's travels and his part in them, of the Holy Apostolic Church, of the Church's Register of Beliefs that had been compiled from missionaries such as Joseph, tramping and recording all over the world, and how Joseph had promised Yevgeny his due for them, his name in print, a copy sent to him from the Church's headquarters in London, how it had been the last thing Joseph had ever promised Yevgeny when Joseph had taken off alone to follow his urge for home, for his daughter, an urge that had been so overwhelming it had eclipsed even Yevgeny, Joseph's faithful companion, translator, and disciple, for so many years; Yevgeny had been left behind without purpose, thrown away like an outworn boot in the mud.

'Yevgeny,' Sholto had creaked out. 'You should know that it's there, it's in the chapel,' and he went on to tell of the satchel he had found stashed with all the rest, the stamps on it from the Faroes, Shetland, another from Orkney, the last from Wick, as the package was shuttled its long route from Iceland to Joseph's home.

Joseph Lundt had left Archangel for Iceland in March 1855, as soon as the first whalers were ready for the off. Sholto couldn't yet understand how it had taken almost ten years for the folder, the register, this Index of Beliefs Yevgeny and Joseph had laboured so hard and for so many years to compile, to reach its destination, but what he did know was that the Helmsdale Office of Post had received it on the 11th of May, 1864, and therein must lie the reason that Solveig had overlooked it, had just put it away with all the rest of her father's belongings, for that was the same year, the same month, that Elof John McCleery, Solveig's husband, had died.

Later, much later, Sholto would learn about the volcanic eruptions in Iceland that had begun at 8.43 a.m. on the morning of the 2nd of September, 1855, and not ceased for another seven months, declared officially over on the 5th of April, 1856. Soon after he wrote to the mayor of every town in Iceland, having learned the basics of the language for the task, eventually pinning down Joseph's route, where he had started, where he had ended up, and was given the name of one Lilija Indridsdottir, to whom he had written his final letter, and got the reply he'd long sought, as had Yevgeny. And this letter told them that Joseph had perished in Storofshvoll on that first morning of the eruption, and that several years later she'd found what remained of Joseph's journal and Index of Beliefs, and had bundled it up, addressed it with sparsity to *The Lundt Family, Helmsdale, Scotland,* sending it off with some fishermen, in the vague hope it would reach the Bean Counter's home. And eventually, of course, it did.

Right now, on this late October night in 1869, it was as much as Sholto could do to ease himself into a position that would give him the sleep he so desperately desired, his chest as tight and agonised as if a cooper had hammered his staves about Sholto's body. Brogar had given him some laudanum concoction from Tobar's extensive collection of chemicals, and it gave him some respite. Brogar himself was now puffing quietly at one of Tobar's pipes that he had selected from the rack to the left of the fireplace, listening to the ewes in the back coops who were snoring softly and without concern, blithely believing that tomorrow would be like any other day.

That it would not be so was apparent to Brogar, who alone in that room was still awake, and though he now had the explanation for the murders, there seemed little satisfaction in the knowledge, not with Solveig lying there like the living dead. All Tobar had wanted for this valley, for Kildonan and the Suisgill, and for Scalabsdale, had been peace, and oddly Brogar could understand the reasoning, even sympathised with it having seen at first hand the mess and noise that gold panners, brick clamps and mines could make. But was it really worth three lives? Maybe four, if Solveig never woke up again, and it was to that possibility that he turned his mind to now. He tapped out the pipe, and stood up slowly, and opened the door to the cottage.

Outside in the heather, Tobar still believed in the rightness of his actions, was only regretful that he would not get more of the silence and solitude he had gone into battle for, that he would not see another fall of snow, another winter, another spring. He'd heard the swans coming in earlier that evening, their great wings whooshing through the air, the soft splash as they'd landed on the loch;. He hoped it was the same two who had nested here last winter, and many winters before that, and that they would still be around the following April getting ready to leave again, with maybe two or three cygnets, their plumage still grey with new beginnings.

He rested his head on the heather, drew in its scent with every breath. His crying was done, his bruised eyes open as much as they could be, his body aching, though not with the ropes that bound him, but because he could see only a part of the land that he loved, that he had immersed himself into, become a part of, could see only a small edge of his loch as it glittered beneath the stars, the last section of the jetty he had built with his own hands having first erected a cofferdam so that he could sink the pilings down to a depth where they would remain sure and solid for fifty years, sixty, maybe a century, after he was gone. He couldn't see the walls of his home from where he lay, but could feel their warmth, their strength, at his back, and took comfort in the fact that his books – the collective knowledge of his own lifetime, and of all those who had gone before him, who had painstakingly written out every word on every page – were safe within.

He heard Brogar's heavy boots approaching, and wriggled slightly within his bonds, though not with fear. All that was gone, drained away, and he wondered what more the man could want from him. But in the end it was a simple thing he asked, and Tobar saw no reason to lie or obfuscate, indeed felt a certain grace that Brogar had asked, and he had given, and in doing so had given back Solveig her life. And when Brogar had gone, he thought on all the knowledge he had learned throughout his life, and all that still lay to be learned within his books, and a truly amazing thought sprung into Tobar's head fully formed. He'd not long left on this earth, would soon be a part of it, absorbed back into its immensity, allowed to rest for eternity, or for as long as the earth itself lasted within the circle of the sun. But there was still a way he could make his mark, leave something of himself behind in perpetuity. And that it had been Solveig's idea seemed so fitting that Tobar, trussed up like a hog ready for the spit, this man, this murderer, this Tobar Strabane, began to laugh.

Tam Japp had finished cursing God, and had started praying. He was cold, his fingers white as dough, and he could see the frost beginning to sparkle on the moors all around him, the low belly-creep of mist coming down the valleys, along the river courses and streams, barely visible in the darkness, but seemingly defined from the night by some small light of its own devising. He should go in, he thought, should ask after Sholto, how he was

286

doing, but he couldn't bear to see Solveig lying there, couldn't bear that the Almighty would be so cruel as to let him think she'd died, then brought her back to life, only to let her die again. Earlier, the first time Brogar had come outside, when he had dumped Tobar so unceremoniously out the back like a sack of goose-guts, Brogar had come over to Tam, explained to him all they had learned about Tobar's whys and wherefores, and the mystery of Yevgeny Constanenko and how it was that he had appeared when he did.

Brogar hadn't stayed any longer than he'd needed, couldn't fathom Tam Japp's grief any more than he could fathom out why Yevgeny Constanenko had come so far on such paucity of information – less so, in fact, for he understood that Yevgeny and Joseph – the wandering minstrels of the missionary world – had been adventurers in their way, and that Yevgeny still thirsted for those days, and had maybe taken this flimsy excuse because he thirsted for those adventures still. And that was something Brogar understood well; he had predicated his whole life on it. And because of it, he had spent the next half hour or so back in the house talking to Yevgeny about the places he had been with Joseph, both marvelling at the fact that Brogar had been to many of them himself, and how easily their paths might have, though had not, crossed.

But this lassitude of Tam Japp's was something else entirely, and Brogar simply didn't care enough to probe it further. He had other concerns, specifically Solveig and Sholto.

The second time Brogar had come out and talked to Tobar, and righted the man's chair at the same time, Tam had kept going over everything they said, his heart black and heavy with all Tobar had done, and when Brogar had gone, closed the door to the cottage, shut out the light, leaving Tam alone in the darkness, Tam had dug his nails into the palms of his hands, and had watched the pair of swans at the loch's end, their whiteness a glisten in the night as they paddled gently here and there, began to bend the reeds towards their liking, making for themselves a nest, a raft, on which to carry on their lives. It seemed heaven-sent, this calm time, and yet the grief inside him had all the while begun transmogrifying, slowly, but without check, turning into a dreadful anger he could no longer contain. Tam Japp stood up, ankles stiff, bones cracking with the sudden movement, and he began to wind his way towards the dark slump in the heather that was Tobar Strabane.

Inside the cottage, the laudanum Sholto had been given had done its work, and he was sleeping, not deeply or well, but sleeping nonetheless, giving him a few hours respite from the excruciations the day had inflicted upon his body.

Yevgeny Constanenko too was exhausted, worn out by his struggles in the loch and by Brogar's earlier talking – yes, me and Joseph went to this place, and yes, we went to that, we went to Kanin and to Kolgayev Island, to Novay Zemlya, and the Yamal, further east to the Byarrang Mountains…Still, it was pleasing, he thought, that his previous life, and Brogar's present one, had almost intercepted on so many occasions, and yet it was here, in Scalabsdale, they had actually met; Scalabsdale, named for a Scandinavian incomer who had arrived here a thousand years before either of them had existed.

Yevgeny had just been dropping off to sleep when he was awakened by Brogar speaking quietly.

'Come on Solveig, come on. Just drink a little of this, just a little bit of it, lassie, that's it.'

Yevgeny looked up, and saw Brogar trying to pour some kind of liquid down Solveig's throat. He was pinching her nose with his fingers, forcing her to breathe through her mouth, and as she opened her lips, in the liquid went, and the effect of it was so quick, so immediate, that it seemed the next moment Solveig's eyes opened and she was suddenly awake.

'Ha! That's it! That's it!' shouted Brogar excitedly, and then he suddenly moved and left Solveig's side, was making for the door at such full tilt his knocked his chair over, and as Brogar opened the door suddenly Yevgeny could hear what Brogar must already have done: a *whoosh-whoooshing* noise, like water rushing down a hill, or a great flight of swans passing low overhead, and then he saw that the night outside was all lit up, jumping and fragmented, as only a fire can do. He shook his blankets from his shoulders and crashed into the outside world, limping, where Brogar had sprinted, round to the back of the cottage, to see Tam Japp standing grimly, like a boundary stone planted in a field, his flint still in his hand, his eyes glinting with the reflected light from the flames that were coming up from Tobar's still-room, where Japp had gone not long before, missing Brogar by only a minute, a rock in his hand, smashing Tobar's still into splinters, watching with satisfaction as the liquor spurted out and cascaded over the table, onto the floor, smelling how strong, how pure the spirit was, and how quickly it would burn.

'What the hell...' Brogar said, as he skidded to a stop beside where Tam Japp stood unrepentant; he had wanted to burn Tobar's entire habitation down to the ground, with no thought for the consequences, only that Tobar should see it go, had turned Tobar in his chair so that he would face the burning still-house, had leant down low and whispered into Tobar's his ear.

'It's all going to be destroyed. Stick around, why don't you, and watch it go.'

But it wouldn't go, as Tobar well knew, as Brogar guessed, because no one with the skills Tobar Strabane possessed would build a still and not allow for an accident, and had specifically designed the outhouse with that possibility in mind, so that fire, if it took hold after an explosion, could not spread to the rest of the house, and especially not to his precious books.

It did burn admirably though, and Tam Japp got some satisfaction in that, and the blaze was so red and intense that even Yevgeny Constanenko, the ice-man who feared he would never be warm again, had to take a few steps back. And the noise seemed to wake something else up too, because as they all stood there gazing at the fire, watching it spark up into the night, they heard a small voice and turned towards it, saw Solveig in her wet white dress standing by the door of the cottage, one hand held to her forehead, the other clutching the stone of the wall.

'What's going on?' she said. 'If that's the brick clamp burning too hot, then there'll be trouble.'

Chapter 36   *Becomes a land bereft of the noise of its citizens*

It was the morning after the night before, and Sholto was alone in the cottage with Tobar Strabane, who had been barricaded by Brogar into the sheep pen, hammered-down planks over its open top preventing escape. Neither Brogar nor Tam Japp had had any qualms about leaving Tobar out in the heather, but Sholto insisted he be brought in, not about to let the man slip into an easy death he didn't deserve; she wanted to watch the noose being put about his neck and the black sack going down over his face, blocking him from the light of the land he patently loved too much.

The human face has its own landscape, can be shaped by hundreds, maybe thousands, of differing expressions and emotions, but Sholto could not for the life of him read what was on Tobar's face as he looked at him through the wood of the byre.

Solveig was sleeping soundly on Tobar's cot bed, and Brogar and Tam had gone out into the dawn to see to Tobar's animals who were blameless for their master's actions and could not be left to starve. The circle of life needed feeding, as did Sholto's curiosity.

'We'd nothing on you,' Sholto said into the morning air that was tinted with the night-time burning, bore a trace of the ash that had fallen on the cottage, coming in through its door, before the wind took it up and lifted the last cinders from the peat turfs that were its thatch. 'If you hadn't tried to do away with Solveig, if you hadn't done that, we couldn't have proved any of this was due to you, no matter how much we might have thought it.'

In his pen, in his cage, Tobar eased his back against the wall, his fingers delved and woven into the thick wool of his favourite ewe. His eyebrows lifted just a little, though he wasn't looking at Sholto, nor at Solveig, but at a

291

small round pellet of sheep shite that had wound up all alone on the tip of his left boot.

'If you'd not got here when you did,' Tobar said slowly, 'you still wouldn't have.'

Sholto stared at him bleakly, trying to find some iota of guilt or repentance in that weather-beaten face as he glimpsed it between the bolts of wood that nailed him in. There was a lot about this man he understood, but far more that remained hidden. They had discovered the most of his scheme the previous night during Brogar's interrogation, but Sholto had been in too much pain to concentrate properly on anything, and still had questions that needed answers, and he knew this small shell of silence that held them both might be his only chance.

'Why the stones? Why the scratching on the stones?' he asked Tobar, and one corner of Tobar's mouth twisted upwards as he turned his head towards Sholto.

'That was you,' he answered without hesitation. 'Heard you were coming in to port. Thought it might...' He hesitated, searched for the right word. Found it. 'Thought it might amuse you,' he said.

Sholto was taken aback. 'Amuse me?' he repeated. 'But Willie Blaine was already dead by then, already in the burn. Why would you even risk going back to—'

Tobar interrupted. 'To the *rood* ground?' He emphasised the word Sholto had used to describe the rock-bluff Tobar had laid Willie's body on, and now he did smile. 'It was rather a whim,' he said. 'I knew all about you by then, about your interest in languages, in signs, in deeper meanings.'

This might have been taken as a compliment, but Tobar's tone belied his words, implied an obscure contempt for Sholto that Sholto found disconcerting. Tobar carried on working his hand through the woolly back of his ewe, taking comfort in her warmth, her inability to foreguess that he would soon have to leave her, that her lamb would be born into a spring he would not see.

'Did you know that the first known exemplar of the Gaelic language in its earliest form was found inscribed upon a stone?' Tobar asked. Sholto shook his head. 'A bit like your shovel,' Tobar went on. 'I liked your paper on it, by the way. Read it even before I knew who you were, or why you were coming here.'

There was a pause as Sholto tried to assimilate this new information, understood now the piece of paper, the little piece of bark, and kicked himself for not recognising that paper – of such good quality – the same paper Tobar had brought out the day he and Moffatt had brought the bowls.

'But why Willie Blaine? Why Robbie?' he asked. Tobar moved his foot, watched the small world of the sheep-shite sphere rolling from it, becoming indiscriminate amongst all the rest.

'Robbie was just there,' he said, 'and Willie was easy pickings. Everyone knew he hated every minute of his life from start to finish. Always grumbling, always out alone and early, away from the rest, and,' he said, sounding weary, weary of questions, of explanations, weary of what he had done and why he had done it, as weary of his life as Willie Blaine had been of his. He let out a breath. 'And the chapel,' he finally said. 'He was part of Joseph's chapel way back when, though didn't live a proper life by it.'

Joseph, Tobar thought, and closed his eyes, felt a dull pain beating through him. *What must you think of me now?* And on thinking that, he had nothing else to say, answered no more of Sholto's questions, asked only one of Sholto, which was for a pencil and paper.

'They're in the drawer of the dresser,' he said. 'Grant me the favour of letting me write out my will and testament.'

293

And Sholto complied, though it took him a while to stand, creak his way over to the dresser, open the drawer, taking out that same paper, taking it over to Tobar's pen, but he did not hand it over.

'Just one last thing,' Sholto said, the sweat standing out on his brow with the effort and pain of shuffling the few yards across the room. Tobar sighed but did not look up, understood the contract, that to get what he wanted he would have to give something in exchange. Such was life, he thought, and death, always one thing in exchange for another.

'When I was reading about Patrick Sellar's trial,' said Sholto, 'I saw two names. I saw Thomas Angus Strabane, and I saw Robert Sholto McKay.'

Two names, he remembered, on either side of the divide, one for the defence, one for the prosecution.

'Ha!' The bark that came from Tobar was not a laugh exactly, more like the snort of a dog that has got grass seeds up its nostrils. Sholto waited. Tobar complied.

'My father. Your grandfather,' he said simply, and though Sholto had already guessed it was so, it was as if some part of the puzzle of his life, and his parents' life, had just clicked into the place that had been waiting for it.

'And the clearances?' he asked, allowing the paper to waft slightly above the wood of Tobar's cage.

'My father's idea,' Tobar answered. 'My father's, built on what the Countess had already done. It should have been a good thing, a grand plan, if it had worked out.'

Sholto closed his eyes, released the pencil and paper from his hand, heard them falling down into the pen, landing in the dirty straw, feeling that he too had landed in some inexplicable way, and that the ground of his past, of his life, was no longer a shifting surface beneath his feet, but had become something solid, something on which he could build, from such firm

294

foundations, the rest of his life.

Chapter 37   *When the men who sought malice seek now only mercy*

Tobar's will was notarised that same morning by Sholto McKay and Brogar Finn, and formally acknowledged two days later when Tobar was delivered up to the High Sheriff and Provost of Dornoch, holder of the County Seat of Justice. Tobar himself was held in the Dornoch castle gaol until the Duke of Sutherland, who was wintering at his Staffordshire Estate down in England, sent consent for his trial to go ahead *in absentia* of the Duke, with the proviso that it be overseen by an official of the High Court of Edinburgh. He didn't deem it necessary to return north to oversee the event, even though he'd grown up with Tobar and knew him well, and indeed it had been only a courtesy he had been asked at all. But with the Duke's letter of grant, he also included a writ of notice that all panning and mining in Kildonan and Suisgill should cease from midnight on the 31st of December 1869, but added the proviso that he would personally involve himself once more in the future of the coal mines and quarries in concert with Solveig McCleery, with the result that three years later, in 1872, the New Brora coal mines were officially opened.

Tobar Thomas Strabane was duly tried and found guilty, sentenced on the 4th of March 1870, which sentence was carried out seven days later outside the Council Offices in Dornoch. In the time between, he had only one visitor, and that was Solveig herself, who came down to Dornoch on the railway every week to bring him food and drink and adequate clothing. They made an odd couple, murderer and survivor together in the damp cells of Dornoch gaol, and yet both felt a link to one another that could not be dismissed. He had tried to kill her, had almost succeeded, and yet he had also given Brogar the information he needed to bring her back to life, that small vial of chemicals that jolted her system out of its stupor, and without which she would probably never have woken up again. And she was grateful to him for that, at least, and for the facts of his will, which would establish a Fund for the Common Good whose primary aim would be to establish that Museum of Heritage Solveig had talked about to Tobar up in Scalabsdale that day of her almost-death. Pride of place, of course, Tobar's library, and the seven fully restored Brora bowls.

And they talked too of other things, of Joseph, and Solveig read to him the letter from Lilija Indridsdottir that Sholto had managed after many months to illicit, that told them of how Joseph had died. And Tobar had actually wept then, not for Robbie, or for Willie or for Andrew, but for his old friend Joseph, whom he had sent to die in such a way in such a place, when all he had wanted had been to return back home to Helmsdale, and only because of Tobar had never had the chance to be happy back on those hills.

This reading of the letter was the last time the two of them met, and the following week Tobar was taken out and hung, to the glee of the gathered crowd. The judge had ordered that his body should be buried outside the walls of the old kirk at Kildonan, but Solveig intervened on his behalf, and instead she took him all the way home to Scalabsdale and buried him there, where he could be near the loch, and stay in the wilderness and silence that had been the heart of all he ever did.

Chapter 38   *And the permanence of rest*

Brogar Finn and Sholto McKay waited by the quay in Helmsdale. The snow had chaperoned them all the way here from Solveig's steading, made their going difficult, forcing them several times to get out the half-size shovels Brogar always travelled with to clear it from their way. They could all have stayed up at Kinbrace and waited out this interruptive spate of hail and storm and snow, but both Brogar and Sholto were eager to be on their way, having been sent word a week before, via Solveig's telegraphy system, that instructions were coming for them today from Trondheim, and from the Company, and that at last they were about to be reassigned.

Sholto's ribs were still giving him a little trouble, but not enough to keep him from this assignation, for despite both he and Brogar being back in their familial land, they'd both had absolutely enough of it, or at least this part of it, and were clawing to get out, more than willing to be aimed like arrows for new horizons, and whatever adventures those horizons might hold.

By God, Sholto thought, as he stood on that crowded wharf in Helmsdale, on almost the exact same spot Joseph's barrels had sat all those years ago, with the long shanks and the short, *by God,* Sholto thought, *but life is good.*

298

Chapter 39   *So spoke the wanderer, the wiser man, as he ended his lament*

31st December, 1869

Vardøya, the Island of the Wolf

Yevgeny Constanenko was looking at the eight-pointed star that is the fortress of Vardø, the northernmost fortress in the world, formerly the dominion of the Scotsman John Cunningham, the very same that Tobar Strabane had so admired. He had landed in darkness, although it was not night, had waited two days out of port for the winds to drop, the storm to abate, the waves to allow his vessel the passage through. The sea was not frigid here, as it would be further to the east going towards Murmansk and the Peninsula at Kola; indeed, it had become the trading place it was on the strength of it, on the warmth of it, compared to other ports along this same stretch of coast. A hundred or so years hence, an underwater tunnel would be excavated from Vardøya to the mainland, but that was yet to come, and now Yevgeny waited for a small boat to ferry him across, listening for the traditional greeting, the shouted words *Eläköön Suomi,* that would alert him – whether he could see it or not – that the boat was pulling up to pier.

After they had all returned to Kinbrace, he and Solveig had accompanied Sholto into the chapel to find the package that had been sent from Iceland. And it was there, just as Sholto had promised him: there was the satchel Joseph had always carried with him, and inside, there was the Index of Beliefs – battered, water-damaged, all the pages foxed, and some of the ink bleeding and running into the pages – but Yevgeny recognised it immediately, and also the sheaf of notes tied up with string that were his own recordings of the thousands upon thousands of words he had translated from the tongues of every person they had interviewed on their travels, and from which Joseph had made the final transliterative entries into his Index.

Solveig had not demurred when Yevgeny had asked if he could take them with him, and wished him well, offering him any help he would need to get it to its proper destination, so that the Holy Apostolic Church could add it to all their other Indexes from all their other missionaries, who, like Joseph and Yevgeny, had crossed, and were still crossing, the face of the world.

That Yevgeny Constanenko's own name would now be added to the report when it was published, no longer seemed of great importance. Neither did all the many masts he might have made and mended if he chose to return to Archangel, which he did not. On his way back from Sutherland, the great Land of the South that had been named and settled by the Scandinavian ancestors whose blood still pumped through his veins, he had thought a lot about what had happened there, and why, and how it came to be that he had become threaded into its events, a rogue northern weave amongst the Kildonan gold.

He had travelled from Helmsdale to Trondheim, and from Trondheim back to Vardø, but he had not rushed his journey; he had stopped here and there along the way, taking his time, figuring his options. And now that he could hear the small boat approaching, could hear the welcome *Eläköön Suomi,* he knew where his end would lie, knew that he had already aligned himself to Joseph's mission and his church, and would take the path Joseph had been unable to travel anymore, that whereas Joseph had chosen home – no matter he'd never reached it – he, Yevgeny Constanenko, would choose away, and maybe never go back.

He had no idea of the existence of the Anglo-Saxon poem, *The Chronicle of the Wanderer*, nor of its literary connections to Old Norse, but if he had, he would have understood its words from first to last, telling as it does of a man driven into exile by the slaughter of his companion kinsmen, and the death of the lord to whose cause he has pledged his life. For thus was Yevgeny Constanenko, storm-blasted, sorrow-hearted, seeking only the wisdom he needed to carry on in the world, make of his life something good, something that could be called worthy by the lord he had loved and lost.

The boat hove too, and he was ready for it, stepped across its rocking boards just as a single church clock in Vardø began to chime the ringing out of the old year, the bringing in of the new.

New Year, New Happiness. He murmured the old Russian blessing as he steadied himself against the pull of wave and wind and wood, thought of Solveig, and of Joseph, and put his hand by habit to the pocket of the jacket that no longer held his icon, lost as it was to the loch in Scalabsdale, and despite all that had happened, or maybe because of it, he truly believed this New Year really might bring happiness of a sort. And by God how he wanted that such a blessing could come to pass as he began his new journey, this new chapter of his life, swearing as he did so that he would live it well.

The Chronicle of the Wanderer

His lord is buried by the darkness of the Earth
The Wanderer begins to tell his tale
Sorry-hearted, he moves along the waterways towards the ice-cold sea
Seeking those who knew his kinsmen, and could give him comfort
For his friends have been slain within their mead-halls
Carried away by wars and wolves and ravens
Regret and sorrow, cruel companions to the friendless
Where now is the horse, the young rider?
Where now the seats at the feast, the revels in the halls?
Where the companions, forced to leave this middle-earth?
Each day brings new desertion and decay to the walls of the city
The weapons thirsty for slaughter
His spirit separated from the bounty of the earth
So he is bound by sorrow
The counsels of his lord have been lost to him
Time passes under cover of the night
And in sleep he lays his head upon the knees of his lord
Who was his gift-seat and his throne
The path of exile has twisted him like gold
And bereft him of his homeland

Alas for the bright cup, and the splendour of his prince
Alas for the mailed warriors who have been put to the sword
He ponders deeply on the darkness of his life
On men buried, dreich-faced, into the earth
And how cruel are the wounds of his heart
And how he longs for the good times passed
The friendless man awakes and sees before him the fallow waves
The rocky cliffs, where sea birds bathe and preen
And knows that frost and hail and snow are coming from the north
That the hall walls will soon be swept by storm and frost
And how terrible it will be when all has gone to waste
But the wise man keeps secure the mind-chest of his thoughts
And those who are eager for glory do not boast
Are patient, and never weak and reckless
Because soon comes storm and darkness
When all that is fleeting is turned to waste
Becomes a land bereft of the noise of its citizens
When the men who sought malice seek now only mercy
And the permanence of rest
So spoke the wanderer, the wiser man, as he ended his lament

302